Jonny Keane and the
JOURNEY OF FORTUNE

By James Damaa

Copyright © James Damaa 2018

The right of James Damaa to be identified as the Author of the Work has been asserted by him in accordance with the Copyright, Designs and Patents Act 1988.

All rights reserved. No part of this publication may be reproduced, stored in a retrieval system, or transmitted, in any form or by any means without the prior written permission of the publisher, nor be otherwise circulated in any form of binding or cover other than that in which it is published and without a similar condition being imposed on the subsequent purchaser.

This book is a work of fiction. Any references to historical events, real people, or real locales are used fictitiously. Other names, characters, places and incidents are products of the author's imagination, and any resemblance to actual events or locales or persons, living or dead, is entirely coincidental.

ISBN 978 1 9993446 1 0

Acknowledgements

There are many contributions to this work that need acknowledgement. Most importantly, my long suffering wife – as well as some of my closest friends – for hearing my ideas, providing encouragement and just putting up with me in general. And without the highly professional input of my proof reader, this work would n ever have been completed.

Finally, for all of the people I have met on my travels over the years. I still remain close to some, I lost touch with others and some I never saw or heard from again. But all have contributed to the stories contained in this book in one way or another. The details have, of course, been changed from real life events, some of which happened to me and some I have re-told from others – but all are shared stories, nonetheless.

After all, what's the point of having a story if you don't get to share it?

For Benji and for Bob

Contents

Prologue

Present Day

Di stood, waiting, to one side of the doorway, listening to her daughter's soft sobbing. She had first heard her crying when passing her room shortly before but, then, based on recent similar episodes and despite her maternal instincts, she had given her some privacy. Now, she hoped she had made the right decision or she would never forgive herself.

But her daughter's cries had already started to calm down, so Di pivoted round to stand in the doorway. The girl was lying, face down, her head at the foot of the bed with her mobile phone carelessly discarded to one side. I knew it, Di thought, it's that phone again. What on earth has she found on that thing this time?

'Amber, are you OK?' she said, as her daughter looked up, teary eyed. Amber sat up and pulled herself back against the bed frame while hugging a pillow. Glancing back at her mother, she then gave a little shake of the head.

Di's heart sank and, after what had happened last time, she resisted the urge to jump into the room to hug her. She knew exactly where her twelve-year-old daughter got her fiercely independent streak from.

'What's the matter, sweetheart?' she asked, patiently.

'Mum, why do people have to die?' the girl replied.

Well, that isn't exactly a new topic, Di thought, surprised, but it's one we haven't talked about for a long while. She took a deep breath.

'May I come in?' she said and waited for her daughter's brief nod back. Di walked in and sat in the middle of the bed. 'Tell me what happened then, Amber. Who are you talking about?'

Amber glanced down at her phone and then back at her mother. 'They died. They were just doing what they loved and they died for it. It's not fair.'

Di looked at the phone and saw a video playing. It was some sort of tribute speech featuring several young Americans talking forlornly to the camera.

'Who are they?' she asked her daughter.

'They're friends of the couple that died. They all work for the same YouTube channel, creating travel videos.'

'And you saw them die? I've told you before, Amber. You shouldn't be watching that sort of thing on your phone. It's not what it's for,' Di said, angrily.

'No, Mum.' Amber said, sighing. 'You didn't see it happen or anything like that.'

'How did it happen, then?'

'They were standing on top of a famous waterfall in Africa. There's a pool at the top that's protected by a natural rock ledge which they were both standing on. But the girl fell off and then so did her boyfriend, trying to save her.'

'Was it the Devil's Pool at Victoria Falls?' Di asked.

'Yes. Wow, Mum! How did you know that?'

'You know I've done a lot of travel, Amber. I've been there, with your father.'

'No way! When?'

'At least ten years ago. More, actually, because it was just before you were born. We went there on our honeymoon. I can show you a photo, if you like?'

'Oh, not another one,' Amber said, rolling her eyes. 'As long as I don't have to look at loads of those old things again.'

'All right, cheeky. I won't show it to you, then. Anyway, that place has always been very dangerous. They should've known that.'

'But you managed to do it safely enough.'

'Yeah, but we weren't distracted trying to take a selfie or film a video or anything.'

'They're vloggers, Mum. That was their job.'

'What's a vlogger?' Di asked, curiously.

'Oh, god, Mum,' Amber replied, sighing. 'Video bloggers. They create videos about their travels.'

'Well, I kind of guessed that last bit. But how do they get paid, then?'

'They get sponsored loads of money by brands that want to advertise on their channels. It's because they know that millions of people watch their stuff.'

Di smiled, admiring her daughter's astute understanding of the situation.

'Well, good for them, then, I suppose. It wasn't that easy in our day, though.'

'What do you mean?' asked Amber, looking at her mother expectantly.

'It was always a lot harder to travel back then. You'll never know, but now, everything's made so easy for you. You can just research stuff using free videos like this. We had to buy books or speak to people. It took time and effort, and we didn't have mobile phones, or YouTube, to check along the way. We barely even had emails at first.'

'No mobile phones?' Amber said, in shock.

'I know. Imagine that. Amazing, isn't it?' Di replied, sarcastically.

'Well, you and Dad seemed to manage just fine anyway. You did loads of travel.'

'And your uncle, too. Never forget him,' said Di, sternly.

'Yes, I know. Sorry, Mum. But I want to do it all too... and I loved their videos, I used to watch them all the time,' Amber said, pausing and rubbing her eyes. 'What am I going to do now, Mum? Why do bad things like this have to happen?'

Di knew she and her husband had created this situation. They were the ones responsible for planting these seeds of desire in their children over the years – no one else. Constantly showing them photos and talking about all their youthful travel experiences. What other outcome could they have expected?

'Bad things happen to all of us, Amber. They certainly have to me, and to your father,' Di said, solemnly. 'That's despite all our fun travel adventures. And remember what happened to your brother last year, when he was just trying to have fun, too?'

'When he was trying to climb up everything? But all nine-year-old boys are a little bit silly like him, aren't they?' said Amber, shaking her head.

'Yes, exactly. I know he broke his arm but he's fine now, isn't he? The point is, accidents happen – to all of us. It's just bad luck, that's all.'

'I know I never met them, but what about our grandad and our uncle? They weren't so lucky, were they?'

'No, they weren't... but we just have to hope for the best in life. That's all you can do, honey.'

'I suppose,' replied Amber, frowning.

'Why don't I show you that photo, anyway? Your father and I actually look quite young. You might even find it funny,' said Di, trying to cheer her daughter up.

Part One

'I was about eight years old when I first began to have the dream. It would always start the same. A flash of light would appear out of the centre of the darkness. The light would gradually draw closer, so that eventually I could see it was square shaped. And still it would come towards me, the light growing larger and brighter, dominating the surrounding black nothingness. The square of light would occasionally flicker back to black with a short suction-click sound.

Eventually, I could see the outline of a shape within the light, a black silhouette framed within the square. The shape is a tree, an unusual tree not found in my home town, unlike anything I have ever seen. The branches are very distinctive; they spread out to grow very straight on the horizontal, meaning the top of the tree looks very flat, like a series of mini platforms. I know now it is called the Acacia tree.

In the background, the light changes from white to a bright blue. Soon, clouds begin to pass by, moving faster and faster as if hours were shooting by in mere seconds. They start to darken from a puffy, light grey to a dark, menacing grey. Within moments, the whole sky is dominated by shadowy rain clouds yet the tree is still in the forefront of the scene. I start to shiver as rain and wind howl past and the surreal viewing window rushes towards me to the point where all I can see is the horizon and the black tree, centred and silhouetted, dominating.

Then, without any warning, the darkness starts to fade. Dark greys turn into reds and browns as the clouds begin to separate. Slowly, I see the start of sun rise as a large orange hue begins to form at the bottom of the sky. I feel myself being lifted into the air towards the tree, floating over it, flying towards the horizon, as if with the wind; I am soaring high to escape remnants of moisture left behind from the storm. Soon, I am embracing warm fronts of air as the sun engulfs the landscape.

I look down and fly towards the ground to see large expanses of yellowy green grass blowing softly in the warming winds. Just before I reach the earth, I pull up and fly along the surface, long blades of grass bristling against my face. The terrain is speeding forward, on and on, an upward incline, steeper and steeper as I rise to the top of a hill. Suddenly, I am at the top and vast, baking-hot plains unfold before me, golden grasses gently shimmering in a rediscovered sun. Yet my eyes can still only fix upon one thing – the Acacia tree.

A frame of darkness surrounds the scene once more, this time shrinking away from my view and towards the tree. In the background, the clouds have fully cleared and the sky is changing from gold back to the bright blue of a midday sun. This image moves away from me as the light grows brighter and brighter, the shape of the Acacia still clearly visible. But the square is getting smaller and smaller against the blackness, and soon it is just a speck of light as it once began.

Then, the light disappears totally. And that's how I remember the dream, initially.'

Chapter One

And As Luck Would Have It

Sitting in his cramped seat, he held a card, ready to turn it over, from the stock pile on his tiny plastic tray. How ironic, Jonny Keane reflected, that he should play a game called patience when clearly he possessed none. He'd already been through the pack sixteen times, as well as changing the build rules four times. It was a long flight after all.

At this moment he was tired and anxious and he needed the outcome of the card to be a good one. As was customary, it would decide his next action. The flight was nearing its end and the terrifying realisation of what he was doing was sinking in. This was beyond any shadow of a doubt, one hundred per cent, pure eighteen carat, unadulterated madness.

The card he had turned over was a Seven of Diamonds. This was good news; he could place this on his Eight of Spades. More importantly, it meant he could now allow himself the privilege of looking out of his window.

Stretching forward, he peered through the small square, where countless thousands of tiny lights illuminated the night-time landscape, blinking at processions of miniature cars snaking around in never-ending lines. As the plane swooped lower and lower towards the runway, he began to see what appeared to be a limitless blanket of ramshackle housing surrounding the airport.

A city that looked scarily overwhelming awaited him, but the guide book that lay open on his lap had at least removed some of the surprises. He knew the population was around twelve million people, and that it was the commercial and entertainment capital of India. He knew that the slums he saw beneath him now stretched for ten miles – and were apparently the longest in the world.

Yet, those stats pretty much covered his total knowledge of Mumbai. Added to the fact that he didn't know where he was going when he got there, and didn't have a chance in hell of finding his brother Bobby and friend Rick who were already there. It was now 6.30am local time on Friday 20th December 1996. Jonny Keane had woken up at home in Hertfordshire, England at 7am the previous day and had barely slept since.

It had always been that way for Jonny Keane – or JK to his friends. Planes, trains, anything that moves – the best he might hope for was to nod off a few times; but now it was nervous energy rather than discomfort that was keeping him awake. After the gruelling routine of an airport journey, check-in, waiting for departure then the flight itself, he was probably not in the best frame of mind for what faced him next.

But he remembered why he was here. It was meant to be, after all. He could sense his luck changing; he just had to get through the tricky patches, like this. His mind wandered again and so he pinched himself. Have faith. But then he began to sweat at the thought of the next stage of the journey.

Needing a bigger distraction, JK decided to carry on playing patience until his next good card draw – with which he would allow himself to reminisce further.

He drew a succession of three terrible cards from the stock pile straight into the waste pile. Finally he drew a Four of Clubs which he was pleased to place on his Five of Hearts.

And so he paused once more. JK had chosen to do this knowing that it would be anything but easy. Of course that didn't stop him from being scared. It had only been two days before on Wednesday that he had finally decided he was going on this trip. It was easily the most spur-of-the-moment decision of his life so far.

Although, looking back, he had slowly, and subconsciously, been leading himself to this moment ever since he had found out about his inheritance less than six months ago. The news had pushed JK, a student, into a taking a year out to travel. Except, so far, he hadn't been anywhere this exciting yet. Mainly visits round the country to see friends and a few short trips to Europe for some sun.

In fact, he considered, he had probably made the decision well before even his inheritance. Perhaps it was just after his father's death, fifteen years before.

It was meant to be. And that's why he would find Bobby and Rick. They were only two days ahead of him so far. He would let nature take its course and, so, he knew he would get lucky. His father had been lucky, after all. And he was lucky too. Like father, like son.

His brother Bobby, despite only being twenty-six years old, was already a veteran of travel, and was five years older than JK. So, of course, this trip was all his idea, and he, along with his old friend Rick, had booked it months ago. They had kept going on at JK to join them, right up to when the boisterous-verging-on-obnoxious pair rang him from the airport on the Wednesday morning to gloat and rub in the fact that they were leaving.

After putting the phone down, jealous thoughts lingered in JK's head and finally he succumbed to his desires. He began to play backgammon on his computer and within an hour he had been victorious, winning three games out of three, and thus providing himself with the outcome he needed to make a decision. He found himself a flight leaving at 5pm the next afternoon and booked on it straight away. And then JK left. That part seemed so easy now.

A seventeen day trip in Goa, home of the hippy-beach-rave scene on India's south west coast. JK wryly compared this with England's commercial and soulless Christmas and New Year's Eve traditions which, with every passing year, he was becoming increasingly intolerant towards. Besides, his brother knew what he was doing; he would look after JK – as long as JK could find him first.

It seemed to be mostly the right decision. All JK knew was that Bobby and Rick were staying at Anjuna Beach in Goa, but he didn't even know what hotel they were in. Goa had its own airport but they had decided to fly to Mumbai instead as the flights were half the price. From there you could get a cheap train down to Goa – the only cost was time, seeing as it took about eleven hours. JK decided that if those two jokers could manage it then he certainly could.

JK knew deep down this was the start of something else. Something much bigger. A grand design; a tribute to his deceased father. He didn't know exactly what that would be yet, but he knew he would be successful. Luck would follow him, just as it had followed his father on his travels before him.

Of course he had not mentioned this to anyone yet. Not to his friends and not to Bobby or Rick. Not even to his mother.

The plane came to a stop on the runway so JK packed away his cards and folded away his tray in the seat in front. He looked up, expectantly, and eventually the seat belt light switched off as a tone sounded. He had completed the flight, the first part of his journey, at least. He was lucky, he knew it. No mix ups, no crashes. His father had survived a plane crash once; so maybe he would be just as lucky, and perhaps even more so. It was meant to be.

An hour or so after landing JK managed to get his conspicuous back pack from the swarming, heaving airport. Taking a deep breath, he nervously headed towards an information desk to ask about trains. Eventually he managed to book a train ticket to Goa. After first gawping at the fee of 1,900 rupees, he quickly worked out that it was a bargain at less than thirty pounds for a first-class, air-conditioned sleeper cabin.

Unfortunately, it was leaving in three and half hours or so. It sounded like plenty of time, but he had to take two bus transfers just to get to the train station. Getting out of the airport alone was the hardest part. As soon as he stepped out from immigration, he felt like prey to a menagerie of watchful hunters. But, luckily, he was not the sole focus of their attention. There were a few other Western-looking travellers, ripe for cash pickings, following him out who would take some of the heat.

All were subjected to the same sort of treatment. Salesmen offering used Crayola crayons in boxes that looked like they had been run over several times already. Parents, grandparents, aunts and uncles dragging their children over to beg for money. The taxi drivers were the worst of the predators. Relentless, seemingly self-multiplying or reproducing, it took immense will power to shake them off. Random strangers asking personal questions like 'What do you do for a living in England?' or 'Are you very rich?'.

After a few embarrassing interchanges, the standard 'This is India, do not worry' reply from the innumerable yet unhelpful airport staff and a tip of fifty rupees to a porter, JK was directed to the right bus stop and learnt very quickly to ignore the beggars that plagued his journey.

Finally, JK got to the train station just in time to encounter yet more chaos. He had almost started to ignore the now constant feeling of dread in his stomach.

Feeling sweat stick to his back in the thirty-five-degree heat, JK fought his way through the teeming masses congregated around, his heavy bag in tow, to find a guard who could speak limited English and direct him to the correct carriage.

In his own cabin, JK felt comfortable knowing that the train was due in Goa at 10.45pm. He was finally able to relax, grateful for the standard of his berth but with a nagging guilt over the conditions he had seen the other passengers were suffering, crammed in like chickens in cages on the other carriages. Their floors were filthy and the stench was potent, even from the luxury of his birth.

Despite the realisation he had paid over ten times the price of their ticket, JK was reminded further of the disparity in India's wealth during the journey down the coastline. As the train rumbled along, he looked out of the window to see poor families living inside scruffy little shacks and make shift homes, merely inches from the tracks.

JK decided it was better if he kept himself to himself and managed to remain undisturbed over the next few hours. Filling up on processed snacks from his packed supplies, he fought the urge to sleep and settled back to read, his gaze interrupted by further sights, goat herders and villagers waving to the train as it rumbled past their fields.

He felt the onset of sleep, and despite a lingering fear of the dreams that awaited him, he knew deep down he needed it. Eventually, exhaustion and heat took over and JK slept for three hours.

He awoke to darkness as the train approached Goa. He gathered his belongings together and readied himself for the next step. Feeling a temporary high from having survived this significant stage of the journey, the realisation that it wasn't over yet quickly dawned on him as he dragged his bag from the train.

He had to get to Anjuna Beach. How far was it? Surely a taxi would be OK? No signposts – none that he could understand anyway. No taxi rank to be seen either.

Surrounded by yet more unfamiliar sights he looked around desperately. Locals with their dark, weathered skin milled around, contrasted by their vivid and unusual clothes. Colourful saris, turbans, loose trousers, long shirts. Women with heavily jewelled noses and wrists. Bustling shops and markets, decorated in yellows, fuchsia-rich purples, every colour you could imagine.

Feeling a cooler evening breeze awaken his senses, JK was suddenly aware of being thirsty. He had run out of bottled water and the dryness stretched the back of his mouth to induce a slight panic. His default was to reach into his pocket for a coin.

He could see two main streets leading off the one he had arrived on at the train station. Perfect, he thought, the coin can decide for me. And so his coin toss of heads determined that he chose to wander off down the first of the two streets.

He instantly felt vindicated as he looked up to see a fat man by the side of the road with some sort of stand. Steam rose from a large pot of boiling water. He wore an indigo-dyed turban with white cotton cloths. He had read about these chaps – they were called 'Chai Wallahs', essentially mobile tea makers.

The thought of that great English tradition, 'the refreshing cup of tea', suddenly moved him into action. JK walked towards the tea maestro as if compelled by some mysterious silent guiding force. Seeing him smile warmly as he approached, JK instantly felt reassured, smiling back and nodding, saying 'yes please' and raising a finger to signify the request.

'English?' asked the tea maestro.

'Yes that's right,' JK replied.

'Ah, very nice, very nice. Where do you go?'

'Anjuna Beach.'

'Ah yes, Anjuna, very beautiful yes. Very nice beach. Many parties, yes! Many girls, yes? Ha!'

JK laughed at his naive smile and then watched him open a red tin to pull out some black crinkly leaves. He put them into the hot boiling pot and stirred the concoction with relish. Letting it stew, he lifted his head up to watch JK as steam drifted between them. He drew smoke from a small hand-rolled cigarette.

'Do you know how I can get to Anjuna Beach?'

The tea maestro looked at JK confused.

'Directions?' JK said hoping this would shed light on the situation.

'Ah…no,' He shook his head, bewilderment deepening.

'Can I get a bus there?' JK asked. But the Chai Wallah just stared back at him calmly, in silence.

'Do you know where can I get a taxi?' JK added.

The man grunted an undecipherable reply, clearly perplexed as he poured some tea into a clay cup.

'Taxi-cab? Car?' JK now mimed driving motions sitting behind the steering wheel of a car.

'Ah yes, taxi, very good, yes,' he said, laughing, and handed him the cup as JK finally saw recognition reach his eyes. As JK held the warm vessel in his hands, the tea maestro pointed towards a shack on the corner of the road opposite.

'Taxi in there, yes, very good. My friends. Very nice price, yes.'

'Great, I mean… er… very good, yes, OK…thank you very much.'

The Chai Wallah now seemed content as he shifted around on the spot, seemingly doing a happy sort of skip as JK sipped the hot, sickly sweet beverage and smiled back at the fat man.

'Very nice, very good tea. Thank you.' JK stood awkwardly at this tea stand trying to think how he could communicate further. He asked how much the taxi might be but, of course, his new friend did not understand. Getting bored of the silent smiling and nodding ritual JK hurriedly drank the milky tea. Thanking him again he attempted to hand him the empty clay cup, which he declined and pointed to the ground. Looking around there were three or four discarded cups so JK threw his down also, laughing.

Waving to the tea man, JK walked off towards the taxi hut. The light blue walls were dirty and an old wooden door had been left slightly ajar. Above it was a small white board with red text written in the Hindi language. Hopefully it meant 'Taxi', but given the total lack of cars and any movement of people nearby he began to have serious doubts.

He nervously knocked on the door and waited. After a while he pushed the door open further and poked his head around. All he could see was a dark passageway. What the hell am I doing, he thought? Is this the standard way for tourists in Goa to get ambushed and mugged? Am I about to become another Anglo-Indian crime statistic?

He didn't really want to walk much further so he shouted out a 'hello'. Someone called back but still no movement. He had no choice but to carry on walking. Just a couple of metres past the passage was a dark room with five men sat on the floor. There was a lamp on a small low table in one corner, the air so thick with smoke he could only just see the brown walls.

A large brocade-patterned rug dominated the floor space, with the men arranged in a circle around it. There was a machete behind the circle in one corner and another knife was laid in front of an older looking man. One of them was smoking a bong as silence fell across the room and they all turned to look at JK, this strange Western intruder.

Late in the evening in an unknown room, an unfamiliar city and a remote country. JK's money, passport, camera, clothes – all of his possessions within easy grasp. Five locals that can't speak English and one tourist who can't speak their language. Lots of big knives. And they've got drugs. JK's immediate thoughts were something along the lines of 'Fuck, bollocks, fuck'.

But then he began to focus his thoughts. Smile. That's a universal, non-threatening sign in any language. Plus a jolly good old Great British 'hello' again. Smile. A man with glazed eyes said something but his tone was less than friendly.

'Taxi?' said JK. It was a desperately optimistic question, matched by the now pathetic repeated gesture of a steering wheel motion. Fear probably stopped JK's lips from uttering a car engine's 'broom broom'. Smile.

To his relief, the man smiled back. Then one of them laughed. Then another joined in. Soon, all of them were having a little chuckle. Keep smiling. One of the men, due to have the bong next, sat up and looked at JK.

'Oh yes, taxi, yes please, I take, I take!' He excitedly gestured with his hands as he spoke.

'OK, very good, thank you.' JK tried to keep his attention on the excited volunteer, while noticing the others relax and continue smoking.

'Where, please?'

'Er, Anjuna Beach, please.'

'Ah, yes. Party beach!' His comments were followed by laughter once again.

'Yes, party town. Anjuna party beach.' JK tried to match his enthusiasm.

'OK, we go now, yes please?'

'OK, yes, that would be good.'

The short, skinny man nodded and stood up, walking round his friends to leave the room. Not wanting to wait around, JK picked up his bags and followed him out without looking at the group. As he left the hut, he saw the fat tea man and waved. Tea maestro shouted something across the road and, during their brief exchange, JK heard something that sounded like 'English', so he knew it was about him.

They walked to the end of the road round the corner from tea man's street and the taxi driver headed towards a battered, rusty and stained white hatchback Lada. He opened the boot and grabbed JK's bag before he had a chance to argue. Rust trimmed the inside of the door he stood behind to hold it open, his head eerily perched on top with a transfixed grin. JK got in and sank into his seat wondering what would happen next as he slammed the door shut.

The taxi journey was another forty-five minutes. As the driver smoked casually out the window, his other hand recklessly steered the car as they weaved in and out of traffic. He occasionally attempted polite conversation with JK in broken English. Once again this didn't progress very far as he told him the basics as best he could. The main problem was trying to explain where exactly he was going to in Goa without the driver thinking that JK was either mad or that he was some naive tourist who could easily be ripped off.

Perhaps both would prove to be true. JK knew he was now getting to the most difficult part of the search. As the car drew near the centre of town he could see the coastline in the distance as the cool breeze blew through the car. Tanned-skinned Westerners stumbled around drunk and stoned. Torch-lit lanterns illuminated tattoos, dreadlocks, glazed eyes – selected features that stuck in JK's mind as they sped past the human street litter.

JK hadn't comprehended how big a place it would be until he saw it but Anjuna Beach was big enough for him to start to get very worried again. If the worst came to the worst, he could just book into a hotel and trawl the beaches until he found them in the next day or two. Surely it wouldn't be that hard, he had thought. But now the doubts had well and truly sunk in and JK began to feel restless once more.

It was now almost midnight. He had told the driver to drop him off somewhere central. He figured that his best bet, before finding a hotel, was to look around quickly now. He paid the driver a generous tip and got out. Standing around on the dusty road underneath a small tree, he could see a row of three rickshaws a few metres away. Two men who he assumed were the drivers were standing in front of their rickshaws, chatting animatedly.

But in one of them, a young looking man sat and stared at JK. He was wearing shorts and a blue and white striped t-shirt. There was something strange about the way he looked at JK. He then began to cycle his contraption on to the road, advancing it forward and then pulling up just alongside him.

'You need taxi?' the young man said.

'Er, no thanks.'

'Where you going? You need hotel? I take you – very cheap.'

'Well, maybe, but I have to find my friends first.'

'Your friends? Hey, we find them together. Who your friends?'

JK was impressed with his English and both amused and fascinated that the chap would even think that this could be possible. Now, he had heard that they worked long hours but surely these rickshaw drivers didn't see every new tourist that arrived? But in a confused and desperate frame of mind and beginning to feel very tired, JK, in the end, just decided to play along.

'Two British men, Bobby from England and Rick from Scotland. They're young like me, my age.'

'What they look like?'

JK tried his best to give simple descriptions, using his hands to help. When he described Rick he saw some sort of flicker in the young driver's eyes.

'Yes, yes I know your friends. I know, I drive Mr Rick yesterday. Very funny man. Big tattoo on neck, yes? Give me very big tip.'

'Yes, that's right! You know Rick?!' JK asked in amazement.

'Yes, I know Mr Rick.'

'Wow! Great – I can't believe it. Do you… do you know where they're staying?'

'Yes, I take you to their hotel now – they staying at the Carlton. Come, come.'

He beckoned JK to the back of his rickshaw as he shifted his feet on the pedals. JK felt like he was living out some sort of bizarre practical joke. Not quite knowing what random event would happen next, the whole scene began to blur in his mind as they zig zagged through the streets, dodging pedestrians, cyclist and cars. The journey became even more surreal with the driver's next revelation.

'It's not very far. I know short cut. I work there also.'

'What? Where? At the Carlton?'

'Yes, yes. I am porter there. I know your friends. I know where they stay. This is how I met them, yes.'

'Oh, OK! Right, fantastic. Thank you.'

Within five minutes or so – it felt like longer to JK – they arrived at the Carlton hotel. Instead of stopping outside the reception they carried on past to turn a corner into a dark alleyway. They stopped a few metres along outside a metal staircase.

He beckoned towards the top of the staircase as JK stretched his head to look outside.

'So what is this?' he asked, looking up the dirty staircase. It was one storey high.

'Your friends, Mr. Rick and the other one. They stay here. That is their room, upstairs, yes.'

He didn't know what to think and slowly lifted himself from the rickshaw. He looked around the narrow street. It was well-lit and seemed quiet enough without being threatening; he had already seen the main entrance round the front and decided that, at the very worst, he could ask at the reception desk for help if needed.

Suddenly he could hear a strange high-pitched squeaking noise. Turning around, he could see a small old man, he assumed homeless, sitting just behind the staircase, near some bins. The squeaking was more of a chirp and, looking down, he realised it was coming from a green canary which was in a small box cage at the man's feet. The bird was flapping its wings and jumping, causing the box to move.

The old man looked barely conscious but the commotion from his pet bird slowly stirred him to raise his head and look up at JK. Despite a scraggy white beard and bushy eyebrows, JK could see his dark glazed eyes widen. A skinny arm appeared through his scruffy and dirty white robes, and a bony finger unravelled to point straight at JK.

He then began to say something in Hindi – a phrase he repeated over and over again.

'What's he saying?' JK asked the rickshaw driver, concerned.

'Him? Do not worry, he is local madman. He is often in town at night, to bother the tourists. Ignore him. It's OK.'

'Uh, OK,' said JK, frowning, as he turned his back on the old man and paid his driver.

He glanced back up the staircase – where would it take him? JK thanked his driver who then smiled back at him with an unsettlingly knowing look before getting back into his rickshaw, about to move on.

'Wait!' JK said to him. 'Please will you stay for a minute? I need your help please. I'll pay you. Just in case they're not home.'

After a brief confused frown, the driver then nodded as his expression changed back to his more customary vacant grin. JK looked up again. A door at the top of the stairs stood next to a dimly lit window. Were Bobby and Rick really staying there?

JK decided to at least go and have a look. As he climbed the stairs, he saw thick cables protruding from the wall. Ascending a few more feet, he then passed an electrical box with live wires hanging loose.

Setting his bag down next to the door, he tried to look through the shutters on the window, but there was no movement. He paused to listen for any sign of life, but still there was nothing. Well, this was it. Somehow he had been led to this moment and it was now or never. Taking a deep breath, he formed a fist and knocked on the door.

No answer. He tried again but there was still nothing. Feeling a distant churning in his stomach, he turned around and saw his driver looking back up from the bottom of the staircase. This couldn't be a con, could it? No, the driver was about to leave anyway – JK had called him back. But then another thought struck him. Maybe there was someone else waiting here to rob him. Or worse.

JK turned back to the door to try one more time but with no success. He closed his eyes and took a deep breath before making his way back down, hopeful he might suddenly be called back up by Bobby. As he approached the bottom, he could see that the old man had walked over to talk to the driver, still looking and at pointing at JK ominously.

'Not home?' said the driver, cutting off the old man.

'No,' JK said, cautiously.

'What are you going to do now?'

'I don't know.' JK paused. 'What does the old man want?'

'He is a fortune teller. Parrot astrologer. He wants to read you. He says you give out strong signals. But he is very old now. Not make much sense.'

This fascinated JK, considering the timing of this opportunity. It had distracted him from the fear of the situation. He eyed the old man up and down who continued to stare back at him. A series of necklaces made of dark red beads poked from the top of his robes under his head. A whitish-grey powder was spread across his forehead, partially concealed by his long and untidy white hair. It hinted at a once-held, understated stature, perhaps now lost.

'How much does it cost? And does he speak English?' he asked the driver.

'No. But I can translate for you.' The driver then spoke to the old man. After a pause, the driver was clearly making a calculation in his head. 'You give to me and I pay him, 500 rupees. Yes, OK?'

JK knew the driver had added his cut but it still wasn't that much. But then he had a realisation that he just had to do it. He knew luck would guide him. It was meant to be.

'OK,' JK said, as he got out the money ready to pay. The driver made the exchange very quickly but JK could not see exactly what had been passed to the old man.

The three of them sat under the staircase in the dim light from some windows nearby and the street lamp at the end of the alleyway. The old man slowly sat down and beckoned JK and the driver over as he silently unfolded a small red mat in front of him. JK glanced around and could see lots of remnants of seeds and nut shells on the floor which he assumed were for the bird. The old man produced at least twenty wallet sized black cardboard sleeves and arranged them in a pile in the middle of the mat. He talked as he did this, and to the side was his canary in its cage.

JK looked to his driver for any translation, but none was forthcoming, as he continued to stare down at the mat with a look of supreme disinterest. The old man then spoke to the bird, tapped the cage and opened its door.

The bird had calmed down now but was still making repetitive but brief high pitched cheep-cheep noises – a more pleasant sound now. It hopped out of its cage towards the pile of cardboard sleeves and began to pull on the corner of the top one.

It did this until it pulled it off the pile and then discarded it to the side. It then repeated this with a second sleeve from the pile. And then again with a third, a fourth, and then a fifth. Finally, it pulled a sixth one off but it did not then return this to the pile – it just turned around and walked back to its cage, all the while chirping away merrily.

The old man spoke – and again, JK glanced up at his driver who continued to ignore him – and then stroked the bird before grasping it with both hands. He then tapped the top of the cage and pushed the bird back inside, closing the door behind it.

The old man opened the sleeve the bird had picked and showed the three cards that were inside, continuing to comment as he arranged them in front of JK. Although JK did not recognise the pictures on them, he imagined they were something like tarot cards. Probably Hindu gods, he assumed. He could see that two cards had an identical picture of some sort of bright, be-jewelled and well-dressed figure, and in between these two cards was one with a more dramatic picture of a much scarier demon-like character.

The old man coughed abruptly and then stared at JK, in silence, with a look of fear in his eyes. After what felt like a minute, he spoke softly, while his eyes constantly flicked between the bird and JK.

'Well,' JK said to the driver, 'what does it mean?'

'He said… uh, he said that you will first need to lose a fortune before you find more fortune.'

'Fortune? What do you mean? Like money, coins, gold, what?'

'He doesn't say.'

'Well, what about losing the fortune? What does that mean? How will I lose it?'

'He doesn't say.'

'Can't you ask him?' JK said, sighing.

The driver spoke to the old man, who appeared to laugh at JK but then said something back.

'He says he doesn't know, but he says it will happen. The gods and the stars have told him. He doesn't ask them everything and they don't tell him everything. But they have spoken.'

'OK, but, does he know if – I mean, does he know when it will happen?'

'Soon. Before you are an old man like him!' Even though the driver laughed at this, JK could tell he was getting frustrated with the whole process now.

'OK, OK, very good. Thank you. Tell him thank you.'

The driver spoke to the old man as he stood up to leave. JK did the same and nodded to the old man, who smiled back. Then, suddenly, he reached out and grabbed JK's arm, saying something as he did so. Watching this, the driver shouted at the old man, who then let go and began to clear his stuff away. The driver turned and walked towards his rickshaw as JK followed.

'What did he say back there?' JK asked.

'Nothing. Just more old man nonsense,' the driver replied, firmly.

JK was suspicious but decided to abandon the question – such was the tone of the driver. His mind raced.

'You want me to take you to a bar now? Try and find your friends? Maybe to the beach?'

JK decided he needed space to process everything he had just seen and heard. He replied on instinct.

'No, it's OK. I'm going to wait here for them. I'm sure they won't be long.'

'OK,' said the driver after a pause, shrugging. JK paid him a few extra rupees for waiting and then the driver climbed back into his rickshaw and cycled off, turning to wave goodbye, which JK duly returned.

He stood in the alleyway and, remembering the old man, turned around to look for him. But he had gone already, leaving JK on his own to ponder his situation. He stared vacantly along the alleyway towards the street light.

I should feel worried, he thought to himself. This was not a stable situation. Anything could happen to him in this place and there was no guarantee his friends would show up. He didn't know for sure if it was even their hotel room up those stairs.

And yet he felt elated. Those words from the old man had struck a chord. They had re-affirmed what he knew already.

It was meant to be. He would wait here. Bobby and Rick would turn up soon, he could just tell.

In his pocket, his hands dug around to find his old keep-sake, which he then pulled out. He could barely see the washed, yellowy-coloured paper that hinted at its age, but it held his gaze in the dim light anyway. The edges were a darker brown colour. He wondered if his father had folded it so neatly into half, and then half again, when he first wrote it, over thirty years ago.

He remembered his father holding him in his arms when he was around six years old. He was sitting on a giant brown armchair in their lounge, drinking whisky in a glass tumbler. He could smell his breath on him as he sang 'Que Sera, Sera' to his mother, who stood in the background laughing. She hovered in a doorway watching them, holding a dishcloth and plate. Distinctive yellow, white and brown rectangular shapes were on the wallpaper behind.

He could still remember what his father had said to him.

'You need to know something, son. Some people are just born lucky in life. You'll know who they are straight away. Of course some aren't so lucky. You win some, you lose some. But it doesn't matter, sometimes it's just because it's your turn...'

'Now, listen, I don't think I'm very lucky. Maybe I am, maybe I'm not. But don't let that worry you... because you are gonna be, Jonny, I know. There's a great fortune coming to you one day – it's waiting for you to collect it. I just know it. Always remember that, son, you are the lucky one.'

He had died not long after that, and so that was JK's only clear memory of his father. JK folded the old piece of paper carefully, placed it back in his pocket and looked up.

He heard some shouting and footsteps from the busy street outside the hotel main entrance. Then the light along the alleyway began to flicker as shadows crossed in front of it. The voices were getting closer and he could now make out that they were male and boisterous; he then saw two figures turn the corner into the alleyway.

Straining his eyes, he was unable to make out their features, but then he realised one of the voices was unmistakeably Scottish. Hope edged him closer as fear held him back.

And, as the light improved, he saw the source of the Scottish voice on the left. A young man, tall and skinny with a shaven head and a neck tattoo of a skull with a joker's hat on. With him, on the right hand side, a man of a similar age, heavily tanned and with a stockier build, although not as tall. JK had never liked the earring he had in his left ear.

'Hello, Rick. Hello, Bobby,' JK said, calmly, as he stepped out in front of them and the grin on his face grew wider, 'Surprise!'

Chapter Two

Lapland Karma

Jonny Keane really hoped he was near his hostel now. It was around 9pm and he was in central Helsinki, where, in the darkness, it had started to rain a light drizzle. He was pretty tired, having just got off a short but cramped flight from Oslo, followed by a long bus ride from the airport. It was towards the end of the fifth week of a new trip and, after Finland, only four more cities across Sweden and Denmark remained in his final three weeks.

Frequently checking the tiny map in his guide book proved to be deceptive. What he thought would be a five-minute walk turned into a twenty-minute struggle with his large backpack. Eventually he did find it, and walked into the lobby heading straight for the reception counter where a plump, young, plain-looking girl stood staring at a computer behind the desk.

He felt relief when he made eye contact with her as he approached. Yet he needed all of his mental fortitude to force a smile as he slid his pack off his shoulder on to the floor. He now wished his brother was still with him after all.

His underlying sense of unease was further encouraged when she told him the hostel was full. Cursing and blaming himself, JK knew that this had been on the cards ever since he had underestimated this part of the journey, not bothering to book. It was his own stupid fault for taking risks like that, he reflected.

And not just those. His playing cards had been stolen after he had left them in a hostel lounge. He couldn't find his dice, either. And what about his medication? It didn't seem to be working but maybe he shouldn't have reduced the dosage in the first place.

This was it; it was all coming together in the worst possible way now. He deserved his fate, dreading whatever would be coming next. Standing still, he couldn't even face getting a coin out of his pocket to decide his next move.

The receptionist looked upon JK's grim expression with pity. She described what he felt to be some token and insincere alternative places to stay in broken English. At least she offered him a seat.

So, he walked towards an old arm chair on the edge of the room and slowly sat down to consult his guide book once more. But nothing would sink in and after a short time, he was just about to walk out when a loud voice shouted at him from behind.

'Hey buddy!'

He turned to see who the greeting had come from. To his left, there were some lobby doors that were open, leading out onto a court yard with partial wooden decking; some metal chairs and tables with umbrellas spread around. A man sat in the light rain, drinking what JK assumed to be local beer. Next to him, a fat dog lay under a table, shielded from the rain.

'Welcome to Helsinki!' was the man's greeting, speaking with a brash American accent. He was young, with teeth braces, but he already had a well-developed beard. He dwarfed the chair he was sitting in and JK could tell he was a great big bear of a man.

He was holding aloft another can of beer, unopened, from a crate, waiting for acknowledgement.

'Hey,' said JK, again forcing a smile and waving while glancing back.

'Sit down, grab a beer. I need to get this crate finished up tonight – help me out buddy, I've got nowhere to store it.'

'Oh, thanks, but I can't, I need to go and find somewhere to stay tonight,' he replied, nervously.

'Stick around. I've got a good feeling about room space.'

'What do you mean?'

'You're wanting to check in, right?' said the man, as JK nodded back. 'Well, I've had an insider tip that there may be a couple of beds becoming available any minute now. Why don't you join me for a beer?'

JK mustered a small laugh as he looked at both the bearded man and the dog, hesitantly.

'Come on man. What's the worst that can happen? Trust me, I'm a walking good luck charm,' he said, laughing.

A combination of those words and his generosity somehow clicked in JK's head. Bugger it, he thought.

The dog, a bloodhound, hadn't moved during the whole conversation and even as JK got up to walk into the courtyard and sit next to the American, the dog remained unflinching as it lay with its head flopped over its crossed paws. Although a different breed, he remembered his own dog from many years ago. Poor old Busby.

'Is that your dog?' JK asked the American.

'No, he lives at the hostel, but he's as grumpy as hell, man – watch out.'

'Really? He seems pretty harmless; he hasn't moved an inch.'

JK bent down to stroke the dog who then suddenly lifted his head up and let out a low, deep bark. Shocked, JK looked back at the American. The dog still hadn't moved his body and quickly rested his head back down where it had been the whole time, staring vacantly across the courtyard, through the doors and back into the lobby.

'Ha, ha! See what I mean? His name is Bertie and he's a fat and lazy hound. He's depressed, supposedly.'

'What?'

'Apparently, the story is that when he was younger, he used to have a brother but he got run over and died, and he's been like this ever since.'

Now, this was interesting, JK thought. Bertie the bloodhound had been separated from his brother, as he had also been separated from his, albeit through his own choice. Was Bertie's depression some sort of omen as to his own? Had he made the wrong decision by parting ways from Bobby a few months ago in India?

JK noticed that a couple of older ladies, who had appeared from a door next to the desk, were chatting to the receptionist. They had their luggage with them. After a moment, they said their goodbyes and walked out, backpacks in tow.

'Excuse me!' the receptionist shouted over to him.

'Yes?' He looked up at her, puzzled, but with a hopeful glint in his eye, as she beckoned him over to the desk.

'Those two ladies have just checked out, meaning we now have vacancies for tonight and tomorrow. How many nights do you need?'

Suddenly, he became suspicious of the convenience of the whole affair.

'Oh, right, er I just need two nights actually, please. May I ask why they checked out at this time of night?'

'One of the ladies had asthma and she said the room was no good for her. You don't have asthma, do you?'

'No, no, I'm fine. Well, I guess that's a shame for her. But good luck for me, eh?' He paid a deposit, gave her his details and turned around back to the lobby to see the American smiling up at him. The bearded man took a large gulp of his beer, wiped his mouth with his sleeve and spoke.

'Well, stranger! It's your lucky day after all. What did I tell you?'

'Yeah, thank you. How did you know that was going to happen?'

'Aha! I heard those two old chicks moaning about the room earlier, just before you arrived. So I kinda guessed that they were gonna check out.' He paused to return JK's smile. 'Anyway, my name's Sean Charles, but everyone calls me Chuck. Where are you from, buddy?' Chuck offered his hand as he leaned forward, and JK accepted.

'Jonny Keane – or JK – and I'm from England, just near London, actually.'

'Well, it's a pleasure, Jonny,' said Chuck, putting on a false posh English accent. 'I'm from Oregon in the United States of America. So, are you travelling on your own?'

Picking up on JK's hesitation, Chuck felt compelled to jump in again.

'No shame if you are, man. I am. So many people do now, it's the best way to meet people.'

'I know. It's not that, but, I…er…had a falling out with someone.'

'Oh, right, I see. A lady friend?' Chuck smiled, raising an eyebrow.

'No, it was my brother, Bobby. I was with him in India a few months ago and we were meant to carry on travelling together. But we don't see eye to eye on everything.'

'Right, sorry man. What did you argue about?'

'Lots of stuff really. We have good days and bad days. And we couldn't agree on where we wanted to go to next. He's already been to so many places, more than me, and I felt I had to come to Scandinavia. So, that was it.'

'Hey, that sounds like my older sister. We fight all the time. And then a few hours later, we make up again. That's just what we do, right?'

JK paused. He didn't feel comfortable sharing the whole depth of his family dynamic with Chuck right now: his feelings about his father's list, still sitting neatly folded in his coat pocket; how Bobby hated their deceased father; they could never agree about those fundamental things.

'Well, we haven't spoken to each other since.' JK let his reply hang in the air.

'Wow. Really? Oh man, that is some fight.'

JK decided to take pity on Chuck's obvious awkwardness.

'Yes, but anyway, I'm sure we'll chat soon. I went home for a few weeks first and then decided to go for it. Eight weeks backpacking around Northern Europe. Then maybe I'll have to go back home and get a job.'

'Hey, fuck man, let's not talk about *that,*' Chuck bellowed, laughing. He grabbed another two beers from his crate and threw one at JK.

'So, have you met many other travellers here? Seems pretty quiet.'

'Just wait till you meet this dude I know! He has his own bowling alley! And he knows the owners of all these cool joints. Do you know Spy bar?' asked Chuck, excitedly.

'Yeah, I've heard of it. It's supposed to be amazing – well, according to the guide book anyway,' JK said.

'Yeah, he'll take us there; he knows the bouncer.'

As the rainfall began to get heavier, Chuck's drunken chatter was still audible over the sound of rain drops pounding on to the wooden decking. Bertie the dog finally moved, getting up and lumbering into the lobby.

'Well, where's your good luck now?' JK asked Chuck, holding his palm under the rain. He knew he had to put on a mask of humour occasionally, having realised some time ago travelling was made much easier if he made an effort with people, rather than default to his antisocial instincts.

'I thought you Brits would be used to this rain!' Chuck barked back.

Although JK had let himself feel partly relieved at securing a place to stay, he still couldn't completely shake off his unease. Watching the slow, wobbling, dark brown body of Bertie half collapse into a new position next to the lobby's front desk had started to bring back more sad memories of his childhood dog, now long gone.

He tried to ignore these as the beer cans continued to appear from Chuck's bottomless crate. It was possible they weren't mixing too well with the diazepam already in his system.

'We had a dog once; Busby was his name.' JK said. 'He was a lovely, friendly golden retriever; a big part of my life when we were growing up. Everyone loved him.'

'What happened?'

'He disappeared one day and never came back. I was about nine years old...'

'Sorry man.'

'I still blame myself.'

'Why is that?'

'I think,' JK hesitated, 'I just think I could've done more to look after him, you know? Stop him from bolting off like that.'

'Don't beat yourself up, buddy. Dogs aren't that smart; sometimes they just run away.'

'Yeah, I know. I can't help it, I guess.' JK looked down at the floor, keeping the real reason for his guilt silent and hidden. He didn't feel ready to share that with anyone yet. Let alone Chuck.

But smile on, JK thought. Chuck was a good luck charm after all.

At 3am, JK, Chuck and various other travellers who had joined their group arrived back at their hostel. JK had done his best to remain friendly and sociable throughout their night out in town, which included a visit to the trendy – and many others that were not so trendy – Spy bar.

Now, entering his dorm room alone, there was no escaping his own thoughts this time – even though he desperately wanted to. He saw his bottle of tablets in the top of his rucksack and, feeling unsteady on his feet, contemplated not taking his medication. But he knew that would probably be worse for him. Perhaps it might make him sleep better. So, he took his dosage.

As he undressed, he thought of his dog again and a tear formed in his eye. He lay on his bed staring up at the ceiling, and hoped that sleep would take him soon.

I always knew why it had happened, even though I had never told anyone. It was a punishment for my actions.

Growing up, we would go to our local park, and within it there was a man-made lake which I would occasionally cycle by. I was nine years old when one day I caught sight of something shining down at the bank of the lake. I stopped and got off my bike to take a closer look.

Down in the soil was a gold chain, a necklace. I looked around to see if anyone could lay claim to it but the clearing around the bank, in front of a small cluster of trees, was empty and silent, so I scooped it up in my hands for a closer look.

It had a solid metal letter 'b' looped on to the chain. I didn't know much about jewellery but I knew it looked valuable. The chain was a series of three or four fine strands with tiny links embedded in. Also, none of the covering colour had worn away, and I had seen my brother wear some cheaper jewellery where the gold had worn off to reveal sliver underneath. It seemed like this could have lasted for a long time, but I wasn't sure.

In any case, I knew I had to keep hold of it, so, after looking around again, I quickly put it in my pocket and picked up my bike, ready to leave.

'What was that you just pocketed?'

It was my brother, Bobby; he had snuck up on me after leaving his bike a few metres away. I had thought he was well ahead of me as I hadn't seen him in twenty minutes. But he had a habit of disappearing like that.

'Oh, nothing, just some stone I liked the look of,' I replied, sheepishly.

'Liar.'

Bobby ran over to me and punched me in the arm, and while I was distracted with the pain, he reached into my pocket and grabbed the chain. He took a closer look and smiled back at me.

'Very nice, Jonny, I like it. Well, I don't want you to lose this so I'd better look after it for you.' My brother was an asshole back then. And not just to me, pretty much everyone.

I was about to shout my protest back at him when we heard something ahead of us, outside the clearing.

We both turned around to hear noises entering the clearing from the opposite end. I strained to see two figures walking to the edge of the lake. I could hear them talking; one was a tall boy about fourteen, perhaps a bit older than Bobby, but the other was a girl, shorter and a lot younger, perhaps a year younger than me. They were both mixed race, and possibly brother and sister. I suddenly realised that they were both from our school. I knew the boy, and the girl was in the year below me, but I only vaguely knew her and struggled to remember her name.

I don't know why but Bobby then suddenly went into stealth mode and ran to some bushes to hide and observe. He ushered me over as he did so, putting his finger up to his lips. I followed him, like I always did back in those days, so we both crouched, hidden as we observed the two kids.

Their voices became louder and more aggressive and then I realised they were arguing. They were looking for something. And I could guess exactly what it was. I heard the girl shout out 'Eddie' at the boy. That's when I remembered her name, Beth Harvey, and that Eddie was definitely her older brother.

Bobby and Eddie definitely knew each other. They had fought at school once, about a year before maybe. I think it was an argument about our dad but Bobby never spoke much about it. All I did know was that Eddie's mother and father had divorced but unusually it was their mother who had left them to go back to Germany, her country of birth. The fight had related to that, and as word spread around school, the watching crowd grew, but I had arrived too late to see it. I think the rumour was that Bobby had provoked Eddie about his mother first. He had said something mean about her having an affair, which Eddie retaliated to with some nasty comment about our dad. He said everyone knew our dad was a cheat anyway and our mum was probably glad he was dead already.

Obviously this had upset Bobby and it escalated from there. It was just one of those nasty school incidents that stayed clearly in your head. I don't know what Bobby had said to start with; he just seemed so angry in those days, always wanting to upset people. He hasn't improved much to this day apart from replacing the anger with recklessness.

In any case, hiding here by the lake, we quickly understood that Eddie had lost his sister's chain. It was a present from their mother, Brenda, and had been hers previously so was of extra sentimental value.

This was my opportunity to say something to them, but, as the scene unfolded in front of us, Bobby had a firm grasp of my arm, and so a mixture of fear and excitement prevented me from doing so. I felt guilty, of course, but not enough to open my mouth.

Eventually Beth and Eddie walked along another footpath away from us, and so we turned around and got on our bikes to quickly escape. I followed Bobby's lead, and he made sure we remained out of their eyeshot by cycling along the edge of the park, next to some railings, and then some trees, all the way to the exit.

I never asked Bobby why he didn't say anything either. In fact, we never spoke again on the matter. I never knew what he did with that stupid chain and whether he gave it back or not.

The next day after we had found it was a Monday, and so we were back at school. When we got home, our mum told us that our dog, Busby, had left the house to chase something out of our drive. He hadn't come back and never did. It was all very sad for our family, and after many hours of searching and days of hoping he would show up again, we just accepted it as bad luck, knowing we had lost him.

Several other things since then have made me stop and think about stealing that chain. Over the following years at school, Beth became more and more badly behaved, getting into fights with other girls, and forever arguing with teachers. She became a smoker and got piercings, and whenever I saw her around, I felt a twang of regret switch on in my head, and guilt rushed into my stomach. I guess feelings of rejection, by your own mother, and especially for a girl, must really affect a kid

That's when I first realised there was luck in this world, both good and bad. Call it what you want: karma, yin-yang, superstition, a supernatural force, magic – whatever, but it was all around me. I knew that anything I did had meaning, and could come back to have some effect on my life later on.

Having discussed their travel plans during their drunken night out in Helsinki, Chuck and JK knew they were heading in the same direction and decided to stay together for a while. Separately they had both accepted they would never be close friends, but supposed it was better to have a travel partner. Most significantly, JK thought Chuck would bring him good luck.

So, a few days later Chuck had swayed JK into going on a trip to the Arctic Circle.

'How many saps do you know that have ever been somewhere like that? You can say you've done it. You've gotta do it man,' he had said.

And after JK had chatted to various backpackers in hostels, bars and on trips, they had all agreed with Chuck, that he should take a detour from his planned route and go north to cross the Arctic Circle.

So, they booked a one-way flight to Rovaniemi, in Lapland, northern Finland. They arrived early on a clear morning after a flight that took less than an hour and a short journey on the shuttle bus to a hostel in town. Rovaniemi was very small, and yet the roads were very wide and bare. You couldn't see many trees or bushes, the buildings were spaced out and they all looked quite new, yet they lacked character.

This town couldn't be older than forty years, JK had guessed. After checking in, unpacking and having some breakfast, Chuck and JK walked around town. It was still very quiet, even though it had now passed 9am.

'I see you bought some of that amber shit?' Chuck said to JK, looking down at a pendant he had round his neck.

'What, this? Yeah, I got it in India.' His tired reply was the most he could manage after their early start.

'They tried to con me into buying the same crap when I was in Tallinn, in Estonia. Some bullshit about good luck.' Chuck's reply confused JK.

'Well, I quite like it anyway,' JK said, struggling to form the words. 'In any case, I thought you thought you were a lucky charm?'

'You mean that crap I threw you in Helsinki when you were checking in? Hell man, that was just me being a little bit crafty, as I guess you Brits would say. Nothing lucky about it, dude.'

'Oh, right. Fair enough.' He avoided eye contact with the big man as he continued to stare back at JK. JK started to scratch his head.

'Don't tell me you believe in that hocus-pocus too?'

'Well, I can't see what harm it does. I mean, if it's true, I'm not losing out by wearing it, am I?'

'Oh man, that is fucked up. You've spent forty dollars on a worthless stone because some local con man told you a load of mumbo jumbo.'

'It was more like twenty dollars and I don't think *she* was a con man. It was a really nice lady who worked at my hostel.'

'Yes sir, that sounds right, you wanted her! And she knew it. She's seen a thousand young, fresh-faced pricks like you before, and was hearing that cash register *ting* as soon as you walked in through her door!'

'Oh, for god's sake. OK, yes, I happen to believe in luck, so what?'

'And don't tell me – God too, right?' Chuck rolled his eyes.

'No, no, I'm not religious or anything – but I'll admit I've always been the superstitious type. That's just the way it is. Anyway, I thought it was us Brits who were supposed to be the cynical ones, not you Yanks,' JK snapped back, wearily.

'Superstitions. This should be good – like what?'

'Black cats, walking under ladders, touching wood when you say "touch wood" – all that sort of stuff.'

'Huh. A bit old-fashioned, isn't it?' Chuck's smile was starting to fade now.

'Probably, I don't care; I remembered all those silly little things my parents, aunts, uncles or their friends used to tell me – I guess it gave me a bit of a fright when I was young and impressionable. If something scares you, even if it's just the idea, it does stay with you.'

They walked past a large building site which was eerily quiet, with no workers to be seen. On the surrounding boards, they saw some posters for what was being constructed, the garish and cunningly titled 'SantaPark'. This would be an amusement park for kids with all manner of rides, sweets, toys and events dedicated to Father Christmas. The longer they walked in silence, the more quickly it became apparent that they were the only ones creating any sort of noise on the streets.

Chuck started to mumble some local history to break the silence. Supposedly, this was the original home of Santa Claus. In order to cross the Arctic Circle, they had to go through 'Santa Claus Village' which, unlike SantaPark, was always open. Chuck took great delight in confirming that the village had been expanded by an American settler in the 1950s.

Rovaniemi had been a small village which was starting to boom on profits from access to good ski runs nearby in the winter. The original settler had decided to make the most of this by exaggerating the Santa Claus legend – starting a year-round tourist attraction in the Arctic Circle. That probably explained the strange time-warped feel of the town in contrast to the rest of the country, JK thought.

'What do you reckon? This place doesn't seem to have much soul, does it, Chuck?'

'Yeah, it looks like a dump. It reminds of some towns in the States I've been through. It seems very new.' Chuck frowned.

'I don't really understand it as I'm sure the Finnish would've had a settlement here centuries ago. It just looks like it's got no identity of its own. Maybe it's just a tourist trap.'

'Maybe it's the daylight thing,' Chuck said, licking his lips as he prepared to roll off another stat. 'You know in summer, they only have one hour of darkness all day?'

'Yeah, I'd heard that. It's the reverse in winter, only one hour of light all day,' JK replied, straight-faced, knowing that he had stolen Chuck's thunder with his equally impressive knowledge.

'No wonder they have the highest suicide rate in the world. Poor fucks,' Chuck smugly added.

They walked up a street to the bus stop that would take them to Santa Claus Village and the Arctic Circle. A black cat crossed the pavement in front of JK as he approached.

JK looked up at Chuck, and he glanced back. Remembering their earlier conversation, he decided against saying anything as they spotted a bus driving up the road ahead of them.

On the way to the village, they made another stop where a couple of young men with Down's syndrome got on. They were with a lady who was helping them and were on their way to the village too. Chuck made an extremely distasteful scrunched up face at JK, sticking his tongue in his bottom lip to mock them. JK turned away, shaking his head.

'Look at that,' Chuck then said, tapping JK on the shoulder.

JK dreaded what he was up to next but turned around anyway. As the bus pulled away, JK saw over Chuck's right shoulder, through the window, four magpies standing in a group on the grass.

'Good day sir, good day sir, good day sir, good day sir,' JK said, softly.

'*What?*' Chuck asked, amazed.

'Well, you'll probably laugh at me but it's a superstition thing.'

'I knew it! Jeez, you *are* crazy. I saw you look at me when that cat crossed in front of us earlier.'

'That was good luck!' JK replied.

'It's bad luck in America, pal!'

'Not in England, mate. If a black cat crosses you, it's good luck.'

'Whatever dude, I don't believe that horse shit. Those stupid birds are supposed to be bad luck back home too – I just wanted to see your reaction! So how does it go again?'

'You have to greet a magpie with "good day sir" each time you see one, otherwise it's bad luck. And if you say it without seeing one, like I just did, you then have to say it backwards. Ris yad doog.' JK started to scratch his head again, more violently this time.

'Oh god, dude, that is fucking psychotic! Is that a British thing?' Chuck's eyes were wide in amazement.

'Yeah, it is. I suppose it is kinda weird.' JK laughed, insincerely, avoiding the gaze of Chuck once more.

'Kinda? It's kinda fucked up, is what it is. We don't have any shit like that back home in the US.'

They arrived in the village and did the touristy-type stuff that was expected of them. They met 'Santa', getting a comedy-staged photo with him, saw the reindeers (Chuck decided to throw stones at one of them), bought some tacky souvenirs, and of course, their main objective, they crossed the Arctic Circle.

But walking through this fake village still gave JK a strange feeling. He could imagine that in the thick of a bright winter, with a snow carpet laid down and everyone wrapped up warm, it would be quite a sight. But now, in the spring, it wasn't exactly a welcoming place: it was cloudy, a bit chilly with a strong wind, and there was no beauty around, just silence, exposed soil, small patches of grass, patchy bushes, trees that only had half their leaves – browns and greys everywhere.

Abruptly breaking this silence were the sounds of wind chimes and bells. Overall it had quite an unsettling effect on JK, as if the town was hiding some dark sinister secret.

They stopped for lunch, just after Chuck had cleared his throat and spat on the pavement outside. His lack of manners was starting to grate on JK now. Inside one of the tourist buildings they found a creepy, dank-looking cafe. On the walls hung a series of sketched black and white paintings, which the owners had intended to look authentically historic. A child in an old dress; an old man just staring out into the distance; a middle-aged woman – also dressed a lot older – in a similar pose. Perhaps it was their eyes, JK thought, but they just looked scary.

JK ordered a very safe and simple meal of burger and chips, but Chuck ordered a more tourist-influenced dish: reindeer pizza. After waiting for almost forty minutes, with Chuck muttering and swearing has each minute passed, their plates eventually arrived where they sat.

'Oh boy, I can't wait to tuck into Rudolph!' exclaimed Chuck, as JK rolled his eyes and realised he no longer cared about hiding his disgust.

'You're pathetic! And this place is so weird,' JK said.

'Now what's up with you, dude?'

'Well all those pictures for a start. They look terrible. And how rude are all the staff here? They just seem to stare at you blankly, wait ages to speak to you, and they never smile.'

'I thought that's what all you Europeans were like? Customer Service ain't your thing, is it?'

'Yeah, funny – only when it's American customers, though! I dunno, I just think this whole town gives me the creeps. It's just too false; something doesn't feel right.'

'What, you mean like it's haunted? You've been watching way too many Halloween movies, dude.'

'Well, not haunted. Have you ever seen a film called "The Wicker Man"?'

'Yeah, that's a great movie. Maybe you're right. All the locals could be in some secret society or cult, or Satan worshippers or something, and as soon as all the tourists have gone, they all come out chanting and then burn stuff!'

Chuck was laughing now, but JK wasn't.

'OK, you don't have to take the piss. I'm just saying, it's a bit weird.'

'Well, it's gonna get weirder too. Look, some more window-lickers have arrived.'

JK looked up to see what Chuck was talking about and shook his head at him again. Around twenty mentally disabled people had entered with five carers. It was some sort of group outing; they had seen them going around the village all day in smaller groups.

'Now they give me the creeps,' Chuck said, stuffing his mouth full of pizza.

'Try and show a little bit of class for once, Chuck,' JK replied, quietly.

'Jeez man, I'm only kidding. Try and take the bug out of your ass, why don't you?'

And from this moment onwards, their relationship during the rest of their village tour was irreparably broken. They alternated between petty arguments or awkward silences, including during the whole of their bus journey back to town. On arrival, as they stepped off the bus, they briefly looked at each other.

'Right, well, Chuck. I'll see you back at the hostel. I've gotta make some calls and run some errands in town.'

'OK man. I can wait around for you if you want; I can kill some time in the stores.'

JK really wanted some time alone. He stumbled on his reply.

'Well, to be honest, they're some private calls I need to make back home mate… and, er, I could be a while,' he said, knowing his attempt at subtlety had failed.

'Oh right, dude, I get it. I'll see you later then.' Chuck turned away sharply but JK could tell from his eyes that he had upset him. JK was about to say something back but Chuck had already rushed off, to cross the road.

Sighing, JK decided to carry on up the main street to the shops. His evening was a solitary one, having completed his largely fabricated chores, he returned to the hostel and did not see Chuck for the rest of the evening. After eating a small and extremely unappetising self-made dinner alone in the hostel dining area, he watched some TV before heading back to their dorm room.

With the awkwardness still lingering in his thoughts, JK lay in bed reading with Chuck's empty bed hovering in his eye-line, his things spread out everywhere in a chaotic mess – normality for Chuck. He felt himself nodding off, and switched the light off before Chuck had returned.

Santa and Christmas Day was never that good a memory for me anyway. Although last year had been a good one, getting drunk with Bobby and Rick in Goa, it didn't really count as a 'proper' Christmas.

For a long time my family Christmases had been getting worse and worse. Come to think of it, twelve years ago was the first one I can remember as it was so awful. It was just Mum, Bobby and me all together at once for a change. Normally Bobby would go off round friends. But we had lost our dog earlier that year, and Busby had obviously kept most of us happy in the years after Dad had died. He'd been a great distraction, but with him out of the picture, my god, we had a sorry family scene in our house.

Mainly, the strain had been on Bobby. He was the one who just wouldn't try and make any effort to enjoy it. It made it so much harder for our poor mum. She just wanted to spoil us, but not with extravagant presents as we didn't have much money. It was the cooking, the decorations, the music; she really went to town. The almost-perfect illusion, even though, every year, both Bobby and I would hear her crying downstairs, later in the evening, after she thought we'd gone to bed.

But no, Bobby would never play along. Each year he would get more irritable with it. 'What's the point?' he would say, or 'Why do you bother, Mum? It doesn't mean anything anyway.'

I remember one year I tried to bring up the subject of my father, and what he used to do with us at Christmas, because my memories of him were so lacking. My mum seemed nervous to answer but slowly started to share a few things. I got excited as I was finally starting to learn more about this mysterious figure in my life that everyone avoided talking about.

But as soon as Bobby walked in the room, things changed. My mum looked even more cautious after he appeared, but I enthusiastically brought him into the conversation to see what his memories of Dad were.

'Him? You want to know about him?' Bobby had shouted back at me. I quickly nodded, staring at him, and was just a little bit scared by the angry look on his face. Mum had got up to try and grab him.

'No, Mum. Leave me alone. It's about time we told him about our dear old Dad, don't you think?' Bobby shook off Mum's approach. He must've been around fifteen or so by then, so was more than strong enough for Mum to think twice.

'Please, Bobby, just leave it, will you?' Mum looked distraught.

'Our dad was a complete asshole, that's what he was. He drank too much, gambled too much, and treated us like crap. You wanna know about him at Christmas? Well, he's the reason why our family Christmases' are so shit every year compared to everyone else's. If you ask me, he's better off dead. Better for everyone, including you. So, don't fucking ask me about him again. In fact, you're better off just forgetting all about him.'

My mum slapped him across the face, and he grabbed her hand as I could see his eyes blazing in anger. He held it but after a couple of seconds, he let go and stormed out of the house. Mum looked at me with pity, but couldn't hold my gaze. Then she turned around and went upstairs.

Bobby never really explained why he felt that way about Dad, and Mum never talked about it. We had similar arguments over the years that followed, although nothing quite as dramatic as that. Everything was always buried by Bobby and Mum.

And for the last few years, Bobby was away for most of Christmas travelling anyway, so it was an even more sombre affair with just my mum and I, as we both got quietly drunk and fell asleep in front of the TV.

Merry Christmas, I thought, as I tried to hold back a tear.

JK had been unable to sleep much once again. Another side effect of his medication and a reflection of his current mood. Chuck arrived back at 2am but JK had kept his eyes closed and buried his head in his pillow. At about 6am, he decided to get out of bed and explore the local area, leaving Chuck snoring in a bunk bed opposite.

It was light outside but cloudy and, initially, it had turned out to be a disappointing walk. Their hostel sat just off a main highway in and out of town with very few walkways to any nature.

Eventually, he found a path leading to the river bank and decided to wander and see where it took him. Time dissolved as various fears and worries kept re-surfacing into his thoughts. Before he knew it, he realised he was heading back into town towards his hostel again.

Feeling a wave of tiredness hit him, he decided to buy a coffee. He found a small cafe at the end of the road on a corner, and recognised that the connecting road was the long main road that his hostel was on, perhaps a ten-minute walk away.

Sitting alone by the window, he ordered and stared out at the empty streets, watching them slowly start to awaken, as cars and pedestrians gradually appeared. The hot black coffee arrived and he let the aroma float up across his face as he waited for it to cool down. He felt his body start to relax as the sun began to become more prominent through the clouds. Although he knew that he daren't feel optimism, he did realise that he had suddenly, and unexpectedly, started to experience a tingling of anticipation.

JK looked up and saw a man approaching, along the main road but on the opposite side to the cafe. The figure was quite large, and as he got closer, JK could see the profile was quite familiar; it was Chuck. He wondered why he was up so early.

Then, out of the corner of his eye, he spotted something small crossing the same main road, but much further back than Chuck was now. JK squinted, straining to see what it was. It looked long and thin, although the front end of it was much bigger, almost like a brown snake. It was crossing the road from JK's side towards Chuck.

Looking back to Chuck, JK saw that he had now started to cross the road too, in the opposite direction as the unidentified object, towards JK. Coming into focus, JK could now see what it was. A family of ducks, bizarrely enough; a full-grown mother at one end and six little ducklings trailing behind in a line were attempting the hazardous journey.

It was a wide road and Chuck was concentrating on the traffic on his side so hadn't seen them yet. They had made it about half way across their side of the road when a large lorry approached them. The driver didn't know what to do and so slammed down hard on the brakes. Although he was slowing down, it was obvious he was still going to hit them, so he had to swerve sharply to his right, as there were pedestrians to his left.

It was disastrous either way. On the other side of the road another car approached, which Chuck had just crossed behind. He stood, watching, in the middle of the road, perhaps ten metres away. The other car now slammed on its brakes too to avoid contact with the truck that had just veered in front of it — but it was too late. They crashed almost head on.

The impact of the crash jolted the truck hard and the straps that held its load — rows of metal scaffolding poles on the open trailer at the back — momentarily went slack. At this moment, several of these poles were sent flying straight ahead off the cabin, which was turned at right angles to the trailer section, up the road in the original direction of the truck. In their path, Chuck was still standing, looking back, transfixed and startled.

JK would never forget that image of him, standing motionless, split seconds before one of the poles flew horizontally into the middle of his throat. He was knocked backwards, and collapsed to the tarmac from the weight of the pole, protruding out in front of his neck. And, as he gargled in his own blood, he caught his last sight on earth.

The family of ducks, which had scattered in the commotion of the truck, first breaking and then its subsequent crash, had now all reconvened into one line again. They were attempting the crossing again, further up the road, behind the truck. All in one piece and a happy family again, oblivious to the surrounding chaos, they made it successfully across the road this time.

Chapter Three

Fate, Festivals and Fallacy

A car horn sounded outside their house. Waving back to their mother, JK closed the front door and walked down to Bobby, sitting in his blue and purple Mini at the bottom of the driveway. The engine was enthusiastically ticking over.

It was an old car but it was one of the few things Bobby had taken great pride in, enhancing it in some way whenever he could afford to. It didn't really fit with his carefree attitude to life, a fact that made JK smile. Chrome was everywhere and JK had just noticed the most recent additions – two bright yellow plastic discs with smiley faces painted on – attached to the front bumper. JK climbed into the passenger seat.

'About time, JK! Let's hope I don't get bored by any of your nonsense about good luck – we've still got two whole hours to kill,' Bobby said, as he drove the car off their drive and onto the road.

'All right, don't start on me this early. Are you sure this thing is going to make it all the way to the festival? It's a death trap,' JK fired back, smiling.

'Shut up! This is a bona fide classic – she's a beauty!'

Laughing, JK switched on the radio to one of Bobby's pre-set stations that played dance music. As a loud bass beat blasted out from the speakers, he had to turn the volume down.

'She? Next you'll be telling me that you've named it.'

'*She* has been with me all the way, I'll have you know. Ever since I bought her six years ago. Remember, it only cost me a hundred quid?'

'Yes, Bobby, I remember. But since then you've spent four times that on the engine and three times that on the body work and chrome. And what about those stupid smiley faces? They'll get nicked in no time in the car park.'

'Bollocks they will. Anyway, I needed a summer addition, mate, it's a tradition now. One of my part-time jobs paid for it. They were only about forty quid.'

JK smiled and leant forward to turn the volume back up. As they made their way to the motorway on a clear Friday morning in August, he yawned and stretched on the seat. He felt cramped already and could only guess how his brother felt, who was several inches taller than him. He stared out of the window and realised this could be their last bit of fun together for the summer of 1997.

He didn't often spend much time at home nowadays. Neither of them did. But JK was on holiday from university after a year out travelling, and so was only staying there temporarily. Suddenly he realised that he wasn't used to the things he had seen round the house these last few weeks.

Their mother had starting putting pictures up of their father, after having years of barely seeing anything related to him round the house. He didn't know why; whether it was for his own benefit or some other reason entirely, he had no idea.

The few pictures they had of him had always made him look so scruffy. A crumpled shabby appearance, his dirty finger tips and finger nails with ground in oil and dirt from the garage he had run. His curly brown hair with a full beard and moustache that hid most of his face but a pair of enigmatic, yet sad-looking, eyes stood out.

JK looked across to his brother and could see he had the same tight brown curls of hair just like their dad, minus the beard and the grey hairs of course. Perhaps Bobby had the same cheekbones as our father, he thought, but couldn't be sure.

But now JK finally noticed that it was their eyes. Bobby's eyes had always stood out; everyone would always comment on them. And JK could now see how that was the one true similarity to their father, their unusual amber eye colouring.

Immediately, deeper memories were evoked in JK. His father digging into his pockets to find loose change only to bring out all manner of buttons, nuts, bolts and other small mechanical parts or assorted unidentified junk. His constant talking, mumbling almost, through a mouth that used to scrunch up under his beard whenever he smiled, like he was unintentionally doing a comedy gurning action. A whiff of whisky on his breath.

'Is everything OK, JK?' Bobby said, interrupting JK's daydreaming.

'Oh, yeah, of course. I'm probably sill half asleep,' he replied, awkwardly.

Silence hung in the air, as JK struggled with the urge to discuss anything further with his brother. JK guessed that Bobby probably hadn't seen these recent photos. He had only popped in for a quick cup of tea with their mother this morning. But JK knew he had to speak to Bobby about this eventually, and tried to test the water gently.

'Mum seems a bit different, don't you think?' JK asked, casually.

Bobby paused before replying and glanced at JK before turning back to the road.

'Not really. Why do you say that?' Bobby asked.

'Well, she seems that bit more talkative and positive. Just overly keen to get on with me, maybe.'

'That's difficult for anyone, to be fair, JK!' Bobby said, smiling.

'Ha ha! You know what I mean. Haven't you noticed?'

'Not especially. I guess I should be round there more often than I am. But she never phones me,' Bobby replied, coldly.

'Well, nothing new there Bobby. And what about… what's with all those… photos?' JK finally asked, with trepidation.

'What, you mean all those tacky Charles and Diana ones from the eighties?'

JK smiled for a second as he remembered their mother's fondness for the Royal family. This had often embarrassed both JK and Bobby when visitors to their home saw the various pictures of the famous 1981 wedding that she had on display.

'Oh god, those things? No, I was trying to forget them! I never really worked out why she liked them so much anyway; she never even mentioned the Royal family.'

'I think she wanted to try and surround herself with good things to remember from that time. There was enough happening to us already for her to think about.'

JK knew that Bobby was referring to the death of their father.

'Yes, well, anyway, I didn't mean those photos,' JK continued.

'Really? Well, I don't know what you mean then – I haven't noticed any others,' Bobby replied, blankly.

'Oh, come on. Didn't you see them earlier? There were loads of them on display. I think she's gradually been putting more and more up, starting a few months ago, before I last went travelling.'

JK could see his brother frowning now, and yet he still refused to respond.

'You really can't bring yourself to even say his name, can you?' JK finally asked.

'What do you want me to say? I didn't tell her to put those pictures up. And I never would. It's none of my business anyway – I don't live there anymore. Come to think of it, you're only a temporary guest, so it's none of your business either.'

'Our father? None of our business? Can you even hear yourself sometimes?' JK snapped back.

'Do we really have to do this again? You know what I think of him.'

'Yes, I know, I know. You hate him. But why has Mum put these pictures up now? He's been dead for so long.'

JK had never really understood why their father died so early in his life. Initially he couldn't accept that it was an accident, or bad luck, or a purely random event. As a child, attempting to grow up and understand such serious emotions, he had been convinced there should've been some meaningful reason for it to have happened.

Of course, he never found one; but thanks to his brother Bobby, after a while it didn't seem to matter as much. Just being around him had helped JK overcome that need to find a reason all the time.

Bobby didn't need a reason to explain his father's death. It wasn't that he didn't care; far from it. He had completely internalised it a long time ago, but his way of outwardly accepting it was to be permanently angry at the world, and he wanted to take everyone down with him. He struggled to form lasting friendships as somehow he would always find a way to upset the people that cared about him.

For as long as JK could remember noticing, Bobby was a wild child who did not take anyone or anything seriously, never worrying about reasons or consequences. He was the definition of spontaneous and, of course, from an early and impressionable age, JK had always admired and wanted to be a little bit like him.

He certainly knew that he would always be the more sensible one of the two of them. Bobby's behaviour helped remind JK what the impact of their father's death was on the whole family. With the kind of incidents that his brother put them all through, JK tried to stop looking for reasons all the time and instead focus on a more positive reaction to their father's death.

Yet, JK had struggled with this balance: his constant fear, worries and dread eventually resulted in a depression that squeezed him from the inside, and it often outweighed any desires he had for a positive outlook.

So, the two brothers existed in a state of limbo, knowing that they were each trapped in their own emotional maze. They knew they could probably help each other out of it but were just unsure how. It had always been that way.

'I can't help you, JK. You need to speak to Mum. I don't have a clue what she's doing,' Bobby said, curtly, looking at traffic on his right, waiting to enter a roundabout.

'You mean you don't want to help me.'

JK could see Bobby's cheeks redden as he turned his face back to him, angry at his response. At the same time, through the windscreen, JK glimpsed the driver of a car as it passed by – an attractive woman – who made eye contact with him. A pretty young girl, perhaps twenty-one years old. There was traffic on the roundabout and she stopped her car not far in front of them.

Unfortunately, Bobby had not seen this car and, still angry with JK, glanced hastily over his right shoulder to see that he was clear to pull away and accelerated onto the roundabout. He managed to hit the brakes before he built up too much speed, but it was too late, and their car slammed into the back of the girl's car with a loud crunch.

'Fuck!' shouted Bobby.

'Are you OK?' JK asked.

'Yeah. Fine… Are you?'

'Yeah, I'm OK. We should probably check them, though.'

Bobby put his hazard lights on and had just seen that the car in front had switched theirs on now also. He opened his door and got out.

JK watched as Bobby walked across to the driver and then saw him also glance to the back of the car, where JK could see lots of bags. Bobby started talking to the driver and then JK saw him nod before he jogged back to their car.

'She's fine – it doesn't look too bad. We're gonna drive off the roundabout, straight ahead, and then pull into the hard shoulder to exchange details,' Bobby said, breathlessly.

'OK. Does she have any passengers?'

'Yes, just one. Another girl. Both remarkably good looking,' he said, smiling, to which JK rolled his eyes.

Within a few minutes both cars had stopped on the hard shoulder. JK could see there was minimal damage to the other car, just a dent in the rear bumper. The driver, with long, luxurious blonde hair, and her passenger were already standing beside their car, waiting for Bobby.

Bobby and JK got out and approached the girls.

'Hey, look, completely my fault, girls, I'm really sorry. I wasn't looking. Are you both OK?'

'Yes, we are, luckily. Just a bit shaken up.' There was definitely a frosty tone from the blonde as she eyed Bobby with suspicion.

JK looked back at their car and couldn't see any other damage at all besides the small dent, although he suspected there would be some scratches on the bumper if he were to look closer.

'Well, the damage doesn't seem all that bad. I'm sure our insurance will easily sort this out.'

The passenger, with jet-black hair and dark skin, then leant across and whispered something to her friend, who then looked back to Bobby.

'OK, that's good. I'll get my details in a sec,' she replied with a smile, and let her words hang in the air, before she continued, 'So tell me, boys, you don't happen to be going to the same festival as us, do you?' The girl had switched to a more optimistic tone now.

Her passenger had seen bags in the back of the boys' car in the same way JK had, and had just made an educated guess they were heading in the same direction. They exchanged details and introduced themselves, agreeing to meet up later.

Just as they turned around to go back to their cars, JK looked back at the driver at the same time she had looked back at him, catching the gaze of her unmistakable blue eyes once more.

'Look, we really are sorry about this, Di,' he said.

'Don't be silly, JK. No one was hurt. C'est la vie – such is life,' she replied.

'Que sera, sera?' JK asked, with a pretence of mystery.

'Whatever will be, will be. Yes, very apt, JK,' she said, laughing back at him.

Bobby stood at his car door, feigning a look of disgust.

'Oh jeez, sorry about my younger brother's cheesy old song reference, girls. You know there will be lots of young and trendy people at this music festival, right, JK?' Bobby laughed as the two girls joined in.

He looked at JK with a glint in his amber eyes, exerting his sibling dominance, and JK returned a wry smile.

'Anyway, I prefer "Shit happens, then you die",' said Bobby, as he smirked over at Di, as she shook her head.

'That's even worse, Bobby. Both you boys need to sharpen up your chat-up lines. Hopefully see you later. But try not to crash into anyone else before that!' she said, getting back into her car as her friend laughed and did the same.

Bobby and JK got back into their car, silently watching as the girls pulled away from the hard shoulder. Shortly after, they found a gap in traffic and set off down the motorway, following them.

The next morning, JK lay in his sleeping bag, watching sunlight filter through the flimsy tent walls. The light was slowly massaging his senses into 'awake' mode, fighting against the grubby, sweaty and humid air in his nostrils, as well as the pain running through his alcohol-impaired head and sleep-deprived muscles.

His sensory recall was completely confused as sporadic sights, sounds and feelings from the previous day sparkled into his brain: standing proud in a massive field, spoilt for choice as he-people-watched among a crowd of over 90,000 sun-crisped, booze-stewed subjects.

He had flash-backs of the previous evening, swaying along to the tunes along with tens of thousands of strangers surrounding him. Yet, they all felt like friends as they sang as one, long into a perfect summer night. There was a last rousing encore rendition of 'Disco 2,000', an anthem of the time for JK and his group.

The intensity of emotion, and of mutual happiness, on that first night was as genuine and pure a moment that he had ever had in his life.

Yet now, JK felt the low coming. Perhaps it was the hangover, but he knew his body well enough by now for it to be more than just that. Or perhaps because he hadn't taken his meds recently: a few days earlier he had been feeling good and hadn't felt the need to.

Since then, however, little things had slowly begun to confuse his emotions again. Why did he feel like this now? Last night, the festival had provided a certainty of feeling along with a huge crowd; an unstated, yet undeniable, tangible positive energy penetrated his mind and body, a strange but welcoming natural high. Seeing complete strangers – both nearby and in the distance – smile, cheer and raise their arms in unison to a shared sound and vision. It had engulfed him like an infectious and invisible fog; and just for a few moments last night, he had been able to switch off and think that everything, everywhere, in his life was good.

It was inevitable, he reasoned, that he would come crashing down eventually.

He permitted himself another sardonic smile as waking up got easier, but not enough to warrant any strenuous movements.

He could hear his friends slowly emerging from their tents. Lying still, the first voices he heard were Bobby and his Scottish friend, Rick.

'I can't believe you did that last night, Bobby, you filthy bastard! Show your face,' Rick shouted back towards the tent he shared with Bobby.

'What?' replied Bobby, sheepishly, still in his customary jovial and good-natured tone, but staying within the anonymity of his tent.

'You know what! You're a sick man!'

There was a pause and then a rustling from the tent as Rick sat waiting for a reply on the tarpaulin entrance. Rick sat with Georgie, Di's passenger in the car that JK and Bobby had crashed into the day before, along with a couple, Chris and Katie, who were Georgie's friends. They were on the edge of a small circle they had formed to enclose all four tents in their group.

'Morning, everyone!' Bobby half emerged, looking dishevelled but with a mischievous glint in his eye. 'What time is it? You're all very keen, aren't you?' he muttered, sarcastically.

'8am. Breakfast time I reckon,' replied Georgie, as she fiddled her long straight, black hair into a pony tail.

'Good idea. Where the fuck are my sausages anyway?' Bobby said, straight faced.

Rick grabbed a semi-crushed beer can from the ground and threw it at Bobby, who ducked in time, and then clambered out of the tent, laughing as his checked short-sleeved shirt hung off his skinny frame. It was completely undone at the front, revealing a spectacular tan and a giant scorpion tattoo on his flat stomach.

'You're fuckin' rude, mate – especially after what you did with *your* sausage last night,' Rick responded.

'Yeah, you can have a sausage, as long as you try not to stick it in any candle flames this time,' Chris replied.

JK decided that now was as good as any to make his appearance, considering he had no chance of going back to sleep with the many stupid early-morning hung-over conversations continuously chattering around the campsite. He pulled on a cap to disguise his bed-head, and a pair of sunglasses in an attempt to get used to the ever-increasing sunshine.

'Morning all,' JK said, poking his head through his tent door. 'Would someone tell me what you lot are on about?'

'Don't you remember either – god, how hammered were you last night?' Rick shot back at him.

'Completely wasted. I feel awful. Top night, though. So, what was the –'

'Top night indeed, gents,' interrupted Bobby.

'Don't change the topic, Bobby. Do you plead guilty of the infamous cock and candle incident?' Rick turned back to Bobby.

Georgie, Chris and Katie laughed out loud.

'I don't know what you're on about, mate.' Bobby shook his head in denial, but was struggling to suppress a knowing smile in the corners of his mouth.

'You fucking know! When we got back to the campsite last night? We'd got some candles out. So had Di. Then we all lit them. Remember that?'

'No. Where is she anyway?' Bobby asked.

'She's in the tent, getting ready,' said Georgie, who was sharing a tent with Di.

'And can probably hear every word of your defence, you liar,' continued Rick. 'Then you asked for her help to show her "an amazing trick". Remember that?'

'No,' Bobby looked back at the rest of the group with fake innocence.

'Idiot. Yeah, he remembers. You told her to hold the candle steady, level with your waist, and not to let go, no matter what happened,' Rick said, laughing.

'Yeah, it was something like "You're not in any danger, I promise",' said Chris.

'You do remember being incredibly drunk, don't you, Bobby?' Katie, Chris's girlfriend, decided to chip in.

'Ah, yes, guilty. I remember that – but I think we all were.'

'Aye, he's not wrong there,' piped up Rick. 'So then, Mr Bobby Jenkins, do you finally remember exposing your penis and then, in one swift movement, placing it on top of said lit candle, and, thus, extinguishing the flame?'

'Nah, sorry, I still don't remember, mate,' Bobby said, laughing with the rest of the group.

'Di's face was a picture!' said Rick, turning to look at Georgie.

Then the entrance to their tent unzipped and Di looked out, sitting up on her sleeping bag. She looked at Bobby, let out a sigh, and held both hands in front of her eyes, grimacing dramatically.

Various laughter and cries of 'Good morning!' greeted her. In one motion, Di lifted both her hands to feign an excited wave to everyone, and then began to tie back the blonde hair that hung limply around her head.

JK noticed that her pale skin still had a healthy glow, despite last night's excesses. She scanned the group and caught his stare; her startling blue eyes were irresistible to him.

'Morning, candle girl!' Bobby shouted towards Di.

'Pig!' she replied.

He stood up abruptly, and began walking towards Di's tent.

'I dunno about any of you lot, but I am dying for a piss,' he said, adjusting his baggy shorts as he approached.

'How lovely!' Georgie muttered towards him as she huddled low into her knees.

On his way to their tent, he grabbed a half-used candle from the floor, unlit, and then stopped to hold it up with one hand in front of the girls. With his other hand, he then slowly edged down his shorts, pretending he was about to recreate last night's infamous moment.

Then, just as the top of his pubic hair was on display, he suddenly dropped the candle and jumped to turn around, grabbing his shorts with both hands and pulling them down to reveal his bare arse to the girls. They screamed and threw their hands up to half cover their faces, but then started to laugh as he ran off, his backside still exposed to the world.

Rick volunteered to go and buy breakfast for the group and took Chris and Katie with him to help carry it all, leaving JK sitting with Georgie and Di.

Georgie adjusted a brown jumper, tied around her waist, with a look of surprise spread across her face.

'Hey, you do realise Bobby wasn't wearing any shoes?' Georgie asked, as she pointed back.

'What, just barefoot?' Di replied, turning around to get a view of Bobby, who was by now far out of sight.

'Oh, that. Yep, he does that all the time,' JK said.

'Really, why?' Georgie asked, intrigued.

'Because he's weird! I dunno. He usually mumbles something about it being more comfortable in summer. It's just the way he is.'

'But it's disgusting – look at the place!' Di said, and laughed.

'Oh, I don't think anything of it anymore. I've seen him turn up down the pub, at the park, even at the local supermarket like that. He's a nut job, I'm telling you. Always been that way.' JK suddenly thought how many worse stories he might have, but then Di spoke up.

'So, JK, do you mind if I ask you a personal question?' she said, cautiously.

'No, not at all,' JK replied, without hesitation. He felt that he would always be intrigued by her aura of eternal optimism.

'Earlier, Rick called him "Bobby Jenkins" I think. But he's your brother, isn't he? How come your surname is Keane?'

JK paused, but was ready with an answer, as it was one he had had to give before.

'Ah, yes. I can see how that must look weird. So, when he was eighteen, he decided to start using our mother's maiden name. But I didn't, I kept our father's surname.'

'Oh right, I'm sorry, I didn't realise your parents were divorced,' Di replied, feeling embarrassed as she looked down at her feet.

'No, no, it's OK. Actually, they're not divorced; our father passed away when we were younger.'

'Oh, right… I'm really sorry, again.' Di stumbled on her words and Georgie shifted on her camp seat, awkwardly.

'Don't be. You weren't to know. Besides,' JK paused, 'families can be a funny bunch,' JK continued with a smile, trying to lighten the mood.

'Completely agree with you on that one, JK,' Georgie said, smiling back. But JK could feel the tension as now Di was avoiding eye contact with him.

'We just disagree about our dad sometimes. I guess we agree on wanting to travel, though. And do lots of it.'

'Yes, Bobby mentioned that to me yesterday. He's been to a lot of places, hasn't he?' Georgie asked JK.

'Well, he's been doing it a lot longer than me – he's five years older. I've only just started really.'

'Do you think he'll keep going? How can he afford it?' Di said, interested again.

'We both had inheritance funds that were released when we reached twenty-one. So I've only just had mine. But Bobby, well, I think he spent his a long time ago. Every time he comes home now it's just to work for a few months and then go off travelling again. He's been in that cycle a few years.'

'Sounds tiring. I'm not sure he'll be able to do that forever. Surely he'll burn out one day, and then he won't have any roots to settle into,' Di said with concern.

'I'd agree but he doesn't really think like that,' JK said, and laughed.

'And what about you? Don't you think like that too?' Di said bluntly.

'Er, well, no, probably not. I'm not sure, though. Like I said, I'm only just getting started. I think I want to achieve certain things. But Bobby doesn't really have a grand plan or anything. He just wants to enjoy himself as much as possible.'

'What's your grand plan then, JK? Why are you two so different?'

'I don't know. I've got to finish my degree first. But, I guess I want to copy my father. He did a lot of travel at a young age, so I want to try and emulate that eventually. He seemed to think it was a good idea, and always had a lot of stories to tell. So, I'd do it for him really.'

'But Bobby doesn't want to do that?'

'No, he's doing it for himself. Just because he can. He doesn't care what our father did. And now he's addicted to the lifestyle, I think.'

Di looked deep in thought as she softly nodded at JK's response. He felt it was strange that she was so interested in his brother's life decisions.

'Well, I bet Bobby sure has a lot of stories to tell, doesn't he?' Georgie commented.

'Yeah, he has a few. But I've got some too. Like from my recent trip to Lapland – I bet you'll like that even more,' JK said with excitement.

A few hours later, JK and the rest of their group were in the middle of the festival grounds, in between the two main stages. The sun continued to shine brightly as they sat and quenched their thirst in the striking afternoon heat.

Occasionally JK would switch off from his friends to people-watch, in an attempt to zone out and relax. One group in front of them kept catching his eye during the afternoon. They were sat down in a rough circle, three girls and four boys. All were in their early twenties, he guessed.

There was sexual tension in their group. Two couples were clearly in a relationship; they were open with their affection, holding hands, kissing and hugging each other without a second thought. With the others, there was nervousness, and it was less clear who liked who. Some laughter and flirtatious glances; some occasional brushing of arm against arm; some playful hitting.

JK smiled to himself as he recognised the similarities with their own group. The thrill is always in the chase, after all, he thought. He struggled to understand how Bobby had managed to charm his way into Di's good books. She had clearly taken a liking to him, but with Bobby, you could never tell what he was feeling. He was so brazen; it never quite seemed genuine, just a show for everyone.

Rick, on the other hand, was clearly up for anything. He had been outrageously flirting with both Georgie and Di since they had met, and it was getting a bit much. As for himself, JK knew he didn't have a chance with Di, so had tried to stop thinking about it. But more than anything, he was still feeling queasy from the morning and just hoped that it didn't show.

JK was suddenly attacked as a blur of curly brown hair lurched towards him. Bobby's stocky frame and broad shoulders made quite an impact, as he rugby-tackled JK around his midriff, knocking them both to the floor.

'Surprise! I'm back,' he boomed, as he stood up.

'Thanks for that. What's up with you? And where's our drinks?' JK grumpily replied, as he dusted off dried mud from his elbows and knees.

'Oh yeah, sorry, the queue was massive. I got bored, so I left. But I was given this, cool eh?' He held up a small football with festival sponsor logos printed all over it.

'Yeah, great, it's a football, Bobby.'

'It just seemed right at the time, my friend. What can I say? What have you guys been doing, anyway?'

'Nothing really. Just chatting about nonsense,' Georgie replied.

'Sounds about right. Let me guess, festival toilets?'

'Yep. Disgusting,' said Di, 'Oh and, of course, travel.'

'Obviously. As if there is anything else to talk about!' Bobby paused and took a look at JK for a moment, who sat quietly looking down. 'Fancy a game, brother?'

Somehow, he always seemed to know when JK needed a distraction.

'What game?' JK replied, cautiously.

'I have an idea.' Bobby dropped the ball at his feet and put his hands in his pockets, jumping up and down sporadically. He then grinned, bent his arms at his sides and looked down at his feet, flicking the mini football up in the air. He caught it and then theatrically stepped forward with one arm outstretched, holding the ball.

'Hold this a moment. I just need something to write with.' Bobby threw the ball to JK, then looked around and saw a lively group of five or six girls about ten metres away who were jumping and giggling. They were in some sort of matching blue and yellow fancy dress, possibly Swedish football outfits, and they all had painted faces.

'Can I borrow your hat a minute?' Bobby didn't wait for an answer and yanked the army print fishing cap off JK's head, put it on and marched towards the girls. JK and the rest of their group watched him chat to them for a few moments, heard some laughter, then they handed him something. In exchange, he took off the cap and gave it to one of them, turned around and walked back towards JK.

'Hey, that was my cap!' JK said, annoyed.

'A small price to pay for sorting out our travel plans.'

'What?'

'Got it,' he said, holding aloft a small blue face paint crayon. 'Now, chuck us the ball.' Once JK had returned it he started to scribble on the stitched segments with the crayon.

'Come on, get on with it. You have a captive audience now,' Rick shouted.

Di and Georgie walked over to take a look and let out a puzzled laugh.

'This is how you like to make decisions, isn't it, JK? Well, here we go!'

JK, with a growing sense of unease, watched Bobby hold the ball just above his knees then throw it up, in front of himself. He then wound his right leg back before kicking his foot through the ball as it dropped. They all watched it soar in the air and then land about fifteen metres away, narrowly avoiding the Swedish girls with face paint on.

Bobby and Rick shot each other a glance before they sprinted towards the ball.

'I think they might have done this before,' said Georgie, sarcastically.

'Probably,' was JK's limp reply.

Rick got to the ball first and, after looking at it, shouted out 'USA!'

'Nice. Right, whoever is nearest has to chase it,' shouted Bobby.

'What the hell is he doing?' Di asked JK.

'I have no idea.'

Rick threw the ball low towards him and, quick as a flash, Bobby turned and kicked high through the ball. JK looked up and lost sight of it against the bright sun as it sailed through the air again. It fell out of the sky and landed at the feet of Georgie and Di.

'Watch it, you nutters!' shouted out Di, as Bobby and Rick sprinted back over.

'Wait, don't pick it up yet, what does it say?' said Bobby, in between breaths.

'What, on the top? It says "New Zealand". Is that good?' Georgie asked.

'Sounds great to me. What do you think, JK? Fancy going there?' Bobby left his question hanging in the air optimistically.

Inside, JK felt sick. He couldn't reconcile this as a valid way to fulfil his travel ambitions. But he knew he had to say something, or risk looking really stupid in front of the whole group.

'Er, yeah, I guess. When though, Bobby? I thought your money had run out?'

'Oh, you know me. I'll make it work. We can wait a little bit – I'll save some cash like I normally do. Right, Rick?'

'Hell, yes, Bobby,' Rick said, laughing.

'Oh, can we come too, or is it boys only?' said Di.

'Why not – the more the merrier!' Bobby laughed as he picked up the ball and kicked it in the air again.

And so, much to JK's annoyance, this continued for a little while until they all got bored and confused with the various travel permutations and additional related trips they each wanted to customise the journey with. He knew they wouldn't stick to this plan and so had no intention of using Bobby's suggestions. JK fully suspected his brother to have forgotten it all by the morning anyway. But now, he felt sick with a fear of having made such trivial deciding on a proper travel plan.

It was getting busier around them as they edged their way through the crowds. The sun was setting as they waited, with alcohol infused excitement, for the next big act to come on. It was a warm early evening, and the remaining low rays of sunlight put everyone in mysterious, yet appealing, contrasts of shade and brightness.

JK had tried to get into the vibe but his stomach and head were both throbbing now. He also chose to decline the pills that Rick and Bobby had discreetly offered, although the girls did not. He watched as their eyes rolled and jaws started to go slack.

Soon, Bobby had disappeared again and they were all dancing together. At some indeterminate point, JK was shocked to turn around and see Di kissing Rick. He stood motionless, staring as they continued, before eventually turning away and trying to subtly blend in again.

As if on cue, Bobby stormed back into the circle, jumping onto JK's back. His bare feet were black now, but no one cared anymore. They stood and watched as the big screen which had previously been inactive suddenly flashed with a bright white light. Guitars started to sound. The lights flashed back on-to the main stage, as they saw the band members running on, the guitars kicking into the gigantic sound setting.

JK struggled to remember the order of what happened next. He had heard the start of a very old song being covered by the band. He hadn't recognised it at first, but when a distinctive element of the song arrived – played with a saxophone in the original and now replaced with guitars by this band – he suddenly had a flashback of sitting as a child with his father singing it to him.

JK then blacked-out and collapsed.

It was early the next morning, a Sunday, as JK now laid awake in bed. He vaguely remembered being drowsy as his mum helped him from her car late the previous evening. As a result of his medication and the alcohol he had consumed, he fell asleep as soon as his head had hit the pillow.

It was infrequent but not an uncommon occurrence for him to pass out like that, so Bobby had known what to do. Although JK had quickly come back round, his brother had taken him to the first aid tent to see if there were any serious after-effects. As ever, JK had just felt extremely tired and, after disagreeing with his brother at length, decided to head home, taking one of the special festival buses to the nearest station. Then he had called his mum before he got on a train, and asked her to meet him at the other end and take him home.

Now he lay on his side, staring at a piece of paper that he held on the pillow. It smelled in that way only old paper can: a dry, dusty, almost vinegary, smell, long faded by the sun. The edges seemed to be a very dark brown colour, whereas the centre of the pages were a lighter, yellowy tone. All in all, it was in pretty good condition, considering.

It was the list of countries that his father had visited. His mum had given it to him over a year ago now. But she had sowed the seeds long before that. She had kept going on about how much he loved his travels, how he had seen thirty-two countries by the age of thirty, and stuff like that.

JK had always been fascinated by those stories when he was younger. Whenever he watched any wildlife documentaries, he thought of his father's travels, and wondered when he might have the chance to do it himself.

His mum had told JK that his father had written it just before his previous employers at the airport had made him redundant. He had been lucky to have that job, as it had given him so much opportunity to travel, but after losing it, he had started his own business in a garage, and wasn't able to travel much after that.

But his father had never stopped mentioning it; he always felt sad that he never got to add to his list, and that's why he had kept such good care of it.

England	1959	Sweden	1966
Wales	1959	Denmark	1966
N. Ireland	1960	Jamaica	1966
Scotland	1960	Barbados	1967
France	1961	USA	1967
Spain	1962	Canada	1967
Germany	1963	Hawaii	1967
Italy	1963	Egypt	1968
Portugal	1963	Turkey	1968
Switzerland	1964	China	1969
Belgium	1964	India	1969
Austria	1964	Australia	1970
Holland	1964	Hong Kong	1970
Tanzania	1965	Singapore	1971
Kenya	1965	Thailand (the crash)	1971
Greece	1965	Malaysia (last so far)	1972

JK knew that his mum had met his dad in the middle of 1965. She went on about how he had charmed her with all his stories about Africa; that he had been to see safaris and things like that, and load of other exotic places in Europe. They got married not long after, sneaking on a flight to Greece for a cheap honeymoon while he was supposed to be working. They had some exotic holidays after that, too, often combined with his work.

He had moved to England as a mechanic from Ireland, for work, when he was eighteen. Several years later he met Alison, his wife to be, and continued to work hard to provide for his family; a sensitive and caring man, but also somewhat volatile, and impulsive. Although it was accidental, it was this combination that had led to his death.

Aside from the tales of travels, JK was amazed by his father's career. Leonard Keane had worked under his own father as a trainee mechanic from a very young age, perhaps fourteen, and was obviously a fast learner. Through a combination of some good fortune, his own skill and charms, plus his father's contacts, he got a job at Heathrow airport as a transport mechanic within a few weeks of arriving in England. Over time, the job grew to be more of a consultancy role that enabled him to go to visit other countries' airports in an advisory capacity, likely as a result of his skills and his personable nature. Or perhaps that's where the good fortune came in.

However, in 1972, after thirteen years in the job, he had been made redundant and it all changed. Using his redundancy payoff, he was able to start his own garage locally. Although he had some additional income from his occasional dubious dabbling as a used car salesman, over the following nine years, he worked very hard on his business. A fire at the garage while he was there proved to be disastrous.

After escaping the fire initially, he must then have had one last desire, one essential object, one crucial final thought that he couldn't let go. He was spotted jumping back into the site before being trapped in the flames, never to re-appear.

Those are the facts that JK knew from his family, but they hadn't really talked about him much since. Bobby and his mother became very defensive on the subject whenever he had brought it up. So, while it was clearly quite a sensitive issue for them, JK always felt slightly removed from it.

JK had a handful of sketchy, memories of his father. Like the first time he took him and Bobby to Hampstead Heath in winter, a snow-covered layer everywhere the eye could see. Attempting to sledge down one of the big hills in a red plastic, but laughably small, sleigh.

His love of jelly beans, which he would always buy for his sons, inevitably causing fights between them as they attempted to share the giant kilogram bags he brought home.

Alison, and most people that knew him, called him Lenny. He would sing to his family in the evenings after he came home from work, pretending to dance with everyone. JK remembered creeping out of his room down the stairs late at night to find him asleep on the sofa, snoring, with a glass of whisky in his hand, fascinated to see if he would ever drop it. He never did.

And some of JK's memories were not so good, like waking up to him arguing with their mother after he'd arrived back, drunk, at 3am. JK had sat huddled next to Bobby on the stairs, watching him cry as they listened to the resulting drama. He had felt bad, because he wondered if he should be crying too. Lenny had been drinking excessively for a few years by then.

By the time of his death in 1981, JK was almost six years old and Bobby was eleven. This time held strange memories for JK, but mainly all he remembered was lots of tears, lots of fuss and lots of visitors.

There was a family fall-out about a year or two after his death, when a few shady characters claiming to be associates of Lenny Keane turned up at the family house. They were demanding money, and it transpired that he had large gambling debts that needed to be paid off. Even though there had been some business insurance pay out to Alison after the fire, this extra debt still made things financially difficult for the family for a few years.

It had tainted Alison's memory of her husband permanently after that. She had put up with his drinking, his escalating mood swings, his frustration with his job for near enough the previous sixteen years of marriage.

Drinking had been an escape for him, but when she had found out about the gambling, it was the breaking point. It also led to some really unsavoury rumours about him among so-called family friends, with Bobby suffering all sorts of unfair teasing and accusations from kids at school as a result. Not that he complained – he rallied round his mum during that time to make sure she was OK.

JK had been too young to really appreciate what all that meant at the time. He had thought about it many times since and, even though he didn't like the way it had affected his family, he still had a void of emotion, like he had been cheated, missing out on forming his own genuine emotions.

He couldn't hate him – but he couldn't love him either – because he didn't know him. All those brief moments, those fleeting recollections, were not enough for JK to form a proper picture in his head.

JK just wanted to understand his father, have his own private knowledge of him, and it had kept nagging away at him for many years. His interest in travel had now become the substitute for a shared interest with his dad, and a useful distraction at the same time.

And now, as he lay on his bed, he wept with frustration at how unfair it was that he couldn't really talk to his mum or brother about it, as they had already made their own minds up about Lenny Keane.

Then a knock sounded at his door and his mum, wearing an old blue dressing gown, stuck her head in. He quickly hid the piece of paper he held, sliding it under his duvet.

'Sorry, I heard you were up, so I just wanted to see if you were OK after yesterday?' she said, speaking softly, with a look of worry etched on her face.

'Yeah. I'm OK, Mum. What time is it?'

'It's about 7.30,' she replied. 'Are you sure you're alright? You look upset. I can call the doctor if you want me to?' She looked down at the floor and began to play with her uncombed brown curly hair nervously.

JK couldn't deal with seeing his mum worry like this; usually, she was the one that would console him. He wasn't sure if she had ever really got over Dad's death – she had had a few boyfriends since, she even almost remarried once, but that fell through.

'Honestly, I'm fine, Mum. I was just… thinking about Dad.'

With this admission, JK had certainly surprised his mother, but also himself.

'Really? Why is that, Jonny?'

'I think because you put all these photos of him up round the house, and you seem, er, a bit different recently?'

She paused, and looked around the room to avoid eye contact. Eventually, she stared back at him.

'Well, I just wanted to feel good about him again. Since your trust money became available – when was that, a year or so ago? Well, I could see that he could finally do something nice for you, that's all. I could see that it would make a difference to you. And your travel plans.'

'I see. But what about Bobby? When he got his trust fund, ages ago, didn't you feel like that then too?'

'No, not really. You see, Bobby only sees the bad in your father, none of the good. And I used to feel like that too, back then. But now, well, I guess I'm tired. Too much wasted energy resenting him. I want to try and remember the good things while I still can.'

'Well, that's very good of you, Mum,' JK said, and smiled, 'I just wish Bobby would try and open his mind.'

'Yeah, well, sadly, I just don't think that will ever happen, Jonny. I have tried to get him to do that many times before.'

They were both quiet for a time, looking at each other. JK had the feeling she wanted to tell him something else, but she remained silent still.

'Mum, I think I'm going to have a shower now. I don't suppose you're making tea, are you?'

'Yeah, sure, Jonny, see you downstairs in a minute?'

JK grunted an 'OK' as his mother left the room. He then reached over to his stereo remote, which sat on the bed-side drawers, to switch it on. Enchanting music played from the speakers – no vocals, just slow, serene and lucid tunes. Jean-Michel Jarre, JK thought, but couldn't be sure. Perhaps it was called 'Oxygen' or something; it was purely instrumental, and not even that recent. It struck him as a strange choice for a radio station which usually stuck to a very commercial play-list.

Although he felt uplifted by the conversation with his mother, only a muted optimism started to flow into his mind and mix with the prevailing worry that remained. He still held the list under the duvet and then remembered the travel conversations he had had with the girls he met at the festival.

Distracted, he noticed the tune from the radio again, as it began to grate on him. He stretched to reach the remote and switched it to BBC Radio 1. Strangely enough, they were playing another old instrumental track, which was also pretty unusual for them. He'd heard it before but, again, couldn't quite recognise who the artist was. Intrigued by the tune's mellow nature, he decided to leave it on, as he sat up in bed, yawning and stretching.

He thought back to when he had first met both Georgie and Di after his brother had crashed into the back of them. JK had really thought that Di and his brother would hit it off. He was amazed when, instead, she had paired off with Rick – someone that JK had been less fond of, even if he was Bobby's best friend.

He wondered what they were all doing now and if they were still getting on. He hoped they would remember him and not think him too weird for fainting and leaving the festival the way he had.

JK turned around to the window behind his bed and opened the curtains. It was bright outside, but the main road that they lived on was as quiet, as you would expect this early on a Sunday morning. He spotted an old man walking his dog along the pavement on the other side of the road. Another pedestrian, a younger man in his forties, approached him.

Then he saw the old man stop and say something to the younger man. Their body language was not that of two people who knew each other. Yet, it was as if he was telling the stranger something very important. This certainly struck JK as unusual for this part of the country. They lived in a fairly reserved suburb of greater London, where strangers didn't really speak much to each other – the occasional bit of road rage apart, that is.

He again thought about Di and how beautiful she was, letting out a resigned sigh. At the very least, he hoped that she would stay in touch. Seeking distraction from his thoughts, he flicked between another couple of radio stations, but they were all playing slow, melancholy tunes.

Suddenly a strange sense of dread hit JK in the stomach. He saw the two men outside were still chatting, and so he turned the radio back to Radio 1, where the instrumental track was just finishing with the lyrics 'Life… isn't death everything'.

Then the DJ's voice cut in, someone who was normally quite upbeat, but today sounded extremely reserved and sombre, as she confirmed the name of the track 'Song for Guy, by Elton John'. She continued: 'We'll be going to a full news bulletin shortly. Our thoughts go out to all those who are finding this hard to accept. We'll continue with some more music for now as we all struggle to come to terms with today's awful news.'

Then, the Jean-Michel Jarre track that he had heard on the other station earlier began to play. Once more, he flicked back to some other stations – but they were all playing sombre songs with no announcements.

JK ran downstairs to the lounge and flicked on the TV to BBC One; but he could've chosen any channel, as they all had the same story. There had been a car crash in Paris at 12.30am overnight. A passenger had been declared dead at hospital by 4am, with a press conference announcement at 5.30am.

Today was Sunday 31st August 1997 – the day of Princess Diana's death.

Chapter Four

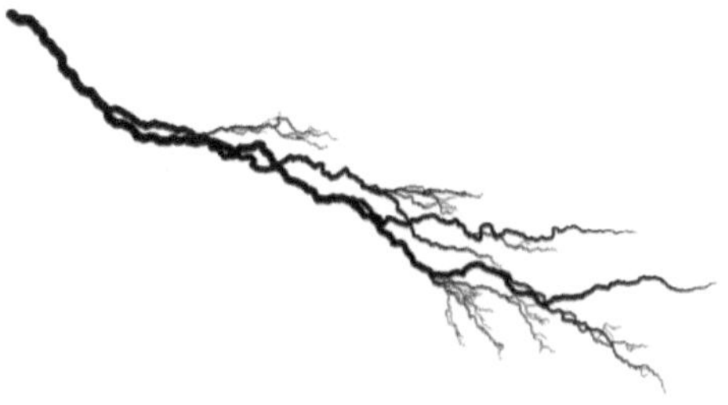

Lightning Never Strikes Twice

Diana Jones stared out the window at the rain hammering down and the wind forcing itself upon the landscape. The surface of Lake Zurich, normally so calm, was rapidly moving as waves swelled to disproportionate sizes for the usually placid retreat. Charcoal-coloured clouds peered miserably overhead and threateningly loud cracks from occasional lightening bursts exaggerated the gloom.

She sat next to her friend Georgie in their still-damp clothes, having both arrived dripping wet at the café earlier. Now, as another lightning bolt cracked on the horizon, they both jumped in their seat and exchanged worried looks.

'Di, this is pretty bad. I think it's getting worse. How are we going to get back to our hotel?' said Georgie.

'I don't know. Maybe we can get a taxi?' Di replied.

'From where? I haven't seen any cars go past for a while now.'

Di looked around the cafe. There was an old man at one table, a couple of older ladies at a table at the back and, other than a waitress and a lady behind the till, there was no one else inside.

'Perhaps we can call one? Or, failing that, maybe someone here would offer us a lift. Surely it has to blow over eventually,' Di said with a feigned air of optimism.

'Let's hope so. I guess we can just keep ordering coffee in the meantime,' Georgie replied, as she sank low in to her seat and crossed her arms.

'Still think we had the right idea?' Di said, as she took a large sip from her cup and emptied its contents.

'What do you mean, to go inter-railing? It was your idea!' Georgie said, smiling.

'No, silly, I mean the route we took. Cold countries first, ending in hot. I bet you can't wait for Italy and Greece now, right?' Di replied, as she waved the waitress over.

Georgie was right, though. It had been Di's idea to travel. Although they had both agreed to take some time off together a while ago, it had only really taken shape recently since Di had split up with her boyfriend, Rick Marshall, a few weeks earlier.

'Oh, yeah, definitely. I'm so over this storm now. But yes, it will make the last bits even better by the time we get there. Bring on the Mediterranean heatwave already!'

Georgie attempted an enthusiastic smile as the waitress arrived and they ordered another round of coffees. Di could tell she remained concerned. It wasn't just the storm. She knew Georgie well enough by now to recognise her subtle expression of mood. Then their silence was interrupted again, as the wind shook the window frames.

Another loud crash came as lightning hit the surface of the lake, closer to them. Along a road outside, fifteen metres away from the window and parallel to the lake's lowered banks, several trees stood, shaking.

It hadn't been a bad breakup between Di and Rick. They weren't dating long enough for it to really hurt either of them. In truth, she had known quite quickly – not long after she and Rick had first got together a few months ago at the festival – that it wouldn't last. But they were having fun and it seemed right then to continue.

Still, Di had known it was coming. Although Rick was funny and spontaneous – not to mention good looking and athletic – he was also dismissive, reckless and often uncaring. They were character traits she knew she would never have the patience for over any length of time. She suspected they probably only got together due to alcohol and drugs in the first place, which was unusual for her. She remembered thinking at the time that she needed to have some more fun anyway. She had finally been ready again.

Di guessed that Georgie would know all this – but she didn't know everything. The extra complications. Why she had felt the need to suddenly take this trip now. That's probably what her good friend Georgie couldn't figure out.

'Come on then, Georgie, spit it out,' Di finally said, as their fresh coffees arrived.

'What do you mean, Di?' Georgie said, looking confused.

'Oh, don't play innocent with me! You've been trying to dig something out of me since we left Germany.'

'Eh? Dig what out?'

'I don't know. Gossip, anything.'

'Well, I just want to make sure you're OK. After, you know, your breakup.'

'I'm honestly fine. I instigated it, remember?'

'Yes. But this reaction – you know – seems strange?' Georgie said, hesitantly.

'What reaction?'

'This trip. Originally, I expected a few weeks lounging in the sun, flirting with men, but when you organised this whole extravagant European gallivant – and at such short notice – it just felt like you were running away or something.'

'Don't be ridiculous.'

'Di, did Rick hurt you? Not emotionally, I mean. We all knew you were never suited to each other. I mean, did he *hurt* you?'

'What? Oh god, no. I would never let him do that. He was a bit of a prick sometimes, but nothing like that.'

'What, then? What happened?'

'Honestly nothing. We had a few arguments, nothing serious, but, like you said, we knew we weren't suited so I suggested calling it quits and he had no real objections.'

'Just like that?'

'Yep, just like that.' Di turned away from Georgie and stared out at the storm.

'Well, there's something you're not telling me.'

Di didn't say anything.

'Fine, be stubborn. We're not going anywhere fast. I can wait.' Georgie slumped further down in her seat and crossed her arms.

Tension brewed as they sat silently, watching the thunderstorm progress in front of them. Eventually, Di released a sigh.

'Look, it's complicated, Georgie. I just felt like I couldn't see where my next relationship was going to come from. We'd made some good friends with Rick, JK and Bobby and had a lot of fun. I guess the breakup meant I could lose all that, and so I started to panic. I needed to go and do something a bit different. And not have to think about proper adult stuff, like relationships.'

Di hoped her response would convince Georgie, but instantly knew it hadn't as she stared back at her suspiciously.

'You won't lose them as friends, surely? No one has had a falling out, have they?'

'No, not that I know of.'

'So what else is it? What are you afraid of?'

'Well, let's be honest, my relationship track record isn't great, is it?'

Di let her reply hang in the air as yet more thunder cracked nearby. At this, the waitress, who had just been chatting to the woman behind the till in animated fashion, came over to the girls and asked them to move tables, to one further away from the window, next to the old man's. It seemed like overkill to Di, but they obliged and got up as the waitress moved their coffees for them.

'OK, so now I understand you. You're worried you'll never get a boyfriend, just because of what happened to you five years ago?' Georgie said, as she sat down.

Di shrugged, avoiding eye contact. Georgie was only half right – but Di didn't want to get into it now.

'Look, Di, come on. You were just a kid, sixteen years old. I know it must have been terrible – well, I can't even begin to imagine. But it was just bad luck – really, really bad luck – sorry that's such a clichéd understatement – and it was a long time ago now.'

'Maybe. But I can't just forget, you know?'

'Of course. And you shouldn't, either. But you're allowed to move on with your life.'

'I know, I know. I think I have.' Finally, Di turned back to Georgie and they exchanged smiles with an affectionate gaze, as only two close friends can do.

'Good. I mean, you do know that nothing like that will ever happen to you again, don't you?'

At this, Di suddenly laughed, to which Georgie raised a puzzled eyebrow.

'You sound like my mother. She said something like that to me once. Not long after it happened, when I was really upset. "Lightning never strikes twice," she said. Pretty apt now, huh?' Di said, as she cocked her head towards the window.

It was still hard for Di to talk about her past, and she felt a twang of guilt using it now to partially cover up her story to Georgie. But talking about it now was nowhere near as hard as it used to be.

The death of her boyfriend in a motorcycle accident had destroyed her emotionally, and it had taken her a long time to recover from it, if she ever had. She hated the expression, but Justin had been her first true love, having known each other since they were thirteen.

The lateness, the missed dinner date, the lack of a phone call, the waiting, the confusion, the annoyance, the worry, the absence, the lack of information from anyone. And the deep, growing fear. And then, eventually, the phone call, but not from him. His father, with the news that was never to be forgotten, the broken, tearful sentence that still replayed in her head every day: *I'm sorry, Di, he's… he had an accident on his bike this morning. He's not… he didn't… I'm so sorry, but he's…*

She had dropped the phone as she collapsed. When she came to she withdrew from the world, unable to form words for several days. Then her grief changed to anger: *Why him? Why her? Why had she been punished? What had she done to deserve it?*

This quickly changed to depression and loneliness, as his loss was too large a hole to be easily filled by life's inadequate daily routines. But slowly, quietly, she started to get on with a life, of sorts. She could still barely talk to anyone for weeks, let alone try to form new relationships.

Yet, eventually, she did; and generally, these boyfriends tended to be the complete opposite of Justin: safe, non-adventurous boys that played by the rules. So they wouldn't remind her of him. It had certainly kept her mum happy. It did, that is, until she would stop seeing them after a few weeks. Either bored or annoyed with them, or – very rarely – afraid that she might form some real attachment to them.

But that wasn't the way to recover; she knew that deep down it was just a way of avoiding her real feelings. She was afraid of getting close to anyone again, especially anyone who she could feel genuinely close to. And who might then replace Justin in her memory.

She still felt scared, even now, and needed the distraction. She had even more complex emotions forming too: hope as well as fear. Hope that someone else, new and real, could actually make her feel normal again. But she wasn't going to tell Georgie that just yet.

'Well, Di, you say that now but… just look at that!' Georgie suddenly pointed to the horizon. The clouds had started to clear and the sky was brightening. The rain was easing and the thunder and lightning had stopped. Shortly, the sun became partly visible, still covered by some thin clouds. More and more blue sky appeared as the storm clouds receded out of view.

'Wow...that is...amazing. I wonder if there'll be a rainbow,' said Di, looking round at the people in the cafe. The two ladies at the table at the back exchanged beaming smiles and were chatting loudly now. The old man had barely registered any change, seemingly half asleep throughout. The waitress and the lady at the till were laughing and pointing back outside.

'Look at that, Di, you were right!' Georgie said, also laughing.

A full-frontal view of a huge rainbow now rewarded their patient cafe vigil, connecting the last edge of the escaping clouds with a bank on another side of the lake. As the sun shone brightly, the last clouds disappeared to leave clear blue sky everywhere overhead.

Taking advantage of the improved weather, the girls had got on a bus and returned to their hotel room to snack, freshen up and get changed out of their now-dry clothes. By around 3pm, they had gone out again. As their hotel was next to another part of the lake, they decided to take a leisurely stroll along it and take in some alternative views. This would be on their way into the centre of town, eventually heading for a restaurant they had heard was good for dinner.

The sun's heat was sweltering and Di and Georgie had quickly worked up a thirst. They found a drinks stall and ordered lemon iced teas, sipping them while sitting on a grass bank. Despite being one of the busiest parts of the lake, with many ferries and boats passing through, it was a spectacular scene: the calm waters reflected the clear sky, framed by natural green beauty, all set among air so fresh it provided an assault on Di's senses that she imagined would be unrivalled anywhere else in the world.

The moment was serene and Di felt a strange excitement growing inside her. The hairs on the back of her neck had begun to stand.

From behind, Di heard a voice shouting out and turned round to look. Georgie was squinting in that direction already. They could see two youngish men walking towards them, waving and shouting. Eventually they heard their names.

'Oh my god,' Georgie spluttered, taking off her designer sunglasses.

'It can't be, but...that looks like Bobby,' Di said, straining to make out the features of their faces.

'It is! And that's JK behind him!' Georgie said, beaming excitedly as she got up.

Stunned, Di stood up also, as the boys ran the last few metres to join them. Di looked at Bobby in fake annoyance as he stared at her with a mischievous glint in his eyes. The four quickly embraced.

'What the hell are you two doing here?' Di said, laughing.

'We were just passing, so we thought we'd drop in,' Bobby replied, cheekily.

'How on earth did you find us?' Georgie asked.

'Hey, come on! We knew roughly from your email saying when you'd be here.'

'So, you came all the way here, just to see us?' asked Di.

'No, it just so happens that part of our trip was to come here for a weekend anyway, to see our friend, Stefan. Remember, we met him at the festival?' said Bobby.

'Er, not really. But there's a lot I don't remember from that festival!' Di replied.

'That's probably true for all of us!' Georgie said, laughing. 'But tell us about the rest of your trip then – yet another one? Where else have you been this time?'

'Oh, this? It's only a short one. I wanted to keep the little brother company, make sure he kept practising his travelling skills before he joins the big league,' Bobby said, looking at JK. 'This is just our quick, get-fucked-up-in-Europe, trip!'

'You have such a way with words, Bobby,' said JK, rolling his eyes as the girls laughed.

'Quite simple, really. Two weeks, three countries, three cities. Amsterdam, Zurich, Prague. In and out, quick. Clubs, dancing, pills, booze… and, er…' Bobby paused. He had said the line many times before and was caught up in his usual excitement, before remembering at the last moment who he was speaking to.

'Yes?' Di asked.

JK watched with delight as Bobby squirmed.

'Birds. That's what he was going to say,' JK offered.

'Oh. That's nice for you,' said Di, looking annoyed.

'Yeah, alright, thanks JK… It's just a bloke's expression. It doesn't mean anything. It's all just hot air,' Bobby stuttered, going red in the face.

'That much is certainly true,' Di said, with a knowing smirk.

'Well, anyway, as we were here, and if we could get our timings right, we thought we'd surprise you!' Bobby said, desperately trying to change the subject.

'Yes, that you did! How long have you two been planning this?' Georgie asked.

'Hey, it wasn't me! I only found out this morning,' said JK, as he shot an accusing look to Bobby.

'Yes, guilty, it was me. Maybe only for a couple of weeks, I think. I don't do a lot of planning usually, as you know! Anyway, we couldn't remember exactly where you were staying, only somewhere near the lake. So, we had a morning stroll and here we are,' said Bobby, holding Di's gaze momentarily before JK interrupted him.

'Well, he says a stroll but I reckon we've been on our feet for at least four hours. We tried about five places and got soaked in that thunderstorm,' JK said, with a hint of annoyance.

They had all sat down on the grass bank now. Bobby looked over the lake and Georgie smiled at JK with her habitual flirtatious trick of biting her bottom lip. Di saw this, not sure Georgie was even aware she was doing it anymore.

'Guys, this is so random. Where is your mate Stefan, then?' Georgie asked.

'Oh, he's massively hungover. So we left him asleep,' Bobby replied.

'Yeah, like we should be!' said JK.

'Big night, was it?' Di asked.

'Yeah, you could say that! Stefan is an organiser of The Zurich Street Parade, a big techno music festival they have every year in mid-August. Just under half a million people went this year. Come to think of it, I'm sure you and Rick had a long conversation with him about it at the festival we just went to,' said JK.

'What, the one you bailed out of early?' said Bobby, cheekily.

'Ha ha, brother. Very funny. Yes, that one. It was only a couple of weeks after the Zurich Street Parade you see,' JK continued. 'Come to think of it, where is Rick, anyway?'

JK noticed Bobby look away and then Di and Georgie exchanged a quick awkward glance.

'He didn't fancy coming. I'll explain more later. So, your mate Stefan is pretty well-connected here, then? Lots of party invites?' Georgie asked.

'Yeah. He got us into the top clubs and he has this massive, luxurious rooftop apartment in the centre of town. He's a great bloke,' Bobby enthused.

'Hopefully we can meet him later. So, we were going to carry on walking along the lake into town. Are you guys OK with that?' Di asked.

'Of course,' replied Bobby, with a wink.

They stopped at a bar at about 5pm which had a seating area outside, overlooking the lake. They ordered their drinks and sat on the grassy banks in the late afternoon heat, the sun was still shining strongly.

JK was sitting with one leg flat and one bent, towards his chest, which he bounced up and down repeatedly from his foot. He was deep in thought as he began to scratch the sole of his other foot. Sometime previously, he had been walking with Georgie, in front of Bobby and Di as they talked in their separate groups.

Georgie had informed him of Di's breakup with Rick. It had surprised him and was further compounded shortly after when he had stolen a glance back at his brother to see him holding hands with Di. Now, they sat close to each other and remained in deep conversation.

'So, what's Zurich like, JK? You've been here a couple of days longer than us,' Georgie said loudly, noticing his agitation. She was trying to distract him but also engage the other two.

'Oh, it's a beautiful place. There's an interesting mixture of people, though,' JK replied. 'I mean, you've got at least three distinct cultures all merged into one.'

'German, French and Italian?' Georgie replied.

'Yes, but they don't seem to have an identity of their own. I don't really see them as that friendly a bunch,' he continued.

'I'd agree with you there, mate. You couldn't have had a more quiet train journey than the one we had yesterday. There was just no-one talking,' Bobby added.

'Well, I suppose in Zurich it's predominantly a German culture, very efficient and reserved,' JK confirmed.

'So, no train is ever late, then?' Di quipped.

'Yes, that's right. Everything is by the book; they have rules and regulations for anything you can imagine. Even doing the laundry in Stefan's apartment block – you have a slot on a roster which you can't ever change. And, it's banned to do it at all on a Sunday!'

'And the miserable bastards that work in the shops don't even attempt to make eye contact with you,' Bobby said, laughing.

JK, who had finally stopped scratching his foot, continued to talk about the city as well as their recent Amsterdam visit. Di was impressed at how passionate about it all he was – she could tell from the desire in his eyes and the fervour of his gestures. She wondered if he had made his mind up about his future travels yet.

'So, JK, what are you going to do when you graduate. Do you know yet? Not long left for you, I guess?' Di asked.

'No idea yet – after this academic year, I've still got my final year next year. I had to repeat my second year, you see, because of all the time off I had – various travels and sickness. And I don't think they'd be that happy about me jaunting off for this two-week stint either,' JK said, shifting awkwardly as he swapped the position of his legs.

'Good thing you didn't tell them then, brother! And I'm very glad you took my expert advice,' said Bobby, as he flashed a smug smile to the group.

'Yes, because that's served me so well in the past,' JK replied, sarcastically.

'Oi. Don't you forget I'm your wiser and more experienced elder.'

'Elder, maybe!' JK snapped back.

'Well, you could've told them if you really wanted to. Like I've always said, travel makes everyone a better person; in fact, it makes just about everything feel better. So, it was the right thing to do, in my opinion. Anyway, it's only for two weeks – you can easily catch up on your boring studies later,' Bobby replied.

'Maybe. We'll see,' said JK.

'And what about your big round-the-world trip? Is your brother still bullying you to do one?' Di asked.

'I am not! He wants to do it!' Bobby said.

'I might do it. I dunno if I wanna go on my own, though.' JK sheepishly looked at his brother. He had been drinking quickly and swirled the remaining dregs of his beer around the bottom of the glass, swapping it from hand to hand. Di and Georgie both looked back to Bobby.

'What? Surely you aren't turning it down, Bobby?' Georgie asked.

'Well, not exactly. We've discussed it and I told him I might not be there for all of it. I've done a lot more travel – as you all know! I can't do it forever. Anyway, he can easily go with some uni mates or something,' Bobby said, deliberately avoiding the gaze of Di.

'My god. Something sensible actually came out of Bobby's mouth. Somebody write it down,' said Di, as she smiled at Georgie then finished her drink.

'If your heart is set on it then you should do it,' Georgie added, trying to get involved in the conversation.

'I guess you're right, there's plenty of time. I'm sure it'll get sorted one way or another,' JK said, but Georgie could tell from his tone that he was attempting to downplay his interest.

Bobby lay back on the grass and, as the sun finally found a cloud to hide behind, rested his sunglasses on top of his head among brown tufts of hair – hair that had recently been trimmed, but a lot shorter than normal, JK noticed.

'What about you, Di? All OK with you? I was sorry to hear about your breakup with Rick,' JK said, and as he snuck a glance to his left, he saw Bobby try to casually look up.

'Oh yeah, thanks, I'll be fine. It wasn't exactly a long-term deal,' she replied.

'Well, I'm sure it could've been awkward, seeing as we all know each other,' JK said.

'It shouldn't be. We're going to remain friends. We ended it on good terms.'

'Have you heard from him recently? Is he OK?' JK continued.

'I have,' said Bobby. 'He sounded fine. You know Rick. He doesn't really do emotion anyway.'

'Oh, so you knew about their breakup, then? You never mentioned it to me?' JK said, looking surprised.

'Yeah, I meant to yesterday, and then we all got hammered and I forgot. Sorry, JK.' JK looked disappointed, staring back down at his empty glass.

'Here, give me that. I'll get a round in,' said Bobby, as he stood up and stole the glass off his brother in one motion.

While he was at the bar, Georgie pulled out a CD Walkman, which they set up to play over her portable speakers.

Di pondered on her feelings about Bobby turning up so suddenly. Initially, she wasn't sure that it was just his idea, and that perhaps JK had played a part too, wanting to make the effort to see Georgie.

But now, since their arrival, that didn't seem likely, as JK hadn't paid Georgie any particular attention. Also, she was very happy to notice that Bobby had barely taken his eyes off of her, and she was more than happy to return his attention.

Then Georgie interrupted Di's day-dreams by reaching into her bag and pulling out an A5 notepad and pencil, handing them to JK.

'There you go, take this and work it all out,' she offered.

'Work it out? How do you mean?' he replied, confused.

'I mean, where you want to go, for how long, how much money you need and when you can get it by. Then you can work out when you can go. You can make a start while Bobby is at the bar so he isn't distracting you.'

'Oh, come on, Georgie, that will take him ages! We just wanna sit and have a drink by the lake and chill in the sunshine. He can do that when he gets home,' Di said, concerned, as she raised an eyebrow in Georgie's direction. She was trying to enjoy the moment and it just didn't seem like the time for JK to think about those finer details right now.

'Why not? Now's as good a time as any. He can still sit there and drink while we talk, it doesn't matter. We've got time – we're on holiday.'

'Yes, but -' Di began, but Georgie cut her off.

'I've learnt that if you feel passionately about something then why wait? Do something about it now or it may never happen. Only if he wants to, that is.'

'She's got a point, JK. You may as well have a go – we could help you,' Di said.

So, JK sat with the notepad and pencil, scrawling ideas for his trip of a lifetime. They talked about which countries inspired them, and exchanged rough guesses of the time and money required for each.

Bobby soon returned, carrying an ice bucket containing a bottle of Prosecco and four stem glasses. He was just as bemused by JK's task as they all were with his choice of drinks, but he happily got straight back into his usual repertoire of offhand ideas and observations. After a couple of hours or so, the combined effect of music, sunshine and alcohol had sunk in.

JK was extremely satisfied with his progress; he held open the notepad – two pages side by side with his plans – for them all to see. Georgie took it for a closer look.

On one page was a very rough map of the world with countries and cities marked with crosses, a line connecting them all. On the other side was a list of those places, followed by details like the length of stay and cost of each, and then with further info like accommodation, travel and spending money required. JK said he had a final figure of what it would cost in mind, and some dates of when he could expect to have saved enough money to cover it.

Georgie passed the notepad back to JK, and he turned the page and started to doodle. With these thoughts and conversations of wondrous sights, he day-dreamt and the others watched him sketch an idyllic beach.

He added detail of palm trees, clear white sand with clear skies overhead, and a calm ocean in the background. He had added a hammock between the trees with a figure lying in it, basking in the sun with sunglasses on and holding an enormous cocktail glass complete with umbrella and assorted fruit chunks.

'Hey, you. No doodling, this is serious business!' said Bobby, interrupting the tranquil moment. He had a drunken glint in his eye that betrayed the stern expression he wore on his face.

'I assume that is meant to be you, JK?' Georgie asked.

'Yeah, but I guess it's just a pipe dream. My quest's Holy Grail: the perfect beach photo,' JK replied. 'I'd love to create this for real one day.'

'Why can't you?' asked Georgie. 'Why don't you write "pipe dream" at the bottom of the page? Then, whenever you look at it, it'll give you the reminder you need. Maybe some sort of incentive for you to make it all happen.'

'You know what? That's a good idea.' JK lifted the pencil to write the words.

Suddenly, from nowhere, they heard a commotion on the grass in front of them, as a rapid and heavy thudding of footsteps approached. JK looked up to see a large, excited dog running towards him like an unstoppable train, just as a tennis ball bounced past his face. Laying down, drunk, he lacked the leverage and energy to move either himself or the notepad in time.

The ball rolled onto the pad and the dog followed milliseconds after. Grabbing the ball in its slobbering mouth, the dog could not change its momentum and crashed into JK's head, trampling all over the pages of the notepad spread open in front of him. The collision was only brief, and wasn't painful; the random shock factor would likely have shaken him up more.

Looking confused, the dog stared at JK with the ball in its mouth and let out a strange muffled bark. To make matters worse, the dog was soaking wet from a recent dip in the lake. They all sat up, shocked, and heard the owners call over to the dog.

'Stella! Stella! Sorry, oh I am so sorry!' a lady shouted over to them.

'Oh, no problem!' JK managed to blurt out in a startled daze, still on well-mannered English-autopilot.

'Stella!' the lady beckoned.

Stella, a healthy looking black Labrador, was clearly quite friendly but certainly not the brightest animal you would ever encounter. She looked over at her owners, back at JK and then trotted off back towards them, now seemingly oblivious to the whole episode.

The group looked down at the notepad. The pages JK had just spent over an hour planning his dreams on were now soggy, covered in mud stains, creased and ripped. JK had a look of death on his face and it appeared as if, in that moment, he wanted to kill Stella the dog.

Trying to suppress a laugh, Di turned round to look at Georgie and Bobby, who were both sniggering themselves by now. This set her off too, their laughter exploding upon seeing JK's rage-ridden expression as he held up the notepad to show them the damage Stella had inflicted. Upon scanning all their faces, his demeanour slowly changed and then he too began to laugh.

Di closed her eyes and wallowed in the moment. When she opened them, Bobby put his hand on hers and their eyes simultaneously met.

She knew Bobby's spontaneous effort to come and see her really meant something to him. And it felt more special to her as a result.

Time seemed to slow down as a private happiness radiated between them, intimate and yet unspoken. In that instant, Di knew that, whatever happened next for her and Bobby, they would eventually be together.

Three days later, well after the boys had left for Prague, the girls were on the move again. They had continued down into northern Italy by train, and were currently waiting in Milano Centrale railway station to leave for Rome.

They had arrived via a quick visit back to nature, to take in the unspoilt beauty of Lake Como, and had then had a pleasant couple of days in Milan, the city of culture for the usual shopping, sights, bar and cafe type activities.

They had a carriage to themselves as they sat down, waiting for their train to leave. Di had taken out her diary, ready to update it that morning. Georgie sat opposite, trying to read an Italian guide book, but instead, slumped in her seat and stared out of the window.

They were both tired and frustrated. Last night, one of their twin beds in their hostel had collapsed so they had to swap rooms in the night to share a double bed. And on their way into the station, they had got soaked as the weather had turned bad once again. Heavy grey clouds hung overhead, darkening the skies, even though it was just a little after 10am.

They both turned to look out of Georgie's window. There was a train on the tracks next to them and in the carriage opposite, there were four young local boys, between sixteen and eighteen years old, all laughing and waving. All harmless at first glance, but then they saw that they were making lewd gestures, rubbing their chests, grabbing their crotches and waggling their tongues. Just at that moment, the girls' train began to pull away, leaving the boys in the station.

'Thank god! Finally we're moving!' Di said.

'Those boys were *awful,*' Georgie said, grimacing.

'Um, yeah, they looked like they were getting really excitable. Could've got nasty, I reckon,' Di agreed.

Silence descended on them as Di looked at her diary on the seat next to her. Unable to concentrate, she stared out at the countryside passing by instead. They had three hours to kill before they got to Rome.

Bizarrely, even though it was still raining, some bright sunlight was now warming up their carriage. After the darkness of the station, some rogue rays of light were poking through in between the grey clouds.

Di viewed her best friend, Georgina Shah, knowing that she was more free-spirited than herself. She didn't seem phased one bit by the whole travel routine, constantly encouraging them to keep going, making sure they were enjoying themselves.

Georgie took off her jumper to reveal a sleeveless white t-shirt underneath. Her black hair was tied back in a ponytail which hung over her heavily-tanned shoulder. She had always had a great figure and been a big hit with the boys; they'd both had lots of fun watching her torment the many boys she deemed worthy.

Besides her looks, she oozed a calm and quiet confidence. Her fierce independence came from a liberal upbringing, a result of an ex-Christian mother and an ex-Hindu father who had both been rebelling against their own parents for years. While she wasn't one for making huge emotional outbursts, when she did react, with happiness or otherwise, you could tell it was genuine and not for effect. Di had always thought her sincerity was quite disarming.

'What about JK, then? He seems to have resisted your charms,' Di said, with a smile.

'Me? Nah, he seems to have a lot else on his mind!' Georgie replied.

'Yes, I noticed. Do you mind? I'm sure you were flirting with him.'

Georgie paused.

'He's kind of cute, I guess. In a vulnerable, sensitive, brooding kind of way. But I think he may have too many issues going on there. A little bit too complex, even for me.'

'Yeah. Like his travels. He finds decisions like that tough to make. He'll weigh up the pros and cons, the consequences, see if it's his destiny and such like. All that worrying is just part of who he is. I think Bobby finds it all a bit annoying,' said Di.

'I know what you mean, but I've actually found it quite endearing, after a while.'

'Yeah, I suppose it is. Especially given how much emotional baggage he seems to be carrying about his father. And god knows I know a thing or two about that.'

Her reply hung in the air as Georgie paused to consider her next comment.

'And what about you and Bobby, then?' Georgie said, smiling directly at her.

Di closed her eyes and shook her head. She knew Georgie would guess eventually; it was only a matter of time before she brought this up.

'Shit! Was it that obvious? We were trying to be discreet,' Di replied.

'Yeah, afraid so. Even JK knew, and I assume Bobby hadn't told him either. Thanks, friend, by the way.'

'Oh, come on, Georgie. It was so complex because of the whole Rick thing.'

'How long has it been going on? Does Rick even know?'

'No, not at all. It's barely even started. We guessed we liked each other straight away but didn't do anything because of Rick. And then I knew it wouldn't work out with Rick anyway.'

'Really, why?' At Georgie's question, Di became uncomfortable.

'Well, er… mainly because he had some really strange habits in the bedroom department.'

'Oh my god! How am I only hearing about this now? Like what?'

Di remained silent and blushing.

'Come on Di, you can't say that and then tell me nothing!'

'Look, it's all a bit embarrassing and I'd rather not talk about it, OK? All I'll say for now is that he's seriously fucked up,' Di replied with a stern look.

'OK, OK. But I am so curious now, you'll tell me one day, right?'

'Maybe. Anyway,' said Di, desperately trying to change subject 'after the break up, me and Bobby kind of happened at the same time. It was, you know, inevitable.'

'Check you out, you little mistress-of-deception, you,' said Georgie, laughing.

'Please don't. I feel bad enough as it is. And please don't say anything to anyone else yet. It's too early after Rick. I mean, him and Bobby are so close – I'm petrified people will think we were cheating on Rick behind his back.'

'Weren't you then?'

'No! We really didn't do anything while I was with Rick. It was just talking, honestly. Obviously, since Rick and I ended, well, that's different…' Di blushed as Georgie laughed again.

They both looked away, escaping to views of the countryside speeding by, either side. The only sound was the train running solidly over the tracks. They could feel the vibrations underneath, loosening minute dust particles from the old seat covers that floated up and around, flickering in the occasional rays of sunlight that invaded their carriage.

Gradually, they relaxed and discussed their next moves in Rome and beyond. Di managed to update her diary in between day dreaming and watching several fast trains speed past. Later, they stopped and heard English voices behind, as two men and a lady boarded and sat at the back of their carriage. The clouds had returned to block out the last of the sunshine and the rain got heavier.

After about forty minutes, thunder started to sound. Despite this, Di noticed, with some surprise, that Georgie was dozing off, curled up in the corner of her side of the seats. The rain was now torrential and the train was starting to slow down again.

'Look, Georgie – I think we're stopping. Where are we?' Di said, nudging her with her foot.

Georgie stirred as the train came to a halt alongside another train. They weren't in a station, just in the middle of the tracks. It could've been a signal point or maybe the driver had stopped to talk to the other train driver. They weren't sure, even after a brief announcement was made in Italian.

They looked across to see the carriage opposite was empty. Suddenly, a door burst open inside it and the four young lads they had seen earlier in Milan station confidently barged through. They glanced across to their right, and then saw Di and Georgie.

'Hey, signora sexy! Ti amo!' one of them shouted at Di.

'Oh shit, it's them again!' she said, flustered. 'Is that the same train? How the hell did they get ahead of us?' she asked Georgie.

'Maybe it's a fast train that overtook and now it's broken down,' Georgie replied.

The boys resumed their efforts in trying to get the girls' attention, waving and banging on the windows this time. They could hear them shouting.

'*Desidero il vostro corpo,*' and

'*Desiderate avere sesso?!*'

'Do you know what they're saying?' Di asked Georgie.

'"I want your body", I think, and "Do you want to have sex?" or something.'

'Yuck,' Di replied.

'Just ignore them. They'll give up eventually – tossers.' Georgie turned away, frowning.

They certainly didn't give up. As they opened their window, Georgie got up and checked that theirs was shut before walking over to sit down with Di on the same side. Their shouting got louder.

'*Lascia per fare l'amore!*'

'*Desidera scopare?!*'

They had no idea what they were saying, but Di severely doubted it would be suitable for polite dinner table conversation with her parents.

'OH MY GOD, OH MY GOD! LOOK WHAT HE'S DOING!' Di suddenly shouted.

'Gross! That is sick,' Georgie echoed.

One of the lads, maybe about eighteen, stood at the window staring right at the girls. He had exposed his manhood and was now masturbating feverishly and unashamedly in their direction while his friends were laughing in the background.

Di's jaw dropped as a strange, unsettled feeling formed in her stomach.

'I think this is a perfect time to use the phrase "I don't know whether to laugh or cry",' said Georgie, trying to lighten proceedings.

For an unknown reason, the girls seemed unable to move, stealing a glance in between covering their eyes with their hands. It was like they were watching a car crash, fixated and quivering, at the spectacle. They began screaming, shouting and swearing back at the boys. The young lad finished, and then proceeded to flick his ejaculate onto their window.

'I think I'm going to be sick,' said Di.

Hopeful that this was the end of the ordeal, they glanced back at the boys. Then, sadly for them, another of the lads stepped forward, laughing. Not wanting to be outdone, he then repeated the performance of his predecessor. Still the girls tried frantically not to look, in total disbelief at the events unfolding.

And then, suddenly, they all disappeared. The girls started to panic, thinking that they were getting off their train to come and find them. If their train was broken-down then they might have to join the girls' train anyway.

But, to the girls' immense relief, the boys' train pulled away shortly after, with no more to be seen of their young Italian friends.

Di, still in shock, looked back down to her handbag and her diary, sitting loosely inside. She couldn't help but laugh out loud. Georgie, who was looking afraid and now confused as well, watched Di pull the diary out and hold it up.

'Dear Diary, how on earth do I describe what just happened?!' she said.

'Well, at least they're gone now. But we're still not moving,' Georgie replied, tentatively.

They sat in silence, waiting and watching grimly, as thunder cracked around them. A large forest dominated their view outside, but then, at regular intervals, they saw lightning break the sky on tree-tops along the horizon.

'Not another storm,' Di sighed.

Lightning flashed brightly outside their carriage.

'Shit! It's getting closer,' said Georgie.

Suddenly, right in front of them, there was a large crack! A lightning bolt had hit a tree with an explosion of light, sending sparks and branches shooting against their window. The girls had both jumped out of their seats and screamed, and now stood on tip toes, stiff with fright and holding on to one other.

They watched thin smoke trails rise from within the remains of the shattered tree. The trails quickly evaporated in the pounding rain as the broken, ragged branches blew in the fierce, unforgiving wind.

Chapter Five

It's Only a Matter of Time

The brothers stood side by side, surrounded by a large crowd of people, all of them looking up at the Old Town Hall to the famous clock. It was mounted proudly on the Hall's southern wall and the minutes relentlessly counted down, towards the hour of three in the afternoon, as the excited noises of the tourists grew louder. They filled up at least half of the Old Town Square of Prague, staring towards the great time piece: the Orloj.

'How much longer do we have to wait for this, JK?' Bobby asked, loudly.

'Seriously? You know when, and you're asking me that while we're staring at a clock?' JK shouted back.

'Yes, thanks, I can see the time. You know what I mean. Does it start on the hour, or earlier?'

'Just before, maybe three minutes I guess,' JK said with a sigh.

'Well, it better be worth it, brother,' Bobby shouted.

'Come on, Bobby, it's a medieval astronomical clock, almost six hundred years old, and the oldest one still operating in the world. Look around you; this display has got to be worth it, right?' JK looked at his brother who returned his stare with a wide-eyed look of bemusement.

'Besides, we've already waited ten minutes. It would be a massive waste to leave now,' JK continued.

'Well, the same old show happens every hour. It's not like it won't happen again if we did miss it,' Bobby said, with his customary smug grin on his face.

JK rolled his eyes and took in the scene around him. There must have been at least seventy people standing immediately around him, possibly one hundred. He had seen and heard various nationalities: Japanese, American, German, Italian, Dutch and many more. Children of all ages, the elderly, even dogs, were all assembled for this moment. He wondered how many people came every hour of every day just to see this show.

At the back of the square he noticed the black uniforms of the local police officers, who were watching the proceedings. Several of their cars, with 'Městská Policie' written in large letters down the side, were parked at the edge of the square, which seemed strange, he reflected, for a regular tourist event.

He looked up at the clock, remembering what he had read in the guide book much earlier that morning, now buried deeply in his rucksack. The structure protruded from the wall and was beneath the building's main tower, also housing a smaller clock, standing several metres above. It was a complex design; its original workings had been in operation from the beginning to the present day, and it was divided into three parts.

Firstly, at the top of the centre piece was an arch, underneath which were two doorways where 'The Walk of the Apostles', the main event, was due to appear. This was an hourly show of figures where the Twelve Apostles and other moving sculptures were presented. In between the doorways was an angel-like statue and, above this, a gold bird figure sat in a rectangular alcove.

Secondly, underneath this, in the centre, was a spherical clock dial representing the position of the Sun and Moon in the sky and displaying various astronomical details, such as the signs of the zodiac around a smaller ring in front of the main clock. Both circles were illustrated in ornate gold lettering and numerals on a navy background. The main clock was a mixture of orange, navy, sky and light blue circles and more gold lines crossing the circle. Four sinister figurines stood by the clock, two on each side. JK knew they were due to move as part of the show, and one in particular, the skeleton, had caught his eye. It had stuck in his mind from his earlier research.

Thirdly, in the lower part, a calendar dial, with medallions representing the months, and a series of pictures in circles on a gold background. There was an inner circle of circular pictures with one large picture of a three-towered castle in the centre. Four more figures accompanied this feature, although they did not move in the show. To the bottom left, a chronicler and an angel and to the bottom right, an astronomer and a philosopher.

JK's eyes began to close as stood staring up, feeling the heat of sunlight shine on his face. He was tired yet agitated, having forgotten to take his medication once again. Although it felt like days ago that he had been reading his guide book, it was a diluted memory of a torch-lit vigil in their hotel room that was actually from this morning.

The account of local legend, that the city of Prague would suffer if the clock is neglected and its good operation is placed in jeopardy, had transfixed him. It was said that once the Old Town astronomical clock stops running for a long time, the Czech nation will suffer bad times and the skeleton was supposed to confirm this fact by nodding its head.

Based on the legend, the only hope was represented by a boy born on New Year's night. Once the astronomical clock is in motion again, the boy is supposed to run out of the church, across the square, to the Town Hall. He has to run very fast to arrive before the last strike of the clock. If he makes it, it would end the skeletons dark power and avert all evil.

JK could not shake off this description; its memory had possessed him. Once he had read it, it had been one of his hardest acts of willpower to restrain himself from asking his brother if they could go and see the show right away.

On each occasion that time got closer to a new hour, JK had become more and more agitated, to the point that Bobby had asked him if he was unwell during breakfast. And each time he had held back his urge to run away, into the square to see the show.

As the morning had progressed, he had noticed how ornately the city's buildings were decorated, and yet even the sunshine could not clear what he felt to be an underlying aura of sinister darkness. The overhanging arches on narrow alleyways, tall darkened walls with harsh edges and gothic statues overlooking his every move that morning.

His unease accelerated as each hour approached and he remembered the skeleton figure once more. And when JK and his brother had visited some gift shops, he observed a seemingly unlimited supply of wooden puppets, with their dead-eyes staring back at him. Every aisle he had walked down and every corner he had turned, rows and rows of inanimate bodies hung, motionless apart from infrequent and almost imperceptible swaying in the natural drafts of silent rooms, watching him, waiting for the next hour to strike.

And still each hour passed without incident and he resisted trying to see the show of the great old Orloj – until now. He felt sweat running down his back, and on his forehead. He knew Bobby would not notice this, given the crisp sunshine in a clear blue sky they now faced. The time was just on the hour.

'OK, JK – Mr. Culture – tell me what happens now.'

And just as Bobby had finished speaking, the skeleton figure pulled a bell cord with one hand and held an hour glass in the other. He continued to pull the chord as a bell rang and the other three statues shook their heads. Then, the two doors above opened up to reveal figures of the Twelve Apostles, who had been set in motion, rotating round to face out as they passed by the openings.

JK pointed up at the skeleton as the background noise from the tourists got louder but the bells continued to chime.

'These figures represent the four things that were most despised by the city at the time the clock was made,' said JK, pointing from left to right as he continued, 'vanity,' he said as he pointed to the first figure, a man who was admiring himself in a mirror, 'greed,' pointing at the next one, who was holding a bag of gold, 'and the end one is lust.'

'You missed one. The skeleton,' Bobby replied.

JK paused.

'He represents death,' he shouted back, eventually.

'Why are they all shaking their heads?'

'Because they aren't ready to go yet.'

The procession of the Apostles above the four figures was coming to an end, and as it finished, they went back inside and the doors closed. The gold bird above, a cockerel, flapped its wings and crowed in its alcove. Finally, the chimes of the hour sounded out within the square. They rang three times and left a brief silence before the hum of tourist chatter returned to the square.

'Right then, JK, let's go and get a fucking drink,' Bobby boomed, trying to prompt a reaction.

Bobby looked across to his brother who stood rigidly, eyes locked in on the clock in front of him.

'Come on, bro. We don't want to miss those models that are in town, remember? We might spot them.'

JK blinked as he finally registered his brother's voice, feeling the crowds escaping as space opened up around him.

He looked back to his brother and began to smile. Suddenly, he became distracted by movement behind Bobby's shoulder, at the far end of the square. A loud whistle sounded out as he saw two police men running toward them.

Bobby turned around swiftly as they approached, and with several tourists still blocking the way, the police officers did not see and barged into him. As he tried to remain on his feet, Bobby let out a soft yelp and grabbed the nearest thing he could hang on to, which happened to be JK's rucksack. As he wrenched it from his shoulder, it was thrown open and fell to the floor, emptying its contents as it did so.

The police officers were barely knocked out of their stride and carried on running past, to the edge of the square and round the corner.

'Fucking hell, what was that all about?' Bobby asked, as he got up off the floor, dusting his knees and elbows, checking for any scratches or dirt. JK did not even look up and was squatting over his bag, frantically grabbing at his things as he picked them off the floor. Heads in the crowd had turned and were staring at them both now.

'No, no, brother. Don't worry about me, I'm just fine,' Bobby said, sarcastically.

'What? Oh, right, are you OK?' JK barely lifted his head as he glanced at Bobby but then quickly returned to his task.

'All good. Just curious as to what all the fuss was about. Who were they chasing?'

JK uttered a barely perceptible huff in acknowledgement as he now stared at his bag, confused.

'Well, come on. We both definitely need a drink now. Enough of this sightseeing. I told you it never ends well, does it?'

Again, JK didn't answer. He had just unpacked his bag, and was now re-packing it. And then a look of nausea and fear came upon him.

'What's the matter?' Bobby asked him.

'I think I've lost something,' JK said, slowly and softly. 'The list. I've lost the list.'

JK stared out at the dim candle-lit room simmering with people, beyond the edge of the leather-bound booth he sat at with his brother and two beautiful local girls. L'Fleur was a

1920s jazz-styled cocktail joint, a five-minute walk from the Old Town Square. Crystalline chandeliers above the wooden panels added some sporadic lighting along the length of the bar. There was a stained window in the back, and long velvet curtains draped across the windows at the front to add to its darkened, glamorous appeal.

'He's called "Reaper of Prague" to us, you know?' said one of the girls, with a deliciously mischievous smile. Her black hair formed a shoulder-length bob around her perfectly-shaped face, with high cheek bones and a wide-eyed stare.

'What? All those police were just for some petty local criminal?' Bobby replied, straight-faced but JK knew he was clearly trying to provoke a reaction.

'Not just criminal. A monster!' the other equally stunning-looking girl replied, enthusiastically. Her blonde hair was in contrast to her heavy dark eyeliner which added a sultry air of forbidden and illicitly-corrupting pleasure. But the look, for both girls, was engineered, and purely intentional, JK thought to himself.

'Yes, he killed four prostitutes already in Prague,' the brunette added, with a sour look of disappointment at Bobby. She flicked a quick look back at JK, taking a sip from her glass, and continued, 'You must watch out, too. Police say he is nearby, right now.'

JK felt the exposed brick walls start to sway slightly in his vision, a natural consequence of the third round of cocktails they had consumed. JK wondered if these girls were really drinking the same drinks they had recommended to Bobby and himself. Of course, they looked the same – tall, dark, translucent glasses with dry-ice smoke pouring from the top – but, surely, they could not be as ridiculously strong as the absinthe-based, tourist-monstrosities that littered their table?

Bobby and JK had not been sat down for long before the girls had joined them, and their conversation had moved on quickly: where they were staying, what they had seen, the incident at the clock show.

In common with many other attractive women he had noticed in the bar, both these girls shared a chemically enhanced look: their eyes were enlarged and they had very dark pupils. JK smiled at the situation, knowing that Bobby, who ordinarily did very limited research, had specifically chosen this bar. He found it incredible just how outnumbered the men were here.

Every time JK had glanced up, he caught a glimpse of another creature of wonder appear from a dark corner, impossibly smooth legs in between an expensive-looking long, flowing dress, a tanned shoulder and neckline adorned with subtle jewellery. They sported exceptionally 'light' fashion with dramatic sweeping fabrics that hung loosely from their skinny limbs, yet somehow still clung tightly to their torsos.

Their movement was economical, effortlessly gliding in and out of the few vacant spaces across the crowded bar floor. Even though their appearances were brief, they stood out in the darkness, floating like glowing ghouls with faces of angels, each a shimmering blur of colour and light.

There were plenty of good-looking men there too, making an effort to get in the swing of things, wearing tight shirts and trousers and wearing extravagant hair styles. JK couldn't help but think that the bar seemed to be some sort of informal stage show for Prague to parade its most beautiful people to the discerning tourists. Not that he and Bobby were, he thought, but at least they could do a good job pretending.

JK wondered if Bobby had realised yet that these girls gave the same welcome to a lot of new tourists to the bar, if they met certain criteria. But, suddenly, the two girls stood up, the blonde pointing and saying 'bathroom' as they left and walked away from the table into the mass drinking horde surrounding them.

'How about that, bro?' Bobby said, smiling.

'Yes, Bobby. I suppose there is a small chance that they might not be actual whores,' JK replied, sarcastically.

'Oh, who cares. I know they aren't genuine but, come on, man. I mean, wow, how hot are they?'

'Very. But don't pay for any more of their drinks – you know you won't get lucky with them.'

'Just enjoy yourself. You never know what will happen. This place, hey? I heard there's a fashion show in town this week. I swear there must be loads of models in here tonight.'

'Maybe, but I think those cocktails are making me ill. I don't want any more.'

'Fair enough, let's just order some beers, then. Still, they worked though, right?'

'What do you mean?'

'You forgot – for a few minutes at least – about that fucking list. I hope so, anyway.'

'I suppose. But I still need it back, Bobby. It's important to me.'

'It's meaningless and you know it,' Bobby replied, rolling his eyes.

'Don't start this with me now, Bobby. I'll fucking walk out,' JK snapped.

'OK, OK. Calm down, JK. Surely you can't be that surprised by my reaction by now, though. This is our father we're talking about.'

'I guess not. But it's still quite a list of achievements though. I think it's a pretty good memento of him – and I don't feel the same way about him as you do, remember?'

Bobby looked at JK silently with pity for a moment and then turned back to staring at the bar.

'Well, maybe you should, JK. I'm not sure our father did all that travel for the same reasons as us: the right reasons, that is. I don't think you should be copying him, anyway. Maybe one day you'll realise that.'

They continued to look away from each other as music played around the bar and the background noise of conversation and drinks being made enveloped their awkwardness. After some time, Bobby ordered two beers from a waiter. The girls had not returned.

'What about you then, Peter Pan?' JK said, deciding finally to interrupt their silence. 'When will your travels ever end? You can't keep this life up forever. Especially if Di is someone you really like.'

Bobby looked down at his near-empty cocktail, smiling wryly as he swirled the remnants of the drink around the bottom of the glass.

'Yeah. You might be onto something there, JK. It definitely can't last forever. I do know that,' he replied, sheepishly.

JK was taken aback; it was a side of his brother he didn't get to see very often. Guessing that the cocktails were taking their toll on Bobby also, JK saw his opportunity to ask something that had been bugging him for days now.

'What about Di? After all that cloak and dagger stuff you pulled in Zurich, she must mean something to you.'

'She's a nice girl, sure,' Bobby said, with his most polished straight face.

'What? Oh, come on, I saw how you were with her. I was there too, you know. You can't fool me.'

'Huh. Like I said, who knows what the future holds, little brother. It's early days yet.'

'Yeah, but you like each other, right?'

'OK, OK. Yes, we like each other.'

'A lot.'

'Oh, fuck off now, JK. You won't get any more out of me, no matter how pissed we are,' Bobby replied as they both laughed.

Their beers arrived at the table but the girls did not return. JK had spotted them watching from afar and speculated that they had figured he and his brother were too 'low-end' as tourist potential went, and had decided to wait for the next willing targets to appear.

JK and Bobby continued to drink and have fun people-watching at the bar. As more tourists arrived, they observed a similar pattern of various good-looking girls weigh the visitors up and then approach them.

Sometime later, they heard some raised voices at the entrance as a security guard went from the bar to assist the two doormen. A large group of visitors were trying to gain entry all at once, but were not being allowed in. The discussion became more heated and then the bar manager came over to join in.

JK watched with concern but Bobby was taking a great interest in events at this point. The manager walked away from the group, back to the bar to make a phone call. Almost at the same time, someone in the group started shoving the doormen, who had no choice but to push the whole group back and out of the entrance way.

'Come on, let's go,' said Bobby.

'What, now? Why, for them?' JK asked, a bit confused.

'Yes, I think I know that girl,' he replied, pointing to a young girl in her twenties, with dark skin, standing near the front. 'Beth? Beth! Is that you?' he shouted out, but no one looked back and he knew he had not been heard. JK's mind raced as he struggled to see the girl's face, but she had already moved out of the doorway.

Within a few more minutes they had paid their bar bill. And as they were walking out, they could see flashing lights through the windows from the police cars that had just arrived. JK looked at his watch and saw that the time was nine-thirty pm. He remembered the Orloj, and then his missing list, and began to worry once more.

Outside the bar a chaotic mass of bodies was squashed together around the entrance. The night was cold but JK didn't notice, given he was sharing the air with so many others. Along with his brother, they tried to squeeze their way past several doormen and security guards – some of whom had joined in from other nearby bars – onto the pavement.

The security staff were jostling and shouting at a younger group of fifteen people, who had now been pushed back into the cobbled streets. Two police cars were parked behind them and at least five police officers were now walking among them. JK and Bobby managed to slowly edge their way outwards, to the back of the group.

'What about this Beth?' JK shouted out to Bobby, who was still frantically looking around.

'I can't see her anymore,' he shouted back.

The group did not look like normal tourists. They were of a similar age to JK, but they were very aggressive, shouting and jumping at the police and security staff. A lot were clad in leather, with bleached or coloured hair, some with punk-styled spikes or Mohicans, and various facial piercings too. JK then noticed a lot of them were speaking German.

A few onlookers had started to arrive around the edges of the scene, on the pavements on the other side of the street, opposite the bar. Bobby approached the manager of L'Fleur, who was stood watching, concerned. He spoke to him briefly while JK watched.

No actual violence had occurred and no one had been detained by the police, yet. There was lots of talking and shouting with the officers, who formed a natural human barrier between the bar and various individuals in the group.

Suddenly, a young man, who must have been their ring leader, began singing and shouting in an attempt to whip the group up into a frenzy. He wore a bright pink t-shirt underneath a black leather waistcoat and had bright blonde spikey hair. Gradually, a few started to join in with the singing.

JK noticed that a few of the group would occasionally walk off, away from the crowd, and then some other new members would join them. Yet he had no idea where they were going to or coming from. Then, Bobby returned to stand next to him.

'They're student protestors. From Germany,' Bobby said.

'Really? What are they protesting against?' JK replied.

'No one knows exactly. Some sort of political thing. The manager hasn't seen them before. He thinks it could be related to the fashion show: they use feminism as their main protest, but then it's a bandwagon for loads of other things, like animal rights, capitalism, etc., etc. Fucking students eh, JK?'

'Ha, ha. Very funny,' he replied. 'But what about your mate, Beth? Is she one of them, then? Who is she?'

Bobby paused, looking unsure how to reply.

'Yeah, I guess so, but I can't find her. Apparently, there's been similar reports across the city today; they seem to be spread around the bars in Old Town tonight. She could be nearby, so maybe we can go and find her in a bit,' he said, looking away from JK, knowing that he hadn't fully answered his question.

'So, are they dangerous?' JK asked.

'Don't think so. Just minor stuff so far, like shouting and a bit too much drinking. The police are here just as a precaution. They want to make sure no tourists are harmed.'

'Yeah I get it, and they wouldn't want the restaurant and bar takings to suffer, would they?' JK replied, but his mind began to wander to the events earlier at the Orloj, and the 'Reaper of Prague' the beautiful girls had then told them about.

'No, and no one seems that worried, anyway,' Bobby said.

The singing continued as JK waited for Bobby to make a decision. He expected him to volunteer some more information about Beth, or at least say they should move on somewhere else. But, unusually for Bobby, he seemed unable to respond as he stood staring, fixated by the noisy crowd in front, as if paralysed by the spectacle.

'Come on, Bobby. Who is this Beth – do I know her?'

'Not really. You've met. A long time ago,' Bobby replied eventually, with a resigned sigh.

'Really? From school?' JK uttered in sharp reply.

'Yes. Elizabeth Harvey. I think she was in your year. You probably remember the fight I had once with her older brother, Eddie.'

JK stared back at Bobby, wide-eyed, with shock. He tried to process this information, but all he could think of was the memory of their necklace that he had stolen.

'But that was like twelve or thirteen years ago or something, wasn't it?'

'No idea. I can't even remember what I fought Eddie about now, either.'

'Their mother left them, didn't she? Weren't you fighting about that, or about our dad?'

'Maybe. I got into a lot of fights back then. I mean, I can't remember what started it, anyway,' Bobby said, trying to clarify.

'Your big mouth, probably,' said JK, who still had the sense that Bobby was holding back some information as a thought struck him. 'But, hang on a minute, she was only about nine years old then, same as me. So how do you remember her so well now?'

Bobby shifted his footing where he stood and shrugged his shoulders dismissively.

'What's that mean? Did you stay in touch with them or something? Don't tell me you and Eddie became secret friends?' JK asked. 'It was that necklace we stole, wasn't it? Did you ever give it back?'

'Oh yeah, that necklace. I had forgotten all about that. As a matter of fact, yes, I did give it back to them, much later, though. It was from their mother. I couldn't really keep it, could I?' Bobby laughed back at JK.

Angered at his brother's flippant reaction, JK was about to shout back at Bobby for further clarification but was robbed of the opportunity. At that moment, the leader of the students, who had been singing, suddenly started shouting what sounded like orders for the group. And then, all at once, they started running from the pavement, away from the bar, along the street going back towards the direction of the Old Town Square.

The police blew whistles and shouted back at them. But it happened so fast that it must have caught the police off guard. A couple of officers started to run after the group, while the others remained with the bar security staff. JK could see one of them talking into his police radio, presumably to report the situation status and alert officers in other locations.

JK felt his customary feeling of unease deepen in his gut. He looked at his watch again and saw it was now nine forty-five. And then Bobby started a light jog in the same direction as the group, not wanting to go too fast and draw attention to the police. JK knew and dreaded what was coming next.

'Come on, JK, let's see where they end up,' he said, turning round to beckon his brother.

'Why? Just to find Beth?' JK replied.

'Stop worrying, bro. Trust me. I'll tell you all about it, I promise,' Bobby said, with his mischievous glint in his eyes. And after a brief pause, JK shook his head and slowly followed after his brother, now several steps ahead, in pursuit of the rowdy young group.

They ran up the cobbled streets, quickly passing two pubs where they saw more police but no further students. JK knew where they were headed; it was inevitable. They approached the Old Town Square, back where they had been earlier in the day.

He began to feel sick again, a combination of nervous energy mixing with his underlying fears and the alcohol. He fought the urge to look up at the clock tower ahead of him. He could see a large group of people and knew it was the students, not just tourists, all gathered underneath the Orloj, waiting for the next display to appear.

JK stopped and watched his brother carry straight on into the group. He checked his watch and saw it was now five minutes to the hour.

'Shit,' he muttered to himself, as he shifted his rucksack on his back and carried on ahead towards Bobby.

He joined the edge of the crowd but could not see his brother anywhere. He tried to move in closer but any progress was extremely difficult. It was so noisy all around: angry shouting, drunken singing, a constant chatter in a multitude of languages and a sea of faces.

But then, JK clearly heard the bell chime and he knew the show had started. The shouting of the crowd got louder, and he again stopped himself from looking up to the skeleton figure, continuing to stay at eye level, looking for Bobby. The bell started to sound ten times as the clock struck the hour. On the last chime, he finally saw Bobby, talking to a girl.

Beth. Now JK remembered her. Not the little girl from the time in the park when they had found the necklace. But an older girl, several years later. He now realised who she had been to Bobby. They had hung around together while JK had been doing A-

levels. Bobby never really introduced her to him or their mother; she never seemed to
stay for very long.

She wore a green army style jacket which was covered in several badges, ten or so
on either side: CND, 'meat is murder' and the female symbol with a raised fist in the
circle. Several earrings and piercings – on her lower lip and through one nostril – stood
out from her brown skin. Her long black hair was tied up straight at the back but then left
to hang out in natural curls behind her head.

JK slowly approached them as they continued to talk. Beth's face was pretty but she
held a stern look as she spoke to Bobby. JK knew from her body language that she
wasn't happy to see his brother. As Bobby saw JK arrive, she then turned in the same
direction to notice him staring at her.

'JK, there you are. Well, I found her. Beth, you remember my younger brother don't
you?' Bobby said.

'Ah, Jonny Keane, yes. Hello,' she said with a heavy German accent.

'Hi,' JK replied, tentatively.

'Ah, but you look shocked to see me. I guess this is all a bit of a surprise, isn't it,
Bobby?' she said with an unmistakeably aggressive tone. Bobby viewed her nervously.
'Well, JK, we weren't very good at communicating back in those days, but your brother
and I, we used to fuck each other. On and off for a few months. Just one of life's
journeys. We all make mistakes en route,' she continued, bitterly.

'Oh, right, I see,' JK replied, hesitantly. He noticed the gold necklace around her
neck. The letter 'b' hung from it.

'You like my necklace? Yes, that's a good story, too. That's how we first met. One
day I lost it; eventually, he found it and gave it back to me. Lucky me, I guess.'

'So, you live in Germany now?' JK asked.

'Yes, very perceptive, JK. Looks like you got the brains in the family. I moved out
there to be with my mother three years ago, when I was eighteen. I'm at university in
Berlin now studying politics, with my friends: these guys you see all around you tonight,
having fun.'

'So, you're happy? I'm glad,' said Bobby.

'Well, I'm glad I can satisfy your guilt, Bobby. It's a great life, thank you. But, what
about you, Bobby? Are you still chasing the perfect dream?'

'Come on, Beth, that was a long time ago,' he replied.

'You don't give a fuck about anyone other than yourself. And you never did,' Beth
said. She turned around and saw some other people moving out of the square.

'Anyway, I've got to go now. It's good to see your brother isn't as fucked up as
you,' she said, looking straight at Bobby, who stared vacantly back. JK thought he could
detect the slightest hint of fear in his eyes. Beth glanced at JK, and then back to Bobby.

'You haven't told him yet, have you, Bobby?' Beth said, but he could only stare
down at his feet. 'Oh, you really are a piece of work, aren't you? Fucking hell, I thought
my family was bad but you guys are something else. Good luck, JK. And good luck to all
of you,' Beth said.

And with that, Elizabeth Harvey ran off to join her fellow student friends, who were
on the move once more. The two brothers never saw her again.

'What the hell was that about, Bobby?' JK pleaded.

'Forget her. She's just bitter – she never got over our break-up. She wanted to
continue but I didn't. Simple as that,' Bobby said, dismissively, doing what he did best.

'Really? She was pretty intense. Seemed like she had a major axe to grind with
you?'

'She was like that before I met her, and probably always will be. Truth is, we both used each other for what we wanted at the time. But, she probably loved me for years before we got together. I think I broke her heart.'

'Bastard… But what did she mean at the end? What haven't you told me, Bobby?'

'No fucking idea. Maybe she was just being spiteful, to get back at me by trying to fuck with your head. She knows you have OCD. I told her.'

The answer seemed credible to JK. Enough to give him pause and let the words sink in at least. Yet still he couldn't shake the uneasy feeling buried deep within. Her arrival was some sort of bad omen, he knew it. And as he eyed his brother suspiciously, he saw Bobby looking back at him expectantly as if to see if his answer had satisfied him.

He took this as a sign that he was definitely being lied to. Bobby was hiding something from him, just as he suspected his mother had been doing for several years now. Perhaps they were hiding the same thing. He had no idea.

'You're lying, Bobby. I know it. You're full of shit.'

'I'm really not, JK. Look, it's been a long day and we've probably drunk too much. Let's just go back to our hotel, shall we?'

'You know what, Bobby? Ever since I lost our father's list, all this shit has happened to us,' JK suddenly blurted out.

'What are you talking about? What has happened to us?'

'Those girls telling us about the Reaper of Prague, the students, the police, Beth.'

'So what? None of it was that bad, was it? No one got hurt?'

'And now you, lying to me,' JK said, more calmly this time.

'I told you, I'm not lying.'

'I know you are. I need that fucking list, Bobby. It's not meant to be like this.'

'The list? His list of countries that he saw? I've already beaten it, I expect. Not that I care. And you will soon, too. We're not like him, so what does it matter what's on the list anyway? You won't win any prizes from him, thank god.'

'Stop doing that. Stop acting like you own our joint history. You don't. I'm entitled to my own memories of him,' JK snapped back, fighting back tears.

'Who cares what he did, JK? He's gone and when he was around, he didn't care about us much anyway let me assure you. You weren't old enough to remember but I was.'

Bobby's reply stunned him into silence – he said the same thing every time. The argument always ended this way, always said with such conviction, such strength of belief. And every time, JK did not have an answer back for his older brother. The words pierced JK's weary mind, festering, spreading and circulating like a toxin.

'Its bad luck, that's all. I'm meant to be lucky. We both need the luck,' JK said, hysterically.

'Calm down, OK, JK? We'll sort this out, don't worry.'

This briefest of brotherly vigils was instantly shattered by the sound of a police siren. Flashing lights penetrated the Old Town Square as the remaining tourists from the Orloj show meandered around. Their happy spell broken, they looked on in shock as seven armed police ran at full pelt through the square.

JK, his mind in another place, was blindsided by their onslaught, the impact catching him hard on his left shoulder. His rucksack flew to the ground as he stumbled but managed to stay on his feet.

Both the brothers stared at the ground; the contents of the bag were strewn across the stone floor once again. A folded and frayed piece of old paper, browned at the edges, had been dislodged from within, buried among some clothing.

It was unmistakeably their father's list.

Part Two

'The dream changed a few years later – say, when I was about twelve years old. The startling opening vision of the light and the tree is the same: the clouds, the storms, everything, right up to the part where I am flying above the earth, on top of grassy plains and following the ground's surface up a hill.

As I reach the top of the hill, I encounter an infinite and flat landscape before me once again but I don't notice a tree anymore. Instead, I am drawn towards the sight of a large male lion, his mane effortlessly blowing in the occasional breeze, a welcome respite as he sits basking in the hot sun. His glorious tan-coloured fur reflects and shimmers in the intense sunlight as his lean, muscular torso rhythmically expands and contracts with every breath.

Untroubled, he peruses serenity spread before him, his kingdom in peace. Then, the lion lifts his head up with sudden alertness, his amber eyes watching closely some movement far in the distance. Following his line of sight, I see a lioness only twenty or so metres in front. She also watches the same movement far ahead. I follow this line once more and see yet another lioness, the same distance apart. Still I can see more lions, younger males and females, spread out in a perfect straight line. The pride of lions, ten in all, has spotted the blurred movements of wildebeest running on the horizon.

They are ready, watching and waiting to take up the challenge and catch their prey. But I don't stick around to see the kill. I am rising in the air once more, getting hotter and hotter, flying high above the lions, invisible and unnoticed. From the blue sky I fly into the clouds, into the white; and out again, only to find myself in a blend of new colours this time. With sweat dripping from my forehead, I turn and realise I have just flown through a rainbow as I see the translucent reds, yellows and greens emanating from the edge of the clouds.

I fly back down, low, to see what will happen when the rainbow reaches the ground – but there is nothing, only grass and earth, and the closer I get, the less I can see. The rainbow disappears from view and I look up to see the Acacia tree once more dominate the grassy horizon. The lions have disappeared also and the sky begins to cloud over and darken. Ferocious rain crashes to the floor and thunder cracks violently in the air above.

A final drama of lightning bolts arrives, flashing intermittently above the tree, in silhouette once more. Just as suddenly, a cold, quiet air then envelopes the scene as it starts to shrink again, and the now familiar black frame surrounds and approaches me. The flashing lightning in the background is intense and dazzling, but as it gradually slips away, it grows fainter and fainter. Nothingness engulfs the vision before me – in an instant, it returns to total blackness and my dream ends again.'

Chapter Six

Those Wise Old Coyotes of the Strip

He sat on the enormous ageing coach, shuddering along its journey, as loosened dust particles lingered on his eyelids and the edges of his nostrils, tantalising his senses along the edge of consciousness. JK worried exactly what the hell the small green tablet he had taken earlier was. Whether it was a prescribed sleeping pill or not he couldn't tell, but something weird was now happening inside his head.

He was stupid for taking it in the first place, JK reasoned, given he was on his own medication already and that he hardly knew the girl he had accepted it from for more than a few days. Ronnie had seemed nice enough: her broken English was quite charming, and her self-deprecating sense of humour seemed too genuine to be an act.

Now, JK wondered if she was asleep herself, as she sat, slumped, in the row just behind him. Veronica was from Argentina and had introduced herself as Ronnie to other fellow travellers. She had a fuller figure and a friendly face, with instantly disarming and welcoming large brown eyes. Her wavy, long black hair and tanned brown skin were faring well in the American West so far.

They had met in a hostel in San Francisco and had got on well enough. It made sense to travel to Las Vegas together, their mutual destination now. And at least an hour ago, JK had accepted her tap on his shoulder, looking round to see her hand, offering a tiny pill of mystery, and a pair of innocent, optimistic eyes staring back at him.

He just couldn't stand those cramped overnight journeys, whether it was on trains, planes or disgustingly smelly coaches, like the great lumbering Greyhound bus they were all currently suffering in. Anything for an easy life, he thought; he couldn't understand how anyone slept on these things at all.

JK's knees scratched against the seat cover's dusty blue and black woollen material, his legs cramped up against the back of the seat in front. His elbow stuck into the loosely hanging, fat-ridden arms of the large woman he sat next to. The air on board was humid and dank with the smell of sweat and cigarettes. A baby sobbed for attention from its comatose mother a few rows in front.

His neck was arched back painfully on the vertical head rest. Blackness engulfed the window view to his left. He speculated where they might be as he glanced at his watch. It was just past 11pm and he hoped it wouldn't be too long before they arrived.

A car's headlights shot by in the opposite direction, forgotten in an instant, as their bus crawled along a lonely road, weighed down by a low-budget mixture of tourists as well as local passengers from Arizona, Nevada and California.

His mind wandered, and, despite an unusual headache, he was grateful to have finally begun his trip. The delays to his grand travel plans had happened because, in the last three years, JK had been distracted by a number of key events. He had managed to graduate with a degree in Statistics before pondering – and beginning – a career at a large market research agency. Finally, he had taken the time he needed to save enough money to top up his depleted inheritance and get his travel dreams back on track.

Interspersed with all this were more raucous holidays with his brother, a few months where his depression had worsened, followed by multiple family arguments. Yet, somehow, he had largely recovered and now barely needed to take his medication. But, even though it had been weeks since his last dose, he knew it could stay in his system for a while. Now he realised it could be having a side effect and wished he had asked to check the bottle from where that sleeping pill came from.

His eyelids started closing and his head began to drop, stirring when the coach went over a bump on the road before going back to the normal smooth terrain. He saw the lights of the highway speeding by outside – brief interruptions to the blackness with no one else in sight. He dreamt while staying awake.

Yet the dreams didn't seem real, a strange collage of personal moments, his sights and experiences over the last few weeks in the USA and Canada. Nothing had seemed real recently; it was now March 2000 and finally his world tour had begun. Ahead of him, a big, scary unknown was now wide open.

Almost fainting as I looked down, impossibly far, through the glass floor at the top of the CN Tower in Toronto. The Niagara Falls from the Canadian side. Poutine and the Olympique Velodrome in Montreal. A New York hostel in Harlem, where two people were discussing last night's murder at a newsagents next door. A hot dog for breakfast and sleeping on the subway the same night. Lobsters in Boston. The surreal sugary sweet 'World of Coca Cola' in Atlanta.

The big cumbersome Amtrak trains slowly grinding across the country. Train tracks seemingly on water through a lake to New Orleans and the colourful French Quarter. Another long wait due to a car suicide on the tracks. Orlando for jet skiing on a lake with alligators and water snakes. The beautiful people of Miami. Ernest Hemingway's house in Key West with thirty polydactyl cats. 'Yard Dog' cocktails and snorkelling in Key Largo.

Walking along the streets of Vancouver, city skyscrapers illuminated as impressive silhouettes against the night sky. Rivalled with day light, where imposing snow-capped mountains were interspersed with spectacular views of pine tree forests.

San Francisco, modern art, trendy bars and rickety cable cars down steep streets. A tiring walk halfway across the Golden Gate Bridge. A trip to Alcatraz Island, the escape of 1962. Hundreds of sea lions at Pier 39, quite endearing in a strange way, like cranky old aunts, moaning great uncles – weird, noisy and smelly.

A rockslide just outside of San Francisco, a lucky escape. The picturesque walk through the forest, almond and walnut trees growing all around, the natural beauty of Lower Yosemite Falls and the Mirror Lake. A raccoon, scrambling around outside my tent late one night in our campsite. Putting chains on the wheels for extra grip, it's wet and snowy on the mountain tracks. Every journey is tiring. Long delays to our journey, hours of waiting, reading, dozing, eating, staring. Long trains, long roads, long walks: connecting us everywhere we go in North America.

Just as JK had nodded off into a normal sleep, he was cruelly awakened once more. The brakes of the coach pressed hard as it pulled to a stop at a service station, where the driver informed everyone that there would be yet another ten-minute comfort break, even though they were already an hour behind their scheduled arrival time.

Watching the driver get off, JK stood up and turned round to tell Ronnie he was popping outside briefly, who nodded in return. His head spun as he walked along the aisle, thinking he might be sick.

He wondered whether a trip to the restrooms was needed, but hoped, at the very least, a walk in the fresh air might do him some good. But as he rested his arm on the side of the silver bus, head bowed, he felt the pain in his gut increasing. He walked through to the grimy, dark and cold public toilets, in a small irrelevant town he had never heard of, and would never remember or return to, and sat, waiting for the pains to subside.

They did not, and he eventually gave up, deciding instead to make himself sick. Feeling temporary relief, he cleaned himself up and returned to stand next to the coach to get some air and clear his head.

JK sighed in relief, absorbing the calm silence that had momentarily spread across the bus station. And that's when he first met Jo-Jo Knox.

'Hey, compadre, is this bus going to Vegas?' an American voice from behind JK said, startling him.

He turned round to see a tanned white man who was of a similar age to himself, yet much taller and leaner. His dress sense was exuberant, wearing army print shorts, with a blue gilet partially covering a bright orange t-shirt underneath. His face was clean shaven, and a blue baseball cap with a white and red 'Cubs' circle logo on the front mostly covered his short brown hair.

He smiled broadly and, despite the ridiculously large sunglasses he wore, behind the brown-orange lenses set in a thick black plastic frame, JK could see his eyes gleaming back at him.

'Yes, it is,' JK said, smiling back at the unusual character he faced, still a little unsure about him.

'OK, that's good. You seen the driver around?' he replied. Seeing him shift his backpack, JK knew that he was a fellow traveller, despite his American accent.

'Yeah, I think he's in the toilet,' JK said, pointing back at the direction he had just come from.

'Well then, I'll just get me some fresh air for a moment, if you don't mind that is?' Puzzled, JK looked at the stranger, and then realised his intention as he pulled out a packet of cigarettes.

'Oh right, yes, no problem,' JK replied.

'Smoke?' the stranger said, offering the pack and pulling out a lighter.

'No thanks. I was just stretching my legs.'

'Uh-huh. You been on the road long?' he asked.

'A few days or so, from San Francisco.'

'Nice. And you're headed for Vegas too?

'Yes, that's right.'

'I figured so. You doing a tour of the USA, right? So, where else you seen?'

'Yes, and Canada too. I've been out here a few weeks now, started in Toronto and worked my way down the East Coast. Then I flew to Vancouver and have been going down this coast too.'

'Hell, yeah, that sounds good to me. But you missed out the middle!'

'Oh, well, I've seen loads of the States and loved every minute of it. I just couldn't do it all,' JK replied.

'Heck, that's some of the best parts of the country!' he interrupted. 'Like Chicago, what a city! The windy city – in my home state of Illinois, although I'm from a little town called Champaign, which you probably haven't heard of, but it's in *downstate* Illinois actually, yes sir. But you've also got New Orleans, Dallas, Austin etcetera, etcetera. Trust me, hombre, you should see the middle too, it ain't all bad bible-bashing KKK types down there, you know?' the stranger said, laughing.

'I know, I know, but it's just time and money I guess,' said JK, returning a chuckle.

'True enough, friend, true enough. Say, I'm being mighty rude now, ain't I? I should introduce myself, I'm Joseph Johnson Knox, but there ain't no airs and graces with me – y'all can just go ahead and call me Jo-Jo, I don't mind. Where are you from, friend? England, obviously?' He offered his hand to JK as he inhaled from his cigarette.

'Yes, that's right, from near London. My name's Jonny Keane, but you can call me JK. I don't mind, either,' JK replied with a smile as he accepted the handshake. 'So, if you're from Illinois, how come you've got a Southern accent?'

'Ah-ha, JK, that is very perceptive. Yes-sir, that is a good question, my man. Well, I'm not sure. Me and all my friends just started out talking like this one time when we was little. I mean most of the people in my town don't talk like us, so I don't really know why, if I'm honest. Although you don't have to go too far south of us to hear the real red necks of America, like in Kansas, for example. Sorry, but I have a tendency to waffle. I'll always try and stick to one story, but you'll have to forgive me if I get a little lost in the telling. Once I get started, there ain't much that's gonna stop me. Heck, I may get a little side tracked and veer off the subject on the way, but I'll get there in the end. Yes-sir, I guess I just do love a good yarn, that I surely do.'

JK was not used to such a vivid introduction from the travellers he had previously met and was so taken aback by the man's expressive demeanour, he momentarily could not form words to reply. He just stared, wide-eyed and open-mouthed, back. When Jo-Jo eventually started to frown at him, JK realised that must have appeared strange.

'Oh, yes, sorry, I er, I'm not quite with it. I think I must be half asleep. I'm still pretty tired from the trip, you see. Anyway, you must've had an unusual journey here from Illinois, then? What brings you to Vegas?' JK eventually managed to ask.

'I was on a bit of a road trip with my best buddy, Andy Robson. He's a big, dumb, Canadian moose. Well, actually, he's not all that dumb – if anything, most people would probably say I'm the dumb one. We went down through the middle and along the bottom of the States – hence my glowing tribute for you earlier. Those places I said, plus El Paso, Santa Fe, Phoenix – hell, I've probably forgotten a few. Anyhow, who cares? We've been having an absolute ball the past few months. I can't even begin to tell you all the stuff we got up to 'coz there just ain't the time.'

'That's great. Where is he now, then?' JK asked.

'Ah, he had to fly back home to Canada early because his dad got sick. It sucks, man. But hopefully he'll be OK and he can come out and meet me somewhere else later. So, what about you, JK – what's your story? You don't seem the traditional British backpacker type?'

JK raised any eyebrow, unsure as to how to interpret the comment. Reacting to this, Jo-Jo quickly continued.

'As in, you seem a bit older, and this isn't the normal backpacker route, is it? Don't all you Brits normally go to Thailand?'

'Yeah, I suppose some do. I just had my own plans. I might go to Thailand one day, though. And as for my age, well I would've gone earlier but I wasn't sure if I was going to travel on my own or with my brother, you see. Plus, I had to save money – boring things like that.'

'Gotcha. Is your brother here now, then?'

'No, but he's on his way, I think. He's done a lot of travel already and he's older than me. I'm meeting him in Vegas, although I'm not sure how long he's staying with me for. He kinda does his own thing, you see,' JK said.

'Ah, a bit of a free spirit, an untameable beast, eh?' asked Jo-Jo.

'Something like that. Although maybe he's finally found a girl who can tame him. Not sure she is that happy about him coming out here to see me, though,' JK said, wincing at the memories of the arguments Bobby had had with his long-term girlfriend Di before he had left. Goodness knows how many more they had had since.

Jo-Jo laughed with JK before the coach driver appeared out of the doorway leading to the station facilities. He walked towards the bus and shouted out 'All aboard' to several passengers who were standing around.

'Ah, hold up now, I better just sort my ticket out, JK. Good talking to you, my friend. See you later,' said Jo-Jo, and with that, he turned his back on JK to approach the driver, pulling out his wallet as he walked.

JK walked through the bus door, climbing up the steps and onto the aisle to his cramped seat. He checked on Ronnie, who was asleep behind him.

Shortly after, he felt a tap on his shoulder as Jo-Jo walked past him and nodded. He carried on up the aisle looking for a seat on the now almost-full coach. Eventually, he found one of the few spare ones available and sat down.

JK's seat was warm from the heat of the wheel below it. Apart from when the coach went over small bumps, perhaps stones in the road, there was no let-up in the throbbing rotation, a constant vibration up his leg and spine for hours.

His head began to feel heavy once more, and he lost all sense of time as they drove along the mostly smooth and flat road. His mind became a trance-like wasteland of exhaustion and nervous tension, flitting between REM sleep, memories and flashes of current surroundings.

It was gone 1am and only darkness could be seen outside. Eventually, a dot of light appeared, far in the distance, growing larger as they approached it. The strange mirage on the horizon grew bigger still, a huge mass of light now, but JK couldn't make out if it was just one thing, a car, a truck, a building.

He forced himself awake and sat up to get a better view of the oncoming spectacle. A few different colours among the huge mass of light emerged. As they continued to forge ahead, JK slowly comprehended that it was neon light he could see.

It was everywhere – among buildings, signs and streets – and, as they continued along the highway, it transformed into what he came to realise was 'the strip'. The entrance to a place where dreams were realised or shattered on an hourly basis.

After the driver announced that their next stop in a little under ten minutes would be their final destination, Jo-Jo turned back to see JK smiling at him. They were finally arriving in Las Vegas.

By 2am, JK, Ronnie and Jo-Jo had arrived in a cab at a hostel in Fremont Street. JK knew it to be where his brother was staying but he hadn't told him when he would be arriving. Given the time, JK decided against enquiring what room Bobby was in.

They finished checking in, completely drained, but the excitement of arrival was carrying them all through. They picked up their bags, and Ronnie, who had a separate girls-only dorm, disappeared off to bed.

As the boys walked off to their dorm, JK spotted a hand-written sign on one of the walls opposite the reception desk:

MINIR AND POP'S GRAND CANYON TOURS

Our local and experienced guides show you things the book doesn't tell you about! Action-packed 12-hour round trip includes:

* Hoover Dam visit
* Lunch in authentic Arizona locals' bar
* Exploration of Grand Canyon National Park: Desert wildlife such as Snakes, Tarantulas, Cattle, Deer, Wolves, Coyotes, Mountain Lions, Joshua and Cactus Trees
* Sunset views

* Leaves every Tuesday and Friday
* MaxiMum 8 persons
* $30 p.p. (includes lunch and at least 4 beers each!)
* Book at reception

Must wear strong footwear for walk on uneven / rocky terrain – no sandals

It sounded pretty intriguing to JK, only because they had been discussing a similar trip earlier during the cab ride from the bus station. Jo-Jo had seen JK reading the sign, and took a look also.

'What do you think, Jo-Jo?' JK said.

'Yeah, sounds good. May as well quickly ask the chief at the desk.'

'OK, and as its Thursday morning now, I reckon we have a day's rest and could try and book for the Friday slot.'

'Uh-huh, go for it,' replied Jo-Jo, as they both turned back round to face reception.

'Er, Hi. We were just wondering about your Grand Canyon tour, there,' JK said, pointing towards the sign.

'Oh yes, what would you like to know?' replied the young Chinese man behind the desk.

'Well, we were thinking of doing a similar trip ourselves at some point. Is it too late to get on Friday's slot?'

'No, not at all. There are four places left at the moment. I can pencil you in while you decide,' the receptionist replied.

'OK, that's great, but if we wanted to know a bit more info about it then who should we speak to. I mean, is it well recommended?' asked JK.

'Absolutely, we've had no complaints yet. All our guests have always been very happy with it. The two guys that run it both work here; actually, I think I've seen one of them still around tonight. He normally hangs around quite late. He'd be a good person to ask.' Looking over his shoulder the receptionist paused to see if he could look down the short corridor behind him.

'Yeah, OK, that sounds good. What's his name?' JK asked.

'That's Minir – but let me just see if I can find him. And I have a good idea where to start first – I shouldn't be long,' the receptionist said with a smile.

As he walked away from the desk, Jo-Jo poked JK in the arm to point to another sign, further away on one of the corridor walls, in stark red handwriting.

<u>CAUTION TO GUESTS:</u> WE HAVE A HOSTEL THIEF. SEVERAL PAIRS OF SHOES & OTHER PERSONAL ITEMS HAVE RECENTLY GONE MISSING. WE ADVISE ALL TO LEAVE VALUABLES IN THE HOSTEL SAFE. ANYTHING ELSE THAT IS LEFT UNATTENDED IS DONE SO AT YOUR OWN RISK.

JK raised his eye-brows with concern, and just as he was about to speak, a double doorway opened from the opposite side of reception. Above the doorway was a sign that read 'Hostel Bar'. The receptionist and, following just after, a man of medium height and lean build with a light blue polo shirt and shorts walked out towards them. He had short black curly hair, and a dark complexion.

'Here they are for you, Minir,' the receptionist said.

'Oh, hey guys, welcome to Las Vegas!' Minir replied smiling, 'So, you wanted to know a bit more about our Grand Canyon tour? We'll get to that, but how you doing?

You just got in, eh? From where?' Minir directed a wide-eyed glance to them, flashing white teeth in a wild grin. JK couldn't quite determine his accent, but guessed some sort of Arab, maybe Turkish or Moroccan.

'Good thanks, a bit tired, I guess. We've just got off a Greyhound bus from San Fran and Yosemite National Park,' JK replied.

'Yosemite, eh? See any scary bears?' Laughing, he held up his hands, scrunching his fingers to imitate claws while making a muted growling sound.

'Sadly not!' JK laughed, giving Jo-Jo a puzzled sideways look. What was more concerning to him was that both of Minir's eyes appeared to be severely bloodshot and unable to focus.

'So, how about the Grand Canyon then, partner?' Jo-Jo continued.

'Ah, yes, yes. Well, let's go into my office and we can have a little chat while you guys have a little drink and relax.'

'OK, right, well, can we just get rid of our bags first?' replied JK.

Looking down, Minir noticed all their stuff still at their feet.

'Oh sure, sure, no problem guys, you go ahead. Come find me round here in a few minutes or whenever you're ready. No rush. I'll still be around.'

They quickly dumped their bags in their dorm, and JK had a quick scan around for his brother, but couldn't see him. They were in agreement that this Minir character was a bit of a joker but decided to go and hear what he had to say anyway. JK waited near the reception area for Jo-Jo who was in the toilet. He saw Minir leaning over the desk, chatting to the receptionist and overheard the tail end of their conversation.

'Look, all I'm saying is that maybe you need to slow down, Minir' said the receptionist. 'Some people have complained and said it was dangerous, so you've got to think about it, at least.'

'Yeah, but why does he have to be so rude? He's speaking bullshit, man,' Minir replied.

'He's the boss. Think about it, if you get caught drinking enough times, they'll take your licence away and you won't be able to run the trips anymore.'

'Hey, but come on, man, that won't happen, will it? That's bullshit.'

'But if it did, how will that look on us? Think about it from his point of view. And how would you be able to afford to stay here anymore?'

'Oh, this is crazy; it's making a big drama…' Minir trailed off as he saw Jo-Jo and JK approach. The receptionist awkwardly turned round, back to his computer screen.

'Oh, hey guys. You ready now? You wanna come have a drink?'

'Hell, yeah, that'd be swell,' said Jo-Jo.

'Yeah, thanks,' JK replied.

'OK, great, great. Let's go, come into my office! This way, guys.'

Minir turned round and walked up the corridor, pushing open a door towards the end. The boys followed him through into a large low-lit room. There were no windows and a long red sofa faced a huge projector screen opposite.

There were ashtrays spread across a small coffee table in front of the sofa and a few empty glass tumblers. It was a sparse room but it was clean and fairly tidy.

Behind the sofa along one wall was a cabinet with glasses and several bottles of spirits spread across the top. Next to it was a fridge. There was another open door, which JK could see went through to a bedroom and bathroom.

'So, guys, sit down, have a drink. What would you like? I've got beers, whisky, vodka – whatever you want,' said Minir.

'I'll have a beer then, thanks,' JK said.

'Yeah, ditto, partner,' Jo-Jo added.

'OK, no problem, coming up. Sit down, sit down, relax.'

JK and Jo-Jo sat at either end of the sofa. Minir walked round to the cabinet, opened the fridge and pulled out two bottles of Budweiser, flicking off the tops. He poured himself a brown spirit, over ice, and then fiddled about with a black box behind the sofa. Suddenly, a light flickered on in the centre of the screen in front of them as Minir walked round to hand out the drinks.

'Hey guys I don't even know your names?' Minir said. He sat on a tall wooden chair next to Jo-Jo on the left of the sofa, sipping his drink.

'Oh yes, sorry. I'm Jonny Keane. But most people call me JK.'

'Joseph Johnson Knox, that's my full handle, but there ain't no airs and graces with me – y'all can just go ahead and call me Jo-Jo, I don't mind,' he said, laughing, and then looked back at JK. 'Hell, it's the same intro every time! You'll get to learn that about me pretty quick.'

'Great, great. Pleased to meet you guys, so cheers!' He raised his glass and they followed suit. 'So, where are you both from?' Minir continued his questioning as he bent over and fumbled on the floor for something.

'Champaign, Illinois, yes-sir,' said Jo-Jo with relish.

'Near Chicago, the windy city? A small world, huh?' Minir said, laughing. Jo-Jo nodded back with a raised eyebrow and a confused smile, unsure as to how to interpret their host.

'And just near London, England,' JK responded.

'London, God save the Queen, eh?' Minir laughed and continued to sip his drink.

Seeing that whatever he was looking for wasn't on the floor, he put his drink down, got up and walked back around to the cabinet. 'Now where is that fucking thing? It must be up here. So, you guys are on a big trip eh? Going round the world?' He said standing behind them.

'Well, I am, but we just met now on the Greyhound bus,' JK said.

'Hey, that's great guys. Are you having lots of fun? Doing what you wanna do? Ah, here it is!' After grasping a long black remote control, Minir walked back round to his chair.

'Hell, yes,' Jo-Jo replied.

'Good, you guys enjoy yourselves while you're still young – not an old man like me, eh?' he said, laughing as he sat down. Pointing the remote at the projector box behind them, he flicked a switch as the huge screen came on to show a naked woman.

'So, do you guys like dirty movies? You like to party? A bit of "rinky-dink"?'

Minir laughed out loud as hard-core pornography began to play out in front of them. Jo-Jo and JK looked at each other dumbfounded as they both began to shift uncomfortably, taking turns to gulp down a big swig from their beers. Minir provided running commentary on the graphic action happening on screen, laughing and occasionally cheering and shouting. He wasn't really looking for his guests' reactions as he spoke and JK got the impression he had been drinking for quite a while that evening already.

'So, er, Minir, what about your Grand Canyon tour, then?' JK asked, awkwardly.

'What? Oh yeah, that… No problem, we go to see the Hoover Dam first, then have some lunch and some drinks, go up to the Canyon to see the views – it's very beautiful. We try and catch the sunset, have some more drinks, have some fun. Sound OK with you guys?'

'Yeah, sounds great. Do we see anything else?' JK continued, but could now see that his questions were a futile exercise.

'Ooooh, look at that, that girl is bad!' Minir screeched, suddenly realising JK's question was hanging in the air. 'What? Oh, no problem, man. We can sort it out tomorrow. There's plenty of time. Don't worry! We'll have some fun, guys, I promise. Lots of fun!'

JK smiled wryly at their predicament as the explicit scene neared its climax.

'Ha, that is unbelievable. That woman is not nice, you would not take her home to your mothers, no?' Minir shook his head and smiled in their direction.

'Eurgh, that is disgusting,' JK exclaimed, wrinkling his face at the sight before him. Following Jo-Jo's lead, he took another big swig from his bottle, and as the movie ended, they both sat quietly, completely, ill-at-ease.

Minir attempted some small talk about his background, telling them he used to be in the Air Force and now he lived at the hostel in exchange for doing the odd bit of work for the owners.

They limply tried to keep the conversation going but after a few minutes of this, Jo-Jo looked at JK, raised his eyebrows and flicked his head towards the door. JK nodded back to him as they both took a final large sip of beer each.

'Hey, Minir, we're pretty tired after that long coach trip. I think we're gonna hit the sack,' said Jo-Jo, taking the opportunity to instigate an exit before Minir could put on another show for them.

'Yeah, we'll have a chat tomorrow,' JK added.

'Hey, are you sure guys? I have lots more beer.'

'No, no, it's alright, thanks. We really need our beds now,' JK reinforced.

'OK, guys, no problem. Come and see me tomorrow or whenever you want, OK? I'm going to take a piss now. Anyway, I'll see you at the bar – goodnight, my friends!'

Minir walked to the other door as they returned his 'goodnight'. And as he left, they felt like they had been released from some sordid miniature universe.

'Well, that certainly was an eye-opener,' Jo-Jo whispered, looking back to Jo-Jo.

'I know, I feel dirty. Remind me not to get *any* sort of advice from him again,' JK replied.

'So, let's get the hell out of here, man.'

Shortly after, in their dorm room, they lay in their beds. They fell asleep almost instantly, soon forgetting their vivid introduction to the hostel.

Much later that morning, JK had found his brother at the hostel's self-serve breakfast. Along with Jo-Jo, they started walking from the south end of the strip, north along the South Las Vegas Boulevard. A late lunch at the Mandalay Bay hotel interspersed with various visits to casinos and bars en route.

Now, the sky had begun to darken and a gentle breeze pushed around and in between the three young men as they stood in a line, tired and in disbelief. They were watching the free Pirate show outside the Treasure Island Casino.

Everything they had heard about this town had so far been true. They watched, transfixed, as the performance unfolded, overflowing with showmanship and extravagance, symptomatic of all the things they had seen that day.

At least thirty dancers and acrobats, with highly elaborate and colourful costumes, were diving around in the water with a background of mock-ships, caves and sandy beaches. Fireworks, huge sound systems and other complex stage props drew in massive crowds from any nearby streets.

'Seriously, Bobby. Where the hell is Rick?' JK wearily asked his brother.

'I don't fucking know, do I?' Bobby replied angrily.

'We've been looking for him all afternoon. He can't have any money left by now. Honestly, I don't know why you invited him in the first place,' JK snapped back.

'Fuck off JK. You know he's one of my best friends. I've known him for years and you've known him a pretty long time yourself.'

'Yeah, exactly, and he's got worse and worse recently. Spends all his money on drugs and he can't hold down a decent job. It's no wonder Di hates him so much. If it weren't for her, you'd probably be in the same state as him.'

'Fucking hell, JK. How many times have we helped you out overseas? I've fucking lost count. Just try and remember that, bro.'

'Hey there, dudes, it's OK, don't stress it. We've seen quite a few sights today and had a mighty fine late lunch to boot,' Jo-Jo said, shifting awkwardly.

'That's very polite of you, Jo-Jo, but, Bobby, aren't you worried? You know what Rick can get like. He's been out all night – I assume he's carrying something? JK asked.

'Well, of course he is. But he's not stupid. Well, not when he's sober, anyway. Like you say, it's been all night,' Bobby replied, suddenly realising he needed to try and think of a solution. 'Come on, the show's ending, let's try along here. We haven't been here yet. It's heading back to downtown, nearer our hostel, anyway.'

After around twenty minutes, they found 'Slots a fun', fittingly, just before the 'Elvis Presley Way' turn off. It was a lot smaller and low key than the previous casinos they had seen.

'He's got to be in here; this is more up his street, I reckon,' said Bobby, expectantly. JK nodded and they continued towards the entrance.

On walking through the automatic double glass doors, they entered a glowing and carpeted casino lobby. Ahead, they saw a commotion and approached with caution. Two security guards were grappling with a man, while another few spectators looked on, concerned. Then they realised they recognised the young bald man, who was now being frogmarched back towards the front doors.

'Leave me be, will you? I haven't done anything wrong,' the man pleaded to the guards.

'That's Rick!' JK shouted at Bobby.

'I know,' he replied, transfixed.

'Come on then,' JK said, as he walked towards Rick. Bobby, and then Jo-Jo, followed out through the doors. They saw one of the big security guards standing over a shell-shocked Rick lying crumpled on the floor.

'JK, Bobby, thank fuck! Help me out here,' Rick suddenly shouted on seeing them. Bobby approached one of the security guards as the other one turned to walk away back through the doors.

'You know this person?' the guard said to Bobby.

'Yes, he's my friend,' he replied.

'Well, your friend is very lucky we haven't called the police. He should quit while he's ahead and just keep moving.'

'What's the problem?'

'The problem is that he was being drunk, loud and abusive to our guests. He can't afford to pay for his drinks and he was in possession of some contraband, which we have confiscated. The Las Vegas Police Department would not have been so forgiving, let me assure you,' the guard said, sternly.

'Oh, OK, I'm very sorry. He's not had any sleep, you see. I'll look after him,' replied Bobby, sheepishly.

'Yes, you should do that, friend. I would suggest he goes home to sober up and get some rest, right now. He's not welcome back in here,' the guard said, as he glared one last time down at Rick, before he turned round sharply and walked back into the lobby.

'Fucking hell! What is it with you?' Bobby shouted at Rick.

'What, man? I've just been assaulted!' Rick replied, desperately trying to keep a straight face, but with the glint in his eye giving him away. He turned and saw JK and Jo-Jo staring down at him.

JK tried to return his smile but his patience was wearing thin. He looked at Rick's gaunt frame, and his vacant, wide-eyed stare. He now had even more tattoos than JK could remember, with new ones up both arms and on the other side of his neck. JK began to feel pity for him.

'Hello, trouble. How you doing, Rick? Are you OK?' JK said, looking down.

'Aye, just the fucking Americans trying to get off on a power trip. Nothing I couldn't handle. How are you, anyway?' Rick replied, as he took Bobby's outstretched hand and stood up. After shaking JK's hand too, he looked at Jo-Jo. 'Who's this then?' he said, somewhat abruptly, as he bent over to brush his jeans down with his hands.

'Jo-Jo. He's an American too,' replied JK, smiling.

'Hey there. No fear: no power trip here, man,' Jo-Jo said, and as he smiled, did a mock salute to Rick and offered a hand.

'Glad to hear it. Pleased to meet you,' he replied, taking his hand.

'So, do you guys ever meet up in a normal setting?' Jo-Jo asked, laughing.

'Not Rick, that's for sure,' Bobby replied. 'You do know you were this close to getting arrested, right Rick?'

'You're lucky. You know how intolerant the police are out here,' JK interrupted, shaking his head in frustration.

'I didn't start it. He couldn't understand what I was saying and it just escalated, that's all. Once he pushed me, I wasn't going to stand for that,' Rick replied.

'You must be wasted,' Bobby said.

'Aye, totally. Are you going back now? I could do with a shower.'

'Yep, let's go. So, tell me, how much did you burn?'

'Enough, let me tell you.'

'Come on, Rick.'

'Fucking hell, I dunno, a grand maybe?'

'$1000?'

'Aye, I guess.'

'That is impressive, dude. What were you playing? Win anything back on the way?' said Jo-Jo.

'Aye, the odd one, here and there. Blackjack tables, Wheel of Fortune, Video Poker machines – everything inside these places is basically the same, you know?'

'Well, luckily for you they look different on the outside or we might never have found you. What was your favourite casino?' JK asked.

'No fucking idea. I can't remember; they've all merged into one. I didn't spend it all on gambling, though, if you catch my drift,' Rick said, with his customary crazed glint in his eyes. As Bobby let out a chuckle and JK rolled his eyes, they walked back to the road side to hail a cab.

Arriving back at their hostel, they walked past the busy bar and heard a diverse assortment of travellers' accents: Irish, German, Aussie, Kiwi and Scandinavian.

'Who wants a drink?' Bobby said, enthusiastically.

'Aye, I'm in, but let me go shower first,' Rick said.

'Don't you want to sleep?' JK said, surprised.

'I'll be alright, don't you worry. I'll try and grab a quick fifteen minutes of shut eye and then, maybe I'll take some special medicine. You want some, big man?' Rick asked Bobby with some glee, knowing what reaction he might provoke. Bobby shot a nervous glance at his brother.

'Maybe later,' he replied, as JK returned a look of disgust but remained silent.

'And I just need to quickly get changed, so I'll see you in a few minutes,' Jo-Jo said, breaking the awkwardness between them as he walked off with Rick towards their dorm room.

'OK, I think I'm ready to talk to some normal people now,' said JK, grumpily. He followed his brother into the bar as they ordered a round of beers.

Ronnie, JK's travel companion from San Francisco, approached them.

'Hey, JK, how are you?' she said, smiling, as she held a bottle of beer.

'Oh hi, Ronnie, yeah, very good, thanks. How about you? Have you been enjoying Vegas?'

'Oh, you know, it's fun but it seems a bit, well… fake, don't you think?'

'Yeah, I know what you mean,' JK replied, and seeing that Bobby was looking at him expectantly, he continued, 'Ronnie, this is my brother, Bobby.'

'Aha, you finally found him, then? Hi, Bobby, I've heard a lot about you.'

'Hi. All good, I hope?' Bobby said, smiling cheekily back at her.

'Some, but not all,' she said with a laugh. 'So, how about you, Bobby. Have you been to the casinos yet?'

'Yeah, most of them, but they all seem mostly the same–' his reply was interrupted by the return of Jo-Jo, who greeted Ronnie with a great big hug, as she shrieked in delight.

'Hi Mr Jo-Jo Knox! I bet you must just love Vegas! Have you been here, like, one hundred times before?' she asked with mischievous glee.

'Hell, no! This place is crazy, and always has been. I only came here once as a kid, with my parents. But I think I feel the same about it now as I did back then,' he replied.

'How do you mean, like a kid?' Bobby asked.

'Well, you know how you feel sick after gobbling a whole packet of candy in like, one minute? Well, just suppose all the innumerable but questionable pleasures of Vegas is the candy,' he said, dramatically gesturing with his hands and continued, 'It's like some sort of super-sweet brand of hedonism. And once it starts to wear off, then it's a real crash and burn, you know? How would you Brits say it, a downer?' Bobby and JK nodded, as they all laughed.

'Well, it doesn't have to wear off just yet. We can stay a bit longer, surely?' Bobby said.

'Are you guys doing the Grand Canyon trip tomorrow?' Ronnie asked them.

'Yes, are you?' JK replied.

'Yeah, Minir will make it interesting,' she replied, trying to keep a straight face.

'Oh yes, I bet he will. We met him on our first night,' Jo-Jo replied.

'He's harmless fun. Speak of the devil,' Bobby said, as both Minir and Rick appeared in the bar entrance. Minir greeted everyone with a handshake.

'Hey, Minir, are we all still booked on your tour tomorrow? What time does it leave?' asked JK.

'Yeah, no problem, guys – you're all in. We say to be ready at 11am but there is no rush. It never leaves that early. Hey, just excuse me a moment, I need a drink,' he replied, and then headed straight for the bar.

'Standard,' Bobby said, under his breath, laughing.

'Assuming his usual position for the next ten hours, no doubt,' Jo-Jo added, who then walked off with Ronnie to a table where one of her friends had beckoned them over.

'That was pretty quick, Rick. Couldn't sleep?' JK asked.

'Aye. Buzzing now. Eager to get back on it,' Rick replied, his maniacal eyes even wider than normal and his giant black pupils seemingly eating up any sight that was in front of him.

'You're a nightmare,' said Bobby, shaking his head.

'So, tell me. Your yank pal, what's his name again?' Rick asked, looking straight at Bobby.

'Jo-Jo,' JK replied, but Rick didn't even glance at him.

'I think you should watch him. I saw him checking out our stuff earlier when I had my shower.'

'What?' replied Bobby in disbelief.

'I don't know if he took anything but I'm pretty sure he was thinking about it.'

'What, you think he's a thief?' said JK.

'Aye, there's been some thefts here, after all.'

'Yeah, I saw the signs. But they were here before we arrived, actually,' JK snapped back.

'Well, whatever. I'm just saying I don't trust him, that's all,' Rick continued to look at Bobby, as JK shook his head.

As the drinking continued, the group at the hostel bar grew larger. They decided to venture out, en masse, along downtown Las Vegas, gradually veering further and further away from the hostel. Eventually, by 3am, well past the hour of rational decision making, Bobby, Rick, Jo-Jo and JK had separated themselves from the rest of the hostel travellers and came to the end of a street as they contemplated their next move.

They heard from a distance what they assumed was another bar or club on the corner. Passing by the large windows, they stopped to look in on the small enclosure at the front. It was hard to discern what type of bar it was but they were encouraged to see about forty people, a large majority being girls, crammed inside. The dancing, shouting, laughing, drinking – the sweat and heat was causing condensation to run down the windows – all giving it an appearance of a miniature night club.

Eagerly looking for the entrance, they were eventually disappointed to see a sign saying 'Private Party' above the door. They had one last stare through the windows of hope, ready to admit defeat and turn around to finally go back to their hostel. Just then, a group of five or six attractive girls of similar ages caught them looking and started to laugh and wave at them.

Realising they were equally drunk, they decided to have a bit of fun and wave back. This mutual mimed flirting performance carried on for a few moments when suddenly the girls turned to talk to each other. They were debating something, and when they turned back to face the boys, they began to beckon them in, luring them into the mysteries of implied treasures. Laughing out loud, the boys did not hesitate to take the bait, and walked round to a side door where two of the girls opened it for them.

A few hours later, several 'Death Wish' shots (Tabasco, cinnamon snaps and 76%-proof white rum) flowed through their bodies. It all seemed like such a fantastic idea at the time – and still did – when they crawled into their beds at 7am.

The next morning, all four of them had slept through an alarm after someone, unbelievably, had had the presence of mind to set one the previous night. So, instead, even later, they did eventually awake, to a loud and persistent knocking on their door.

'Hey, come on guys, the tour is going,' a voice called out.

'What the fuck is that?' Bobby said, as he squinted towards the thin shafts of light coming from under the door.

'Guys, sleepy heads, we'll go without you!' The accent was familiar.

'Shit, it's Minir! What time is it?' said Jo-Jo, sitting up in bed.

'Oh fuck, it's eleven already,' JK replied, looking at his watch.

Jo-Jo darted out of bed to open the door as JK shakily stood up. The door opened for them to see Minir standing there, who, for a change, wasn't laughing. Their sleep-deprived and intoxicated perception did not register at the time that Minir was wearing what appeared to be a medical outfit: a plain white, shortened tunic-shirt with loose turquoise slacks.

'Come on, guys, we gotta get moving. Everyone's downstairs waiting.'

'OK, Minir, sorry about that. We'll see you down there in a sec,' replied Jo-Jo as he closed the door with a strained look on his face.

' "No rush to get up for the trip. It never leaves that early" – what a load of bollocks!' Bobby said, under his covers.

'What an asshole! Anyway, come on, let's go. No shower time, neither,' Jo-Jo replied.

Suddenly, Bobby jumped up and kicked the still sleeping Rick below his ribs. A loud groan emerged from him.

JK rubbed his eyes and pulled on a pair of trousers as Jo-Jo went into the bathroom. By the time JK had pulled out his wallet and camera, Jo-Jo had already emerged. Within three minutes, they had left their dorm and walked down to the car park, where a white 4x4 minivan sat with the engine ticking over and Minir stood, ready to open the back doors.

JK and Jo-Jo acknowledged Ronnie and as they did, Bobby and Rick pushed in front of them to take their seats. Bobby had a cap on pulled down low to shield his eyes and Rick had sunglasses on, but JK suspected he was already asleep as his head hung limply to one side.

The remaining people on board eyed all of the four late arrivals, who could barely grunt an acknowledgement, suspiciously. It was far from spacious, and as the last to enter, JK was grateful to have the back row to himself, avoiding the direct stares of the other people on the trip.

Minir climbed in up front to drive. Next to him, in the passenger seat, was a very bony old man with long wispy and greasy grey hair, poking out from underneath a red baseball cap that said 'POPS' above the peak. His skin was blotchy and taut against his cheeks, and he gazed over at the late arrivals with a friendly smile.

JK quickly realised that those glazed wide eyes and rigid grin were the same semi-permanent characteristics that his younger compatriot, Minir, also had.

Minir's first action was to pull four cans of beer from a cooler box sitting next to 'Pops' up front and pass them down. JK looked around the passengers and saw they already had one, including Pops, who subsequently raised his can, laughing. JK wondered if Minir had one hidden too. Jo-Jo and Bobby, in the seat in front of JK, both did a bad job of hiding looks of disgust as they accepted theirs. Rick hadn't even moved.

'OK, everyone in? Everyone ready? Everyone got a beer? Then let's go!' Minir didn't wait for any answers. He looked in his rear-view mirror and immediately zoomed off in reverse out of the car park. Out onto the open road, he began his tour introduction.

'Well everybody, welcome to Minir and Pops' Grand Canyon tour extravaganza! I shall hand you over to my co-pilot on my right. Some of you may know him as the hostel cook, but he is also a veteran of Vietnam, an Air Force legend and a god damn hero of the United States of America, *Mr* Pops!'

'Well, thank you for your kind words, Minir – our pilot for the day and also a veteran of the United States Air Force. Please can I ask you not to distract your driver today with any questions that he won't know the answers to anyway!'

Pops delivered the speech in a rasping hoarse voice, turning round to his audience every now and then like a true professional.

'Unless it's to buy him a beer, of course,' Minir interrupted, laughing.

'Of course, or to buy me one – all bribes, I mean tips, gratefully accepted! Your emergency exits are situated there, there and here,' Pops continued, pointing at the side windows and front windscreen.

'That concludes our emergency evacuation procedure, so I'll hand you back to your pilot now. Minir, I think that should cover just about all our insurance demands!'

'Oh yeah, in the event of an accident to either your pilot or co-pilot, buy them more beer and everything will be OK again,' Minir added.

The two of them continued this over the next thirty minutes or so, each time doing their best to out-do each other, laughing as one. It certainly made for a relaxed atmosphere within the group when everyone introduced themselves. They were left in no doubt as to what the spirit of this tour would be.

By the time of the first stop at the Hoover Dam, Sam (English), Susannah and Camilla (both Danish) were openly chatting. It was an unremarkable stop, as the tour guides did little to explain the surroundings to the party, besides 'it's a big dam, with lots of water', as they took photos. Bobby lost his hat over the edge of the dam due to the wind.

They continued to drive into the desert, stopping to look at some soft gold mixed into the surface soil. Not long after, they made another stop, which Pops described as a 'hearty lunch in the middle of fokin' nowhere' at a bar populated by rednecks and retired alcoholics. There was little surprise in the group on seeing that their tour guides were good friends with quite a few of the residents.

Their 'hearty' lunch consisted of a stale French onion dip sandwich, washed down with a few jugs of beer. Some people were already on their third cans of the day since the tour started.

JK, Bobby and Jo-Jo had recovered from last night and were chatting openly to the others. Rick was still half asleep as Bobby attempted to engage him.

'Come on you big wimp. I thought you Scots could take a hangover,' he said.

'Fuck you, big man. Just tell me when we get to the Canyon,' Rick replied, grumpily.

'Hey, look,' JK said, pointing at the table where Minir and Pops were chatting with the locals. 'I knew it. Minir is still drinking. He didn't have any lunch either. Pops might have managed a bite of a sandwich, I think.'

'No great surprise, bro. I saw a can of beer in his coffee cup holder when we got out of the van earlier,' Bobby replied.

'I doubt he drinks much coffee. It might confuse his body, which is used to a strict intake of alcohol only,' Jo-Jo said, laughing.

As country music played over the radio, the resident, trembling, staggering old drunks were trying, unsuccessfully, to get a dance with the three girls on the tour. They were the only girls under thirty present in the building and, possibly, the whole town.

'Hey, Rick, it's your tune, mate. I'm sure one of these old drunks would love to see your famous dance moves,' said Bobby, prodding Rick as he spoke.

'Seriously, fuck off,' he replied.

'Come on, you'll blow their minds. Especially with those fancy new shoes, Rick.'

Suddenly, Rick sprang into life, as his eyes opened wide. He looked down at his feet to the clean and immaculate green-brown hiking boots with a high ankle support.

'Eh, what about these shoes?' Rick was alert now.

'I've not seen them before. Nice though, special walking ones, are they?'

'Aye, I bought them just for this trip. Didn't wanna show off, like,' he replied, awkwardly.

'Oh right, you never mentioned it,' Bobby said, surprised.

'Eh? I don't have to tell you all my fucking business, do I? Anyway, why do you care so much about my fucking shoes?' Rick had suddenly gone red in the face.

'Alright, calm down, Rick,' Bobby replied.

'Yeah, go easy, Rick. I think we're all just a bit bored. We've been at this desert hillbilly bar for over an hour. Am I the only one who's wondering why we're here?' JK said with dismay.

'To see the desperation and dregs of American humanity, of course,' Jo-Jo said, shaking his head.

Within twenty minutes, every one of the tour guests had now started to grumble and so Minir and Pops packed them all up to go on their way.

Following along the Colorado River that entered the Grand Canyon, 277 miles long, their ride became increasingly bumpy. Although their minivan was a 4x4, no one apart from the tour guides were sure if speeds of 95kph were an entirely wise idea. But they all tried to put these details to the back of their minds, knowing that a stunning view was approaching.

Minir had a plan for their arrival at the viewpoint. He began to build up their excitement levels, saying they were getting closer and closer, only metres left to go. Then, just as they were getting worried how close to the edge of the Canyon they were, and the fact that he had not reduced his speed much, he drove off the edge anyway.

But, of course it was all one big joke to Minir. He knew the area and that there was a false ledge, where the decline from it was a smooth one, leading down to the real ledge below, where he did finally stop, naturally this time.

'Great – at least he's not pissed out of his head as well,' JK muttered, under his breath.

They soon forgot his hilarious gag once they registered the view before them, and quickly got out of the van to absorb it completely. Layers upon layers of textured red rock rose up high from a wide base that narrowed towards the blue sky. Deep oranges shone brilliantly in the sunlight, and contrasted with the dark reds, browns and purples in the shadows. In between two such colourful rock faces, a deep valley snaked in and out across the landscape, one of many across the horizon. A natural collision, across the vertical and horizontal, had been carved through the millennia, as if an unspoken drama of history hung in the air around them.

But soon, as the sun began to set, danger bells started to ring in their heads again. Pops had taken on the unlikely role of a rock climbing guide. JK considered their situation, as they climbed along a steep ledge, a one-mile drop below them.

He was sure that when Pops had been in the Air Force he had been fit and healthy, in both body and mind. Now, their tour leader had a sixty-year-old alcoholic mind inside what looked like the body of an eighty-year-old skeleton. All the while, even with a severe case of the shakes, he balanced a slim cigar in one hand, and his can of beer in the other.

JK admired his tenacity as he attempted the climb in no more than a plain green t-shirt, jeans that hung off him and trainers that looked like paper-thin gym shoes. It seemed comically strange that, just moments before beginning the walk, he had reminded everyone to make sure they wore strong footwear.

Despite the lunacy of this sightseeing tour, the beauty of the fading light brought a momentary calm to the group. They stopped in silent awe of the desert.

'OK, folks, let's just have a walk to the viewpoint before the sun goes down,' croaked Pops, breaking the quiet. One of the girls, Camilla, had refused to walk and remained behind, standing by the car with Minir. The rest of the group slowly eased their way along the edge. Behind Pops, leading from the front, were Sam and Susannah, followed by Rick, Bobby and Ronnie.

'What the fuck are we doing, man?' said Jo-Jo, standing at the back of the line, with JK just in front of him, completing the set.

'I have no idea,' JK replied. 'Instead of bats, mountain lions, goats, rattlesnakes, coyotes and racoons as promised, we got rednecks, alcoholic geriatrics and Vietnam veterans.'

'Wait, dude, we did see *one* deer,' Jo-Jo replied, sarcastically.

'Hey, at least we got to do *this*,' said Bobby, in front of them both, as he turned back to face them, waving one arm across the view ahead.

And suddenly they heard a loud shout from in front, followed by a short scream from Susannah.

Pops and Susannah were crouched over the edge, looking down. Ronnie, Bobby, JK and Jo-Jo rushed closer to see a wider ledge, two metres below them. On this, Sam was standing over Rick, who was curled up in a ball of pain, grasping his right ankle. There was a long, deep graze on his forearm and blood began to ooze from the wound.

'Rick, are you OK?' Bobby shouted down.

Rick could only grimace, shaking his head as his eyes remained firmly closed.

'Rick?' Bobby shouted again, desperately.

'My ankle… I think it's broken,' he replied, limply.

Bobby climbed down to him, and with the help of Sam, and then JK and Jo-Jo, lifted Rick back up to the higher level, and back along the ridge to their van. Pops tried to help, prodding Rick's ankle in the most painful way possible. He at least found a plaster for Rick's arm wound, cleaning it first with some sort of alcohol he had in a hip flask.

Minir grabbed an old t-shirt from the boot, soaked it in the cold water from the now empty cool box, and wrapped it round Rick's swollen ankle. They helped him into the back seat, propping up his foot, as everyone else squeezed in around him.

They cut the tour short, driving home to their hostel in the dark.

Minir, his face pale and sweaty, was now driving more erratically than at any point before, swerving all over the empty roads. Before long, flashing sirens approached from behind and the police pulled them over.

Minir got out of the minivan and everyone watched as he casually sat on the bonnet of the police car, chatting to the officer. Pops then got out to join the conversation.

'Look at this, will you,' Jo-Jo said. 'A male Arab nurse, and a pensioner in a baseball cap. Smiling and gesturing with a cop in the dark on the freeway. I wonder what they're saying.'

'The cop looks pretty suspicious,' JK replied.

'Do you blame him? I just hope Minir has a better excuse for his driving than "it's the wind" this time.'

'Are you feeling any better, Rick? Bobby asked, having just turned round to see Rick, sitting on the back seat, rolling his eyes and sighing at Jo-Jo's continued commentary in front of him.

'Aye, a bit. Ankle still hurts like fuck, but not sure it is broken after all,' he replied.

'That's great,' said Jo-Jo.

'Aye. No thanks to you.'

'What's that?' Jo-Jo replied, taken aback.

'My new shoes. I only fell off that ledge because I wasn't used to wearing them.'

Jo-Jo turned to JK and Bobby in confusion.

'Er, yeah, but how is that my fault, man?'

'I only bought them because you fucking stole my old pair.'

'Oh, fuck you, man, I did not. You gave them to me.'

'Fucking cheeky bastard. And he's even wearing them now, look,' said Rick, pointing down at Jo-Jo's feet.

'They are Rick's shoes,' Bobby said.

'Wait a minute. Yesterday, you were gonna get rid of them, and, seeing as I don't like to waste an opportunity, I asked you if I could borrow them for this trip. And you said yes, man.'

'Oh, that's fucking convenient. I did no such thing.'

'How on earth can you remember anything that you did yesterday, Rick? You were off your face, as per usual,' said JK, angrily.

'Alright JK, there's no fucking need for that,' said Bobby.

'Aye, don't stand up for him. He's the hostel thief, I know it,' Rick shouted back, as the rest of the group in the minivan looked on awkwardly.

'Fuck you, man,' Jo-Jo said, shaking his head.

'Don't speak to him like that,' said Bobby, sitting next to JK, as he reached over his brother to push Jo-Jo, only managing to make scuffed contact with his shoulder.

'OK, but why would I wear his shoes now, in front of him, if I'd stolen them? That's fucking lame and you know it,' Jo-Jo said, as JK sat up in between them.

'Yeah, and that fucking thief was around before Jo-Jo and I even arrived at that shitty hostel. In fact, I've got a much better idea of who the real thief might be!' JK shouted, as he turned round to glare at Rick.

'You're lucky I can't move my ankle, otherwise I would fucking jump over the seats and slap the both of you,' Rick replied, behind them.

'Yeah, shut up, JK, you lunatic. He's hardly going to make this up,' said Bobby.

'Why not? He probably needs the money, seeing as he's blown it all on gambling, pills and coke. Some friend, Bobby,' JK said, watching his brother shake his head and close his eyes. 'I don't even know why he's here in the first place. Di hates him. So, come on, Bobby, why exactly did you bring him anyway?'

'I said, fucking-shut-up.' Bobby grabbed his brother's shirt as they both stared at each other, red faced.

Outside, Minir had just stood up, getting off the bonnet of the police car. He and Pops shook hands with the police officer and were now walking back to the minivan, unaccompanied, with relieved but tired looks on their faces.

Bobby quickly released his brother as they entered, and a tense silence welcomed them. Despite Minir's assurances that he knew the officer, no further explanations were required as no one asked any questions. They all sat, contemplating their fate, and then continued their journey in silence, desperately waiting for it to end.

JK allowed his mind to wander once more, and he started to question his future plans. They couldn't be any worse than what lay in store for Minir and Pops. How many more trips before the police arrested them, the hostel sacked them or they drank themselves to death? It was only a matter of time until karma caught up with them, or with any of us, he thought.

He turned to look at Bobby, now nodding off to sleep, and then stared out at the road in the pitch-black night again. JK knew his brother would be loyal to Rick, and he had to consider what that now meant for his dream ambition – his long-awaited world tour.

Chapter Seven

North Shore Nirvana

'But aren't you ever worried about the plane crashing?' JK asked Steve, who stood confidently over the pool table with a cue in his hand. He stared back at JK intently for a moment and then smiled.

Steve, a young commercial airline pilot, was impossibly cool. He was still dressed in his uniform but had removed his jacket, while the top button on his shirt was undone and his black tie hung loosely round his neck. With slicked-back black hair, he was close to JK's height of six foot but had more of a thick-set appearance.

From the opposite corner, Jo-Jo sat watching them, sipping a beer. The bar, with a night-time view overlooking the beach front in Waikiki, Honolulu, was the unlikely setting of a spontaneous drinking session with an all-British aeroplane flight crew.

'Shit, JK, I wish you'd saved that question to put him off his shot, not your own. Now get on with it,' Jo-Jo said, as he laughed and shook his head.

'Hey, it's OK. I get asked that all the time. I happen to know a lot about it,' he said, with a mixed English and American accent. With two stunning air hostesses in tow, also in uniform, the cock-sure pilot was completely at ease with the inherent risks associated with his profession.

'One in every 1.2 million flights,' he continued, 'Those are the odds of crashing.'

JK let the numbers sink into his head and nodded back at him before looking down at the table again. He didn't normally care about games of pool, but suddenly queasiness started to develop in his stomach as the pressure on his next shot grew.

'Oh, and the odds of dying in a plane crash are one in 11 million flights,' Steve added, 'So, in answer to your question, no, not really. I never worry about it.'

JK found his directness unsettling, and paused again. He leaned over the table and stretched out his left hand over the blue baize, resting a wooden cue in between his thumb and index finger. If he sank the number eight ball he had lined up in his sights, it would be three games all. He pulled back his right arm, ready to push the cue tip through the white ball, but hesitated one last time.

He repeated the odds he had just heard in his head and then stood up. *The odds of a plane crash are one in every 1.2 million flights. And the odds of dying in a plane crash were one in 11 million.*

While JK knew they were exceptionally long odds, something about his current surroundings had compounded a familiar unsettling feeling. It was one that he never seemed to fully get rid of, and one which returned to him every few months.

He thought about his father's travels, as well as his brother's and his own. But more importantly, JK realised, he could not doubt the accuracy of these odds given the source. It made sense that Steve would know these things for his profession.

Perhaps it was excitement at the progress of his travel ambitions, entangled with his complex family history. Not only would JK soon overtake his father's unwitting travel legacy, but his recent break from his brother's company had left some tiny lingering doubts at the back of his mind about the validity of his decision.

But those odds have nothing to do with my next shot, he reminded himself.

'Are you OK, JK?' Jo-Jo asked him.

'What? Oh, yes, fine. Absolutely fine. Sorry, I got distracted,' he replied.

'Are you sure it's not the pressure?' said Steve, with a smug smile.

Finally, after JK caught the eye of one of the girls staring impatiently at him, he bent back down to the table and lined up the shot. As he pushed his arm through, he felt a perfect contact with the cue ball. He had nailed the angle spot on, with the white hitting the black crisply, sending it rolling towards the top-right corner and dropping into the pocket. Feeling relaxed again, he lifted himself off the table and smiled towards his opponents.

'Good shot, Jonny. Looks like the next one will have to be the decider, then, as it's getting late,' said Steve.

'Oh come on Steve. Live a little!' said Faye, a tall and curvaceous blonde with a healthy golden tan.

'I'd thought you'd be more tired, considering we've just come off the long shift across the Atlantic,' he replied.

'You should know Faye better than that by now,' said her friend, Karen, as they both laughed, standing next to each other.

'Like I told you earlier, we just want to unwind a bit before we get home,' added Faye.

'Yeah, but losing pool to these two backpackers doesn't count as unwinding in my book,' Steve replied, with a faked look of disgust. 'I knew we should've changed uniforms at LAX like I said. We were off duty by then anyway.'

'We didn't have long to make that connecting flight and, besides, if we had got changed, I don't reckon these two would have been brave enough to challenge us to a few games of pool,' said Karen.

Karen was shorter and skinnier than Faye but her tan was more pronounced. Her dark features and piercingly sharp stare led JK to suspect she had some Asian family heritage, but he couldn't be sure. Both girls seemed to have the stereotypical good looks and heavy make-up associated with air stewardesses.

However, they had been friendly enough when Jo-Jo decided to introduce himself with a pool challenge, along with JK, only a couple of hours ago. The five of them had been leisurely chatting and drinking ever since.

Jo-Jo and JK had flown in from LA, flying into Honolulu on the main island of Oahu. It was to be their last stop in the US before moving on through the Pacific Islands. They had already spent just over a week on the island in a hostel in Waikiki beach, outside of Honolulu.

'Well done, my man. So, what do you fancy doing after this?' Jo-Jo asked JK.

'Whatever, mate. Let's explore outside and see if that nightclub they recommended looks busy, as it's a Monday night after all. Or maybe we'll find somewhere else. What time is that bus to the North Shore in the morning again?'

'8am, I think. It's an hour or so on the road, I'm afraid.'

'Nice. Well, we can sleep it off on the bus, then,' JK said and smiled.

'Oh, sorry, but I couldn't help overhear. You're going to the North Shore tomorrow?' asked Faye. Steve and Karen were both looking over too.

'Yeah, that's right,' replied Jo-Jo.

'Wow, that's cool. So are we. Steve's dad has a place on the coast and we're all going to stay there for a few days.'

Strangely, Steve avoided eye contact with them as both Karen and Faye looked on at him expectantly.

'Oh, that's great. Where are you staying tonight, then?' asked Jo-Jo, to break the silence.

'Just a hotel nearby,' replied Faye, awkwardly, having spotted Steve disappear to the restrooms.

'May as well rack the balls up, Jo-Jo,' said Karen, as she came and stood right next to him, thrusting the side of her hip against his.

'Yes, ma'am,' he replied, and drew away from the table to put a coin in and retrieve the balls. As they continued to flirt, JK glanced over to Faye who was eyeing him curiously.

'So, Faye, have you been to the North Shore before?' he asked her, with slight trepidation.

'No, but Steve raves on about how much better it is than Honolulu. I've been there though,' she replied. 'What about you?'

'The North Shore? No, never.'

'And Honolulu, I assume this is your first time here? What do you think?'

'Well, we've been here a week already, but it's got a great vibe, hasn't it?'

'Yeah, it's always hot, and that ocean colour. Such a cool, deep blue.'

'I didn't particularly know much about Hawaii, apart from what it says in the guide books. I think I had quite unreal expectations anyway, you know? All those glamourous scenes from the movies, *Magnum, P.I.*, documentaries and so on. They must've implanted seeds in me as an impressionable youngster.'

Faye nodded and laughed. 'You're right. I think they completely mythologise the island and its sun-glazed carefree lifestyle. So, has the reality lived up to it?'

'I'm not sure. It was great to start with; everyone seems to be upbeat, with a positive outlook on life. But, the last few days, apart from the weather and how near we are to the beach, it hasn't seemed that different to mainland America: the huge sky scrapers, shopping malls, strip clubs, Irish bars, casinos. In fact, there's probably more variety of fast food here than in the big US cities.'

'Well, don't worry, JK. Luckily, the North Shore is nothing like that. It's not commercial at all; it's basically deserted. But I totally agree with you. There are tourists everywhere – Japanese especially.'

Overhearing, Karen laughed as Jo-Jo was shaking his head.

'This is the United States in five simple words: fast food, insincerity, cars, tips, irony,' said Karen, with a glint in her eye as she looked straight at Jo-Jo.

'Hey man, that's my country you're talking about! But hell, you're probably right,' he replied. At which point, Steve finally returned from the toilets.

'Ready for the decider then?' asked Faye.

'Yeah, fancy a wager on it? The losers have to buy a round of shots for everyone, how about that?' Steve replied, boldly.

'Game on, man,' Jo-Jo replied.

As they began the final frame, JK wondered if it was just as curious for this flight crew to talk to two backpackers as it was for Jo-Jo and himself to talk to them. They'd told them their route, where they'd seen so far, and what they liked and didn't like. They seemed genuinely interested, and even shared a few tips for various future destinations. But JK still felt like they were the poorer class traveller cousins.

JK was also interested in the interplay within the group. Jo-Jo and Karen were obviously hitting it off, but he couldn't tell if Faye was interested in Steve or not. JK could tell that Steve was – as he himself was too, even though he suspected he had no real chance.

He was fascinated to watch Steve's approach, as he made obvious attempts to impress Faye. Steve was clearly aware he was a good-looking guy, and endeavoured to give out an aura of control. When Faye was a spectator, he maintained a dialogue with her just by eye contact, deliberate smiles and decisive, firm movements during his periods of play at the pool table.

But JK decided that it was Faye who was in control of all of her admirers. She kept her flirtation to a minimum with Steve without being cold or dismissive, just leaving the door slightly ajar for him to continue. She would also spontaneously involve JK in an exchange that he hadn't been part of if she felt that he was being ignored. Likewise, when JK had instigated a discussion, she made sure she was the first to join in, much to Steve's chagrin.

All the time, JK knew she was manipulating both himself and Steve in whatever fashion she chose, and he was revelling in it. He'd heard about good-looking women that could do this, or seen it in some trashy Hollywood movies, but it was the first time he had seen this behaviour first hand and he was very wary of her as a result.

Jo-Jo had somehow just fluked two balls in one shot, meaning he and JK only had one ball plus the black left, to the four balls that Steve, Karen and Faye had. He mucked up his last shot to leave an opening for Karen, who duly potted two in a row but could not convert the difficult shot that followed.

JK crouched down to pot their last ball, leaving an extremely difficult final black. He looked over to Faye, who was smiling over the rim of her glass at him. Noticing her uniform again, he remembered what Steve had told him earlier.

The odds of a plane crash are one in every 1.2 million flights. Yet, his father had had one and survived. And he'd said I was lucky too, JK remembered.

JK shook his head and focused back on the black. He pushed his shot wide as the ball ended up rattling in the jaws of a pocket then rolled back to the middle of the table. He stood up, disappointed. It was Steve's turn next, who smiled as he bent down at the table.

'No pressure, Steve. The flight crew are about to beat the backpackers in the inaugural Waikiki cup,' said Jo-Jo, desperately.

Steve gleefully potted another two balls and left the final black. He stood up to take a sip of beer then calmly walked back to the table. He refused to look at anyone before lining up the final ball in his sights. His right arm snapped into the shot with controlled power as the black surged up the table and disappeared satisfyingly into the far-left pocket.

He stood up to be greeted with a pat on the back from Karen and a gentle hug from Faye. Handshakes were exchanged all round as everyone put their cues back in the racks around the table.

'Sorry to remind you, but we'll take those shots now please, gentlemen!' said Steve, smugly.

And as Jo-Jo continued to flirt with Karen, JK walked to the bar, inwardly fuming at his miss as a deep resentment towards Steve built up inside him.

As Faye had promised, the North Shore of Oahu was a deserted and peaceful spot, safely away from the commerce and hustle and bustle of Honolulu's capital city. After their hectic trip round mainland USA, JK and Jo-Jo were grateful for the peaceful setting to chill out for a few days; just the beach and quiet.

It had been a late night with the flight crew, which made their early bus journey painful, but on seeing their accommodation, their tiredness was instantly forgotten. It was spacious and yet tranquil in an idyllic setting, more so than any hostel they had ever seen before. Situated metres from the beach, the perimeter to the grounds was surrounded by palm trees. One small central white building was the reception, restaurant and bar. The one and only supermarket in the area for miles around was just a ten-minute walk away.

Rows of wooden huts were lined up in front of the reception building, flanking either side of it. Making their way to their cabin, they found small decks surrounding the entrance to each hut. Each hut had two 'bedrooms' with three single beds in each room as well as a shared toilet and bathroom. The standard of these dorms was very simple, and given the sweltering hot sun and the surroundings, this was rather an appealing change for them.

There were barely any other guests in the hostel and it appeared they had the run of the place to themselves. They unpacked their bags, headed to the restaurant and ordered an early lunch with some cold beers as they stared out at the ocean.

'Man, this sure is the life,' Jo-Jo said, wearing his ridiculously large sunglasses again.

'Yep. Peace and quiet. Bliss,' JK replied, and took a sip of beer.

'But, you know, I just can't help but think,' Jo-Jo began to speak, but tailed off.

'Think what?' JK said, eventually.

'Oh, come on, man. You must be thinking the same.'

JK stared silently at Jo-Jo, seeking clarification. Eventually, Jo-Jo began to smile at him.

'Yeah, now I *know* you're thinking the same as me.'

'What, that it's a little too quiet? That we might get bored?' JK said.

'Exactly, look around you. There's no one here.'

'True. Well, you got Karen's phone number. Maybe they'll want to meet up with us. You could call Steve's house now? They did offer.'

'I thought you'd never ask, compadre. Hang tight, I'll be right back.'

And with that, Jo-Jo walked briskly off to reception to use their payphone, having noted it when they checked in. He called a number that was scrawled in lipstick on a napkin by Karen, which still had an odour of sweat and alcohol. He had collected it from a neon-infused night-club at 1am that morning, during a lustful, public display. He remembered the repeated joining, and separating, of their lips, tongues, hands and various clothed extremities.

Once the plans were made and the conversation ended, Jo-Jo walked back with an even brisker step to relay them onto JK. They sat and finished their drinks, then left to hire body-boards and snorkel masks. They took a quick taxi to the supermarket to buy some beers before beginning a long walk along the beach, away from their hostel.

They encountered a simple view of paradise in silence: clear white sands and deep blue water, rows and rows of palm trees, with no sound apart from the soothing lapping of the ocean's tide onto the beach. With the sun baking on their backs, there was no litter, no cars and barely a soul in sight.

Eventually, they stopped at 'Sunset Beach', the scene of more dramatic beach views and their meeting point with the others. The surface of the sand here was more varied in height with undulating hills and troughs. It was an occasional home of the surfing world championships, but it was almost deserted for their visit. As JK and Jo-Jo sat waiting, they watched two surfers put on hugely impressive displays, breathlessly riding the massive waves before violently crashing down in front of them.

Shortly, they could see the girls approaching. Faye wore a short red dress with a thin belt, her blonde hair hanging loosely on her tanned shoulders. Karen wore a yellow vest-top with brown shorts.

'No Steve, then?' JK asked Jo-Jo.

'Yeah, Karen mentioned he might not come, but she was a bit vague. I know his father's house isn't far that way,' Jo-Jo replied, pointing in the opposite direction the girls had walked from.

'Oh, hello, fancy bumping into you here!' Karen shouted, as the girls got closer.

'Well, I didn't think the views round here could get any better, but y'all just changed that now, didn't you?' Jo-Jo shouted back, with a broad grin on his face.

Jo-Jo was first to warmly embrace Karen, and the others greeted each other with a distinctly less vigorous exchange of hugs.

'Did you catch any of the surfers?' JK said.

'Yeah, a bit. Pretty cool. What a great life those guys have,' Faye replied.

'Yeah, swimming, chilling out, drinking...' he agreed, trailing off.

'Picking up chicks, lying in the sun, getting a tan,' Jo-Jo added.

'No wonder they're *sooo* fit looking, really lean and strong,' Karen said, licking her lips.

'You gals don't mince your words, do you?' Jo-Jo said.

'You just wait till we get a drink inside us,' Karen replied, sharply.

'Speaking of which, I assume that's what's in your bags?' said Faye, pointing at the rucksacks both JK and Jo-Jo carried.

'Hell, yes!' Jo-Jo yelped, excitedly, grabbing his bag and unzipping it in one smooth motion. He tossed over a couple of beers for the girls and they all sat in the sand, facing the sea.

Both Faye and Karen were confident girls. Karen had a skinny and, at times, slightly ungainly body, but her jovial demeanour combined with sparkling eyes gave her an unusual appeal.

Faye's long blonde hair partially hid her face and an occasional melancholy look. She was direct when she spoke to people, and her confidence was sometimes confused as abruptness, but soon became friendly once the ice was broken, especially with a drink in her hand.

'I have to say, you girls were hilarious last night,' JK offered.

'Ah yes, all those cheesy eighties and nineties songs. My highlight was that beautiful rendition of "Angels". Thanks for that girls,' Jo-Jo said, smiling. 'What else was there? "I Should Be So Lucky" and George Michael's irrefutable classic "'Cause I gotta have faith"!'

'They were singing everything you told them to by the end! And dancing!' JK added.

Faye and Karen looked at each other embarrassedly, oozing groans of regret, while still managing to smile.

Then Jo-Jo stood up to perform a rendition of one of the songs at the girls' expense, dancing with an intense mock-enthusiasm.

'Oh my god,' Faye put her hands to her head, suddenly remembering as she bit her lip in a regretful smile. Laughing, Karen threw her arm out to punch Jo-Jo.

'OK, you're boring us now,' she shouted, as Jo-Jo sat down looking very smug with himself.

'So, where's Steve today, then?' JK asked the girls.

He noticed that they exchanged an awkward glance before pausing. Karen eventually stumbled a reply.

'Oh, him, yeah, we found out he's a bit of a control freak.'

'That's a bit harsh, Karen,' replied Faye.

'Is it? You agreed with me earlier.'

'Well, he just wanted to tidy the house up before his dad got home.'

'Right. Has he been away for long, then?' JK asked.

'Not sure. But he was coming back any minute now, and Steve didn't want loads of people round the house unannounced for when he got home. So, it seemed fair enough for him to ask us to pop out and give him some space,' Faye replied, looking away from the boys uncomfortably.

'Yeah, but come on, he still could've come with us. He seemed like he just wanted us out of the way as he couldn't bear us touching his stuff. All a bit weird. He always comes across as a bit arrogant, to me, anyway,' said Karen.

'Hey, well, you know I like to give people the benefit of the doubt and all, but I've got to agree with you there. I'm not sure he ever wanted us two to come and visit you at his place either,' said Jo-Jo after gulping his drink.

'Well, let's not be too mean as we still work with the guy, OK? And he's got all our stuff now,' Faye said, with a resigned shrug, 'and may even turn up later.'

'I doubt it,' Karen said.

'Well, if not, it's more beer for us then,' JK said, raising his can to the group. Faye smiled as they all took a sip at the same time. And they continued to talk and drink, interspersed with swimming, snorkelling and a few attempts at bodyboarding.

After a few hours, the desire to explore returned and they resumed walking along the beach. Far away from JK and Jo-Jo's huts, they had mostly found long stretches of isolation. Now they were amazed by the natural hive of activity that suddenly confronted them: the shore had become a wide expanse of polished bed rock terrain mixed in with white sand.

Little rock pools formed at their feet as the foaming sea spread casually over the uneven surface. Large brown rocks with rounded edges sat undisturbed while errant smaller grey and black pebbles nestled on top of small pits filled with white shingle.

Creatures, both living and dead, littered the shiny wet carpet surrounding them – a thriving universe in a coastal microcosm. Sea shells, cones, spirals, red and brown stripes, star fish, a sea purse, cuttlefish shells, crabs. Gulls flapping their wings, squawking for scraps, flitting to and from the ground. Sea weed, dark and green, dragged along by the tide, the larger pieces getting caught up among the bigger boulders and the smaller wispy strips inescapably ending up back at the ocean's edge.

Faye and JK followed behind Karen, who walked alongside Jo-Jo with his bare, dark-skinned back in the sun. He wore a faded navy cap and had seized a long stick from the trees on the shore's edge about 500 metres back, poking it into the sand as he moved along. Further on up the rocks, he stopped to look down at something in one of the pools. As the others caught up, they bent down to see a load of tiny hermit crabs, all of different colours.

'Ah, look, aren't they cute?' Karen said.

'I think they're horrible. They remind me of spiders,' Faye replied.

'Say, why don't we pick four. We could have a race!' Jo-Jo said, excitedly.

'Yeah, good idea, mate. Let's take them to that big rock over there,' said JK, pointing towards a large grey stone that had an ideal long, flat surface.

'I am not picking up one of those things!' Faye shrieked.

'Sorry, mi' lady! I'll carry yours, then,' Jo-Jo offered, sarcastically. 'Right, everyone choose one and name it. I'm having that one and I'm calling it "Ernie",' he said, pointing to a little, blue-shelled crab. The others looked at him blankly. 'Ernie Banks? Number one all-time Chicago Cubs Hall of Famer?'

'What's that, a sport?' said Karen, as the blank looks continued in Jo-Jo's direction.

'Jeez, you Brits kill me. Yes, it's a sport. *The* sport – baseball,' he replied, sighing.

'Oh, how boring!' said Faye. 'OK then, I'm having that one and he's called "George". See his white stripes on his brown back? I think they look like highlights. "I gotta have faith", after all!' Faye pointed to hers and Jo-Jo picked it up, along with his, and walked to the flat rock a few metres away.

'Come on, Karen – I would've thought you'd be great at picking up crabs!' Jo-Jo quipped, as he walked away.

'Ha fucking ha! Which one do you want, JK? Do you mind if I have this little yellow one? It kind of matches my top,' Karen asked.

'No, you go for it,' said JK, as Karen picked hers out and went to stand next to the others at the rock.

JK was left with one black and dark green coloured crab of about medium size. He paused to think of a name.

'I guess I'll have him, then. I'll call him… Leo.'

'Your star sign?' asked Faye.

'Yeah, and my dad's,' he replied.

'OK, OK, let's get to the race! Get over here, JK. We can't hold these bad boys forever, you know,' said Jo-Jo, ushering him over.

They stood holding their crabs over the rock at one end. The rock was about two metres long and Jo-Jo stood in between the others.

'Right, when I say go, we put them on the rock at this end. Whichever one gets to the end first, wins. Or, if they start running off the sides, whichever is the only one left standing on the rock at the end is the winner.'

'Wait, Karen's doesn't have a name yet,' said Faye.

'How about "Karen", it's got her top on, after all?' said Jo-Jo.

'Oi, you. No, I don't want that thing named after me,' she replied.

'"Crab"? Or how about just "Hermit",' said JK.

'OK, OK. "Hermit" is fine. Just get on with it, he's gonna pinch me in a minute!' Karen cried out.

'Alright… Go!'

Everyone except Faye leaned forward to place their crabs delicately on the rock. They stayed in this position to watch the crabs scurry across the surface sideways. This didn't last too long for the yellow one, as it quickly reversed direction and walked back ten centimetres through the starting point and off the edge of the rock.

'Well, that was a waste of time! You're useless, Hermit!' Karen complained, laughing as she watched the others continue. Jo-Jo's crab was already in front, about halfway up the rock, but JK's was approaching fast.

'Come on, Leo! Go on, my son, go!'

'No way, Ernie's pedigree will see him through. He's got it sewn up. Come on, boy!'

Suddenly, JK's crab climbed in front of Faye's brown and white one and started to attack it.

'Hey, that's not fair! He's bigger than my crab. Disqualify him!' Faye shouted.

'Come on now, Leo, plenty of time for that later, keep going,' JK said in front of her.

'Cheat! Leave my George alone, Leo,' she replied, shouting. 'It's raping my crab! Your crab is a pervert, JK!' she squealed.

Finally, "Leo" ceased his assault and carried on moving but was still twenty centimetres behind "Ernie" who rapidly approached the end of the rock.

'Yes, he's doing it, he's gonna do it… YES! He's done it! Ernie wins!' Jo-Jo leapt up and pumped both fists inches from JK's face.

'Pathetic,' JK said, shaking his head.

'Looks like Ernie's class remains! What a win!' Jo-Jo added.

'Whatever, Jo-Jo! I clearly had a word with my crab before-hand to let you win. I told him to make it look like a contest, but he got distracted,' JK said, smiling at Faye.

'I want him reported,' Faye said, pointing at JK.

'Yeah, that Leo crab, he's just a big bully,' added Karen.

'Yeah, yeah, losers! I promise not to mention this too much for the rest of the day,' he replied. 'Now, let's all celebrate my win, shall we?' He pulled out more drinks from his rucksack and shared them round. The post-race analysis continued as they started walking back along the coastline towards Sunset Beach.

When the sun finally started to lower in the sky, they stopped, deciding to sit in wait until they were rewarded with the view that the beach's name promised. As more drinks and snacks appeared, their sun-and-alcohol-drenched exploits further relaxed the group of travellers who spread themselves out along a ridge in the sand banks.

Their conversations had become more personal, finding out about each other's lives back home: first pets, families, education, music, movies and aspirations. The orange sun fell closer to the horizon as the sea became a calm, silky-black background.

Karen laid flat, her head on Jo-Jo's stomach. He lay at right angles to her, with his arms behind his head, eyes closed. Separated by a few metres, JK lay side by side with Faye, and as he inhaled a deep, comfortable breath, he tasted salty air and felt the cool sea breeze caress his cheeks.

It gave him further opportunity to think, prompting an urge to share with Faye.

'Faye, I'm curious about your job. Do you get to enjoy any of your travel?'

'Yeah, definitely. I mean, it's different to you backpackers. We don't stay that long anywhere but we still get to see some great places, and I guess we're on a much higher budget. But I'd love to be in your position. Aren't you enjoying yourself, JK?'

'Yes, of course. Why, don't I look like I am?'

Faye smiled back and then looked away before replying.

'You do, but you're quite... reflective at times, and I wonder what's going on in your head.'

'Yeah, I get that a lot... It's... depression. I feel OK at the moment, but it's something I've struggled with over the years.' It was JK's turn to avoid eye contact this time.

'Hey, you don't need to feel embarrassed. I've got an uncle who suffers with it,' and as Faye said this, she laid her hand on his.

'Thanks. But I sometimes question why I'm doing all this travel. My father did a lot too, you see, and sometimes I wonder if I'm just doing it as a tribute to him, or whether I genuinely enjoy it or not.'

'What do you mean, as a tribute to him?'

'He died. When I was quite young.'

'I'm sorry, JK.'

'It's OK. But, honestly, I've been feeling really good the last few weeks, as if I'm really enjoying it for what it is now, rather than having to try too hard. Like the randomness of it all.'

She looked at him curiously.

'Like the guide book recommendations – sights, restaurants or whatever – some that disappoint and some that are better than what you expect. Or friends that you click with straight away.' He paused, as Faye stared at him silently.

'The strange habits of strange people that remind you of close friends back home. Amazing nights out where you don't have a care in the world and then suddenly feel homesick on your way home.'

JK could only interpret her continued silence as an assessment.

'Sorry, that probably sounded really cheesy, didn't it?' he added quickly, becoming embarrassed.

'No, no. Not at all, JK. Carry on.'

'Remember we talked about the media depictions of Hawaii last night?' he asked her.

'Yes,' she replied, sitting up.

'It's just, these views, all of this. It's so breath-taking, and no picture or TV programme could ever possibly do it justice. And now I feel like I've known the place all my life.'

He looked into her eyes and finally saw recognition.

'You're actually quite deep, aren't you?' she said, smiling.

'Am I? Maybe I just think too much.' He sat up and smiled back at her. As Faye stared at his mouth, he lent in and kissed her tenderly. Their embrace continued for some time until JK pulled away.

'What about Steve?' JK asked.

'What about him?'

'I just thought, you know, that you and he were an item.'

'No,' she replied, bluntly. She withdrew her hands and looked away, over the horizon. 'Look, I guess I should be honest with you. I did have some feelings for him, and we flirted for a while. But he just doesn't seem interested. Like he doesn't want to let go of his emotions or something, I don't know. Maybe he's a control freak like Karen says. Anyway, I can't work him out. He's just a bit fucked up. So, I've given up.'

'Well, it's his loss, then, not yours.'

Faye smiled at him, and then from over her shoulder, beyond the sand ridge they all lay on, he saw a stranger approaching with a dog in tow.

The man was older and was wearing khaki shorts, sandals, a short-sleeved plain grey t-shirt and a dark blue cap. His dog, a very large brown cross-breed with a luxuriously fluffy coat, ran up to them ahead of its owner.

The friendly dog came up to each one of the group, in turn, to investigate and win their attention. They didn't mind at all and began to play with him. His owner eventually caught up and, on seeing Karen was smoking, asked for a light before they casually began chatting.

He took the beer they offered him and sat down. Introductions came and went without JK really noticing – for some reason he couldn't take his eyes off the stranger. His name was Frank, and he had a mop of dark brown hair with flecks of grey popping out from under his cap, his skin was a heavy brown tan with wrinkled, but not loose, skin; JK estimated his age at fifty-five at the most.

With a friendly face, the stranger had strong features that were probably good looking in his younger days, and now hinted of a rich and varied history. A vertical scar ran from the middle of his left cheek down into the light stubble running along his jaw line. But it was his sparkling blue eyes, suggesting vitality and a wealth of experience, that compelled JK to find out more about him.

'I'm from the mainland US originally but I moved here to Oahu when I retired. So, where are all you folks from, then?' Frank said.

As they replied in turn, JK remembered thinking that all of their backgrounds must've seemed so trivial to him, yet he never showed it. He looked you in the eye, never interrupting, every time you spoke. He sat very still all of the time, with short, controlled movements as he lifted his small cigars to his mouth. Always interested, always polite and pleasant, he had such a world-wise aura about him: tranquil, yet knowledgeable.

'Back in the eighties, I spent a lot of time working in the UK,' Frank said. 'That's where I met my wife. I have to say, that was one of my favourite places I've ever seen. She didn't agree, though. She hated the weather, of course.' He smiled wryly as he paused; then just for a moment, he dropped the smile and his face went blank as he stared back out at the ocean, silently.

JK thought he noticed a flicker of sadness in his eyes just before his dog came over to him, sticking his snout under Frank's chin. He snapped out of his private thoughts and ruffled the hair on his dog's head in return.

Frank turned back to the group, smile restored, and twisted off the bottle top to his beer. On hearing it fizz-click, Frank's dog barked. They all laughed, and then Jo-Jo, who was also about to start a new bottle, opened his to test the dog's reaction. Again, the dog barked and stared expectantly at Jo-Jo, his head cocked to one side, as if waiting for a treat to be thrown from the bottle.

Laughing again, Frank saw the group's interest in his mad dog, Al, and decided to show them a trick. He stood up, facing his dog about a metre apart, and looked him in the eye. Al, looking back up at his owner with his mouth opened and tongue out, panted excitedly, waiting for the trick to happen. Then, Frank suddenly kicked up a load of sand in front of him into the air over the dog's head. Al jumped up and back flipped to try and catch some of the sand in his mouth.

The dog would do this in response to his owner's kicks over and over again, in quick succession. His excitement never dropped, each time returning like a coiled spring to a crouched poise, ready for the next go. No one was sure if Al actually ate the sand, but he certainly had an insatiable appetite for the trick. They all laughed at this spectacle and so Frank encouraged them to have a go themselves.

JK and Faye did first of all, constantly amazed by the dog's relentless energy, never getting bored. Al was starting to pant heavily after a while but his happiness showed no signs of stopping, even after ten minutes of performing. There was also something comfortingly familiar about this dog.

Jo-Jo stood up and put his shoes on, figuring he could kick up more sand compared with the bare-footed attempts of the others previously. Yet as soon as he did so, Al suddenly started growling and then barking at Jo-Jo.

'Woah there, boy, hold up!' Jo-Jo said with concern, and held his hands up, looking at Frank in desperation.

'Oh, heck. I'm sorry. I think it's your shoes, my friend. You might have to take them off. Old Al seems to have a bit of a thing about certain shoes,' said Frank.

Jo-Jo took off his shoes and, to the others' surprise, Al the dog instantly calmed down.

'Wow. What is that all about, then?' Karen asked Frank, with amazement.

'Oh, ask my son, and he'll probably tell you it's all just a load of nonsense really. But I think I've got a lucky dog,' he replied.

JK had noted that Jo-Jo's shoes were the ones he had kept from Rick in Las Vegas a few days ago and was watching on in stunned silence.

'What do you mean? Your dog thinks I'm unlucky? Or my shoes are?' Jo-Jo asked with confusion.

'Not entirely sure. Old Al's getting on a bit now, but it started several years ago. After my wife passed, he would bark at her old shoes. I left them lying around the house for a while, you know?' He paused to take in people's sympathetic looks before continuing. 'I had a fall one day, out walking with him, and busted my leg real bad, and I realised that he'd warned me before, barking at my shoes that very morning. And similar things happened after that, a couple more times, so now I know just to trust his barking at shoes. Probably silly, I guess.'

'Shit, man, that's unbelievable,' Jo-Jo said, staring at JK.

Karen and Faye both turned to look at JK also, who by now had gone pale.

'JK, what's up? What happened?' said Faye.

'Well, the dog, he's… he's right,' he replied.

'Really?' said Karen.

'Hell, yes. The guy who owned these shoes before me, he was a friend of JK's. We were with him a few days at the Grand Canyon when he fell over. Almost broke his ankle,' Jo-Jo said.

'There you go. My lucky dog, that's Al. Always listen to him. That's why I can't fly anymore,' Frank said, in a philosophical tone. He had deliberately let his reply hang in the air, knowing he would be asked to, and wanted to, explain his story.

'You can't fly anymore? What, you mean you're banned or something?' Karen asked, intrigued, as the sea breeze suddenly picked up around them.

'Kinda. It's just a vow I made to myself. You see, I've had my fair share of chances already.'

Immediately, JK eyes were wide in alert, but the whole group was sufficiently intrigued not to interrupt.

'Come on, Frank. You can't say something like that and not explain yourself,' said Karen.

'I've survived seven different plane crashes.' He smiled, looking straight back at her.

'What? That's impossible. Didn't you get hurt? Didn't anyone die?' JK said, stunned.

'A bit of a mixture. The first time it happened, in my early twenties, I was running late and missed a business flight. No big deal, I just caught a later one. But then I found out later that the flight I was supposed to catch crashed, killing twenty-three passengers. Lucky, right?' Frank looked down at his cigar burning between his fingers in the fading light.

'Yeah. Then what?' JK replied in excitement.

'A second time, about five years after, another business trip, in Thailand, on a small passenger jet. It had a bad landing and crashed just off the runway. We picked up a few cuts and bruises – nothing too serious, but the whole plane had been lucky to avoid worse damage. Luck again, I guess.'

'When was that?' JK asked.

'Oh wow, now you're stretching me, kid. Er… let me think… maybe 1971, I think. It's funny; I do remember chatting afterwards to a British guy who had been on the flight too. We joked that you could easily disappear after a plane crash if you wanted to. In those days, there were no detailed passenger manifests or anything. And it's even funnier now, given how many times it happened to me, I could've disappeared over and over again. I'd be invisible by now! In fact, you're lucky you can even see me at all!'

JK continued to look disturbed but stayed silent again.

'So, what about the other crashes?' Faye asked.

'Flight number three, that's how I got this scar,' Frank said, pointing to his face, 'but they were all a similar story, small business flights in the seventies when safety standards weren't as high. Minor damages, no deaths. Apart from the last flight, that is.'

Frank's tale of misfortunes added to his infectious charm. He was in complete control of his life, and totally at peace, exuding contentment and security. JK looked across the faces of the girls, who both appeared to be hanging on his every word during another expertly placed dramatic pause; he was an immensely likeable character that they had all warmed to.

'So, what happened?' Karen said, with desperation.

'Well, it was about eight years ago now. It was a holiday with my wife, in Australia. She had mostly managed to avoid flying with me previously, knowing my history.

Eventually, after a few years, she thought I'd broken my jinx and that it was safe to fly with me. Against my advice, I should add. Well, we experienced engine failure in mid-air and had to make an emergency landing, which we just managed to do with all passengers un-harmed.' His dog sat still at Frank's side, watching them, and the only sound they could hear was that of the waves breaching. The clear night sky had now revealed its beautiful stars.

'Then, a few days afterwards, she experienced heart problems. A heart attack, possibly brought on by the stress of the flight. The docs could never be sure, but I knew that's what it was. They couldn't save her. I was there with her at the end, which was some comfort to me.'

'My god, that's horrible. I'm sorry,' Karen said, echoing what they were all thinking.

'Yeah. So that's why I vowed never to fly again. You know, I got to cheat death seven times and I don't wanna push my luck. Seven is a lucky number, right? Now that I'm retired, I guess I've got no need to fly that much anyway. I just go fishing. My son, on the other hand, he loves flying. He's a qualified pilot and he's not had a single crash yet! Talking of which, I should get going, as he only got home today.'

Besides the stars in the night sky, the only light provided was the occasional flickering of cigarettes and a couple of beach fires some distance away. But it was enough for JK to see the faces of the others as the realisation of who Frank was finally began to sink in.

'Wait a minute, is your son Steve? Steve Fleetwood?' Faye asked in astonishment.

'Yes, that's him. I'm Frank Fleetwood. Do you all know him, then?'

'Karen and I are part of the flight crew with him. We've been staying at your house!'

'Oh, wow! You guys, that is crazy! Well, what are you doing out here? Why isn't Steve with you? I got home a few hours ago and he was there saying he was going to wait for friends to come home. That must be you, I guess?'

'He said he didn't want to surprise you,' replied Karen, smiling.

'That boy, he needs to relax and live a little. I've always said that. Anyway, come on, let's have another drink at my place. I'll walk with you. I know the quickest way.'

Jo-Jo stood up and, after some more gentle encouragement from Frank, grabbed Karen by the hand and together they walked off in pursuit of Frank and his dog. JK looked at Faye and offered his hand to her, and she accepted. They followed their friends, quickly disappearing in the darkness.

They arrived at the Fleetwood family home at around 9pm and while the night air was still warm. The house was a building of grandeur, with a spectacular wooden decking veranda at the rear that was their entrance from the beach. They walked together through the first section, beyond a row of trees providing a natural separation to a more secluded garden. They could see lights were on in the house.

'Steve must still be up, then,' said Faye.

'Yeah, let me go grab him. Make yourself comfortable, I'll bring out some more drinks,' said Frank, as he walked away, into the house.

They spread themselves out across the various wooden chairs positioned around a large swimming pool, illuminated in a cool blue light.

JK marvelled at the scene, adding to the confusing allure he felt towards the Fleetwood family. He knew now that the same self-assured personality traits that both Steve and his father shared – comfortable in themselves and in their lives – came from their wealth.

However, the mystery to him was how they dealt with the fluctuations in luck over the years. They could still manage to hold it all together and be successful in their lives. He was envious of their coping mechanisms, thinking it was impossible for anyone to live like that. Everyone he had ever met had some sort of issue, a hang-up, resentment or grief, stress from their job, their family or their finances. He thought he could spot it in people; even if he had only known them a few minutes, he could usually spot something was wrong – maybe not to know exactly what, but to know there was a problem.

Yet this contrast of good and bad fortune was turning over and over in his mind. How could he be so content with his life? It filled him with wonder that this was even possible. He yearned for what Frank had.

But he couldn't help think his own fate was somehow connected to all this. His father had said he would be lucky. He had survived a plane crash too, and now maybe this stranger, Frank, shared this same luck. Maybe there was a reason he was meeting these two people now. He had to find out; he had to be sure.

'Are you sure you're OK, JK? You've been pretty quiet since we left the beach,' Faye said to him.

'What? Oh yes, I'm fine. Just taking in this place. Nice house, hey?' he replied.

'Yeah, man. Beats most of the hostels we've been staying at,' said Jo-Jo.

At this point, Steve, with his father, appeared to greet them all.

'Hey, you. What happened? We had a great time on the beach all afternoon,' said Karen. JK could see Faye was directing a hurt look at Steve, but he tried to avoid eye contact with her.

'Yeah, sorry guys. I did some tidying up, then my dad arrived and we caught up. I think I fell asleep for a bit and then by the time I woke up I thought it was too late to come and find you anyway. I had a feeling he might bump into you though, how funny,' Steve replied. He didn't appear as confident as usual and JK wasn't sure but it looked like Steve had sore eyes, as if he'd been rubbing them.

'Well, we raced hermit crabs, surfed, swam, drank, kissed. It was terrible, really,' Faye said, sarcastically.

'You know, I'm still feeling pretty tired,' said Steve. 'I might hit the sack early. I want to make sure I'm fully rested for the next flight.'

'But that's not for another three days,' replied Karen.

'Yeah, I know, but I never drink two days in a row. I just wanna rest up in between.' Faye frowned and looked across at Karen who returned a wry smile.

'No problem, hotshot. Hopefully we'll catch up tomorrow?' said Jo-Jo, trying, as ever, to lighten a growing tension.

'Yeah, of course, and you guys, you're both welcome to stay over. Isn't that right, Dad?'

'Fine by me. Stay for some breakfast – it's a lovely spot, in the shade down here, in the morning,' Frank replied.

'Cool, it's set then. Night all,' said Steve, and quickly disappeared, without waiting for anyone to return his farewell.

After a few moments, once Steve was well inside the house, Frank handed out some glasses with ice, and started to pour a yellow-coloured punch out of a large jug.

'Your son, is he OK?' said Faye, with concern.

'Yeah. I think he gets a bit upset coming home. Memories of his mother, you know.'

'Oh, of course, sorry,' she replied, softly.

'Hey, what *is* this stuff, Frank?' said Jo-Jo with a look of surprise as he took a sip.

'If you like Pina Coladas, you'll like these. My home-made variation,' he said, with a laugh. 'But really, don't worry about Steve. He'll be fine in the morning. And you guys really are welcome to stay. We have loads of room.'

'Thanks. If that's OK with you, JK? It's probably getting quite late to try and get back to our place anyway now,' said Jo-Jo.

'I would drive you but, you know,' Frank interrupted, shaking his glass.

'Yeah, makes sense. That's great, thanks Frank,' JK said, and then suddenly stood up and said, 'Hey, do you mind if I use your phone?'

'What's up, JK?' Jo-Jo replied.

'Well, we should probably just tell the hostel we won't be back, in case they call the police or something,' he replied, nervously.

'Ha. You worry too much, JK,' said Karen.

'I understand. A very sensible young man. No, not at all. It's just through those patio doors to the right,' Frank said, pointing to the house.

JK went inside and quickly found the phone on a long sideboard table. He grabbed a card from his wallet with their beach house hostel phone number and called to confirm they wouldn't be home that night. He then stood, motionless, his eyes wandering around, as if for inspiration.

Underneath the table he saw several pairs of shoes, in various sizes and states of disrepair. It was easy to recognise which ones belonged to Frank or Steve. But one pair stood out. They were women's shoes, and were partially covered by another larger pair of men's boots. The very old brown leather had started to fade and was covered in tears and tufts. He assumed they had belonged to Frank's wife.

JK picked up the phone again, and started to dial a different number. A number he had memorised, but now he just had to make sure he got the international country calling code correct. It would be about 9.30am UK time.

'Hello?' answered a female voice.

'Hello, Mum. It's JK,' he replied.

'Jonny! Are you OK? Where are you?'

'Everything's fine, Mum. I'm in Hawaii.'

'Hawaii? Wow, lucky you! Are you enjoying yourself? What time is it there?'

'It's about 9.30pm, I think. Yeah, I'm having a great time. You'd love it here.'

'Oh, that's good. I'm glad.'

'Look, Mum, I can't speak for long. I'm at a friend's house on their phone. I just wanted... I just wanted to ask you something.'

'OK, that's fine. Ask away.'

'I need to know something about Dad.'

There was a pause on the other line.

'Hello? Mum? About his travels. I just need to know where he went in 1971, when he had the plane crash?'

'1971? I can't remember that far back.'

'Oh, come on, Mum. I think it was a business trip. One of his last, maybe, before he set up the garage.'

'What about that list he wrote? You have it, don't you? It's probably on there. Don't you carry it around with you still?'

'Well, I used to. I have it but just not on me at the moment.'

'OK, as long as you haven't lost it. I know it means a lot to you.'

'No. It's in my bag which is back at our hostel.'

'Well, why do you need to know now? Can't it wait?'

'Sorry, Mum, I wanted to… I just needed to… check something. Can you remember?'

'OK, OK. Let me think. Hang on a minute.' Another pause. 'I think it was Asia somewhere. He went all over there in his last few years on that job before he got made redundant.'

'Thailand?'

'Yes, yes, that's it. I remember now. Why, what were you checking?'

'Oh, nothing important. We were talking about plane crashes and I just needed to know. You know how I get sometimes, Mum,' he said, trying to be jovial.

'OK, well. Just you take care of yourself, Jonny,' she replied with concern.

'Don't worry, Mum, I'm fine. Now, I really have to go, sorry.'

'OK, write to me soon, Son. I love you.'

'I love you too, Mum. Bye.'

'Bye, Jonny.'

He replaced the phone and let out a heavy sigh. Turning round to go back outside, he saw Faye standing at the patio doors, watching him. She didn't say a word, but offered him her hand. She led him upstairs to the spare room she was staying in and, after closing the door, kissed him on the lips.

They silently undressed in the darkness. The room overlooked the swimming pool, and with the curtains half drawn, streaks of light occasionally cast their bare skin in a blue hue, contrasted against the blonde hair on their heads.

They took it in turns to explore each other's bodies. In one continuous movement, he gently drew his fingers along her long legs, around her taught stomach to her back, and from the base of her spine upwards. She caressed his face before stroking his head through his uneven tufts of hair.

They embraced, and kissed again. The intensity quickly escalated into passionate intercourse. Eventually, as Faye sat astride JK, she leant forward and then grasped the pillows either side of his head, in the throes of climax.

JK was still awake at 1am that morning. He was full of a nervous excitement as Faye slept peacefully next to him. The day's events had given him an immense feeling of optimism for the future, that he would be lucky after all, just as his father had told him.

He certainly felt lucky right now. He had met the Fleetwoods, as if it was meant to be. He had met Faye, and had experienced a wonderful place, the most beautiful beach he had ever seen. Now, at least, he had something tangible in his mind, something that was absent before – his own personal nirvana to visualise. He now knew how it felt and could always return to that feeling.

He got up slowly, walked to the mirror and smiled to himself. He hadn't felt this happy in some time. Yet, his mind kept returning to the contentment that he had seen in the stranger, Frank, that he was so envious of. How could he hang on to that feeling?

He thought, the future would never be this good; it would never rival this. He shook his head, suddenly realising how ridiculous he was being. Enjoy the moment while you are in it, he reminded himself. He couldn't understand why he had suddenly stirred up such negative feelings in his head at a time when he should be grateful for such good fortune. He frowned, wishing he could empty his head.

He walked over to the window, noticing that the pool lights were now off. Then, he saw a slight movement in one corner of the veranda. There, Steve was sitting opposite Frank. On hearing a muffled sound, he quickly ducked back behind the curtain.

Peeking out, JK could see that Frank was passed out on a chair. Next to him lay Al the dog, also fast asleep, along with an empty whisky bottle. And then, upon seeing Steve's cheeks were wet, glistening in the night, JK realised what he had heard. It was the sound of Steve sobbing as he sat watching his father. Frank had fallen asleep and was holding his late wife's shoes closely to his chest.

133

Chapter Eight

When Opportunity Knocks

JK shivered as he stood outside in a temperature of 3°C, questioning the clothing advice the tour company had given him. How could shorts be appropriate in the middle of winter on New Zealand's South Island?

And why, exactly, were sunglasses essential? He had broken his last pair several weeks before but, nevertheless, he knew he only had five minutes or less to find a new pair before his coach would leave. The engine was running and his fellow travellers were already queuing to get on. He looked along the main road, strangely deserted at 8.30am, to a service station on the corner opposite, and sprinted across towards it.

Although he didn't really expect to be able to get a decent pair from a petrol station, at least the flimsy, metal bug-eyed shades he ended up with cost less than $15 NZ. He ran back and climbed aboard creating a good-natured fuss among the group of people he had kept waiting.

As they drove away, JK wondered what the store manager had thought of the spectacle. Perhaps he was used to the sight of the twenty or so loud young backpackers from England, Ireland, Canada, Denmark, the USA and more countries that this bus network brought through his town every three or four days, all year round.

After three weeks in New Zealand, JK and Jo-Jo had already seen so much. The tour had been a handy way of getting round the country and an even better way of meeting people. They could stay on the bus as long as they wanted, following the natural route round and, if they found somewhere they liked, they could get off and stay a few days longer. Their bus driver was also important, as he often acted as a guide – although not today as it was a special trip – and as a rep to book hostels and activities for them all.

It was all very professionally run and JK certainly didn't care if it wasn't what some travel snobs – like his brother, Bobby – might call the 'real authentic experience', i.e. researching and booking it all independently. They had managed to get a fantastic group of people to stay together, all having fun and getting to know each other, and the country, at the same time.

'Oh shit!' JK said to Jo-Jo, next to him.

'What, man?'

'I've just realised I forgot my pack for the hike.'

'How, dude? We've only just been given it?'

'I must've left it on the chair at the hostel.'

'You douche. Well, luckily, we haven't gone far,' Jo-Jo replied and stood up to face the front. 'Elvis! Yo, Elvis! Stop the bus!' he shouted out to the driver, who quickly agreed to turn the bus around.

In return, they both received more good-natured abuse from their travel companions surrounding them, and just smiled back at it all. Five minutes later, they had returned to where they started, past the service station, and JK ran outside to pick his stuff up. He was slowed down by the heaviness of the equipment, containing a rain coat, ice axe and boots. The soles of the boots were lined with steel-grip crampons.

As they got moving again, excitement simmered around the bus. It was a short journey to the Franz Josef Glacier, and anticipation was high as incessant chatter surrounded JK and Jo-Jo.

'My throat is sore as hell,' said Jo-Jo.

'Are you really that surprised? You must have copped off with half the bus by now,' JK replied. He sighed in frustration at Jo-Jo.

'Yeah, I know. I just wish I knew who gave me the lurgy. Too many possible suspects on this bus.'

Jo-Jo was now sporting a goatee beard and wearing a bright red beanie hat. He turned round to chat to two girls who were newer to the group, Steph and Fiona, clearly eager to lay some ground work for later. JK preferred to play it cool for now, and maybe make more of an effort as the day progressed.

As the coach journey came to an end, they were briefed by the lead guide while still on board. He stressed the dangers, the importance of concentration and the need to stick with their guides. They were then split into three groups of ten or so with a guide each. But JK could see Jo-Jo was hardly paying attention anymore. He wondered what had prompted Jo-Jo's change in attitude since they had arrived in this country.

As they stepped down off the bus onto some rough stone-ridden ground, they saw a gigantic white tongue of ice before them. The scene would make a tourist's dream postcard: layers of flat brown rock in the approach terrain, turning to the larger grey and black rocks, before the start of a brilliant blue-white solid chunk of ice with textures that were impossible to make out from this distance.

The ice stretched on and on, in between mountains and up to a clear blue sky. JK's breath created steam on the fresh cold air, causing a slight pressure on his cheeks as he marvelled at the view.

Their hiking groups would take different routes, but Jo-Jo and JK stayed together, along with the new girls. The rest of their group had all met anyway. They sorted their equipment out before setting off, securing their boots, shades, woolly hats and a small back pack containing little energy snacks and a water flask. Finally, they found out why they needed rain coats when there wasn't a cloud in sight; they were going to get very wet from crawling on the ice.

Jo-Jo pulled out a small metal tin of Camacho Minis and lit a cigarillo, as he caught JK staring at him. Once again, he was wearing the famous retro-style 'Blu Blocker' shades that he seemed to have been wearing non-stop since they met, even though the past few weeks in New Zealand had offered little opportunity to use them. JK was grateful, this time, to be spared from an accompanying lecture on the merits they provided the wearer by cutting out the glare from snow and ice reflection.

'What's the matter with you?' he asked JK.

'You look ridiculous,' said JK, shaking his head.

At which, Jo-Jo jumped on the back of JK, pretending to attack him with his ice axe as the two girls laughed in delight.

Jo-Jo's huge orange lenses set in a thick black plastic frame did not complement his green rain coat, army print shorts and beanie hat combo. They would look more at home on a red-neck deer hunting trip. But Jo-Jo knew this – he always played up to the image – and that's why he loved them so much. It gave him an opportunity to be centre of attention. Even their group guide laughed when he saw Jo-Jo.

JK guessed he didn't look much better in his cheap petrol-store shades either. They all looked pretty bizarre in these outfits.

' "I know not all that may be coming, but be it what it will, I'll go to it laughing",' said Jo-Jo, cryptically.

'What's that?' JK replied.

'It's from my man, Herman Melville.'

JK shook his head as the girls looked up at Jo-Jo, confused.

'This man in front of you now, believe it or not, is fairly well read,' said JK, sarcastically. 'He happens to be a fan of *Moby-Dick*.'

'Hell, yes. I studied it for my thesis. Also known as *The Whale*. The quote seems pretty apt now, don't you think?'

JK rolled his eyes as he knew what was coming. He had seen the routine before.

'Go on then, Jo-Jo. Get it over with – show them your tattoos.'

'Hell, I've only got two. But now you've said it, I've got to, don't I?' Jo-Jo smiled and took off his rain coat. His fleece top and shirt came off in one go, to leave him standing, bare-chested. He pivoted round so the girls could see the gigantic humpback whale tattoo over his right shoulder blade.

'Had that one for a while. Did it back in the States.'

'Impressive,' said Steph, 'And that one, what does it say?' she said, pointing to the writing inked around the top of his left upper-arm.

'This one is pretty new. It says "I try all things, I achieve what I can." It's from *Moby-Dick* as well.'

'You see, I told you. He's big fan of whales,' JK said, laughing. The girls hadn't even noticed the fish-hook pendant on the necklace Jo-Jo wore. It was a whale-bone carving which he had only purchased recently, around the same time as he had got his second tattoo.

'Do you have any, JK?' asked Fiona.

JK hesitated to answer, inwardly shuddering at the drunken memory from Nelson a week or so ago. It was something he had been considering for a while anyway. And, once he had admitted this to Jo-Jo, upon passing a nearby tattoo parlour it was the only encouragement that Jo-Jo had needed to get him to do it.

JK sighed and pulled his sleeve on his left arm to his bicep. On the inside of which he revealed a small symbol, a black circular ring with a simple s-shaped curve connected at the top.

'Very subtle. What is it?' Steph asked.

'It's a Zodiac sign, isn't it? Which one?' said Fiona.

'A Lion. I'm a Leo,' JK replied, guardedly. He still wasn't sure he liked it, but had just been dragged along with Jo-Jo's spontaneity at the time. JK had always known that Jo-Jo shared a lot of similarities with his brother, Bobby, and that was probably the reason he liked him.

Even though so many good things had happened to JK since parting ways with Bobby, he had really begun to miss his brother recently. However, at the same time, Jo-Jo's increasingly reckless behaviour was another reminder of his brother's similar bad habits.

They had begun their New Zealand trip in the large city of Auckland. It was uneventful but a useful base from which to finalise their route around the country. They moved north to Ninety-Mile Beach and the Bay of Islands, where they did find excitement: their coach had driven along sand and water; they got an adrenaline rush from body boarding off the top of huge sand dunes; and they had seen the famous 'swell' at Cape Reinga, the meeting point of the Tasman sea and the Pacific Ocean, where legend had it that Maori souls moved north.

They returned down south, past Auckland, through to Cathedral Cove where the sensitive-yet-unhinged Poppy, from Ireland, decided to skinny dip in the freezing sea, naked, in front of everyone. Further water incidents occurred in the spas of Whitianga, where Jo-Jo and JK formed a strong bond with two Canadian girls, Liz and Emma.

At Rotorua, they had experienced a real Maori village, nearby mud pools, hot springs and geysers in the aptly named Whangapipiro (the Maori translation meaning 'an evil smelling place'). They were split into groups with an appointed chief and tasked with performing their own Maori song to the traditional Haka dance, as a new tribe being welcomed. 'Chief' Dave from Scotland came up with the inspirational 'If you're happy clap your hands' for the boys, whereas rival chief Melissa of Washington, DC, came up with the equally rousing rendition of the 'hokey-kokey' for the girls.

The Waitomo caves gave them opportunities to see glow-worms and go black water rafting. Lake Taupo had various extreme sports like sky diving, which the British quartet of Dave, Rob, Jill and Samantha braved. At River Valley, there was jet sprint boating so fast that Lisa (yet another British girl) threw up. After a stop at Wellington, they left the North Island via a ferry to Nelson, and down on to Christchurch.

This is where Jo-Jo's obsession with whales had first surfaced. They booked a day trip to Kaikoura, where they took boat trips to swim with dolphins and watch gigantic Sperm Whales. Riding on a natural high back to Nelson, via Christchurch, they had their drunken night and tattoo experimentation to celebrate.

At Westport, they took a relaxing walk through the forest and lake, and finally, before their arrival here in Franz Josef, they visited the beautiful Lake Mahinapua. This was also a later setting for the long-standing tradition of a cross-dressing night. It was run by Les, who had a long grey beard, and hosted in an old shack where the walls inside were covered head-to-foot in Polaroid memories, depicting the thousands of nameless travellers who had passed through and worn the same borrowed outfits for the night.

Now, their hiking guide approached the group, sternly telling them to get moving, and so their all-day glacier hike began. The crunch of stones and soil underfoot on approach was satisfying to begin with, but soon the feeling was less-than-comfortable. The frequency of the hard, sharp edges of large rocks increased as they came across the true entrance to the glacier.

Tracing the zig-zagging steps of their guide in front, over rocks of varying size and height with small pockets of ice trapped in between, they pushed up from their hamstring and calf muscles and soon it began to feel like the challenge they had originally expected.

Soon the terrain changed again. The rocks had slowly disappeared, having been gradually swallowed up by the volume of ice that took over. Now, their steps were less strenuous but it still required intense concentration as they attempted to get sure footing on the shiny hard surface below.

The level sections were often the most deceptive areas, as they thought they had some stability again. JK fell over, flat on his face, and soon realised that this was over confidence, the same mistake that at least three people in their group would also go on to make.

They traversed higher and higher, their guide ever watchful, taking them at a comfortably unhurried pace. They managed to keep some small talk going in the group, in between the bouts of forced silence, as they walked over steep and narrow ice ledges. On his knees, JK crawled through tight tunnels, barely wider than his shoulders, soon realising why shorts rather than trousers were needed as he emerged with his lower legs soaked through.

Nearer the peaks, their paths became increasingly dangerous and they were grateful for the presence of the guide. Walking across more edges of thin ice, with nothing above, ice ahead and behind, one hundred metre-deep chasms stretching below, some were understandably nervous. Going over one at a time, it was common practice to give a helping hand to the person behind.

Putting so much trust in people like this, after concentrating for such long periods, meant that, on the descent, a lot of tension had been released. Some began to relax but the hard work wasn't over, as they found out once again on encountering smooth level sections of ice. JK, along with a few others, fell again, flat on his back this time, just for good measure, and laughed out loud.

Jo-Jo was in front; JK's designated guardian angel. He turned round to give him a helping hand, getting him back up on his feet. Another few metres on and his collapse might not have been such a jovial scene. Encountering another precarious edge, balancing a drop promising certain death, JK's feet jarred ever so slightly that Jo-Jo threw out a hand and watched every further move he made like a hawk.

Jo-Jo entered another tight ice tunnel and JK squeezed his way through after him. JK emerged to see Jo-Jo sitting on the ice floor, waiting, with a broad grin slapped across his face. He was holding up a chunky silver lighter that sparkled in the sunshine. He rubbed it with glee and showed JK the engraving.

They read the word SKYLINE and a simple outline of a cable car against a mountain range. Ahead, their guide urged them to move on, as Jo-Jo slipped the lighter into his pocket, tapping it as he gave JK a wink, before he resumed walking.

Sometime later, the ice had disappeared from view as they neared the end of the walk. Dark rocks, sharp and unforgiving underfoot, greeted them as they saw their coach far in the distance. Their tired legs and feet yearned for the more responsive feel of the loose, muddy floor in sight as they completed the hike, some seven hours later.

Jo-Jo had wanted one last cigarillo before boarding the bus, and pulled out the lighter JK saw him with earlier from the ice tunnel.

'Aren't you going to hand that in to the guide? It looks expensive,' said JK, to which Jo-Jo looked confused.

'What, this?' he said, holding the lighter up as JK nodded back. 'Yeah, I found it… well, not here, but… yeah, sure, I'll hand it in later. I've just been dying for this smoke for ages,' he replied.

After he had finished, they boarded the bus and began the drive back to their hostel. Physically exhausted but psychologically exhilarated, they eagerly discussed celebrating their great achievement that evening.

Several days later, after yet another stop, this time at Wanaka – probably the most beautiful lake visage they had seen so far – they had arrived in Queenstown, the tourist rendezvous point for all the excitement of the South Island.

Various travellers had come and gone on the bus. Most had decided to stop off and spend a little longer in Queenstown to relax and do all the stuff there was to do at their own pace. For the first few days, there were at least twelve of them but then the numbers reduced as people moved on.

It was the thick of winter, in deep snow, but they didn't care – they were having such a good time. Over the course of a week, they caught a few movies, went for some nice dinners, had a dorm room all to themselves – they could do just about anything they pleased: skiing and snowboarding at Coronet Peak, the luge, a cable car gondola, jet boats, bungee jumps.

It was just one big party town and everyone knew it: fooling around in bars, talking nonsense, drinking, dancing and much more besides. And when one coach load of tourists left, there was another fresh batch, arriving right behind them, ready to take their place. People just got involved – that was the vibe of the place and that's what they'd always remember about it.

By the end, four travellers had stuck together: Jo-Jo and JK, along with Steph and Fiona from Denmark. They were all leaving New Zealand at much the same time after Queenstown to go on in different routes. So, it was an easy but fitting idea they had come up with to celebrate the natural end to their trip.

Late one afternoon on their penultimate day together, JK sat waiting in their hostel's reception. He was usually ready before the girls, and definitely before Jo-Jo – who would take forever, continually blathering on about something. But he wanted to make a special effort today, given it was their big event.

He spied the great big, overweight ginger cat that sat on a comfy chair next to the reception desk. His name was Thomas, and JK wondered if it was likely that the owners had named him after the hostel, or perhaps it was vice-versa, given how spoilt he was. JK and his friends had barely seen him move an inch in all the time they had been there. The cat eyed JK suspiciously, sitting opposite him.

'How is that fat meat-ball, anyway?' said Jo-Jo, as he walked down the stairs next to where JK sat. Behind him followed Fiona and Steph.

'Still very, very lazy,' replied JK. He looked Jo-Jo up and down and saw he was wearing a t-shirt covered in colourfully printed names and logos. 'Aha, is that the infamous t-shirt, then?'

'Yeah, the *world*-famous Queenstown bar crawl t-shirt. I hope you guys are ready?' Jo-Jo replied, as he pulled out three more t-shirts from his rucksack and threw one to each of the girls and JK. 'These are for you. Treasure them. Now, I must admit that I'm a sucker for a good t-shirt, preferably an a-shirt if I'm honest, as I normally rip those sleeves off a t-shirt anyhow.'

'Oh god, it's a bit tacky, isn't it, Jo-Jo?' said JK, grimacing as he held it up.

'You can call it tacky if you want, but I don't care – that's just the way I am. I just love to wear 'em back home. Show all the folks that I've been some place or done something. Anyhow, we've all got to be wearing the shirts, and get the bar staff to sign each one as we go round.'

'Seems like a lot of bars,' said Steph, nervously.

'It's not a big town – it ain't – but seeing as there's only ten bars it makes it a nice, do-able feat. Ten bars, one aim – gettin' fucked.'

'Nice sentiment, Jo-Jo. This is meant to be our final goodbye, our last night out together,' she replied.

'Ah, hell, darling. I didn't mean no offence. I'm just a dumb American,' Jo-Jo replied.

'You got that bit right!' JK interrupted, laughing.

'Shut up, JK. As I was saying, this night means the world to me. I've been looking forward to it for ages. Even got myself organised with these t-shirts for us all.'

'Actually, he has. It's the most organised I've ever seen him. And what were all those rules we spoke about last night? I've forgotten them already,' said JK.

'Not rules. A little protocol, that's all. No time or drink limit for each place or anything shitty like that. Just that our first drink in each bar has to be different every time, and we take it in turns to choose a round of whatever that chosen beverage may be. No consultation or planning or nothin' – we just surprise each other. You all still agree?'

'Yes, Jo-Jo,' Fiona said, rolling her eyes in mock annoyance.

Steph looked through the window at the snowfall getting heavier against the darkening sky, and sighed.

'Don't you worry about that. We ain't gonna let a little thing like the weather stop us,' said Jo-Jo, who was first to zip up his snow jacket and pull his hood over his head. They all followed suit and made their way out into the blizzard.

First up was the Skyline – the Gondola Bar and Restaurant – with a stunning view, high up above town. It was only accessible by cable car and was the furthest bar from their hostel, so they had decided to get it out of the way first. They'd all seen the view already – having been on a trip to do the luge from there a few days before – but it was still an impressive sight up there in the night sky.

'I'm fixin' to order first. Just you wait for these babies,' said Jo-Jo, as he rushed up to the bar while the others found a table.

Shortly after, Jo-Jo returned with four beers and four glasses filled with a dark-coloured liquid that he gleefully set down on the table. The girls picked theirs up to sniff them, and screwed up their faces back at Jo-Jo in disgust.

'What the hell are they?' asked Fiona.

'Gasoline. That's Tequila and Jack Daniels. You are gonna love that good ol' brown stuff,' he replied, laughing.

'That is disgusting,' said JK, taking a small sip.

'Hey, this is meant to be a bar crawl ain't it now, people? You never done one? Hell, this ain't my first rodeo you know? We got us some serious drinking to do here. Let me tell y'all that this here juice is gonna blow your mind.'

He proudly pointed at his chest where the logo for Skyline on his shirt now had a signature scrawled next to it. 'If you go up at some point, the bar man said he would happily do the same for y'all.'

JK looked around the bar, thinking ahead to how raucous he knew that Jo-Jo would get, but he was pleased to see it only had a handful of customers.

' "Looks like I picked the wrong week to give up drinking!" ' said Jo-Jo suddenly.

'Is that a quote from something?' Steph asked him.

'Only the greatest comedy ever made – *Airplane*, of course!'

'Unfortunately for me, I've heard it all before by now. Jo-Jo is a walking encyclopaedia of useless film quotations, with one for every occasion,' said JK.

'Hell, yes. I love all that crap.'

Seeing the girls tentatively take their first sips, Jo-Jo decided to join them and took a large gulp of his own.

'Yessir!' he said, clapping his hands, as the girls grimaced and coughed. ' "Looks like I picked the wrong week to give up taking amphetamines!" '

Steph, opposite JK, to Jo-Jo's left, and Fiona, opposite him, both looked at each other in shock and amusement.

'Time for our first photo, don't you think?' asked Fiona. JK looked to Jo-Jo, who suddenly stared wide eyed back at them.

'Ah, shit,' he said.

'That was your department, Jo-Jo. Don't tell me you forgot a camera.' JK asked.

'No, no. Don't fret it,' he replied, hurriedly. 'Just hold up, we'll do that in a moment. I just need a piss, urgently. And a smoke. See you in moment, folks.' He got up, quickly disappearing to the toilets, opposite the gift shop exit.

'He never sits still, does he?' said Steph.

'Nope. I think we're in for a lively night, ladies,' replied JK. He looked across to Steph, as the dark streaks within her straight long blonde hair looked silver in the low light. He thought he could see a spark of admiration in her eyes as she returned his gaze.

'Let's go get that bar man's signature, shall we?' he suggested.

After they returned, they sat in silence, taking in the picturesque view that surrounded them. Snow-capped mountains dominated the horizon of a violet sky and, beneath them, the lights of Queenstown lit up the darkened land masses, snaking in and out across the black water of the bay.

JK felt contentment as the alcohol entered his bloodstream, relaxing him. He remembered his father's words and, after his last few weeks of travel, he really did finally feel lucky. He knew he would always want more, but now he knew he could justifiably retire his father's list. Eventually, anyway – he still had a long way to go yet.

But to even consider that now, he realised was significant progress for his ambitions towards his father's legacy.

'What a view, eh, girls?' he said.

'Oh my god, it's amazing,' said Fiona. 'And I can't stop thinking about the few days of skiing and snowboarding we've just had.'

'They were great, but so tiring! Do you think tonight will be as big as those nights? I'm not sure my liver can take anymore,' replied Steph.

'Probably bigger,' replied JK. 'I'll give Jo-Jo one thing. He may not be able to ski, but he sure can drink.'

The girls laughed and then JK pointed towards a sheltered balcony outside where Jo-Jo stood waving and making faces through the window. JK noted the lighter he then produced from his pocket – it was the silver lighter that he had found on the glacier over a week ago – to light his cigarillo. JK frowned, but quickly tried to disguise this by standing up and playfully pretending to ski and then fall over. Jo-Jo laughed, shook his head and raised his middle finger back at JK.

He returned to their table not long after.

'I can't believe you mocked my skiing ability. Them lifts ain't much fun for us simple folk who don't know snow slope etiquette, or whatever you call it, being from the flat plains of America an' all. I had to drag my sorry ass in all my kit, up them hills, time after time. Sheesh, that sucked, let me tell you. But once I got up there, I wasn't much worse than you, JK.'

'I know, mate. We were just having a bit of fun.'

'Hell, I know we can't all be as good as the Danish queens over here,' he said, gesturing to Steph and Fiona. 'Are you all born knowing how to skate or ski, or something? Maybe you eat ice for breakfast? I don't know. You were whizzing around those slopes like shit off a shovel!'

They all laughed before the girls took a big gulp of their beers and left together for the bathroom.

'So, Jo-Jo. I noticed you still have that silver Skyline lighter? I thought you were going to give it back to the guide at the glacier?'

'Oh, yeah, that. Well, I didn't actually find it at the glacier, you see,' he replied, awkwardly. 'I found it a while ago and that's why I've kept it hidden. But I thought I'd return it here, seeing as that's where it was from.'

'Eh? That doesn't make any sense. The person who lost it won't be looking for it here, though, will they?'

'No, I suppose not.'

'Come on, man, admit it. You took it for yourself, didn't you?'

'It's not that simple,' he replied, after a pause.

'Why not? It's a nice lighter, after all.'

'Yes, but I didn't exactly, err, *find* it there.'

'What? You stole it? From where?'

'Back in Nelson. But it wasn't stealing in my mind. I was reclaiming it, from some asshole who had stolen it originally.'

'Really, who? Did I meet him?'

'I doubt it. He was in our hostel bar one night. I think you'd gone to bed after our tattoo antics. He was trying to meet other travellers but wasn't even staying there. I found out he was an investment broker in Auckland on holiday and just wanted to meet people, but was showing off about how much money he had, so I don't think he was having much success – surprise, surprise. A big Kiwi dude with black hair.'

'No, I don't remember him.'

'Well, anyway, he was boasting about how he'd stolen the lighter from some poor German dude he'd met the previous week. A teacher on holiday. Do you remember Nick?' JK nodded. 'Yeah, it was him. I liked him. And especially as I did teacher training myself, it really got my goat. Anyway, he was really drunk, so while he was taking a piss one time, he'd left his jacket behind. So, I took my opportunity and made my exit.'

'Wow. I didn't know you had that side to you, man.'

'Yeah, well, I don't normally. Unless someone really deserves it, that is. And he fucking deserved it. You may think of me as one big joker but I know some things really get me all riled up. When I see weak, vulnerable people being taken advantage of, then it kinda makes me angry. There are lots of horrible fuckers out there, and I don't think there's enough justice to deal with it all. I see these fancy investment brokers, politicians, the clergy and what not, folks with lots of privileges, but I don't see that they deserve them. No more than the likes of teachers, doctors and health workers, anyway. They don't get many breaks in life, no sir.'

'Fair enough, Jo-Jo,' replied JK. Jo-Jo sat in his chair, and was shifting awkwardly, occasionally closing his eyes and nodding to himself, as if weighing up an important decision.

'It was like a year or so ago, when I was in Africa. I was on an exchange programme and I hitch-hiked with five dudes who I was convinced were about to kidnap me. On instinct, I jumped out of the moving truck, at one in the morning, on the edge of the Kalahari Desert with nowhere to go. But I survived.'

'That's some story, Jo-Jo. I can't believe you haven't told me before,' replied JK. He watched as Jo-Jo's anxiety levels continued to rise, as he looked all around.

'Yeah, well, there's more. Only a few weeks after that, I was walking through a small town in Nigeria. Then I saw a man being beaten, and then shot. I really thought it would be me next. But it wasn't, and I carried on… You see, that's what I'm all about: taking the opportunities that you get, no matter the risks or the consequences.'

'Wow. So, maybe we should call you, Jo-Jo *Opportunity* Knox,' JK replied, smiling back at Jo-Jo.

'Hell, I quite like that. It might just stick,' Jo-Jo said, as he turned around to see the girls approaching the table and smiled. He stood up, abruptly, and, his beer long finished, he grabbed his spirit glass and downed the remaining contents. 'Anyway, excuse me a second,' he said before leaving the table again, carrying his bag with him.

'Where's he off to now?' said Fiona, as she sat down.

'Oh, I think he needs to return something,' replied JK.

A few minutes later, Jo-Jo returned to the table, walking quickly and looking nervous.

'Hey, you two! *Hit it*, don't baby sit it!' he said, pointing at the spirit glasses they still nursed. They grabbed them and took their last sips. 'Woohoo, that's the ticket. Now, let's get the hell out of here.'

'What's the rush?' said Fiona.

'No rush, but it's pretty dead in here. Plenty of bars to get through yet.'

They got up and put their coats on as JK noticed how fidgety Jo-Jo had become, constantly looking back at the gift shop. He ushered them out the main exit and onto the cable car platform as they watched the snow continue to fall.

After dismounting the cable car at the bottom, back on low ground again, they only had a short walk through the snow to the second bar of the crawl, Winnie Bagoes Pizza. While they were still contemplating the food menu, JK had come back from the bar with a round of drinks he was quickly informed that looked and felt like soggy paper pulp and tasted like acid. They were aptly called Cement Mixers.

'You sly London dog,' Jo-Jo said, voicing the incredulous looks of the girls.

'You're not supposed to like them. I just know they will fuck us up,' he replied, straight faced. 'But may I just say that this last month in New Zealand has been some of the best travel I've ever done. So, cheers to us,' he said, raising his glass to the group as they all returned his cheers and took a sip.

'Fuck! That is disgusting, man!' replied Steph.

' "Looks like I picked the wrong week to give up sniffing glue!" ' said Jo-Jo.

'More *Airplane*?' said Fiona, to which Jo-Jo nodded sheepishly. 'Hey, we forgot to get a photo back at Skyline.'

'Oh man, yeah, that is my fault. But hey, at least we all have photos from when we went there before,' replied Jo-Jo.

'Or we can always go back?' said JK.

'No way man, not enough time if we wanna get this bar crawl done.'

'We could always go in the morning for breakfast?'

'I guess. But it's quite expensive. And I need to pack,' Jo-Jo replied, hesitantly. 'Let's get one done now, anyway.' He reached into his backpack and took out a camera which had a plastic cover on it.

'Hey, did you buy a new camera just for our bar crawl, Jo-Jo?' said Fiona.

'Huh? Yeah, I bought it yesterday, I think. Or, maybe the day before. Well, I needed one anyway,' Jo-Jo replied, stumbling on his words.

JK watched with interest, thinking that he hadn't noticed Jo-Jo buy it, but was quickly distracted as Jo-Jo arranged them all, ready for a group photo. He suddenly pulled in an attractive waitress to take the picture, and then asked her to sign all of their t-shirts. He continued to talk his usual nonsense at her before eventually letting her get on and take their food orders.

'So, Jo-Jo, JK tells me you did some teacher training once. Is that what you want to do for a career, become a teacher? I only ask because I've been thinking about it,' said Fiona.

'Well now, little darlin', it's funny you should mention that because I've been thinking on it some myself, recently. I've got me a fun little yarn I wanna tell you. I know most of you love a good yarn – God knows that I surely do. Well, here's hoping that you do an' all, as once I get started there ain't much that's gonna stop me. Heck, I may get a little side tracked and veer off the subject on the way, but I'll get there in the end. Yessir, don't you go worrying about that,' he said, then paused and smiled as he saw JK roll his eyes.

'Get on with it!' said JK.

'OK, OK! So, two years previous, back in New York at a teacher training college, I met my good pal Andy Robson from Canada. Robbo and I just clicked straight away, you know how it is? We were pretty similar, laid-back, easy-going dudes, looking for laughs and thrills without having to work too hard to get them. In my case, I was never convinced I even wanted to be a teacher. It just seemed like something easy that I fell into at the time. In the absence of knowing what the hell I did wanna do, I saw an opportunity to do something I knew I wouldn't fuck up and might actually enjoy, and so I took it.'

'Robbo and I ended up living together for a year, and after that we went back to our home towns and fooled around, doing some fill-in teaching jobs, our first year at schools and the like. I suppose in the end we both got a bit restless and decided to do a year of touring – we figured we'd find ourselves a full-time job when we got back home a year later. And we've seen some sights, let me tell you. But while we were in the States, his daddy got sick and he had to leave to go back home, part way through our tour. Not long after, I met this young man here, JK.'

'Now, since then, I've heard from Robbo and that his daddy died from cancer. He was devastated, obviously. It was always unlikely that he would re-join me on tour, but he told me he wanted to be near his family which I completely understood. I lost my momma myself when I was a lot younger... So, anyhow, I don't know exactly what I'm gonna do next.'

They all looked at him in silence, shocked at the depth of his answer.

'Wow. Well, sounds like you well and truly kept an open mind, Jo-Jo,' said Fiona, eventually. 'At least you made a start with the teacher training, I guess.'

'Heck, who knows? Maybe I'll go back into teaching one day. Sure, I enjoy it, and sometimes I think I still want to try and do something to help people. But, after everything that happened to Robbo, it got me thinking that you just have to make the most of things while you still can. Life's too short and you're a long time dead. It's like the great Neil Young once said, "Better to burn out than fade away". I've kinda always thought like that anyway. That's why we went on our long ol' road trip in the first place. That's why *any* of us folks here do likewise, I expect.'

They finished eating and paid up and, as the snow fell harder, advanced onward to Shooters Bar. Steph was up next and surprised everyone with her round of Black Russians and some – now obligatory – accompanying beers.

'I think we all need a sing song. Hey, seeing as you guys don't seem to be appreciating my movie references, I feel I need to give you some education on American culture. I think I know the answer already, but do any of you know the seventh-innings song?' said Jo-Jo.

'Er, no. What is that?' replied Fiona.

'It's called "Take Me Out to the Ball Game" and it's a classic bit of baseball, no-less. Now, as you know, I love the Cubs. And just like the movie quotes, I like my sports stats too. I even do some scoring for baseball. I'm one of a select few that still do, mind you, as it's a lost art. Some folks back home don't like me for it, especially when I forget birthdays and anniversaries and what not, but that's just the way God made me, I guess.'

'This is your song? It's really boring,' said Steph.

'Hell, no! That is not the song. But point taken, let me get started, then. I know it well, and so I'm going to sing it right here, for all you people, right now.' And so, Jo-Jo began enthusiastically singing the first verse, receiving sceptical looks from everyone in the process.

Undeterred, he then stood up on an adjoining table and sang it again, louder this time. Even though they didn't have a clue what the words were, eventually they all joined in, slurring and stumbling on the lyrics, and cheering and embracing at its end.

It was a longer walk on to Maggie's Bar. The snow was really beginning to cut through them and their feet were soaking wet. On arrival, they found it to be a small and cosy place with some big, old sofa chairs to relax on.

While Fiona was getting the drinks, Jo-Jo decided to whip off his shoes and socks to place them to dry on a radiator. The others quickly followed suit, before Fiona came back with a jug of Rum Runner cocktail and four glasses.

'We must look really classy right now,' said Steph, as they slouched all over the sofas, bare feet in full view, drinking fluorescent orange cocktails in the tiny, empty bar.

They drank more until their socks dried and then they moved on again. The snow wasn't letting up but luckily their next bar, Chico's, was nearby, so they avoided getting soaked again. There was a pool table which they promptly took advantage of. Suddenly, during one great, long game, there was a massive power failure, likely as a result of the heavy snow. JK found this ironic given that Jo-Jo had ordered a round of White Lightening, a mix of Tequila and Southern Comfort.

Even though all the lights were out, they carried on playing pool anyway. It was an activity that, over the whole course of JK and Jo-Jo's travels together, had taken up a lot of their time. JK, in particular, was a very good player, as evidenced by potting an unlikely last ball black – the whole length of the table – to win their game in the dark, when no one else could barely even see the pocket.

Their sixth bar was called Wicked Willies Bar & Liquor Store and their drink of choice this time, courtesy of Steph – who had stolen JK's turn – arrived in four gigantic curvy glasses, filled with a thick yellow liquid. An umbrella and a straw sat on top of each.

'Sweet Jesus! What the fuck are these?' Jo-Jo asked Steph.

'Pina Colada. Surely you've had one before?'

'Aha! Hell, yes, I have! JK and I both had some back in Hawaii. Now that I remember it, they tasted mighty fine, actually.'

By the time they reached bar number seven – Red Rock – they were all struggling. Especially when JK ordered up some beers and Liquid Cocaine, a dreaded combination of Jägermeister and Goldschläger.

'God-*damn* you, JK, you snake. That stuff burns,' Jo-Jo said, now becoming just a little bit boisterous and ended up challenging JK to an arm wrestle. He accepted, but, with the girls watching and laughing, eventually lost. At which point Jo-Jo rolled up his sleeve to show his right bicep, which he promptly flexed, just to complete his machismo spectacle. 'You're looking at the toughest sonnuva bitch in the whole of the South right here folks! T- U- F- F!'

'You dick! You're such a fucking show off! Hey girls, don't pay him any attention, he's just looking for it,' replied JK.

'Come on, let me try, then,' said Fiona, raising her open palm to Jo-Jo.

'No way, I don't wrestle girls. Not like that, anyway darling,' he said, smiling.

'Sexist pig,' replied Fiona, curtly. Her straight black hair was starting to look frazzled after the constant removal of the winter snow hat, but Jo-Jo was taken aback by her reaction, unable to tell if she was joking or not.

'Aw, shucks, I'm sorry. Look, us Americans do a lot of stupid stuff, bar trash talking and dudes wrestling dudes and the like. It's not a sexist thing.' She eyed him suspiciously, without replying. 'I mean, I know a lot of folks overseas don't like us that much, so please, I don't want you to think we're all like that, now.'

'Yes, I know. I think you're quite smart, actually. So why do you like to pretend that you're not, so much?' Fiona finally replied, looking uncomfortable.

Reading Jo-Jo's desperate glance back towards him, JK tried to help him out.

'Hey, I've known Jo-Jo for about two months now and he just likes to play the fool. Don't ask me why, but he's always been that way.'

JK and Steph decided to walk away and leave the couple chatting. Within five minutes, JK looked back and saw they were now kissing.

In bar eight, The Casbah nightclub, Fiona ordered another round of cocktails, a Tom Collins. Once they saw that monkey nuts were available as a bar snack, they all agreed to grab as many as they could.

'Now, people, this is probably gonna rock your world but, yeah, I eat the nut and the shell an' all,' said Jo-Jo, chuckling before everyone watched him carelessly throw a handful of whole peanuts into his mouth.

Outside their penultimate bar, The Lone Star, they heard sirens as a police car drove down the road, away from them. On seeing this, Jo-Jo raced on inside, ahead of everyone else, and disappeared into the toilets for ten minutes. In the meantime, JK had ordered some Bloody Marys, hoping that they might sober them all up.

When Jo-Jo eventually did reappear, he was nervously looking around the busy club. Once he realised that whoever he was looking for wasn't there, he visibly relaxed. Even though they stayed in the bar for a while, instead of slowing down, Jo-Jo actually accelerated their drinking by buying several rounds of shots.

'You know what? For our last bar, we should do something different,' he shouted, sometime later.

'Like what?' Fiona asked.

'Naked!'

'What?'

'Let's do the drinks naked!' Jo-Jo replied, laughing.

'You are one delusional individual!'

'Anyway, cheers, everyone,' said JK, looking up and down the carnage of their table, pools of various drinks dripping off the far end, empty beer bottles and knocked over chairs among discarded glasses of various sizes.

Fiona stood up and held up her shot glass, and everyone else did likewise. JK could see her rub Jo-Jo's back and then reached over to whisper in his ear. As he laughed, JK turned to Steph, looking at him with an expectant, wide-eyed stare and a sincere smile.

'Wooooo-Hooooo!' Instead of slamming it down, this time Jo-Jo threw his shot glass across the table, sending it bouncing towards the far wall, remaining unbroken.

JK leant over and kissed Steph full on the lips. She then grabbed his hand, and pulled him away from the table and towards the main door, leading him outside.

Jo-Jo and Fiona followed them out, quickly finding them on the nearest street corner, where they were kissing again. They pointed out the final bar of their crawl, a famous Queenstown night club called The World, along the next street, and eventually shuffled to the entrance.

Just before they went in, Jo-Jo looked back to see a police car pull up outside The Lone Star, their last bar, as two uniformed officers got out and walked inside. As he paid the entrance fee to The World and walked through its doors, Jo-Jo suddenly went pale, knowing that his time would soon be up.

He went straight to the bar and ordered some more shots, cinnamon After Shock, washed down with beers that JK had bought. They were all shouting, jumping over each other, singing songs, celebrating the end of their long bar crawl.

The girls walked off to the dance floor while JK hung back with Jo-Jo, who by now had become quiet and withdrawn.

'You OK, mate?' JK said, trying to shout over the loud music.

'I guess. I'm just gonna miss you guys,' he replied.

'Hey, we'll miss you too. But at least you'll have the photos, shirts and souvenirs, right?'

'Shit, they don't really matter, no sir! What matters is that we felt something while we did it... otherwise what's the point?'

'Yep, you're right. We'll definitely have the memories too,' replied JK, trying his best to keep up but could barely hear the conversation now.

'You know what, JK? I love you, man. And I just need to tell you something else, before it's too late,' he said, pausing, as JK nodded. 'Like I said, it's all about the opportunities you get in life. As long as you take 'em, whether it all turns to shit afterwards, or it ends up becoming the sweetest smelling peach, either way, you've got something to remember, ain't you now?'

As the bass music in the club started to give JK a headache, he could only smile and reassuringly pat Jo-Jo on the back, pretending to hear his drunken ramblings.

'Just recently, I've tried to take every opportunity I got, whenever there's even a hint that I might get something good from it. Yeah, I'll probably regret a few decisions later but, shit, I'd surely regret it more if I hadn't taken them. I'd rather it was that way round, too – that's just how I live my life now. Think about that for a moment. Remember that saying, it's "Better to burn out than fade away". Did I mention that to you already?'

JK nodded again, still not understanding what Jo-Jo was talking about.

'Heck, I can't even remember where I was going with all this nonsense, anyways. Like most of my yarns, it's just for shits and giggles, you know? I guess I'll just shut up now.'

At that moment, two police officers appeared on the dance floor and surveyed the other revellers. They looked around at everyone's faces, stopping briefly to look at Fiona and Steph, and then JK, but kept on looking.

Jo-Jo recognised them as the two that he had seen getting out of the police car earlier as, finally, they made eye contact and marched towards him.

JK couldn't hear exactly what they were saying but they began to body search Jo-Jo roughly. They found his rucksack, which was on a seat at a table-booth, and pulled out his new camera. Jo-Jo then became more animated and, just as JK could barely hear the police say something about 'Skyline', they grabbed Jo-Jo by his arms.

He struggled and shouted as they put handcuffs on him. JK, Steph and Fiona frantically followed as the policemen dragged Jo-Jo out of the nightclub to their car.

'You can't do this to me, I'm the toughest sonnuva bitch ALIVE!' Jo-Jo shouted, as he was bundled into the back seat.

It was the last thing JK heard him say for some time and, somehow, despite being in a state of shock, JK then began to laugh out loud, uncontrollably.

Chapter Nine

Dead End Signs in Sydney

JK walked slowly up-hill, along the pavement, trying to keep cool in the sunshine. Rainbow Street was wide with no shade at all, and the heat was compounding his annoyance. There had been no answer at his brother's house, only a few doors behind him now, and he was unsure what to do next.

He had arrived in Australia the previous evening and, after having rested up, he had been looking forward to seeing Bobby today. Perhaps he had had to work late, JK reasoned. Even though his brother's shared back-packer house had no room for him to stay in, somehow no-one else was home either on this sunny early evening in Coogee, a suburb of Sydney.

JK recognised the route; he was heading back down to the beach front, remembering it from his twenty minute bus journey when he arrived from central Sydney. He had seen a large pub on the beach front, which was hopefully the same one he had vaguely recalled his brother mentioning previously.

As he got to the corner of Rainbow Street, he looked along the road to his right and saw an old phone box a few metres away. He had a cheap international call card in his wallet, with some credit remaining, as well as his brother's phone number at work. He approached the phone box and saw it had no door; it was just three sides of a tall box with glass windows, covered in dust, one on each side of where the phone was attached to the back wall. JK took a chance, and dialled the number.

'Hello, Robert Jenkins speaking,' said his brother, impatiently, clearly wanting to leave for the day.

'Bobby, it's me,' JK replied.

'JK! Oh, hi. How are you feeling now – recovered from your flight?'

'Yeah, all fine. I had a good lie-in, although my hostel is a bit shit. I was woken up by loads of noise a few times.'

'Oh no, mate, sorry. Look, I'm really sorry again that I couldn't meet you at the airport but, you know, it was kind of late and I had work today.'

'It's fine, Bobby. Anyway, what time are you finishing? It's 6pm now.'

'Shit, is it? I didn't even look at the time, sorry JK. It's been a nightmare at work and I've still got a lot to do-'

JK interrupted Bobby impatiently as he gazed around the phone box.

'Look Bobby, I didn't call you to hear one of your lame excuses. What time are you going to…OH MY GOD!'

JK screamed as he leapt out of the phone box. Above his head he had seen a large spider, about the size of his hand. He slowly bent down, looking up at the spider the whole time, to pick up the discarded mouthpiece he had left hanging. He could hear Bobby shouting out at him.

'It's OK, I'm still here. I just saw a fucking huge spider – in fact, it's still there, right above my head.'

'What are you doing? Are you in a phone box?'

'Yes, just up the road from your house.'

'What? Why?'

'Because no one fucking answered the door, why do you think?'

'But Rick should be home. Sorry, I know I'm running later than I told you but he said he would be home by now. Are you sure he wasn't in?'

'Well, he didn't answer if he was. And, just so you know, this spider looks evil. It's got a big hairy body and it's staring right at me.'

'Oh, stop being a fucking wimp, JK. What type of spider is it, anyway? It's not one of those funnel-webs, is it? If they bite you, you can die within an hour or something, you know?'

'Yes, thanks Bobby, that's really helpful of you to let me know that right now. I'm standing outside the phone box as we speak, with the cord at full stretch, looking up at it in case it decides to jump on my head.'

'Good thinking,' Bobby replied, trying to suppress a laugh.

'Thanks for your sympathy, brother. I don't think it's a funnel-web, anyway. It's too big.'

'It could be a huntsman. I've seen them round our flat too, I'm afraid. Be careful, they do bite, and it hurts, apparently. They're very aggressive.'

'Great. OK, well, let's hurry up then.'

'Yes, I've got to finish work.'

'Charming. What do you suggest I do, then?'

'Go back to the house and try again. Just one more time. I'm sure Rick is in. You might have to knock pretty loud, though, as he's not been well recently, but it could just be the drugs. He's probably still off his head, knowing him.'

'For god's sake, Bobby, he's always – OH MY GOD!' JK stood, rigid. A bead of sweat formed on his brow as he looked up at the ceiling of the phone box.

'Now what?' his brother replied.

'There's another fucking huntsman! It's just come out of nowhere and crawled up next to the first one – and it's even bigger. I think they're hunting in pairs – ganging up on me!'

'Ha! Well, get a fucking move on then, bro!'

'OK, OK. I'm off. Rick better be in. And you better be back soon, Bobby.'

'Yes, yes, alright. I'll try my best, JK. See you later.'

'Bye.'

JK didn't really want to go back to the phone to replace the receiver as it would mean standing under the two spiders. He continued to hold the receiver, remaining still for a moment as he heard his brother hang up, and contemplated what to do. After a while, he heard the dead-tone on the line and dropped the phone piece. It swung back, as JK simply turned away and walked back the way he came.

He had time to quickly consider what he would say to Rick. They had not parted ways on the best of terms the last time they had seen each other. Eventually he had returned to number 108 Rainbow Street. It was a plain door, an off-white colour, with no distinguishing features whatsoever. He looked at the windows, where the curtains remained drawn, and paused, shook his head and exhaled a loud sigh before ringing the doorbell once more.

He waited, and then pressed again, holding the button for much longer this time.

'This is pointless,' he muttered to himself.

Finally, he decided to knock on the door itself with his fist. He waited again, and was about to turn away when he heard a soft moan from within. Encouraged, this time he decided to continue knocking with his hand as well as ringing the bell.

JK heard more moaning, and then footsteps approaching the door.

JK wasn't prepared for what he saw once the door opened. It was Rick, but a much poorer version of the one he remembered. He had always been skinny, but now he was almost skeletal. His tanned skin hung loosely from his arms, and yet his face was a completely pale, almost grey colour. Underneath his closely shaved hair he had an oily scalp, and could barely keep his eyes open.

'What do you want, man?' he whispered, hoarsely.

'Rick, you idiot. It's me, JK,' he replied, watching, as his presence slowly registered in Rick's eyes,

'Fuck, man! Jesus, is that you, Jonny?' JK nodded. 'Sorry, I'm not feeling myself at the moment.'

'You're telling me. You look terrible.'

'Aye, thanks. Good to see you too, ya bastard... Come in, then, I'm cold.'

JK followed Rick into the house, walking along the hallway and through the first door on the right. An odour of smoke and takeaway food saturated the air, and JK noticed clothes strewn across the entrance to the room. He walked in to find Rick had immediately collapsed onto a sofa, lying flat as he watched a TV in the background.

More clothes, envelopes, other junk-mail and papers littered the floor. A can of Coke and an ashtray, along with some roll-up cigarettes, were on a small coffee table next to the sofa. JK sat down on a single armchair and stared at Rick awkwardly.

'Ah, sorry, do you fancy a drink? I feel like shite so I can't get up. You'll just have to go and help yourself in the kitchen,' said Rick, without moving.

JK realised that he needn't have worried about any residual tension from their last meeting several months ago. Rick was probably in too bad shape now to even remember.

'It's OK, I'm fine. So, are you sick, then?' JK asked.

'Aye, you've not lost your powers of observation, have you?'

'And you've not lost your natural charm either, Rick,' JK replied, shaking his head. 'What's wrong with you then?'

'Ah, some fucking virus. I first got it after I left Vegas, actually, but it's been coming in waves, on and off. This last week, I've been stuck in bed all day – my throat is fucking killing me. Look at these.' Rick sat up and opened his mouth wide towards JK.

He leaned forward and peered in, before sharply turning away at the sight. Rick's tonsils were swollen red and covered in large white blobs of mucus.

'That's disgusting, Rick. You should see a doctor.'

'I have. I just got back, actually. Like five minutes ago. He thinks it's tonsillitis and glandular fever.'

'Shit, man. Sorry. What meds do you have to take, then?'

'Ah, some mega anti-biotics or the like. But, I can't swallow anything either. He said I was dangerously dehydrated and had to get to a hospital straight away.'

'What? Are you kidding? You should go now, then.'

'I know, I just felt really knackered after the walk, and, see, I don't have a car. I'd need to get a bus.'

'Oh, come on, can't your housemates give you a lift? Or you could just get a taxi.'

'They're not here and none of them have cars either anyway. And I'm skint.'

JK rolled his eyes and shifted in his seat uncomfortably.

'Well, look, I can pay for a cab and we can go together, if you want?' he said, eventually.

Rick looked up at JK, who saw something in his eyes that he had rarely seen in him before: gratitude. Rick coughed something quietly under his breath like 'thanks, yes', and JK genuinely felt pity for him. He was in such a sorry state, as he slowly got up to order a cab. He went to his room to get his wallet and shoes, leaving JK to write a note for Bobby, which he left on the coffee table.

The cab arrived and it was only a three-minute ride to the Prince of Wales hospital, where, strangely, it was an English doctor who saw them in A&E. JK wasn't sure why, but he had accompanied Rick with the doctor into a nearby cubicle that had a bed with a curtain pulled round for privacy. After hearing Rick's background story, the doctor decided to run some further blood tests.

Rick sat on the edge of the bed as the doctor produced a large needle from a cupboard. He had to prick Rick's arms several times as he struggled to find a vein. Rick looked down, saw some blood on his arm and then started to sway as he sat up on the bed.

'Are you going to faint?' the doctor asked him, looking concerned.

'Aye, yes… Yes, I am…' Rick said, as his eyes closed.

So then Rick fainted in the doctor's arms as he slowly lowered Rick flat on the bed.

There were certain things that, by now, JK had learned to put up with when he stayed in a hostel. Usually, he had the comforting knowledge that he wouldn't be there long anyway, and would hopefully be moving on to a better place next. It was swings and roundabouts, he figured – his luck would even out in the end.

Keeping his belongings safe in a room full of strangers; putting up with mess or a bad smell; people coming in noisily, late at night and turning the lights on. If he just had a bit of common sense, respect and consideration, then hopefully karma would be good to him over the long run. And he thought that most normal backpackers would follow that rule.

Early that morning, JK lay awake in a hostel in Kings Cross, near the big Coke sign, in the centre of Sydney. He'd put up with people being drunk in hostel dorms before – god knows he had been that person himself. This time was no different.

He had seen – and definitely heard – a sweaty, pale-skinned, chubby man, with ginger hair in a ponytail, awaken in their room with a groan. No one knew him, as he'd checked in while everyone else was out the night before.

JK soon realised he was struggling with a hangover, as he began repeating the phrase 'OH MY GOD' over and over again. His head was wrapped in his arms, hands covering his face, as he repeated his catchphrase, the words partly muffled as he dragged his fingers across his mouth. This ritual, which had started nice and early at 6am, was occasionally broken when he got up and moved to the sink in the room, groaning as he did so, and throwing water on himself.

Eventually, by 7.30am, he suddenly ran from his bed to the toilets outside where he could be heard vomiting violently. Not long after he returned to bed and fell asleep again.

During his first three weeks in Sydney in late July 2000, JK had been putting up with a variety of tiresome habits that stretched his patience to the very limit. His money had almost run out and he was now craving a break from the travel routine. JK had been waiting on his ever-unreliable brother to give him the green light to move in to his place. The possibility of this had seemed to change on a daily basis, and so he had had to find a cheap hostel in the meantime to minimise costs while looking for work.

His time in the hostel had been spent registering with employment agencies, checking hostel notice boards and the internet for backpacker house shares, and squeezing in the odd bit of sightseeing when he could.

JK now looked at his watch and realised, with dread, that he should probably get up. He breathed in a general odour of smoke, dust and damp to which he had become accustomed to throughout the hostel, although it was even worse in his room.

The smell was like a constant coat of dank, stale rain water had been painted on the walls every day using brushes that had been left to fester in mouldy cream cheese. The showers were lukewarm with no power. The toilets were a lottery as to whether they would be cleaned daily and he remembered one particularly unpleasant sick odour that had remained in one cubicle for over four days. Often, he was greeted by cockroaches that sat and waited on top of the toilets; once he saw one as big as a mouse, almost causing him to throw up – perhaps that would explain the smell, he thought.

His roommates were working in the city – not that he ever saw them. Early every morning and late every night, he was woken up as they left for work and returned from post-work drinks. Like him, they hadn't bothered with a house share and all their stuff was spread around the room in cluttered confusion – there was barely enough room for his stuff.

Then, JK smiled, knowing that an end was finally in sight. Today was the day he could check out and move into his brother's flat. And it couldn't have come any sooner, he thought.

As he sat up and stretched, he remembered the girl who had been sleeping underneath him. It was now 8.30am on a Friday, well after she had left for work and he had tried to ignore her charming daily routine. He wearily climbed down from his bunk bed, trying to tread carefully to avoid the domestic assault course confronting him. An aerosol cap used as an ashtray that was knocked over, again, smudging ash into the carpet. A discarded pair of knickers; a used plaster and a cereal bowl with lots of milk still left in it, complete with a spoon jutting over the edge.

He decided to pack his bag straight away and check out as soon as possible. He was going to get a taxi to Coogee, but not till much later. For now, he had to escape this wretched place, to get some air – somewhere, anywhere – away from there.

He walked outside, past the phone box he had used many times to chase his brother. He noticed homeless people and drug addicts standing and sitting around the area, shooting up, with their heroin needles littering the floor. Some had formed a small audience and had begun to watch an argument between a whore, with her arm in plaster, and a homeless Aboriginal man, who had grossly enlarged eyeballs that looked like they were about to pop out of his head. It had quickly escalated into a fight by the time JK, head down, had walked past.

He kept going, his backpack hanging heavily on his back, deciding that it might be his last chance for a while to explore the bustling central business district. A strong London influence reminded him of home at every corner: Victoria Street, Hyde Park, Oxford Street and Liverpool Street.

Within around twenty minutes, he had arrived at Darling Harbour, sweating and out of breath. He soon felt calmed by the sights of rich people's yachts and the fresh smells of sea salt in the air.

It had already been such an interesting city to go and explore and he was excited to do more of it over the next few months. He knew of so many things going on, market stalls, park performers, free concerts, outdoor film festivals or cultural displays.

Market stalls were now being set up for the day by the harbour and he saw a few were already open. The smell of fresh coffee and bacon lured him over to one in particular, where he bought himself some breakfast and sat on a bench nearby. As he watched people mill around, he let the flavoured steam from his cup enter his nostrils and he felt like he was gaining some control again.

A bizarre-looking bird, the Ibis, with a long curved grey beak, wandered around the pavements and park next to the water railings. This species of bird could rarely fly, and standing two-foot tall, it tentatively approached JK, clucking as it inched forward to inspect his sandwich like an alien explorer.

He shooed it away, closed his eyes and began to breathe deeply. He knew he would soon be able to relax properly, but after the last few weeks, he was tired from traipsing round what felt like a hundred soul-destroying recruitment agencies. Tired after having to wear the mask of 'yes I'll do *anything*; it's so *nice* to be given the opportunity; *of course*

I'm available' all day. Wanting to throttle those consultants who perpetuated the cycle, with their helpful plastic smiles, their friendly gleaming eyes, knowing full well that, underneath, they didn't give a rat's arse about him, only the client who was willing to pay their commission.

He finished his coffee and walked to the nearest taxi-rank. He glanced at his watch and saw it was just after 10am. He realised he would arrive at his brother's place – shortly to be his too – earlier than he had promised, but he didn't care.

After telling his taxi driver there was no rush, he was taken on a scenic route through the beach districts, but JK didn't mind. He was trying to maintain calm thoughts for as long as possible, and these sights were a crucial part of Sydney, being so near the city, and each had its own distinct appeal. He looked far to his left and, seeing the coast of North Sydney, remembered pretty Manly beach where he had already taken some surfing lessons not many days before.

They drove through Bondi, the domain of many Irish backpackers as well as those that had settled to live there for good. His final destination, Coogee beach, was smaller and quieter than the other beach areas, but it did have an impressively large bar, the Coogee Bay Hotel. He had already spent a few late nights there, including his birthday only last week, where he got to know a few of his new housemates as well as other local characters he was told would also be regular visitors to their house.

In under an hour he had almost arrived, feeling excited about his new arrangements, but the feeling was mixed with some, now customary, underlying doubts as well. He supposed, after all the experiences he had shared with his brother, even on this trip alone, it was somehow inevitable that they'd end up living together. But, he was glad to see the back of the hostel, that much he was sure of.

Yet, he couldn't help feel some nervousness about his new housemates. He had house-shared before at university, so that wasn't the issue. It was more the fact that it was Bobby who had chosen them: his brother's track record in that department had not been great, Rick being a prime example of that.

As his cab pulled up outside number 108 Rainbow Street, he could see a large handmade mural hanging over the front door that read 'Welcome Wee Jonny Boy'. He allowed himself a small grin, but bristled on the inside knowing whose idea it was. Rick would have taken delight in doing that, just to annoy JK, knowing that he hated any unnecessary attention.

He paid the driver, grabbed his backpack from the boot and walked to the front door before ringing the bell. He could hear loud dance music playing from inside.

'Here he is! JK, you're massively early, bro!' Bobby said, with a beaming smile. They embraced, as Bobby took JK's bag off him. 'You were probably just too excited to see me, weren't you? And, who can blame you?'

'Yeah, something like that. More like I just had to get out of that shitty hostel,' JK replied. 'Thanks for the welcome sign, by the way. That was Rick's idea, wasn't it?'

'I couldn't possibly say. But he is the only Scottish person here, so, you know.'

They walked through the hallway, Bobby stopping briefly to drop JK's bag in his room before they entered the kitchen. They could see into their garden where several people were dancing around a DJ standing behind some decks and speakers.

'Fucking hell, you lot are starting early. Is no one at work today?'

'Well, I took a sickie in the end. I think most people have, or took the day off anyway. It's Friday, the sun is shining and my little bro is moving in, so, I thought, why the hell not? Anyway, you'll soon get the feel for this place – they don't need much of an excuse for a party.'

A bottle of beer had been pushed into JK's hand and he was dragged outside to say hello. Rick was there, already drunk, and managed to give JK one of his trademark fake bear hugs. Their other house mate, Matt 'Matty' Jones from Cardiff, was one of the first to come over to speak to him.

'Welcome, JK. It's finally happened then! Good to have you on board,' Matty said. Like everyone else, he was wearing sunglasses, and was also shirtless, proudly revealing his stocky, muscular torso.

'Hey, Matty. Thanks, I can't believe this party is just for me,' JK said, laughing.

Rick and Matty laughed back, and glanced over at Bobby, who, awkwardly, looked into his plastic pint glass.

'Don't be too grateful – we were having the party anyway,' said Rick, with a spiteful glint in his eye. He was looking slightly healthier now that he had started to put a bit of weight back on.

'Charming, and after I took you to hospital in your hour of need,' replied JK.

'Aye, that's true. And that's why I had to do something for you, JK. Did you like your welcome sign?'

'Oh, yeah, thanks a lot for that, Rick.'

'Anyway, have you got yourself a job yet, JK?' asked Matty.

'Yep, all sorted. I start next week. Just some temp job, nothing special.'

'Like all of us, mate, no worries. Simple, menial office jobs where we know we aren't important but we don't care. You'll survive, like we all do, on a day-by-day basis, ready for your wages at the end of the week.'

'You're not selling the lifestyle to me, Matty,' said JK, smiling.

'Ah, it's easy, trust me. You can pass the day emailing or phoning your mates, afternoon naps, morning hangover recovery naps – all on work time, of course. Then get smashed every weekend, like this.'

'Aye, and you can steal all sorts of stuff too,' said Rick, interrupting. 'Bog rolls, tea bags, tea towels, stationery – whatever useful shit is easily available. Take them back home to a more deserving destination.'

'Are you even working at the moment, Rick? I thought you got fired?' asked Matty.

'Aye, you know I am. I got a new job last week, in another call centre.'

'Good, because you still owe me from last month,' Matty said, with a tone that JK could tell held a thinly veiled threat.

'Don't you worry. I'm on it, Matty-boy.'

'You better be. Anyway, JK, welcome mate. It's gonna be awesome. We've got a cosy little set-up here. It's a quick bus ride into the city for work, you already know the local pub – it's massive and shows loads of British sport – and we've got a nearby tacky night club and the freedom of the beach, which is only a mere five-minute walk away. Now, can I get anyone another beer?'

JK shook his head and, with that, Matty disappeared into the kitchen, with Rick following behind him.

'So, just watch out for her,' said Bobby, pointing out a girl in the garden. She was swaying in time with the music as two tight dark-brown hair plaits bounced off her broad shoulders. She was wearing only a light green bikini top and some brown surf shorts and lifted her arms up to the music, singing sporadic sections of the lyrics.

'Why, who's she?'

'That's Josie, a crazy girl from Leeds. You've replaced her in the house. She only moved out about a week ago. That's when I gave you the call.'

'Oh, right. Why did she leave, then?'

'She used to date Matty. He dumped her.'

'Awkward. So, why is she here now?'

'She lives with his mate, Dave O'Grady from Liverpool. You've met him, haven't you?' Bobby said, pointing out a taller, sinister-looking guy, wearing a cap, surveying the scene as he stood nearby Josie. JK nodded. 'Well, they're all mates, anyway. I'm sure after a few beers they'll have forgotten about it all.'

'You hope,' JK said, with a wry smile.

'Yeah. All that crowd, along with Rick, they really like to go for it, if you know what I mean. I joined in for a while, but I'm kinda getting a bit sick of it now.'

'Could make for an interesting evening, then?'

'You could say that,' Bobby said, leaving his sentence hanging before stopping to watch the party progress. But JK knew his brother had more that he wanted to say.

It was a small bungalow in Coogee, and it was joined to another next door. Their neighbours were also British backpackers – two girls and a boy, all from London – and were regular visitors; today was no exception. Denise and Charlotte were both from Essex, and Danny, the DJ, was from Clapham. He had provided his own decks, which, along with his dark skin, good looks and obvious musical skills, were a focal point for everyone at the party.

The sun shone brightly in the afternoon sky and, as it got hotter, Bobby grabbed his brother to help him set up a barbeque. More guests continued to arrive as the drinks flowed freely. As the afternoon progressed, despite his initial fears, JK gradually began to feel comforted by the 'home-away-from-home' feel his brother had tried to establish among the group of friends.

JK had noticed that, as was often the case with a lot of his British friends, there were a few obvious cliques within the group of party guests. Although Bobby was long-term friends with Rick, he seemed distant from Josie and most of Matty's other friends. And, at the same time, Bobby was very friendly with Danny and continuously flirted with Denise and Charlotte next door.

But JK's comfort didn't last as, inevitably, the party became more raucous. He tried his best to stay involved, chatting with a few drunken lads inside. A sport-fuelled conversation had soon escalated into actual participation along a long but narrow corridor. They rotated sports, from cricket with a tennis ball to rugby, football and then indoor surfing, where they decided to throw a 'boogie' board, a miniature surf board, along the corridor. JK abandoned that particular experiment himself, but watched as each of the other three lads would land on it, face down, before hitting the floor. During one such attempt, one of them cracked a hole in the wall, along with a fracture in his elbow, subsequently resulting in a call for an ambulance.

The evening continued unabated. The music got louder, random strangers turned up, someone produced some bongos and began to play them outside. JK had seen Denise and Charlotte doing some coke at the back of the garden under a tree, and there were open exchanges of pills between Bobby, Matty, Dave and a few of the guests.

Later, the police turned up after a neighbour made a noise complaint, which temporarily dulled the volume for half an hour. Even later, an alcohol-fuelled fight erupted. It began on a small scale when Danny, who had disappeared for a while, came back to find Matty using his decks. Danny had been quite happy for most people to share the decks but he wanted to be in control, and insisted on giving people some tips first. Of course, Matty had just piled ahead without asking him – and even though there was no damage, Danny really objected to it.

According to Bobby, who knew him well, Matty had been in a funny mood all day, being uncharacteristically aggressive towards everyone. When Bobby stepped in to stop the minor scuffle escalating further, Matty decided to give him a 'playful' slap. After

telling him to fuck off – to no avail – Bobby got annoyed quickly and then chucked a pint
of lager over Matty. Then all hell broke loose; Dave threw a punch at Bobby in return,
and Danny decided to get involved again.

In an attempt to slow things down, JK and a few of the others – including the girls –
approached en masse to surround the combatants and formed an absurd-looking swaying-
scrum. But it worked, and after Bobby had taken Matty and Dave to one side, a few
guests began to leave. Danny stuck around, resuming his duties on the decks. Matty, after
convincing Dave to go home, approached Danny to make his apologies, and not long
after, upon realising what state he was in, took himself off to bed.

With the testosterone in the party now mostly diffused, the girls resumed singing and
dancing in earnest. JK realised that he was struggling to keep up, and had a feeling that
this would be a common theme for as long as he lived with this crowd. Wanting to lie
down, he walked to his new bedroom, one he would be sharing with Bobby, only to be
confronted by the sight of an older man, in his late forties, kneeling shirtless on his bed.
He was thrusting vigorously at the waist from behind a naked Josie, on all fours, as she
faced towards JK at the door, gawking at him.

He had been introduced to the man earlier that evening, a local who lived a few
doors away on their street. He was passing by, so had just popped in to say hello. JK
stood at the door, stunned, as neither one of the couple seemed to acknowledge – or was
particularly disturbed by – his presence.

JK weighed up his options and, after a moment, backed out of the room and closed
the door behind him. He had decided the best course of action was to seek out his brother
for one last beer, in the hope that the problem might go away.

The aftermath of the party was felt by all. For JK in particular, it had been the catalyst for
the return of more insecurity and doubt – feelings that something important in his life
was now different or was about to change.

After receiving another tip-off, the police had turned up later on Saturday afternoon.
They unsuccessfully searched their house for drugs before questioning Matty and Rick,
giving them a severe warning. Unbeknown to them, Rick, Matty and Dave had all been
doing small-time drug deals among backpackers in the Coogee area, mainly down at their
local, the Coogee Bay Hotel, where so many of them congregated.

Their landlord had quickly found out also and, on the Sunday, had come round to
read the riot act – they all had come within inches of being evicted. And only a few days
later he returned again, without warning, to remove their kitchen and begin to merge their
bungalow flat with next door, the flat where Danny and the two girls lived.

Sharing a room with Bobby during all of this had created moments of unease;
something was nagging away at JK that wasn't right. They had had the odd tiff, work
was boring and money was tight, but he knew his feelings were due to more than this.

They had both recognised the brewing tension, at least. A couple of weeks later, on a
Saturday afternoon, the two brothers had decided to escape from it all by going for a long
scenic walk between Coogee and Bondi beaches. The day was slightly over-cast with a
refreshing wind that they were both grateful for, knowing it would take a good two hours
to complete the walk.

After the large sandy beach at Coogee, the coast-line varied considerably. Each
section seemed to have its own dramatic effect, the changing colours and terrain giving
specific personality traits. Dogs and their owners walked across the cliff tops with fierce
drops into the unforgiving rocks below. Smaller, intimate secluded inlets where larger
rocks were scattered among small sand banks as the sea lapped in between and over.

Families idled around, fathers standing on the big rocks to fish, mothers grabbing small children to dangle their feet in the water.

JK stopped to take a picture of the view, and, as he attempted to create some space on his digital camera, on the screen he came across a few pictures of the party.

'I don't think I've ever been to a party like that before,' said JK, as he showed his brother a picture of a drunken group shot of them all in the garden. Bobby laughed and looked back at him.

'Yeah, we've had a few in that house, but that one was certainly up there,' Bobby replied. 'I'm not sure the neighbours are going to forgive us anytime soon, either.'

'Or the landlord. We're lucky we're even still in that place.'

'Yeah, well, I don't think Rick and Matty feel like that.'

'Seriously, Bobby? You think I care about those two? After what they did, I'm glad they moved out. Don't you think it'll be better for all of us now?'

'Yes, yes. I know, but they felt like they didn't have much choice, what with all the arguments with Danny next door. Matty said he felt like he was pushed out,' said Bobby, as they continued to walk along the cliffs.

'Well, I'm not surprised. Someone must've scratched Danny's decks during the party. You know how much he loves them. And then, to top it off, he said he had some CDs nicked the next day,' replied JK.

'What, so you think Matty or Rick stole them after the party?'

'Well, maybe. Rick's certainly got previous form, hasn't he? Need I remind you of Vegas?' Bobby had rolled his eyes at the accusing look from JK, who then continued, 'But Danny stayed later at the party than both Matty and Dave. He just thought it was strange, that's all. Considering other stuff got broken or went missing from our lounge on the night.'

'Maybe. Rick certainly didn't want to stick around Danny anymore. No love lost there.'

'Did you honestly not know what they were up to this whole time?'

'I guess I did, but I just tried to ignore it.'

'Well, just imagine if the police had come sniffing around again and they were still living with us: god knows what would've happened. We would've all been evicted and we could've lost our jobs too if our employers had then found out.'

'OK, I get the point, JK. I'm not going to argue with you anymore.'

JK was stunned into silence by his brother's unusually submissive response.

'Speaking of losing our jobs, did you hear about Josie?' Bobby asked. JK shook his head in response. 'Remember that older dude that you caught her having sex with that night, our neighbour? He's married with two young kids. Somehow, his wife found out about it and then tracked Josie down. It's ridiculous to even believe this, but Josie was a supply teacher at their kids' primary school!'

'You're joking?' exclaimed JK.

'No. The wife complained about her to the school and obviously she got fired.'

'Jesus Christ! What an absolute liability that girl is. She did seem completely off the rails that night. All that booze, and the rest.'

'Yeah. She's always been doing stupid stuff like that, certainly since I've known her. I think she got worse while she was dating Matty, but he obviously saw how bad she could really get – and then decided to end it before it did.'

'Wow. Well, I hope she's OK.'

'Me too,' said Bobby, who paused momentarily to look out at the sea. JK instantly knew that he was holding something back from him. Bobby had had an air of melancholy all morning that JK recognised, purely due to its rarity over the years – such was the contrast to his usual blasé attitude to life.

'What's the matter?'

'I think… I think I made a mistake, JK.'

'What do you mean?'

'Coming out here again. With Rick, all of it.'

'What, you mean to Australia? I know you two have been here before.'

'Not just Australia. I think you were right, I shouldn't have come out here with him. Di didn't want me to, that's for sure.'

JK was shocked. It was the first time he had heard his brother doubt his own actions. Especially when it came to his travels.

'Surely, my brother, veteran of travel, is not saying he's had enough of the life?' JK said, laughing.

'Never,' Bobby said, with a restrained smile. 'But I shouldn't have left Di. We'd had a good thing going on back home. And I'm getting more and more sick of Rick.'

'He did seem pretty bad when we left you in Vegas.'

'Yeah, well, in short, since then he's been a fucking nightmare. I never told you, but after you left, I soon realised it was him that had been stealing. He kept trying the same shit, taking advantage of people by ripping them off or nicking their stuff. Makes me start to think that you might be right all along about fucking karma, because that cunt is certainly bringing us fuck-loads of the bad type, that's for sure.'

JK watched his brother silently.

'What, no "I told you so", JK?'

'Well, we've done this before, Bobby. I know you two are friends.'

'I'm not sure anymore. I'm glad he's moved out, too – I've just about had enough of him. But, the amount of drugs he's taking; you know he's been pretty unwell? I only stuck around this long because I wanted to keep an eye on him.'

'Well, at least he'll have Matty and the others to look after him now.'

'Yeah, I'm not sure they will, though. They're not exactly model citizens either. I guess that's why they get on. But I can't worry about him forever. He should know better by now.'

'Yes, he should,' JK replied, as the wind silenced their conversation. They carried on walking and JK knew his brother was still hiding something from him.

As they approached the start of Bondi beach, they came across a lower stretch of coast that had steep sand banks. The tops of the higher ground were a mixture of soil and rock underneath, the surface grass merging with sand as it got close to the edge of the banks. As it was low tide, they walked down the banks onto the flat sand in front of the sea and then turned round to get a view of the land behind them.

Just as they did, a small light-brown coloured dog trotted happily parallel to them, along the top of the bank above their heads.

'Ah, look at that little fella,' said Bobby, as they watched the terrier sit down a few feet away, mouth open and tongue softly shaking as it panted.

'He looks just like Benji, the TV dog,' replied JK.

'Yeah. He's so contented, isn't he? I wonder where his owner is?'

'Dunno, I can't see anyone,' JK said, looking up the beach.

As his short curls blew in the wind, the dog didn't seem to focus on anything. Aside from his slight panting, he didn't make a sound. He just sat and stared far out at the sea in front of them. JK noticed his collar with a pendant hanging from it; it looked vaguely familiar to him.

'I'm gonna get a picture of him,' JK suddenly exclaimed. As he got his camera into position, the dog looked JK straight in the eye and barked.

Just as they heard the click of the shutter, it was literally drowned out by a loud gush of water behind them. A large freak wave had breached against the shore just at that second and, as they turned round to look in shock, they were drenched by the huge sea-spray. Although it was a windy day, the water had been reasonably calm before that – as if it had just appeared from nowhere.

'Fucking hell!' Bobby exclaimed. They looked up at each other, dripping wet and shell shocked by the instant impact. They started to laugh, only stopping when they saw the little dog get up, shake himself off and carry on walking calmly up the beach, without so much as a huff in their direction. As he walked off, JK could just make out that his round silver pendant had a small design on it, perhaps of a tree.

'Well, thanks for warning us, mate!' Bobby called after him, laughing. The dog didn't turn back and soon disappeared from view.

'Oh shit!' JK suddenly yelled.

'What's up, mate?' Bobby replied.

'The camera. It's fucked.'

'How come?'

'I think the water from that wave got in the mechanics; the salt water has busted it up good and proper. It won't wind on; I can't extend the zoom or anything.'

'Well, maybe the photos will still be OK?'

'I hope so, that camera has been everywhere with me.'

Later that day, JK tried to get it repaired but to no avail. But, luckily, his brother had been right. He didn't lose any photos, including the last picture he had taken. It was of the dog, serenely sitting on top of the sand bank, safely enjoying the view of their impending misfortune.

A couple of weeks later, JK awoke in bed at 5am in a confused, chemically induced haze. He had recently resumed taking a diazepam prescription and, stupidly, had also had a few drinks the previous evening. It felt like he was still in a dream as his brother, who now slept in a different bedroom, had suddenly invaded his.

'Di? Diana?' his brother had shouted, as he flung open the door in the dark. JK sat up in bed, looking around and then tried to focus on his brother. He soon realised that Bobby, who had also been drinking with him last night, was now sleep walking.

'What's going on, mate?' JK slurred, fumbling to switch on his bed-side lamp.

Flustered, he sat up in the light, his hair a mess and with a startled look in his eyes. He slowly regained coherent thoughts as a dull pain started to throb in his head.

'Oh, sorry... er... sorry, mate. I just had a dream, thought someone was in here. Really sorry... night,' said Bobby, as he quickly closed the door and walked back to his bedroom, too embarrassed to hear his brother's response.

JK was unable to get back to sleep and, later that morning, finally arose after hearing cooking noises in the kitchen. He had already noticed, after living with his brother again, that each of their own habits had begun to grate on each other; the differences had become magnified and little arguments had crept into their daily routines.

He groggily wandered into the kitchen to see his brother chopping mushrooms and an onion. JK stood in the doorway, frowning at him.

'Ah, good, you're up. Fancy breakfast? I'm making an omelette,' said Bobby.

'An omelette? You never cook. What's got into you, then?' replied JK.

'Oooooh, hark at Mr Grumpy.'

'Do you blame me? That's twice you've woken me up this morning already.'

'What? Oh, yes, I'd forgotten about that. Sorry, JK. We did have a few beers, after all. I spoke to Di last night after we got home from that awful night club – what was it called again?'

'The Palace.'

'Oh yeah, how ironic. Anyway, I spoke to her just before I fell asleep, probably unconscious. So, I guess I must've been dreaming that she was with us, staying here and I got up to try and find her. I couldn't see her in my room and that's when I ended up barging into yours.'

'So, you're making breakfast for me now because you feel guilty?' JK stared back at Bobby silently for a moment, still holding the chopping knife in his hand.

'Can't I even cook my little brother breakfast? I do know how to cook a few things by now, you know?'

Bobby carried on chopping and then walked round the table past JK to the sink. All the time he held it, Bobby had noticed JK's eyes follow the path of the knife as he moved, not saying a word until he had put the knife down. He had seen this fear in JK's eyes before, and knew it wasn't fear of him, but just of an accident happening.

'Yes, I suppose Di has taught you a thing or two,' JK finally said.

Bobby handed his brother a cup of tea who then sat down at the table. Bobby stood at the sink, his back to the window.

'What's up, JK? Are you feeling alright?'

'Me? What about you?' JK snapped.

'What are you talking about?' Bobby grunted.

'You can't fool me. Something's going on with you, and it's not just about Rick, is it?'

'I don't know what you're talking about. What you see is what you get with me, same as always,' said Bobby, and he turned his back on JK to face the window.

The radio played music in the background, filling the conversation void, as Bobby beat some eggs in a jug and JK sipped at his tea, deep in thought.

'That dog was a bit strange, don't you think?' JK eventually asked.

'What dog?'

'The dog on the beach, from our walk a couple of weeks ago.'

'Oh yeah, and then the surprise wave. So, what about it?'

'The way it just sat there, as if it knew what was coming. Then, after the wave, it just fucking walked off, nonchalantly. And it didn't have an owner anywhere in sight.'

'Well, I suppose. But so what? Just a coincidence, bad luck, no?' Bobby replied.

'Really? What about its pendant – did you see it?' JK said, as his stomach started to churn.

'No, why?'

'I saw it. A silver one with a tree on it… Seem familiar to you at all?'

'Er, no, not really.' Bobby looked at him, puzzled.

'Remember Busby?'

'Our family dog? Of course I do. He went missing when I was about fourteen. What about him?'

'Well, he had the same pendant around his neck!'

'Oh please!' Bobby said, laughing out loud.

'He did! You'd remember, you loved each other, you always played with him.'

'Shut up you twat – you're just remembering what you choose to remember. You're seeing what you want to see,' Bobby said, angrily.

'So how come that dog looked straight at me – no one else – and barked, before that freak wave hit us?'

'Yes, *and*? So what? You're going to tell me it's all part of some spooky mysterious cosmic karma, aren't you?'

'No, well... yes, maybe. There was also that dog at Lake Zurich that attacked me ages ago, when I was planning this trip. Remember that? Maybe he had the same pendant too.'

'Oh, come on, I doubt it.' Bobby sighed, seeing JK's eyes glittering with a sort of fearful realisation.

'And there was another dog I came across a few months ago in Hawaii, after I'd left you and Rick. Jo-Jo and I were sitting on the beach with a couple of girls, and this dog and its owner just turned up out of the blue. He'd taught him some tricks to jump and eat sand, but this dog, he... he could read people.'

'Seriously, you should listen to yourself right now, JK. You sound ridiculous.'

'Honest to god. He knew something about my friend, Jo-Jo. He could sense bad luck in people. His owner confirmed it, as he'd done it to him too. I swear to you.'

'Are you honestly trying to tell me that you think the spirit of our lost family dog that went missing sixteen years ago is now following us around the world by inhabiting the bodies of other random dogs?'

'No, I'm not saying that at all, for fuck's sake,' JK snapped back.

'Maybe Busby's still hungry. Did we feed him enough when he was alive?' said Bobby, smirking.

'You're such an idiot. Don't you think it's a bit weird?'

'Maybe he wants to play catch just a little bit more? Or perhaps I've hidden his favourite bone all this time and he still wants it?'

'Oh, fuck you then if you can't open your mind.'

'What does it mean, then?'

'I DON'T KNOW! I'm just saying, that's all – it *could* mean something.'

'Fine. I'll drink up and start reading the tea leaves at the bottom of my cup, get on to reading my palm and then, finally, I'll stay up late to study the stars to see if I can make some sense of it all. Sit tight, I'll get back to you with an answer in the morning.'

JK sniffed in disgust and sipped his tea, observing Bobby as he cooked the omelette. After several minutes, he served up two plates and sat opposite his brother.

'Enjoy,' said Bobby, as they ate in silence. After shifting awkwardly several times, Bobby was the first to speak again.

'Well, look, now that you've told me what's bothering you, I guess I do need to get something off my chest too,' said Bobby as JK looked up at him with suspicion. 'I'm leaving. Going home,' he said, straight-faced.

'What? When?'

'At the end of the month. I booked my flight two weeks ago.'

JK didn't reply, eventually looking down, just using his fork to push the eggs around his plate.

'You're disappointed with me?'

'A bit, I guess. Not for leaving. Just for keeping it from me. I knew something was up.'

'It was hard to know how to tell you. This is your dream trip after all. And I was the one who encouraged you to do it.'

'Well, I coped without you last time, didn't I?' said JK, grimly.

'Come on, JK. Don't be like that. I've done all this travel before. It's not new for me. I'm in my thirties now. Just look at Rick. I can't end up like that, can I?'

'You're right, but why can't you just admit the real reason? That you miss Di.'
Bobby nodded, and mimicked his brother's actions, toying with his food.
'Yep, you've got me there. We're going to move in together as soon as I get back.'
'Wow. It's about time. You two have been off and on so much I've lost count.'
'I know. I'm going to make a real effort this time. No more wandering. Time for Bobby Jenkins to turn over a new leaf.'
'Uh-huh. I'll believe it when I see it,' JK said with a grin.
'It's more believable than being haunted by our old family dog though, JK, surely?' Bobby replied, returning a smile.
'Fair enough, I guess I deserve that.'
'But I mean it, JK. I'm gonna try my best for Di. I love her.'
'I know you do, Bobby,' replied JK. With the awkwardness temporarily lifted they both resumed eating.
'Despite all your good-luck nonsense, JK, I'll probably miss you. Maybe not till after I've gone, but I will, you know?' Bobby said eventually, finishing his breakfast.
'I'll miss you too,' replied JK, as he put his cutlery down. A comfortable silence followed as they sat back and stared at each other.
Suddenly, a loud thud from behind Bobby interrupted them. JK jumped, having first glimpsed something flying fast towards the window. They both stood up and peered outside, under the window. On the soil below was a large brown bird, a kookaburra. It was moving groggily, but after a few moments it righted itself, stumbled a few tiny steps and then flew off.
'Well, that's more than enough weird shit in one day for me,' said Bobby. He finished his tea, leaving the cup in the sink, and walked briskly out of the kitchen.
JK stood, frozen, continuing to stare out of the window.

Chapter Ten

Revelation at Raffles

Jonny Keane woke up peacefully on his twenty-sixth birthday. Stretching out a large double bed, he was enjoying his comfortable surroundings and permitted himself a smile. Somehow, he just felt that today would be one of good fortune. After over a year of his dream round-the-world trip, it was now 29th July 2001, and he was finally on his way back home.

He had only arrived in Singapore last night, straight from Australia, and now sat up in bed, looking over his large hotel room. It was extravagantly expensive by his standards, but he wanted to treat himself. He had achieved most of the travel ambitions he had set out to achieve and so, on balance, the past year had been a successful one – perhaps even a lucky one.

Wearing only boxer shorts, he stood up and looked at himself in a full-length mirror. He felt healthy; although he had put on weight, he was still happy with his physique given that, six months previously, you could see his bones sticking out of his torso and limbs.

He didn't mind that no one would be around to celebrate with him this evening. He had already had a good birthday send off from his friends in Australia and had pretty much had enough of the hostel 'check in, meet and greet, swap routes' routine by now.

He had always planned it that way, knowing he would be able to celebrate properly when he got back home. And, after this amount of time away, he was hoping there would be more than a few people willing to welcome him back with a beer in The Green Man pub, birthday or not.

He scratched at the messy hair on his head and face. As his stomach rumbled, he decided he would shave in the comfort of his en-suite bathroom, before taking advantage of the hotel's 'deluxe' buffet breakfast. He looked forward to it, knowing that it would be of a vastly superior quality to the standard hostel fare he was used to.

It would be a proper start to the long day ahead that he had planned. He remembered the various sightseeing recommendations he had been given, including those from his brother. It had been several months since he had last heard from him and, as he glanced at the telephone on his bedside table, he considered calling him. But he knew that it was still too early just yet – they would all still be asleep back in London.

JK had had a difficult few months in Australia after his brother had left him just under a year ago. It had been a snowball effect: settling in had been difficult for him; his depression got worse; he then stopped working for a while, having a knock-on effect on his finances.

But, gradually, his fortunes had improved. With some help from friends, old and new, he had got back on his feet. Eventually, he resumed working, started to relax and was even able to save some money for a last tour of the country before he left to go home via Asia. The last elements of his trip consisted of another two nights in Singapore, on to Malaysia for three days, then Hong Kong for four days before he would finally arrive back home. He had resolved to go to the more traditionally backpacker-friendly Thailand some other time – there would always be a future opportunity, he reasoned.

He was now in the mind-set of ticking off several easy places on the way, seeing the major sights without getting too involved in the traveller scene, and having fun without hanging around too long. He didn't want to dwell on his impending return home, knowing it would just stir up bad feelings again.

But those feelings were never too far from the surface, and had bubbled even closer to it since he had left Sydney: the realisation that he wouldn't have this lifestyle for much longer; that his escape from the 'real world' was about to end. Now, a bottomed-out emptiness still lingered, deep inside of him, like a predator waiting to pounce. He thought, was this the feeling that his brother had been trying so hard to avoid for so long? And yet, Bobby had managed to survive and had now even returned to 'normality' unscathed.

Shaking his head at his reflection, he walked on to the bathroom. All he had to do was wash those feelings out of his system and enjoy his last few remaining days of travel. He had to make the most of his lucky streak while he was still in it. For now, the future could wait.

The taxi pulled up opposite the lobby of the world-famous hotel. JK's morning of sightseeing had progressed at a leisurely pace and now that he was here, he couldn't help feel drawn into the grandeur and the history of the place. It was an experience he knew he had to indulge in, especially on his birthday. He also thought it was the ideal location to continue his pretence as a wealthy tourist.

A long time ago he had heard his mum talking about it with his brother. It was somewhere their father had always wanted to visit; it was a shame that they had never got to see it together. Since then, his brother had been – and raved about it – and whenever he had planned any of his own travels, JK had always wanted to squeeze in a trip to Singapore, mainly just to see this.

He stood next to a phone box facing the lobby across the road, and looked at the time. It was 4.30pm local time, and so he knew that his brother would be awake by now back home. He opened the door and retrieved Bobby's home phone number from his pocket. As he dialled, he took in the magnificent view from the front of the hotel.

A regally uniformed police guard waited outside the main entrance. With his white helmet and blazer, adorned with brass buttons and a red diagonal belt across his chest, he was an imposing figure, a throw-back to an era of imperial dominance.

'Hello?' Bobby's weary voice eventually answered.

'You'll never guess what I'm looking at right now,' replied JK.

'Not another fucking spider, JK! You're not that lucky with phone boxes, are you?' Bobby's tone had changed to pleasant surprise as he recognised JK's voice.

'No spiders this time, thankfully! How's it going Bobby?'

'Good, mate, good. So, where the hell are you, then?'

'Standing outside Raffles Hotel.'

'Ah, that's great, mate. Very impressive. I take it you've not had the world-famous Singapore Sling yet then?'

'No, but I will later. I thought I'd just take a walk around the place, see the sights first, and then have a drink to celebrate after.'

'Sounds good. You've got to have one in the Long Room, like I did, years ago. It's tradition now. But wait, to celebrate what?' Bobby paused, then said, 'Oh shit, happy birthday, JK!'

'Thanks. You forgot, didn't you?'

'No… well, maybe. Anyway, I knew you were coming home soon – when is that exactly?'

'On 7th August. Not long now.'

'Oh, yeah. It's been ages since we spoke last. Was it February?'

'Yeah, something like that,' JK replied, bluntly.

'Sorry about that, but I've been pretty busy with Di, you know.'

JK paused and just smiled, inwardly annoyed at his brother's casual disregard for not hearing from him for so long.

'Of course. How's it going with Di, anyway? Settled in properly at your new flat now?'

'Yeah, fine. Much better now. It was hard living at her place the first few months, we almost split up. Did I tell you that last time?'

'Yeah, I remember,' JK said, with a heavy tone of cynicism.

'You don't have to say it like that, JK; it's different this time. Getting our own place was the best thing we could've done – we've been so much better together since then. It's been about seven months now. When you get back, you'll have to come over.'

'Yeah, that would be great. I'll be staying at Mum's to start with anyway, so I'll probably need a break soon enough.'

'Definitely. So, how are you, then, JK? Are you still feeling OK at the moment? You would've let me know if you'd felt any worse again, wouldn't you?'

'I'm fine. Actually, I'm good, thanks. I've had loads of fun going up the coast of Australia with mates over the last few weeks, but I'm also pretty tired of the whole travel thing now. I think I'm ready to come home. Another week to go, Malaysia next, then Hong Kong.'

'Fantastic, mate. I'm glad to hear it. Enjoy it while it lasts – let me tell you, it'll feel different when you get back. The novelty of being home doesn't last that long once you realise you've got to get a proper job and lead a grown-up life. It hurts!'

'Well, I'll cross that bridge soon enough – it's got to end eventually, right?' said JK, quickly. He stared out across the entrance to the hotel and watched a car pull up outside. Enjoying his chance to observe, he watched the uniformed guard nod to two men in suits as they got out of their chauffeured car and entered.

'Anyway, mate, I'd better get going. I just thought I'd say hi. It's been great to catch up,' continued JK.

'Yeah, cool, thanks for ringing, mate. Happy birthday again and I'll see you in a few days.'

'See you, Bobby.'

'Take care, JK. Bye.'

Replacing the receiver, JK felt elated at accomplishing his goal. He was glad he had called his brother, and was hopeful about returning home and getting on with a normal life again. Why on earth should I be worried, he reasoned. It was time to move on. Time to find the next high. Time for a drink. With renewed confidence he walked across the road to the entrance of Raffles Hotel.

The more JK had read about the hotel, and the country, the more it had fascinated him. It was built in 1887 and was named after Sir Thomas Stamford Bingley Raffles, an official of the British East India Company, who, some sixty odd years before, had also founded Singapore. Despite being the smallest country in South East Asia, it was one of the wealthiest, due to significant foreign investment and government-led industrialisation. A thriving, modern economy based in part on its strategic location – not that different to its origins as a trading post settlement on the 'spice route' during Raffle's East India Company days.

JK walked round the hotel grounds which were bustling with tourists, and looked up against the clean whitened walls, eventually coming upon a central courtyard. An outdoor restaurant interspersed with tropical gardens looked like a satisfyingly expensive place to eat, but that was the last thing on his mind.

There was enough historical detail surrounding him to delve deeply for hours but, instead, he was content to peruse with a customary check of the prep-reading he had already done. The museum, the Victorian-style theatre, the magnificent and vast lobby with its polished floor and immaculately mannered and poised staff.

He walked into the famous Bar & Billiard room, surrounded by British colonial-era luxury, among fine dark teak tables and chairs, smooth and polished, yet deceptively comfortable. In this huge open room, shiny-grey marble surfaces confronted him and huge white curtains draped the length of the high windows. To his left was the bar – brass plated fittings running along its length as well as at the pump handles – which was manned by two men who were part of a small army of uniformed staff efficiently taking care of business around the room. They all stood proudly in matching black waistcoats, bow ties and trousers, with immaculately ironed white shirts underneath.

JK exited the room and followed signs to the Long Bar. Eventually, he came across a staircase, walked up and then strode through a dark wooden double door frame. The famous bar confronted him. Long it most certainly was, stretching down the whole of the right side of the room, around seven metres or so. As he stared across the seating area, the room had a hazy, almost dream-like appearance.

A sweltering heat lay heavy in the air. Large ceiling fans slowly revolved above his head. Light entered through the window's red blinds. Wooden trellis-style partitions created illusions of alcoves between the tables that lined the edges of the room. Strewn across the entire wooden floor were thousands of discarded peanut shells. It was as if someone had flicked a switch in the room, slowing the rate of time, providing a bewildering yet appealing vision, all at once.

Once again, bar staff with black waistcoats were standing behind brass-plated pumps, watching customers around the room. One of them, while simultaneously drying a fine crystal class, caught JK's eye and returned a smile with a courteous nod. JK felt ever so slightly more important.

He saw a vacant seat at the bar and made his way towards it. He knew what he wanted and it was pretty obvious that the barman would know too. He was after all, a tourist rather than a standard customer, and the Singapore Sling had to be tried. Bobby would never let him hear the end of it if he didn't.

'Afternoon, sir,' said the barman. 'What'll it be?' he continued, with a knowing look.

'Well, it'll have to be the Singapore Sling, I think,' JK said, trying not to sound too obvious, as he made himself comfortable on the high seat.

'Very good, sir.' JK was impressed with how sincere the barman sounded, quickly realising he would probably have had months, if not years, of practice. As the barman carried on mixing the drink, JK saw him steal a glance at the guide book poking out of his small rucksack, before continuing his task.

JK looked down the length of the bar and at the various bottled spirits and glasses in racks spread across polished dark wood and brass fittings. He was fascinated by a picture of a tiger, knowing that they were now extinct in this country, that hung on the back wall, in between the bar level and the top shelf of glasses.

'Did you know, this world-famous drink was invented by Ngiam Tong Boom, a local bar tender, between 1910 and 1915?' the barman informed JK, as he shook the contents of the cocktail and began pouring into a tall glass. Again, JK couldn't work out if it was a genuine attempt to strike up idol chit-chat or whether it was all part of a practised speech for tourists.

'I did not,' replied JK, politely.

'Well, here you go, sir. Enjoy,' the barman said, as he added a cherry and pineapple to the top of the glass.

'Thanks,' said JK, as he took a sip of the bright pink liquid. 'Wow, I actually quite like this. I don't normally like sweet drinks – remind me again, what's in it?'

'Gin, cherry brandy, grenadine, pineapple juice, Cointreau and maraschino cherry.'

'Well, it's all very good, thank you,' JK said, enjoying his new-found relaxation, and deciding to indulge the barman some more. 'Say, tell me. That tiger picture behind you there, what's the story with it?'

'Yes, I often get asked about that. Well, this very bar was where the last surviving tiger of Singapore was shot and made extinct in 1902. It had escaped from a nearby "native show" and was chased underneath the bar. Or so legend has it, anyway.'

They continued a pleasant conversation: the sights of the city; the rest of JK's travels; his future plans. Eventually, JK let slip that it was his birthday, mostly in the hope of a free drink.

'So, your star sign is Leo, then?' asked the bar-man in delight.

JK nodded, intrigued at the reaction.

'Ah, so, did you also know that Singapore comes from the Sanskrit words "Singa", meaning lion, and "Pura", meaning city?' JK shook his head. 'Allegedly, a lion was spotted on the shore by the first settlers, even though lions have never lived here – so it was more than likely to have been a tiger, not a lion.'

Again, JK remained silent, as he stared back in curiosity.

'Leo!' said the barman suddenly, looking past JK.

In confusion, JK turned around to see an older man in a crumpled cream suit approaching the bar from one of the corner tables. He wore round spectacles that had brown-tinted glass, and JK couldn't quite tell if he was a tourist or a local.

'Hello there, my friend,' the man said in a soft, but slightly mixed British accent, smiling broadly.

'How can I help you, Leo? Having a good time? Enough drinks for everyone?'

'Ah yes, we're grand. I think we're off soon, so the good lady wife has sent me over to pay the bill, and who am I to argue with her, I ask you?'

'Ah, you're a funny man, Leo. I'll get your bill. Are you coming back tomorrow?'

'No, not this time. We're flying back home. Gotta go and pack, you know.'

'Shame. Hey, where did your American friend go?'

'Him? Oh, you know, he had to go. Actually, can you do me a great favour there, please, my friend? Could you pass him this if you see him, in case he comes back?'

Sheepishly, the man passed a business card across the bar. Underneath his suit jacket he wore a striped shirt and a badly fastened tie. He ran his hand across his head to smooth a side parting, flattening his brown but greying hair. Looking at his skin, tanned and time-weathered, JK placed him in his late fifties, and was somehow fascinated by him.

'No problem. Here's your tab,' said the barman, as he handed over a receipt on a silver tray to Leo, who removed his spectacles to view the bill.

'How much?!' He raised his eyebrows, feigning shock-distaste.

He caught JK staring at him and smiled back – a broad, closed mouth grin that stretched wide across his face as they made eye contact. And that's when JK noticed the man's eyes: they were amber coloured. A thought entered JK's mind and hit him cold, but in an instant, he returned the briefest of smiles and then turned away.

'How about our normal arrangement: half price for cash, my good friend?' Leo joked to the barman, as he replaced the spectacles on his head.

'Maybe next time, sir.'

'Ah yes, maybe next time, the same old answer. Well, the next time I come to Singapore, I will hold you to that.'

He fished around in his pockets and removed various receipts and coins, to finally find his wallet, paying his bill in notes.

'You keep the change now, and thanks a lot. I must go, as I think the wife is about to kill me!'

'Thank you, Leo, make sure you come back. Goodbye.'

'Bye now.'

He warmly shook the barman's hand and walked towards the exit where a striking looking Asian woman stood waiting, impatiently. She was dressed elegantly in a long, formal black dress with a red and orange shawl around her back and shoulders. It was hard to tell her exact age – but she had clearly aged much better than her partner.

Her long black hair stretched back away from a face that accentuated her strong, beautiful looks. Only an over-heavy application of make-up belied the fact that she was probably ten years older than she wanted to appear. She gave Leo a stern look as he reached her side. She turned around and they walked through the exit and disappeared, side by side.

JK had been completely transfixed by this stranger who had seemed so familiar. He looked back at the barman, who was still smiling at the now empty doorway, for inspiration. Upon noticing JK's stare, he resumed his normal service.

'Such a nice man. So funny, very funny. Shame to see him go.'

'Oh? Where's he going?'

'Home to Thailand. Bangkok, I think.'

'Thailand? He sounded English, or British at any rate.'

'Yes but I think he's been living there for almost twenty years maybe? He got married to a Thai lady. That was his wife with him.'

JK calculated in his head. If it was twenty years, that would be 1981 – just around the time when his father had died.

'So, why was he here? As a tourist?'

'No, business. They met a few people in here over the past few days. Singapore locals, mostly, but some Americans too. I don't think it went well, though. All their visitors seem to go quite quickly, very short meetings. His wife always seemed annoyed. "Lenny, you no good", "Lenny, why you always so stupid, always joking with them, they not take you seriously". She's miserable – luckily, he was the funny one. Maybe not so good for his business though, no? I think she liked to spend his money. I think it's not so good to work with your wife–'

'Wait a minute, you said she called him "Lenny"? I thought his name was Leo?'

'Yeah, it is, but she called him Lenny. I don't know why. Why are you so interested?'

The barman looked at JK with distrust now, concerned at the level of enthusiasm on his face.

'I dunno. I think he… I think I may know him. What do they do?'

'Something like engineering. Consultant, maybe? Here, I have his card.'

The card. JK had forgotten about it. The barman passed it to him to inspect.

On one side was a logo, a lion ready to pounce, with the company and owners' names. On the reverse was a Thai address and phone number.

Automotive? Could this Leo Martin, 'Lenny', really be who JK thought he was?

When, only moments ago, JK had looked him in the eyes – those amber eyes – it had immediately ignited some buried, unspoken recognition, deep inside of him.

Admittedly, he was clean shaven rather than bearded. Although he was shabbily dressed, he was still a lot smarter than JK could remember. He had tidier, if much greyer, hair. His hands were cleaner. But he had the same stupid smile. The same habits, fussing around with junk in his pockets. And the same disarming patter. Lenny.

The barman was becoming agitated as JK asked more questions. For all his expertise in 'friendly barman chat', he didn't know where Leo and his wife were staying in Singapore. JK told him he was going to keep the card and the barman didn't argue, seeing the intensity of his conviction.

JK had no way to confirm that this random stranger – with the bad suit and the smartly dressed but imposing Thai wife – that he had seen for approximately one minute on his twenty-sixth birthday in a bar in Singapore, was, in fact, the first view of his father since he supposedly died around twenty years ago on 10th April 1981. He only had his business card, and not enough money left to buy a ticket to Thailand and find him.

But he just knew it was him.

JK left the 'Lion City' as planned, and spent a few more days soaking up further Asian sights on backpacker autopilot-mode. He saw them, but didn't take any of them in: Jade, monkeys, temples, markets, neon. What did it matter now, anyway?

After over a year on his dream trip, going round the planet, across several countries and numerous flights, that one moment in Raffles Hotel had meant that he now knew less about his world than at any other point in his entire life to date. He had almost beaten his father's list of countries by now: what an achievement, but what did that stupid list even mean anymore?

With each remaining flight, each train, each bus or taxi journey taking him closer to home, he had more time to stew over what it could mean. Round and round in his head, the thoughts circled.

Was it true? Why did it happen? What did it mean? Was he still lucky?

Finally, he did arrive back home, to London Heathrow airport. And, after all those journeys, for the first time, his backpack had been lost in transit between connecting flights. He smiled bitterly at this final twist.

His mum had decided to meet him there, weeping in happiness when she saw him. Cry, shout, scream, punch, rip his hair out, collapse – it felt like he wanted to explode with emotion too. But he did none of these things; he was too confused to even know where to start. It was intoxicating – his brain had become so numb, trying to understand what he now knew, that he just didn't know how to respond to her. He certainly couldn't tell her; instead, he could only manage a stunned silence.

But this wasn't the end of Jonny Keane's journey; it was just the start of a new one. Over the next few years, uncertainty, depression, disillusionment and desperation awaited him.

Part Three

'Then my dream changed again at sixteen years of age – but for the final time. It starts and once more I see a light appear out of the nothingness, growing brighter and brighter as it draws towards me so that I can see the outline of the tree. The background light is muted this time and I can eventually see dark clouds swirling behind as if in the midst of a storm. But the clouds do begin to disappear.

A clearer sky remains and yet the sun is not in view this time. In the backdrop of dull greys, yellows, low on the horizon, merge with browns darkening at the top of the sky. The sun is setting and, as the clouds continue to disperse, it becomes an increasingly dramatic spectacle. Browns split into reds in scores of different hues, dividing into orange streaks that layer into blue and yellow, struggling to stay atop the horizon. Suddenly, the whole sky turns red, with the black silhouette of the Acacia tree arresting in the forefront.

With this extraordinary backcloth, I begin to fly once more. Even as I am rising up above and past the tree, the sun has not yet set; a red blanket continues to coat the sky. I feel cold, a wind cuts through to my bones and a shrill whistle penetrates my ear drums as I soar, looking down at the dark surfaces below. Save for the wind, the landscape is silent and the more distance I travel, the more afraid I feel.

Then, the silence is shattered with a roar of such terrifying volume that I stop moving instantly, the sound of death echoing around me. Finally, the sky turns from red to black as nightfall sets in, and as I stay suspended in mid-air in the shock of the moment, a small tear forms in my eye. But then I am falling straight down. I hurtle towards the ground in a second but there is no impact.

Instead of lying on the ground, I am hovering just above to see three lionesses and their already conquered prey. In between these three ruthless killers lies a wildebeest, hopelessly outnumbered, bleeding from a fatal wound, its legs still thrashing in the last throes of death. Then, in a flash of violence, they launch their final attack. A frenzy of fur and limbs as claws smash down and jaws lock tight. Blood flashes in every direction, the sound of ripping flesh, razor sharp teeth appearing through the slaughter, tendons stretching and snapping; the lions gorge to their satisfaction.

In among the sapping heat, I feel nauseous at the spectacle but my concentration is broken as I hear another roar from further away. I fly away from the scene of carnage towards the roar as it sounds again. As I get closer, I notice that it is a muted, weak, almost dismal sound. Behind a rock and in a pool of mud, I eventually come to the source: an aged male lion.

It is a wretched scene. The once great and mighty king of the pride now lies sick and motionless. Covered in scars, his tatty mane is muddy and matted; his tired eyes look sad and resigned to his fate, their glorious amber centre faded, no sparkle remains. Alone and unwanted, no lions respond to his pitiful calls. They become his last words as he draws his final breath.

But before I have time to grieve for the departed beast, I am suddenly transported back to the tree. A cold light that cannot be explained, hauntingly bright and vivid, shines from behind it. Transfixed, my view of the scene begins to diminish once more as the foreground is swallowed up by the darkness. The final image – it still recurs in my mind even now, even though the dreams stopped after a couple more years – is of piercing white light illuminating the ethereal Acacia tree. In black silhouette, it lingers and then vanishes. Then I awake from the darkness.'

Chapter Eleven

A Marriage of Inconvenience

It was September 2004, on a cold Tuesday morning, when JK leapt out of the bed he shared with his sleeping girlfriend. As he swiftly ran to throw up in the bathroom next door, the tiny bedroom in her dingy North London flat gave her little sound protection. He heard her curse, screaming his name, and he knew instinctively that the end of their relationship was imminent. He ran his head under the cold tap and wiped his mouth, dreading the conversation that awaited him.

'Do you know what time you got home last night?' Laura snapped at him, now sitting up in bed, watching with menace as he wearily walked through the door.

'I dunno – what time is it now?' he replied, sighing.

'It's 7am. You've only been asleep – or unconscious, anyway – for three hours,' she continued, staring at him intently, as he slowly climbed back into bed next to her.

'Yeah, look, I'm really sorry I came home so late and so drunk.'

'Drunk? Late? It was 4am on a Tuesday morning and you could hardly string a sentence together. There's something wrong with you, Jonny, don't you think?'

'Oh, for god's sake. I've just woken up, I'm knackered, I've got a banging headache and I'm going to be late for a job I can barely stand thinking about. Do we really have to have this conversation right now?'

'No, no. It's fine, Jonny. You just carry on living in denial. No need to worry about your behaviour at all – it's perfectly normal,' she said, sarcastically, as she angrily got up from bed. JK turned over, facing away in an attempt to ignore her, before she continued. 'By the way, you were crying uncontrollably, again. And you still don't want to talk about it. It really is quite scary.'

JK had met Laura in March last year at the wonderfully named night club Eros in Enfield. She worked for an impressive advertising agency in central London and knew all the exciting bars in town. He had used her as an emotional crutch for the last eighteen months; he knew she was just as selfish as he was and, beyond her beauty, he couldn't find much substance to the girl at all.

'Nothing to say for yourself at all? Perhaps you have deep and meaningful conversations with your mysterious work colleagues?' she said.

'What's so mysterious about them? You've met them.'

'Yeah, only once or twice, maybe. I guess they must be as equally fucked-up as you, seeing as you're out all the time with them.'

'Well, Laura, you're not exactly perfect yourself, are you? We've all got issues. In fact, we both share quite a few,' he said, pointing at the bottle of pills on top of her dresser.

'Yeah, fine, but at least I try and talk about mine. You just fucking drink. Or cry. Or go off and meet random old family members or people from your past who you haven't seen for twenty years. What are you looking for, JK?'

'I'm not looking for anything. Just because you make a living trying to manipulate people's thoughts it doesn't make you an amateur fucking psychologist, you know?'

'Fuck you, Jonny. You're hiding something. What else am I supposed to think?'

'I don't know. Think what you like. It's my family, it's my business.'

'Your business? What are we doing, JK? We've been going out for a year and a half and the most commitment you can make to me is one or two nights a week, as long as your mates aren't around, or there's no sport on TV. Yet you think you have the right to just turn up at my flat whenever you like, as if it was yours. You can't have it both ways. We just fuck but you don't ever talk about personal stuff.'

'Like what?'

'Well, what about your health? Are you still hallucinating, seeing people?'

'That was one time,' JK replied, shaking his head.

'You passed out. It was scary. It's not normal.'

'My doctor said it's a side effect of the meds.'

'Well, we still don't talk about your family, anyway. You hardly ever mention them.'

'Just calm down, Laura. Look, OK, I'm sorry. I was out of order, fine. Is that what you want to hear?'

'I just think we should be doing something more than this. I don't know where it's going. We could be living together by now.'

'This again. What else do you want from me? Marriage? Kids? Why don't we retire early and move down to Eastbourne right now and just be done with it?'

'God, I'd really like to kill you sometimes. Now you're being ridiculous. Moving in together wouldn't be so weird, would it? Some of your friends have done it. Whereas you seem to have a collection of stuff spread out between your place, your mum's, your friends' and here. Maybe you should try to settle down; it might sort out your issues. I mean, just look at your brother. I used to think he lived in more of a dream world than you, and now he's about to get married.'

'I'm not even thirty yet, what's the rush?' he replied, deadpan.

'Oh, fuck off, JK. You might want to keep day dreaming about travelling round the world again, but we're working full time now. Just because you're incapable of having a mature conversation.'

'Can't we talk about this later, after work?' JK groaned, trying to bury himself under the duvet, only igniting further anger in Laura.

'Oh yes, of course, sure. You just tell me when you're ready. I'll tell you what, why don't you take a bit more time to think about it. Have all morning, or why not all day? Actually, come to think of it, you can have all fucking year if you like – I've had enough of your bullshit and that fucking chip on your shoulder. You can't see what's good for you and what isn't.'

'Yeah, that's it, Laura, go on, just keep going. That's some great melodrama you've got going on there–'

Shrieking her annoyance, she turned to her dressing table, grabbed a handful of assorted beautifying paraphernalia and launched it towards JK's head. He ducked just in time. Hearing the objects smack against the wall, he looked down to see a small nail varnish bottle, a nail file and her razor drop beside him in bed.

'Throwing a fucking razor blade at me will certainly help the situation, though,' he said.

'Just shut up! Why are you always so fucking rational? If only you could be so decisive about what you wanted from your life, maybe you wouldn't hate yourself so much!'

As well as selfish, the beautiful Laura was extremely intelligent. He couldn't argue with her logic; that one statement sobered him up in an instant as he sat up.

'OK, that's what you want, is it? I'll give you fucking irrational then. You're dumped. I've had enough, that's it. How about that? Irrational enough for you?'

Silence. He knew that he was making the right decision. Laura saw the clarity and sincerity in his eyes. As he then saw the subsequent hurt in hers, he knew she was far too proud to cry impulsively.

'Fine,' she mumbled.

'I'll get ready to go and then you won't see me again,' he responded quickly, so as not to lose any of the intent of his earlier words.

'Good! And I want all of your stuff gone as well, or I'll be chucking it out of the fucking window.'

'Fine with me,' he replied, standing up. He hurriedly got dressed, stumbling around the bedroom, packing up the odd thing he could remember that was his: CDs; deodorant; a book; a jumper. There was probably more stuff, but he didn't care – she could keep, chuck or burn anything else as appropriate.

Eventually, as he stood at the bedroom door, he turned back to see tears forming in her eyes, and he felt a twinge of doubt as she began to speak.

'OK, well, have a nice life and now fuck off, you stupid bastard. You moan about your life but I could've made the difference. You had a good thing going with me and now you've just wasted it. You know that, don't you? You've just thrown it away.'

Any guilt he had quickly disappeared as her arrogance washed over him.

'I'll try not to lose any sleep over it,' was his cold reply – it was all he could manage.

'Fuck you, twat.'

Without any further hesitation, he walked out the front door and slammed it shut. He wouldn't see Laura again for a long, long time. Walking to the nearest tube station, he returned to his place, only a few stops away in Hampstead, to shower and go back out again. Back on the tube, back to work, back to kill more time in the office of a meaningless job until the evening, when he could drink again, to block out the nagging questions his heart kept asking his head.

He sat listening, frustrated, twisting the glass of champagne he held at its stem, as the lengthy speech in the background continued to its inevitable emotional climax.

JK accepted that he was jealous it was not him standing up there right now, entertaining a hundred or so guests at his brother's wedding. But it was more than simply envy of the choice of best man Bobby had made. JK knew that he perhaps hadn't been in the best of mental health of late, but even so, where was the family loyalty? After all the time they had spent travelling together, after everything they had been through.

He stared around at the guests, unable to block out the words he could hear. The more he heard, the more contempt he felt, for both the speaker and all those listening now, believing any of the lies they were hearing.

Rick Marshall. He could still barely believe it was him standing up there as he listened to his slow, drawn-out monologue. He had been back in town for at least a year, yet no one had told JK about his return until recently.

He still looked and sounded ill, more so than JK had remembered. His smart navy suit hung loosely off him, a baggy white shirt underneath a skinny neck. His head was still shaven, the grim tattoos still visible on his neck. His signature intense stare, previously only deployed when suitably excited, was now a constant fixture on his face, as if a switch inside had been left on too long and was now permanently broken.

Rick clutched the couple of pages of paper that he read from, slurring and stumbling over his words, mostly in a monotone. The audience appeared to forgive his clear lack of public-speaking skills as the content seemed to come from the heart.

'Sorry, ladies and gentlemen, but I won't be telling you about any of the funny stories we've had together. Not today. Of course, there's loads, but the chances are that if you've ever met either of us before, you'll probably have heard the best ones already,' he said, looking up to smile. 'I'd rather tell you about how Bobby has saved my life. Several times, in fact.'

As Rick paused, JK looked at his face again, seeing tears well up. JK shook his head in disbelief and sighed loudly. But no one had heard; there was an empty seat next to him where his ex-girlfriend Laura had due to be his guest, and the rest of his table were all listening intently as Rick continued.

'I got into some trouble in Australia a few years ago, and behaved like an ass. Sorry, folks, but it's true. Understandably, Bobby almost gave up on me. He left and went home without me. But a year later, after I had hit rock bottom, when I was stealing, addicted to drugs, booze and more besides, and I had driven all my other friends away, he called me from England. He still cared, when he didn't have to. He had a great life. He had moved in with his wonderful wife – and doesn't Diana look beautiful today, everyone?' Rick said, flatly. Yet his words had still prompted a round of applause, while JK rolled his eyes.

'But it didn't end there. I came home, but was still in a bad way. He literally dragged me into a rehab clinic. Which I quit several times, but he kept convincing me to go back. And eventually I stayed long enough to get healthy again. I've left now, and I haven't looked back; I've been clean ever since.' Tears were rolling down his face as Rick turned and stared vacantly at Bobby to his left, raising his glass up. 'So, I just wanted to say thanks, Bobby. Thanks for saving my life, and thanks for being the best friend a man could ever need.' Rick took a sip as everyone in the audience applauded, and JK could even see a few tears being shed.

'Oh, please,' JK snarled, under his breath, but loud enough to receive some strange looks from the people on his table. Bobby had stood up to embrace Rick before, finally, they both sat down. The master of ceremonies appeared and called an end to the speeches and the reception venue staff began serving the wedding breakfast.

JK had long since finished his champagne and so downed yet another glass of wine, looking at the now empty bottle on the table with surprise. His fellow table companions, still on their first glass since they had sat down for the speeches, all knew each other, and yet they still looked at him with annoyance.

He didn't feel comfortable in this setting, even with his work friends who surrounded him. Normally they would have delighted in matching his drinking pace, but now, with their partners in tow and with the formality of such an occasion, their behaviour was more restrained than usual. He could feel their judgement crawling over him, especially from their partners, who he knew less well.

Over the last year or so he had been fascinated and drawn to these characters he worked with, a strange mixture of personalities and classes: one dreaming, eco-friendly northerner stuck in a stalling career; a straight-talking socialist from the Midlands who was trapped in a loveless relationship; and a conservative, public-schooled southerner whose arrogance and womanising masked his resentment at a failed rugby career.

Although they were all so different, JK could draw parallels to his own life, feeling pity and finding solace in equal measure at their various plights, their dissatisfaction with their lives.

But today he was losing patience; he was sick of receiving strange looks from everyone. A few tables along, an old family friend had been watching him intently. The man had an unnerving presence, with his scraggly mop of white hair and a deep scar down the left of his reddened face, where the eye it penetrated was left with a dull, grey veneer. It was a stare that made most people uncomfortable, even JK, who knew him after instigating a meeting with him a year ago to get answers on his father's death. He hadn't expected his brother to invite him to the wedding, though, and on seeing him arrive, he had immediately been caught off guard.

And he had another, more subtle, female observer on a different table. He was sure that her intentions were very different – more pleasant, he hoped – based on the brief glances she repeatedly offered him. She sat with some of Di's friends, including a familiar face, Georgie Shah. JK hadn't seen her in years, and had spoken to her briefly earlier to find out she now had a long-term boyfriend who was with her at the table. But despite their common link, he still had no idea who this mysterious girl was. She was unknown and therefore intriguing to him.

'Didn't you enjoy the speeches, JK?' said the curly haired, deep-thinking bohemian, Tom, sitting to JK's left. He was the most conciliatory of JK's work friends, always the first to try and defuse a situation.

'They were OK, I guess. The father of the bride was good,' he replied.

'Wow, that's a bit harsh on your brother, mate,' said Jimmy, sitting opposite, a man of questionable moral standards but who was always very friendly and talkative.

'He was good. But the groom has to talk glowingly about his wife, and hasn't got much licence to go off-script. He's much funnier in person.' Inside, JK had to conceal the annoyance he felt towards his brother for barely mentioning him and their own travel experiences, let alone the fact that he had not made a single reference to their supposedly departed father.

'Well, that best man's speech was lovely, I thought. Very refreshing that he didn't descend into embarrassing stories and macho-bravado humour,' said Jimmy's girlfriend, Helen, stuffily.

'Oh, come on, babe. It was a bit wet, wasn't it? The best man speech is supposed to be funny. It's tradition.' Jimmy replied to her.

'Would have to agree with you there, old boy,' said David, the last of JK's work friends. He had been public schooled, was tall and good looking and had a commanding aura, often correctly interpreted as arrogance. 'What about you, JK? I didn't really get the sense you liked it either. It should've been you, am I right?'

'I don't know about that, but I've known Rick a long time and, well, I just found it hard to believe him,' he replied.

'People can change. He seemed genuine enough to me,' said Helen. JK noticed Jimmy roll his eyes and knew that he was just as uncomfortable as he was. Jimmy had been having an affair with a girl in the office for months; all his colleagues knew, and he was living on borrowed time with his long term-girlfriend he sat next to now.

'Yeah, well, I know him pretty well and he has plenty of experience at lying. Also, I think I saw him sneak some champagne down earlier today,' JK replied with growing annoyance.

'Really, are you sure that's not just jealousy talking? I mean, why aren't you sat at the top table, anyway?' Helen continued, abruptly.

'Woah, hun,' said Jimmy, 'there's no need for that.'

'It's OK, mate. You all know about my break-up with Laura last week,' JK said, as he gestured at the empty chair to his right. 'They couldn't really put me up there if I wasn't best man, could they? Someone had to look after you reprobates, anyway.'

JK looked to his left, glancing over to the table where the girl he had noticed earlier was sat. He had caught her looking over at him again and so he decided to smile. She returned a brief smile before re-joining a conversation with the man she sat next to. JK wondered if it was her partner and felt a rush of blood to his cheeks. As his head began to sway, he hurriedly poured some water into a glass and drained the contents.

'So, forgive the stupid question, but why is our table called *Glengarry, Glen Ross*?' said the pretty young brunette sitting next to David. She was new to their group – JK couldn't recall her name – the latest date in a long line of pretty young brunettes that David had worked his way through. Although her current state of sobriety was still some way ahead of JK's, she was attempting to accelerate her integration with the group by drinking at a rapid pace.

'It's the table theme – they're all movies,' said Helen, rolling her eyes in disdain.

'Yes, I get that, but why this one for our table?' she replied, sheepishly.

'Aha, that's the best question,' said Veronica, Tom's French-Caribbean girlfriend. 'Probably because these four men are extremely untrustworthy employees, always under pressure, no? The four average salesmen, that's what you like to call each other, isn't it?' She smiled mischievously as she looked around at them all, one by one, waiting to see who would react first.

JK could never tell if Veronica actually liked them or not. She had always come across as being quite aloof, but having said that, the few times she did mix socially with them, she was extremely funny. Of all the couples, she was the most suited to her partner.

'Well, I'm not sure we're under that much pressure. It's not as if any of us have climbed the career ladder that high yet,' said Tom.

'Yeah, we'd have to actually like our jobs for that to happen,' said JK. 'Oh, and I think they sell property in that film. We're not that bad.'

'I don't know, old chap. Selling credit card loans via a call centre is still pretty bad,' said David.

'That's even worse!' shrieked Veronica.

'It's a means to an end, and it pays the bills,' said Jimmy.

'And funds all of your drinking,' snapped Helen back at him.

'We don't drink that much, hun, surely?' he replied, with a fake tone of innocence to which JK and David laughed out loud. Helen shot a look of disgust at him and he looked down at the table and scratched his scruffy stubble. JK then caught him take a sneaky look at his mobile phone under the table.

'I'm off for some fresh air, anyone coming?' David said, standing up and showing a cigarette to Jimmy, as if sensing his discomfort. Jimmy nodded and, along with David's girlfriend, left the table as the rest sat waiting for their dessert course.

'So, JK, do you really not like your job at all?' said Veronica, directly.

'I think I used to,' he said. 'We all did, when we first started there. We worked hard, progressed well, and then management decided to stick us all together in one team.'

'Our little dream team, eh?' said Tom, chuckling.

'Absolutely, we've got lots in common too,' replied JK.

'What do you mean? Do all of you hate your jobs so much then?' asked Veronica, turning to Tom.

'It's just a really political environment,' he replied. 'Some of our bosses are horrible people, you know? That's why we let our hair down so much after work. And besides, you know me, I don't really belong in the corporate environment, do I? We've spoken about this before, Ronnie.'

'Yes, and you know that the sooner you can change it, the better. I mean, maybe you all need a change, if it's such a horrible job? You can still stay friends, even if you don't work together.'

'Don't encourage them, Veronica,' said Helen, as JK could sense her growing intolerance. 'I reckon they've got more than a few things in common. What happened to your girlfriend then, JK? Why did you really split up?'

'It just didn't work out, that's all. These things happen, I guess,' JK replied, annoyed at her abruptness, knowing that she wouldn't have asked this if Jimmy had been present.

'Are you sure she didn't just have enough of your drinking?'

'I drink just as much as Jimmy,' JK replied, coldly.

'Exactly, and you're just as obnoxious as him when you're drunk. In fact, you all are. That's what they really have in common, Veronica,' said Helen, spitefully.

'Boys will be boys, Helen. I know they get a bit boisterous, but I don't think Tom is that bad when he's drunk, actually.' Veronica's reply left an awkward silence hanging in the air.

'Well, if you ask me, I think your Laura has had a lucky escape from all this,' said Helen eventually.

It was enough to clarify JK's thoughts. He and his friends, the four average salesmen, had always been united in their sub-standard approach to their professional lives and an uncompromising attitude to their personal lives.

But now, even though JK knew that they had first been drawn to each other via some unspoken mantra, he now felt those bonds rapidly untying.

'Maybe you're right, Helen. But there are plenty of girls at our office who don't think we're obnoxious when we're drunk, let me assure you. And don't just take my word for it, why don't you ask Jimmy when he gets back? Right, anyway, I'm off to the bar. See you all later.' And with that, JK quickly stood up and walked away.

At the bar, JK collected another glass of wine and stood, watching, as the tables were eventually cleared to make room for a dance floor. His brother was thanking a precession of well-wishers and watched his new wife, Di, tenderly kiss her father. She was quite the spectacle in her strapless, yet simple, long, flowing and pure-white dress. JK realised that he was actually rather jealous of Bobby, of his new-found stability. It was easy to see what a happy couple they were, and he was genuinely pleased for them.

He approached his brother and offered a hand as he tapped him on the shoulder. Ignoring the handshake, instead he opened his arms, which JK willingly returned as they embraced.

'I just wanted to say how happy I am for you, Bobby,' JK said.

'Ah thanks, Jonny.'

'And I'm, er, I'm very jealous of you,' he smiled, trying not to sound too drunk.

'Oh right, thanks... she's amazing, isn't she?' Bobby replied, slightly awkwardly.

'Di? Yeah, she's stunning. Absolutely stunning. But I mean... well, you found something good, after everything.'

'Well, that's just life, isn't it? It all goes through cycles, doesn't it? No one has a bad run of luck forever. It's just a matter of patience. Did you enjoy the speeches?'

'Yeah, they were great, mate. A very entertaining set, a lovely banquet; almost the perfect day,' JK said, trying his best to appear sincere.

'I must say it was a beautiful service. Did you see all the tears? From Mum, and Di's family?' JK nodded with a vacant smile before Bobby continued. 'How are you holding up, anyway? Shame you couldn't bring anyone with you today. What about that girl... Laura, wasn't it?'

JK had always been irritated by his brother's insensitivity, knowing what JK was feeling, and even today, this last comment had managed to get under his skin.

'Yeah, it didn't work out with her. I'm sure Mum told you. Anyway, I'm already on the look-out. Who's that lovely blonde over there, by the way?' JK said, pointing to his admirer from afar.

'Who?' Bobby turned round to check, and JK nodded confirmation. 'Katie? Dream on, my lad. She's taken already.'

'Well, she's the one that keeps looking at me.'

'That's the girlfriend of Di's brother, Paul. They've been going out for years. At least seven. Plus, he's got a few of his rugby club mates here, so I'd watch yourself. I'm not bailing you out if you cause a mass brawl at my wedding!'

'Well, that might happen anyway. I think I upset my work mates at our table,' JK replied, with a mischievous grin. 'I might have drunk a bit too much.'

'Why, what happened?' Bobby looked at his brother with concern.

'Oh, I might have let the cat out of the bag about something controversial. Nothing that wasn't overdue, mind you. Anyway, I've had enough of that job now. My mind's made up. I'm going to quit on Monday morning.'

'What? Why?'

'I've had enough of it. I've become bogged down in the corporate life too early. I just need a break, to try something different.'

'Really, like what?'

'I want to try a new career abroad, maybe in the travel industry. After all, it's in our family's blood, right?'

'Been there, done that, bro,' Bobby said, shaking his head.

'Yeah, yeah, I know. But just imagine, being staff at one of the beach hostels on the Barrier Reef, helping book scuba trips. Or perhaps a barman at a remote island guest house, helping out on fishing boats, chatting to other backpackers in my time off, charming them with the extensive local knowledge and worldly wisdom that I would've gained along the way.' Bobby rolled his eyes as his brother continued. 'And when I'm not working, I could pay for yet more travel, just like you did,' JK said, smiling but without really believing the words coming out of his mouth.

'Like I said, I've done all that but, well, I just don't think that's you. And I'm not sure Mum would be that happy to see you go again. She'd only worry.'

'Would she? But surely she'd want me to tick off a few more countries on my list?' JK left his comment to hang in the air, waiting to see what reaction it might cause.

'That bloody list. Mind you, you haven't mentioned it for a while now. We'd thought you'd thrown it away.'

'What, you and Mum? Is that because it was Dad's list? That figures. What else have you two been saying about me behind my back?'

'What do you mean?'

JK toyed with the idea of telling him about what he had seen in Singapore and then, as he saw his brother's new bride walk towards them, wavered. But he had to say something, and an alcohol-fuelled energy pushed him to take a chance.

'You didn't mention Dad once in your speech. Don't you ever wonder about him? Especially now. Don't you miss him?'

Bobby's face reddened slightly, and he opened his mouth to reply when Di, radiating with happiness, approached and beamed a smile at JK, her blue eyes gleaming as she grabbed him warmly.

'Congratulations, Di. You look amazing, my new sister-in-law,' JK said. His annoyance with his brother had been temporarily forgotten, distracted by Di's beauty, still as stunning now as when he had first met her, several years before. Her blonde hair was tied back neatly with a thin tiara sitting on top of her head.

'Why thank you, new brother-in-law,' she said, and tapped Bobby on his left shoulder. 'Now, hubby, do excuse me, but I think we're about to be summoned for our first dance.'

'Uh-oh,' he replied, smiling. He held her hand and turned away, before looking back to JK. 'Just a second,' he said to Di, before quickly leaning forward to look his brother in the eye.

'Jonny, you don't know what you're talking about. I don't want to talk about that lying, adulterous, drunk bastard at my wedding. Now, please, don't you mention him again today, OK?' Bobby whispered, before walking off with Di to the dance floor.

JK was standing in shock, not knowing where to look. He raised his glass, saw he needed a refill and headed back to the bar; it seemed the most sensible destination for escape as the newly-weds began their slow dance.

Here he bumped into his blonde admirer, Katie, spilling her drink. He realised this was a clichéd but inevitable introduction. Perhaps due to a combination of the occasion, the alcohol and the emotion that she had found him in, it was the most rapid unfolding of a conversation he had ever had with a complete stranger.

After the customary introductions and links to friends and family, they understood each other very quickly. He began telling her his life story and, sensing his increasing frustration with life, she listened patiently. Her green eyes sparkled as if spell-bound, and this only encouraged JK to be even more open with her.

A waiter came round with drinks and they both grabbed refills, irrespective of the contents. They shared a frankness in body language. The awkwardness of her partner being present was acknowledged, and soon he understood how she longed for attention, for someone to actually notice her, her boyfriend being a complete slave to macho rugby club bonding commitments and behaviour.

Within twenty minutes they had finished their drinks again, and putting her glass down on the bar, Katie suddenly looked at JK with powerful intensity.

'I'm going to the ladies now. You can meet me there in a few minutes,' she whispered in his ear. She looked up at him, holding his gaze briefly as her arched neck exuded expensive perfume into his nostrils. Then, abruptly, she walked off.

Once again, he stood, stunned, unable to know what to do. Savouring the moment, he looked around guiltily, seeking eye contact from anyone who might have been spying. From his family; from Paul the boyfriend; from the boyfriend's rugby club clique; from his brother's friends. But no one was watching; he was in the clear.

He edged towards the ladies, waiting nearby. Trying to look inconspicuous, he gave it a few minutes and shortly he heard someone open the door to leave. Looking up, he saw it wasn't Katie. Edging closer to the door, some sort of nervous excitement had taken hold, driving him on.

Then he saw the door open very slightly, when he heard Katie's voice whisper to come in, he did. They then rushed into one of the cubicles like a pair of naughty school children. Grinning like a fool, it struck JK as odd at how luxurious these toilets were. Fully carpeted, with each cubicle a fully contained room in itself, they were completely isolated from the communal mirrors and sinks outside.

Looking at each other momentarily, they locked together in an adrenaline and alcohol-fuelled kiss. The groping accelerated, Katie not being shy in reaching down to his crotch, as he grabbed hold of her breasts and kissed her neck.

As his hand reached her groin, she moaned softly and then, pushing him back, put her hands under her skirt and removed her knickers. But, just as she did this, a loud knock outside made his heart stop.

'Katie? Are you in there? What are you doing?' A man's voice had followed the knock.

Shit, it could only be him, JK thought. The game was up, and such a short-lived one. Katie looked at JK and then her head sunk. He knocked again.

'Katie! Are you in there or not?' He was shouting now.

'Yes, I'm here, alright,' she replied, somewhat deflated.

'What are you doing?'

'I'm on the toilet, Paul. What do you think?'

'Well, you've been ages, are you OK?'

'Yeah, I'm just feeling a little bit sick. I'll be out in a minute, it's fine.'

The finger she had put to JK's lips was redundant; staying completely silent was not a problem. While the nervousness certainly still remained, the excitement had now turned to a sickly feeling in his stomach. Visions of violence flashed before his eyes, to varying degrees of severity. He pictured a group of Paul's rugby friends crowding round a fight, ready to step in when he had finished with JK. He looked at Katie with worry obviously deeply rooted in his eyes.

'Why, what's the matter with you? Do you need me to come in?'

'No, I'll be OK, don't worry.'

'Well, what is it? Why are you taking so long, then?'

JK suddenly got the feeling that this may have happened to them before. He also had an urge to be responsible and take the consequences of his actions. He was certainly beginning to sober up. As Paul clearly wouldn't take no for an answer, JK tried to mouth to Katie that he should go outside and speak to him. She shook her head decisively and began to tidy herself up.

'Honestly, babe, I'm just feeling a bit unsettled in my stomach. Just give me a minute and I'll be out.'

'Well, hurry up, then.'

And then there was silence. JK looked at her in confusion. She clearly had decided what she was going to do. She patted down her long blonde hair and checked her outfit.

'Meet me outside, at the back of the gardens, in fifteen minutes,' she whispered in his ear.

Still nervous, JK listened outside and knew what he had to do. She smiled and kissed him quickly on the lips, before opening the door gently to sneak out of the cubicle. JK listened for any further noises, and then heard her leave through the main toilet door.

As soon as she had done this, he left the cubicle he was in and shot into a similar one opposite, locking it behind him. After a few minutes, he heard someone come in and open the door to the previous booth they had been in. Not long after, this person then left the toilets, and JK could only assume it was Katie's agitated boyfriend.

JK decided to stay in there for a while until it seemed safe to leave. Maybe a further ten minutes passed at which point he slipped out quietly and unnoticed. Returning to the bar with an exultant smile, he could still feel his heart beating and quickly ordered another drink. Looking around, JK could see the dancing had begun in earnest among the guests, and upon seeing the door to the gardens, he remembered Katie's promise.

He opened the large patio door and embraced the cold breeze, seeing the last remnants of sunlight disappearing. Thin, grey clouds diluted the sunset into a purple-orange sky as the odd smoker milled around on the lawn in front of the main reception hall. JK scanned the grounds and saw the miniature maze ahead, where trees and waist-high hedges were interspersed with pink and white rose bushes.

He walked towards the bushes, occasionally glancing over his shoulder to see if anyone was following him. He neared a higher bush and a row of trees at the back, closer to some fences on the garden perimeter, and heard a cough. Startled, he sidestepped back and hid behind the first tree, and peered out.

JK then heard a long sniffing sound and could make out a man standing between the trees further along from him. On closer inspection he saw the shaven-headed and loosely-suited frame of Rick, and understood what he was doing. Rick was now crouching down, holding something small and flat in one hand; while with the other, he held a small piece of paper rolled up into a tube. He then bent over and placed his nose on the tube and drew it along the surface he held, while sniffing again.

After finishing this, Rick rubbed his hands and his nose and turned over the shiny surface he had held in his hand. JK could now see it was a silver hip flask, as Rick then unscrewed it and took a large swig. As Rick turned round, JK quickly tucked his head back behind the tree, keeping still as he listened out for his oncoming footsteps.

But none came, and as JK peered out, again he was relieved to see Rick had departed the trees from the far end of the row, away from JK and back towards the house. He watched Rick disappear to another entrance at one side of the hall, before he saw a girl walking down the front lawn at the other end. JK's pulse raced as he recognised Katie's figure drawing closer to him.

A couple of hours later, inside the hall, a noisy, heaving mass of alcohol-fuelled subjects inelegantly jerked and swayed to the tacky songs playing over the loud speakers. JK's intoxication had reached a ceiling, and he was now content to let his anger simmer close to the surface of an outward appearance of happiness.

He stood next to Bobby and Di at the bar, gleefully watching proceedings unfold, as his mother slowly danced with the mysterious old man with the eye scar. The family guest that everyone had been avoiding talking about was now in deep conversation with their mother, and JK took delight in his exclusive knowledge as to its subject.

His joy was further piqued as he saw the worry spread so plainly across his brother's face, further increasing as their mother and the old man now approached them. He walked with a confident swagger, completely at odds with his appearance. A short man, he had aged very badly, his skin wrinkling and spotted. He didn't wear a tie with his shirt, and the top was unbuttoned down to the third one, where several gold chains adorned his neck; but most people failed to notice anything past his horrific eye scar.

'Chip off the old block, that one,' said the old man, looking at Bobby.

'Yes, he definitely looks like Lenny. Bobby, you might not remember him, but this is your uncle Harry, an old friend of your father's,' said their mother, smiling. Bobby nodded and shook his hand politely, introducing his wife also.

Harry could see the suspicion on Bobby's face.

'Thank you so much again for inviting me, Bobby and Diana. It's a nice gesture for an old man like me.'

'Don't thank us, thank our mum. It was her choice,' Bobby replied, flatly.

'I know. And I've told her already, thanks for reaching out, after all these years,' he said, looking Alison in the eye. 'I know I wasn't that popular in your house for many a year, but it must've taken a real big effort for you to have such a change of heart. Thank you, Alison.' She returned a warm smile and a nod.

'And this one, I saw you only recently, didn't I, Jonny?' said Harry. His mother and Bobby looked at JK in surprise.

'Yeah, that's right. How are you, Harry?' JK replied.

'Good, my lad, good. So, you didn't tell them, did you?'

JK shook his head with a wry smile, remembering his visit to Harry's garage several months ago. He hadn't been that hard to find. JK had made some enquiries at the local haunts that his mother had mentioned over the years, speaking to a few old faces in pubs and cafes around Potters Bar, quickly realising that, ultimately, all old people love to talk. Especially if you buy them a cup of tea, a beer, or even a whisky, in Harry's case.

Sure, everyone knew old Harry Moss, the cheeky local character. A shady mechanic who loved the ladies, the football, a drink and a bet. So, JK had visited him at his garage, Moss Motor Fix Ltd, late one Friday afternoon, and had ended up down a local pub with him not long after.

'Don't worry, Alison. I think he was just curious about this,' Harry said, pointing at his scar. 'I told him I'd paid my debts a long time ago, and so did old Lenny, God rest his soul.'

'You mean, *we* did,' said Bobby, sharply. 'And we didn't have much of that insurance payment left for us afterwards, either.'

'Well, luckily your mum looked after you all, so you paid the right way. Not like me. I got a permanent receipt for my troubles, didn't I?' Harry laughed, horribly.

JK knew about all the scrapes that Harry and his father had got up to years ago: the drinking; the gambling; the womanising. He knew the social circles they operated in back then were 'not the most salubrious', in Harry's own words. At the time, he had wondered how much of it he could really believe, how much the stories had been exaggerated. But now, having heard that the gambling debts were real, he suspected that most of what Harry had told him was true after all.

So JK hadn't been surprised by his brother's earlier revelation, either, of his father's affair. Not only that, his mother had told him months before anyway. It had been a result of yet another argument between their mother and father, at the last Christmas before the fire that had supposedly taken their father. As ever, JK had been too young to remember, unlike his brother.

Lenny Keane had already told his wife he was going home to Ireland to see a sick relative over the Christmas holidays. This had caused enough friction between them as it was, until a last-minute, almost forgotten, Christmas present that Lenny had bought for the boys provided yet another flashpoint. In the bottom of the shopping bag, next to the gift, Alison had found two plane tickets for a Christmas trip to Thailand that Lenny had mistakenly left inside. One for himself, and one for his notorious friend, Harry.

Of course, when he was confronted by Alison, Lenny had denied anything untoward, saying he needed to get away, that the business had made some extra money and that he felt like he wanted to treat himself. So, he still went.

With his lies exposed, Alison knew what sort of holiday they had intended to have, and since then, had always suspected him of having an affair – or multiple affairs – right up until his death a few months later.

And on meeting Harry, JK had eventually managed to build up a picture of his father to confirm all of this, and much more.

'Alright, Harry, no one wants to drag up the past anymore, do they?' Bobby said, angrily. 'Well, no one apart from my constantly unsatisfied brother here. So, what other surprises have you got up your sleeve, Jonny?'

'What's that, Bobby?' JK replied.

'Come on, admit it. You've been dying to tell us about this, haven't you? All your secret investigations about our father. I should've guessed earlier after what you said. You just had to do it today, on our wedding day, didn't you?' he replied, as Di and Alison looked on with concern.

JK's head was pounding now. He forced a vicious smile, and knew this would be as good a time as any to tell them, but paused before he spoke.

'Yeah, I might have a few surprises, actually. Remember Ron Bullock?'

'Who?' Bobby said, confused.

'No, actually, you probably don't. But what about you, Mum?' JK looked at her, and she nervously looked back at him and his brother. 'Surely, you remember Ron, the old family friend?'

But now Alison stayed silent, looking away from him.

'What are you talking about, JK?' Di asked him.

'Well, Mum must know him. I mean, he was the one witness we had that saw Dad die in the fire all those years ago. He saw him dive back in there for something.'

'What did he try and grab?' replied Di.

'No one knows. I guess Dad took that secret to the grave with him,' JK said, provocatively. 'But not even Ron Bullock, the only witness according to the police, saw what he went for. Unless Ron told you, Mum?'

'No. He wasn't a close friend of mine, anyway,' Alison replied, flustered. 'He was just visiting your dad at the time. And I've lost touch with him after all these years.'

'What's your fucking point, JK?' Bobby was getting angry, seeing how awkward his mother felt.

'Just a funny thing. No one else has heard of this Ron guy. Uncle Harry certainly hadn't. He wasn't a local and had no business contacts or relatives that I could find. Yet, it's his name that's on the police report for our insurance pay-out. Maybe he's a ghost.'

'I don't know what you mean, JK. Anyway, can't we stop all this and go and enjoy what's left of the wedding?' Alison said, her head bowed as she tried to subtly wipe away a tear.

'OK, that's enough, JK. Let's go for a fucking walk.' Bobby grabbed his brother by the arm and marched him away, past the dance floor and out through the patio doors. Di watched them leave before she walked across to Alison to comfort her.

Outside, Bobby and JK stood behind the kitchens, at the back exit near a walled enclosure.

'What the fuck is your problem?' he shouted at JK, pushing him in the chest.

'Stop pushing me, Bobby.' JK felt like he was dreaming. His brother was trying to egg him on like he was nine years old again. Bobby used to delight in getting him into trouble. All he had to do was say the right trigger word.

'You're just so wrapped up in your own little dream world. Only thinking of yourself, as always,' said Bobby.

'Don't sweat it, Bobby. I just wanted to see you squirm. And it's too easy.'

'Yeah, that's typical of you. Don't worry about what it might do to our mother. You're an attention-seeking little brat,' spat out Bobby.

'Ah, you don't know the half of it, Bobby. If only you knew. Maybe I do have another surprise for you, after all.'

'Oh, really? Like what?'

'Like our father. You lied to me.'

Bobby stood silently for a moment, taking in the response, as JK's head throbbed.

'I know he's not dead. And you all fucking lied about it, for years. Even our mother. You're all full of shit,' said JK.

Then Bobby leapt towards his brother, as JK tried and failed to avoid the impact. They ended up on the floor, with Bobby on top. He grabbed JK's jacket lapels and held a fist above his face, ready to strike him.

'Go on then, hit me,' said JK, laughing.

'You nasty little piece of work,' Bobby snarled back, dropping his fist.

Eventually, they both sat up, side by side, as their rapid, heavy breath, steaming up in the night air, began to slow.

'I saw him, you know,' JK said, looking straight ahead.

'What?'

'Look at this.' From his breast pocket, JK pulled out a card and handed it to his brother. It was the business card he had picked up three years ago in Singapore. Now dog-eared and frayed round the edges, it had faded brown. He smiled at the similarities to his previous obsession, also an old piece of paper from his father: his travel list.

The problem was that it had given JK nothing. He couldn't find the company listed on any international business directories, it was clearly too small, and it had no website either. He didn't even have any proof that this business still existed. He had rung the number several times. Either no answer or it was answered by someone speaking Thai, and he didn't speak the language. Now he had reached a dead end.

After studying it closely, Bobby asked JK how he had got it. On hearing the answer, he handed him back the card and then suddenly stood up.

'Just forget about him, JK. How many times do I have to tell you that?'

'How can you say that, now?' JK was shaking his head in disbelief.

'Go to bed, JK. You've had too much to drink, and you don't look very well.'

Bobby turned round and walked away, leaving JK sitting there. His head was now in agony as he lay back on the floor and eventually felt himself drifting into unconsciousness.

JK opened his eyes, aware he was now lying in a bed, in his hotel room. He couldn't remember how he had got there and assumed from the daylight that it was the morning after the wedding. He became conscious that someone else was in the room and suddenly sat up to see his mother sitting in a chair next to him, watching with a concerned smile.

'Mum? What are you doing in here?' he said, rubbing his eyes.

'Just checking on you, Jonny. We found you on the floor last night, outside, so we took you up to bed. I kept the key so I could check up on you. I think you had another one of your episodes.'

'Oh, OK. I'm sorry. And… thanks … Are you OK?' he asked, seeing the tired lines round her eyes.

'Don't be sorry. And don't you worry about me. I didn't get much sleep, that's all. Look, I better get going, Jonny. It's time to get ready for breakfast; everyone will be waiting,' she said with a pitiful tone that made JK curious. He forced a smile towards her.

'Thanks, but I'm not hungry.'

'You will come down to see Di and your brother before they leave, though, won't you?'

JK grunted in reply, before Alison got up and walked towards his door. And as she turned back round to face him, he noticed two things. She had a piece of paper in her hand, and she was in tears.

'Look, Jonny. Bobby told me about the card you showed him last night. I knew… I knew you would find out one day.'

Astonished, he watched her walk towards the doorway. She put his room key and the piece of paper on a table, before opening the door.

'I'm sorry. I'm so, so sorry, Jonny. I hope you believe me but I only ever did it to protect you… And I do love you,' she said, and after wiping her eyes, she smiled one last time, before stepping out and closing the door.

He stood up, only in his boxer shorts, and shivered. His headache had also now progressed into deep-set stomach pain as he remembered he hadn't taken his tablets again yesterday. Delaying taking them again now, he knew he had to read the piece of paper.

JK darted towards the table and grabbed out, in a frenzy. He voraciously read the two pages of hand-written content in seconds, before breathing out heavily and reading it all again, more slowly the second time.

The details were sparse, padded out by lots of his mother's emotional outpourings. He had pretty much pieced it together or guessed the rest by now anyway. At the end, she offered herself as willing to talk about it at any time.

That was good of her, he thought, laughing sarcastically, considering she had been lying to him since he was six years old. She had only wanted to protect her youngest son, while he wasn't old enough to form any negative emotions about his father, unlike his brother, who she could tell had already been tainted by the whole of his mother and father's relationship.

His father wasn't dead. He had faked his death in the fire, knowing the insurance pay-out would clear his debts, sparing him and his family any trouble, and also giving him the opportunity to escape from his mundane life. But she and Bobby had known it all along, and had to play along for the authorities to make it look convincing.

She also knew that Lenny Keane didn't love them anymore, but his guilt had meant that he occasionally sent her money for the family every year or so. And she confirmed what JK already knew, that Lenny Keane had since remarried and even his current whereabouts: Thailand.

A tear ran down JK's face as he screwed up the letter into a ball. In a trance, he quickly threw on some clothes and walked out of his hotel room along the corridors of the grandiose, stately hotel.

He ignored various greetings from the guests, loitering with their bags, as he walked by reception. He felt like he was floating despite his feet crunching through the gravel on the driveway.

JK reflected that the morning could be like any other. The first part of the day was always the worst, his mind unoccupied by any daily routines or distractions, when his head was at its most vulnerable to attack, attack from his heart. Those questions that would suddenly arrive in his mind, just as he was trying to switch off.

He dug into his jacket pocket to locate the car keys he had borrowed from his mum. He detested her small purple hatchback, but he didn't have a ride of his own and had been a good son to arrive with her in the first place. He was operating on instinct now, a feeling that he had to escape, and he opened the driver door, inserted the key and turned on the ignition.

It was a long country road from the grand old building, narrow and well protected by bushes and trees, further decreasing the viewing conditions against an already cloudy sky. Despite the concentration required, he couldn't stop thinking about how many lies he had heard over his life.

How much time had he wasted, trying to get to know his father's legacy? How many years had he lost, travelling, trying to imagine how his father had felt? Only to realise now that he knew very little about him at all, and that he was as far away from him now as he had ever been. It was almost as if he had suddenly gone backwards in time. The more he dwelt on it, the more depressed he felt.

A slow tune played on the local radio station, which only served to exasperate him further. He fiddled with it to change stations, anything to get rid of that awful song.

This feels right, he thought. I need to go, I need to leave again. To Thailand, to Asia, and further. This feels right, now more than ever. Maybe I was always meant to go again, to find him, finally, and properly this time. Maybe it was my real destiny.

JK managed a sarcastic laugh as he scolded himself for not concentrating on the road. He braked hard at a junction and waited at the red light, fixating on the old banger of a car that was facing him. It was a rust bucket, but he was sure he'd seen the silver Mercedes before.

The long car had a semi-polished trim hinting at former glory in years gone by. The head lamps were made with yellow glass, and JK thought it was strange that they were on so early in the day, despite the few clouds above.

The traffic lights changed to green and a song came on the radio that always reminded him of his childhood. It had always been on in their house: 'Baker Street' by Gerry Rafferty.

The car crawled slowly towards JK and he was transfixed by the red leather interior. His eye line was drawn magnetically to the driver.

Then, as nausea hit him, JK saw a familiar face. The man's hair was greying, but was still a healthy brown, curly but under control. He was chewing something, and he glanced at JK as the car drew level and then quickly carried on past.

Did he have amber eyes? JK couldn't be sure. Was it you again? Lenny, dear old departed Lenny? Could it be you?

JK had to look round. He turned back but couldn't be sure. He turned round a second time but still wasn't sure. Not his father, again? No, it couldn't be him. Why would it be him, now? He was in Thailand. Why would he be here? For the wedding?

Perhaps I've imagined seeing him again, JK thought. But if he had just seen him again by accident, that would be twice in three years, and in different countries. What were the chances of that? Was his lucky streak active, after all? That looked like his scruffy old car. And he could have been chewing one of his favourite jelly beans. His curly hair. It must be.

JK turned round again. Straining to see through his back windscreen he still had no confirmation. He faced frontwards again, staring vacantly, his car crawling along almost unguided, as a horn sounded from behind him.

The distinctive saxophone tune played on the radio. JK could suddenly smell whisky. He glanced in his rear-view mirror and saw that the car had now disappeared from view completely. He couldn't be sure. It can't be. It's not him.

Not him. Not him.

Shifting to turn round one more time, JK felt himself go light-headed, and his vision turned black.

He passed out, slumping forward onto the steering wheel.

Chapter Twelve

Leo Fortune

JK sat in an open-air cafe in his, by now, usual morning seat, watching the sprawling markets of Pat Pong in Bangkok. Catering for all consumer needs, here you could buy pretty much anything you wanted, as long as you didn't want the real thing. All sorts of knock-off designer-named clothes, bags, jewellery, pirated-DVDs, CDs, pictures – all the cheap junk you needed, plus everything you didn't.

He had arrived in Thailand two weeks ago, and was already being recognised as a regular customer by the stall owners. He spotted one nearby known as 'the rat' who was probably JK's favourite so far. On making eye contact with JK, he approached enthusiastically but JK felt embarrassed that he hadn't yet told him his own name.

'Merry Christmas, mister!' said the small, squat man. His disarming smile acted as a counter balance to his roughly weathered skin and cold, impenetrable eyes.

'Good morning,' replied JK. 'It's a bit early for Christmas, isn't it?' He could never quite bring himself to use the nickname, even though the man so proudly displayed it on the stack of business cards he carried around with him.

'Why, it's first of December today, no? You not like Christmas?'

JK smiled back, and after considering an appropriate response, eventually just shrugged his shoulders.

'Maybe you want some more DVDs today, yes? Make you happy?'

JK faked a laugh and then shook his head. He had already bought more than he needed from him over the previous two weeks. Back then, it had been a thoroughly entertaining and welcome distraction to barter over the price of forty DVDs – he had managed to get him down to about fifteen pounds, and then tested him further to go back to his storage room for a range of older movies. The rat had very rarely let him down, and even if they weren't all high quality or at all legal, he couldn't argue with those prices.

His local friend was clearly less than morally sound and had learnt some impressive tricks over the years to charm his customers. JK remembered what he had said on their first meeting. *'Ah, welcome to Pat Pong – you want shopping or fucking?'* before continuing, *'No money... no honey... no funny.'* He had quickly realised that JK was not the right target audience for this type of sale and so, as a fixer of all sorts, he then went on to offer taxis, DVDs and various other services.

But today was not the day for bartering or for trivial purchases, and the rat eventually left JK alone to finish his coffee. Recently, the mornings had been JK's best time of the day before, inevitably, he would feel low towards the end of the day, as he struggled to make any friends with the multitude of backpackers passing through his hostel. This morning, for some reason, those feelings had arrived earlier than normal.

He had tried to immerse himself in his surroundings, drinking in the go-go bars and meeting up with random tourists. He had hoped to see familiar faces, other travellers he had met in the past, but it would only be by luck as he had made no effort to organise this. He knew he needed help, to talk to someone to try and deal with the turmoil and emotional instability building inside of him. And as his evenings became more lonely, his feelings of isolation and desperation deepened.

Initially, it had been a fun city to see: the traffic, the tourists, the colours, the food, the smells, the temples, the people – everything so vivid and intense, and most of all, memorable. But he had soon grown tired of this place and quickly realised that, even though he was one of the older backpackers here, at least he wasn't the oldest or worst type of tourist in town.

It had left an uneasy feeling in his stomach to see fat, balding men – Germans, Dutch, Australian, and many more Western nationalities – fifty years old and above, walking away from bars with girls a quarter of their age, hand in hand or flirting openly with them. Seeing their cash notes exchanged for drinks and other services.

What he had observed in Bangkok had been disturbing, yet he still couldn't help be grimly fascinated by it all. He had known about the sex trade beforehand, but on seeing it first-hand it had still smacked him in the face. He was staggered at how completely natural it seemed for a lot of them. Was that really their life, he thought?

Their sleazy 'service' industry: tons of pornography everywhere, sex shows and prostitutes – male, female and transsexuals, pre- and post-op. The clients' wealth on display and the locals' joy at seeing this. The touts in Pat Pong, begging, pleading, demanding to drag you in to see one of their sex shows as you walked by. A free market economy in its most unfiltered form.

He hated it, but he knew he had to stay. He was here for a reason, and just had to see it through. Although he was lucky that his car crash a few weeks ago had only been minor, he believed it had proven to be even more fortuitous as it had then prompted him into action. After a speedy recovery from the scratches, bruises and the shock of it, he had quit his job as intended, booked his flights and then, not long after, he had arrived in Bangkok.

He had dared to think that he could track down his father, to resolve his feelings, once and for all. Why do these things happen, he thought? It was fate, and he had got lucky, just as his father had told him he always would be. Now, he just needed to accept and re-adjust to his fate, to try and take control and get back on track. Now was the time to make the most of the situation and find out as much as he could about him. What was the worst that could happen?

So, he took the opportunity and began his search. He still had the crumpled business card from his chance meeting in Singapore, and after advice from a local tourist board, it had been easy to locate his father's business on a map. He had been sitting quietly, holding the card in his hand and, as he finished his coffee, he finally made a decision.

He stood up, located the rat and asked for his help getting a taxi to take him to the address on the card. JK wasn't in the mood for the cheeky pleasantries his driver had tried to instigate, deciding instead to keep his head down and remain generally non-responsive throughout the journey.

It was a good twenty minutes from the Ko San road where he had been staying in central Bangkok. They arrived at a grey-looking street, with very few pedestrians and little traffic for 10am. The few plain-looking buildings were unremarkable and, at one newsagent-style shop at the end, he got out.

He carried on walking south before he saw ahead, on the other side of the road, some green garage doors. Above them was a large blue rectangular sign in black Thai print, with the Western translation in smaller text below. Getting closer, he knew he would shortly be able to read it, compounding his nervous anticipation. It read: 'Leo Fortune Ltd.'

He continued walking until he was standing opposite a front office on the corner of the block, a single entranceway made from glass within a long window next to the garage doors. From across the road, he stood still, frozen with fear, and tried to work up the courage to enter. He peered inside the glass to see who was there and could only make out one female figure behind a low desk.

A pedestrian approached him and so he got out a guide book and started flicking through the pages so as not to appear too conspicuous. They passed without comment, so he looked up again. The person behind the desk had disappeared, giving him the opportunity to cross the road and get a closer look.

Peering through the windows, he could see that the decor of the reception was a lot plusher than expected. The low black desk was trimmed with a silver surface and the walls were of a light, soft-brown colour. There was a long, thin sofa made from expensive black leather across one side of the room facing the desk. There were also some silver doors to a lift to the right of the desk, and a door that backed on to the side of the office which had the garage on the other side, and another door just behind the desk.

A framed picture of an expensive-looking car was on the wall above the sofa. He tried to make out the sign behind the desk but it was hard to read the print. Still unsure, JK walked through the doors in any case, and saw the lion logo from the card on the front of the desk.

At that moment, a girl walked through the small door and sat back down at her desk. Just as she did, she saw him and looked momentarily startled. JK smiled and this appeared to calm the smartly dressed girl, who was around twenty-two years old, with pleasant, if not stunning, features.

'Sawatdee ka,' she said.

'Sawatdee khap. Do you speak English?' JK replied, tentatively.

'Yes. A little. How can I help?'

The ultimate question. He looked around frantically to see if he could find the names of anyone who worked there. He saw a pile of business cards on a low glass table in front of the sofa.

'Ah, yes please. I'm… I'm looking for someone… A Mr Leo Martin. Is he the manager here?' he asked and simultaneously bent down to check the names on the cards. The business cards had changed slightly now. They now read 'Corporate Automotive Hire and Consultancy Services', but the names underneath hadn't changed. Surely it wouldn't be this easy just to walk into his shop, out of the blue, and confront him? JK thought.

'Mr Martin is not manager. That his wife, Mrs Martin. They both owners. Who are you?'

'My name is Jonny. I'm an old friend of his from England.'

She eyed him suspiciously, and then looked down at something on her lap.

'You make appointment with him?'

'No. I'm on holiday and just wanted to visit while I was here.'

'He not here at the moment.'

'OK. Do you know when he will be back? Can I wait?'

'Maybe not today or tomorrow, out on business trip. You wait one moment, maybe Mrs Martin will talk to you. Please sit.'

She ushered him towards the sofa as she picked up a phone. He nodded, sat down and flicked through a glossy car magazine on the table. She spoke to someone in Thai briefly and then put the phone down.

'OK, Mr Jonny. You go up and see Mrs Martin. She is on second floor. You take the lift, yes?'

'OK, thank you.'

After coming this far, JK didn't think there was much else he could do now. If they had been married for twenty years or so then she must know something. He got in the waiting lift and pressed the button marked two. The lift doors closed just as he caught the face of the receptionist viewing him with curiosity.

As the lift doors opened at the second floor, Somrak Martin stood in a small waiting room next to a doorway. Dressed in a smart, all-black business suit, she had her hair tied up again like the first time he saw her. She viewed him with coldness and didn't move.

'Hello. I'm manager of Leo Fortune. My name is Somrak Martin. Your name is Jonny, yes?'

She didn't offer a hand, but he outstretched his anyway.

'Yes, that's right. Pleased to meet you.'

'Please come through to my office,' she said, ignoring his hand and abruptly turning round before walking through the doorway.

He followed her into the room and saw two large desks, one reasonably untidy and another immaculate, which she sat behind. He assumed the other desk was Leo's. There was an empty chair facing her across the desk which he sat in. It faced a window which perfectly framed her upper torso.

'So, why you come to see my husband?' she said, directly, without smiling.

'Well, I'm an old friend from London. I'm just passing through.'

'Really? He not have any friends in London. How you know him?'

'He's a friend of my family from a long time ago. I just wanted to talk to him.'

'About what?

'Personal stuff. I wanted to ask him something about my family. He knew them.'

'How old are you?'

'I'm twenty-nine.'

'We've been married twenty years. We not been to England in that time, let alone mention friends in England. He must not be that good friends with your family, no?'

'Yes, I know it was a very long time ago, but it's something that I need to ask him. It's personal. I can't explain it to you.'

'He my husband. If you can explain to him, you can explain to me. What is your name?'

'Jonny.'

'Yes, I know that. Family name please. What your last name?'

He hesitated. Clearly, she was being protective, but at the very least this woman would be able to confirm whether it was him or not, and whether he gave a shit or not.

'Keane. My name is Jonny Keane.'

Somrak paused. Her brow furrowed as she turned and looked out of the window.

'I knew you would come eventually.'

'What do you mean?'

'I've been expecting you.'

'Really? Why?'

'You are Lenny's son.'

'No, my father died when I was six years old, in a fire.'

She looked at him and laughed.

'You very stubborn. I think you must be his son. But you not very smart.'

'Oh? Why's that?'

'Someone call us, maybe one year ago, from London. Said you were asking questions. So I knew you would come here one day.'

His mind raced. That was around the time he spoke to Harry Moss. He must have called and spoke to her or Lenny. Either way, it was enough information for him.

'I want to see Lenny. I'm entitled to that.'

'You not entitled to anything. I had to work like a dog for twenty years before I even met your father. I did things you not want to know about, probably make you sick. But I became successful business woman before I met him. After, he helped me enjoy myself and we grew business together. And I help him escape his life.'

'Escape? What was he escaping?'

'All he got from your family, your lifestyle, was sadness. Pressure. Debt. Violence. Now he can enjoy his life without any of that.'

'You're lying! I don't believe you,' JK snapped.

'Believe what you want. He's been in my life for a long time, and not in yours.'

JK choked back tears as he stared at her with hatred for a moment.

'But… but he still has a family,' JK stuttered to respond. 'He owes them an explanation, at least.'

'He not owe them anything. They owe him! They owe him freedom, but I gave him that instead. And he gives me it too. Even now. Can you give him that?'

'I know he has a life here. I'm not trying to take it away.'

'I don't want him to think about you. I don't want him to think about old family. I don't want him to remember old life.'

'I just need to speak to him. You can't stop me.'

'You not think so? I have a team of ten drivers and twenty engineers. We have some of biggest corporate clients in Bangkok. Sometimes, they have to do unusual things. But they do them, because I tell them to. Do you understand?'

'I'm not afraid of you.'

'Where you staying? Backpacker? Maybe Ko San road, yes? I know many hostel owners in Bangkok. I can easily find you.'

'I'm going to talk to him. You can threaten me all you like.'

'You are a little boy. You are farang, alone in a big city. You don't know what you doing. You should go home, back to your family. Otherwise you will get hurt.'

'Do you think Lenny would like that? Do you think he would want you to threaten his son?'

'I'm doing it for him, he doesn't need to know.'

'We'll see. I'm going to find him,' JK said, feeling his face go hot with anger.

'You go now. And you leave Bangkok in two days, OK?'

She pointed to the door and turned away, picking up the phone. She barked something in Thai as JK stood up and glared at her. She frowned back while talking and pointed violently again at the door. Eventually JK turned round and left, walking into the open lift.

When the doors opened at reception, two men were waiting for him. One fat and the other slim but tall for a Thai man. They both shouted at him in Thai and then shoved him. He stumbled and turned around, but then decided against fighting them back. They shouted at him again as he stood defiantly, and then pushed him out of the doorway.

The fatter one walked onto the step and pointed up the street. JK smiled at them both and again stood his ground. They made a rush for him and then stopped, just a few metres onto the pavement. JK flinched but then decided to turn round and walk away briskly.

He quickly found a cab and on his way back home, reeling from his experience, considered his options. It was a less-than-satisfactory outcome, but I'm not going to give up yet, he thought. Not for that crazed, manipulative bitch. He wasn't sure how seriously to take her threat, assuming it was just for show to start with, but he wasn't going to take any chances. He needed to get Lenny alone, but if she caught him, he felt sure she would follow through on her earlier promise.

If Lenny was away on business, it was pointless him turning up there again in the next two days. He had pocketed one of the new business cards from reception and had seen some Thai printed on the back that he hoped was their opening hours – which was confirmed later by the rat.

Three days later, he got a cab out there again, just before closing time. He got out two streets before their office and approached from a different direction, staying well back but close enough to still have a view of the entrance way. Feeling like a fool, he put on the cheap sunglasses and cap he had bought from the Ko San road markets, but not from the rat this time, who must have had a day off.

After about twenty minutes, he saw Somrak leave with a man, a white man in a suit, who he assumed to be Lenny. They walked round the corner and JK started moving towards them. He just managed to see them turn another corner as he reached the top of the road before hearing a car engine firing up and he stopped on the edge.

Peering round the wall, he saw a black Hyundai estate car pulling away in the opposite direction. He made out that they were the two passengers in the car, with Somrak driving, and took a note of the parking space and the car number plate.

Now it was just a matter of getting lucky. If he hung around long enough, he might find a day when Lenny was in but she wasn't. The only way he could check without drawing attention to himself would be if her car wasn't parked in the usual place. He made a routine over the next few days of turning up in the morning to see if her car was there. If it was, he went home. He varied the times he arrived and the mode of transport he used to get there. He even changed his outfit – different caps, coats, glasses, etc. – and came to quite enjoy the distraction.

As this continued, she was in each time over the following days. One time he saw Lenny arrive on his own, in a silver Toyota, but knowing that her car was already there, he decided it wasn't worth the risk of approaching him. By the Thursday of the following week, he finally saw that she wasn't parked in one of her normal spots, but Lenny was. Of course, JK knew that this didn't mean she wasn't there and so he went back to town, deciding to return to the office at closing time to inspect again.

By 6pm it was wet and dark as he arrived. The office closing time was 6.30pm, but he had to be sure of seeing Lenny. The lights were still on in the building as he spied from an opposite street corner, sitting in a bar where he could view the doorway. Recently, while drinking, he had taken to smoking cheap cigars, the thin Café Crèmes he had first tried with his friend Jo-Jo years ago. And he now opened a square tin and lit up another, as he sat nervously, sipping his drink, watching the rain pour down. It got to 7pm and he wondered if Lenny was still there or if he was out entertaining clients and therefore might not appear for a long time.

At 7.20pm he was just finishing his fourth vodka and tonic and was considering leaving. Then, he saw the second-floor lights go out, and he quickly dug into his pockets for cash to pay the bar bill. He threw it onto the table, knowing it was more than enough, but then sat still, waiting for any movement in reception. After a while, he saw Lenny open the door, lock up and leave the building.

A waiter arrived with his change but he ignored it, stood up and walked out of the bar. Lenny was walking quickly along the street without an umbrella. He had a long coat on with the collars pushed up to his ear line. JK watched him turn the corner towards the road where his car was; so then he decided to take his chance, running as he crossed the street.

'Excuse me!' JK shouted, but Lenny didn't hear, as the rain soaked them both. 'Lenny!' he tried again.

'Yes? Do I know you?' Lenny turned round, a few metres from his car, to look at JK. JK stood in silence, once again transfixed on seeing his father's amber eyes.

'I think so, Leonard. Don't you remember me?' he said, eventually, and he took off his cap. Lenny looked at JK and ran his fingers through his wet hair to straighten his fringe.

'Leonard? My name is Leo Martin. Lenny to my friends. And I don't know who you are,' he said, defensively, as JK resolutely held his confused gaze.

'My name's Jonny Keane. I'm twenty-nine years old and I'm from London. I haven't seen you in twenty-three years.'

JK paused and saw something in Lenny's eyes sparkle as he pondered his next words. Rain droplets ran off his nose, but JK couldn't find anything funny about that: he could only picture an ageing family photo of Lenny with a beard, holding JK as a baby.

'Well, I hope you're enjoying Bangkok, Jonny. But I think you're confused, I'm not sure I know what you want from me.'

'Don't you have anything to say to me?'

'I don't know what you mean. I've never met you,' Lenny's voice began to croak, betraying his emotion.

A pressure point built in JK's chest as Lenny viewed him suspiciously.

'Dad. It's me. I just need to understand. Please talk to me.'

Lenny continued to regard JK cautiously. Something was happening behind those amber eyes, and JK thought he saw a tear well up, or a hint of moisture at least, but then he quickly looked away, fishing in his pockets for his car keys.

'I'm sorry. I don't know who you are. And I have to go now.'

'Please, Dad. Don't do this. You know why I'm here.'

JK walked towards him with his right hand outstretched, attempting to grab him. Lenny stepped back, abruptly pushing his keys in the car door.

'I can't help you. I'm leaving.'

'No, Dad, please. Don't go.'

JK tried to grab him again, but the wet coat easily slipped from his grasp as Lenny opened his car and sat down, slamming the door behind him. JK banged on the window as the engine started. Lenny didn't look at JK as he doggedly concentrated on his steering wheel, reversing and pulling out of his parking space.

Rain ran down JK's face, mixing with his tears, as he watched Lenny pull away. Then, a few metres down the road, the car stopped unexpectedly. JK felt his heart pounding in his chest as he waited for movement from inside the car. For a moment, time stopped as JK tried to find the strength to move his legs, cross the road and go over to the car.

But then, just as JK had finally begun to move, the car pulled away once more, and for the last time. The rear lights got smaller and smaller as Lenny Keane disappeared from JK's life again.

His mother and brother had known that JK was going to Thailand, and had received two emails from him since he had left home. The first had been very matter of fact and perfunctory, confirming his arrival in Bangkok and where he was staying, with but had very little other detail.

His second email had been fractionally more involving, almost optimistic in its nature, in that JK had mentioned he had been enjoying the weather and was starting to make progress on his task.

But that's when the contact had stopped and so, naturally, his mother and brother had begun to worry about JK. And well they should have as, since he had finally located his father, JK had taken to drinking and smoking heavily and, at the same time, had abandoned taking his medication.

And now, in the third week of December, JK couldn't face a return home in time for another miserable Christmas. He knew it would be even worse than previous years by returning empty-handed, having failed in his mission. He was wallowing in depression, and as his intoxication levels increased, so did his mind's imagination as he began to see and hear things that weren't there.

He spoke to random strangers as if they were old friends, often breaking down in tears during conversation. He would become agitated at fireworks, thinking his life was in danger. He became known to the local bar owners and, despite never trying to become friendly with any prostitutes, even they were cautious of him.

But then, on another humid evening, completely unannounced, his brother and his old friend Rick had arrived at JK's hostel. Dragging their bags behind them, they had walked into reception and spotted JK sitting at the bar, on his own and staring into space.

'There he is!' said Rick.

'Brother! What the hell?' said Bobby.

JK looked up, his spell seemingly broken, but he said nothing as he stared vacantly back. Bobby threw a nervous glance at Rick and then returned his focus to JK.

'JK? Are you OK?'

'What?' he replied, before recognition finally sparked in his eyes. 'Bobby? Rick? What… what are you doing here?' He stood up, managing a half-smile as his brother approached to embrace him. JK accepted this and the following handshake from Rick.

'Just like old times, eh, JK?' said Rick, who smiled but there was a subtle tone of pity in his question.

'Yeah and I'm playing catch up, as per normal. You two have been to Thailand loads before. This is my first time,' JK replied, nervously.

'Yeah, but we've never been out here for as long as you have. What's it been, like, five weeks? We thought it was time to drag you back home,' replied Bobby.

But JK didn't reply, not offering any natural prompt to continue the conversation and so Bobby knew that his brother wasn't his usual self.

Ignoring his tiredness from the journey, and before they had even checked in, Rick spontaneously suggested that they go straight off to watch some Muay Thai at one of Bangkok's large Thai boxing stadiums. Despite some reservations, Bobby agreed, recognising Rick's attempt to provide an enjoyable distraction.

They dragged JK along with them, and Bobby once again tried to get his brother to open up to him over the long tuk-tuk drive en route.

'So, I guess you're wondering how Di let me come out here so soon after our honeymoon?' Bobby asked JK, who could only manage to raise his eyebrows at him in response.

'You certainly have an understanding wife there, Bobby,' said Rick.

'Yep. We were all quite worried about you, JK.' And as JK remained silent, Bobby felt the need to fill any awkward pauses quickly. 'But Christmas was coming, and none of us wanted you to be on your own. Di has her mates, and it's only one year, after all.'

'She didn't mind us having one last lads' trip, then?' said Rick, laughing.

'Well, in your case, Rick, she knows, like I do, that the only way of getting you to behave is to keep you on a short fucking lease. If that's even possible!'

And still JK said nothing. He held the strange look in his eyes that Bobby had noticed earlier, a vacant, emptiness. He ignored anything in his immediate vicinity but was still seemingly focusing nearby, as if he could see something that no one else could, but was afraid to admit it.

During the Muay Thai, Bobby's suspicions were emphatically confirmed. It was a lengthy, colourful and noisy spectacle, and even away from the fights in the ring, the various scenes happening all around the stadium were fascinating to observe.

The vibrant blues, greens, reds and yellows that decorated the fighters and fans in the stands. Non-stop clapping and a rhythmical and slow drumming in the background. The local crowd's unintelligible racket occasionally rising to shouts at the loud crack of a fighter's knee or shin across the body or head of their opponent. The unofficial bookies who wore leather jackets, commanding respect in the stands while smoking thick cigars, as their many punters flocked around them, feeding their success with copious amounts of cash notes.

They had already been watching for three hours when it first happened. Just as ringside attendants brought torch-lit flames in between rounds, JK had fainted at his seat. But he had recovered quickly, and so they remained to carry on watching.

Then it happened again, half an hour later at the same break between rounds as the flaming torches circulated. Again, JK had come round very quickly, but Bobby was now so concerned about his brother that he demanded they leave immediately.

They all rested up, and the next day, they quickly found out that it was the King of Thailand's birthday, as they encountered various street celebration festivals, displays and markets. Despite several indirect attempts asking if he had found their father, if his search had been successful, JK had still not responded in any meaningful way to Bobby, whose concern deepened.

By the evening, they had begun drinking in the midst of 200,000 people that were celebrating on the city streets, and they were treated to a huge firework display. On seeing Rick bring back three bottles of beer, JK looked at him, puzzled.

'I thought you had cut all that out now, Rick?' said JK, as he looked at his brother, expecting a similar reaction.

'Aye. I fell off the wagon. Bobby knows already.'

'Yeah, it was a while ago when I found out, just after I got back from my honeymoon, wasn't it?' asked Bobby, as Rick nodded.

'It was much early than that, Bobby. I saw him drinking at your wedding, you know?' JK said, forcefully. It had been the most passionate thing he had said since Bobby had arrived in Bangkok. 'You're a mug if you think he's changed at all.'

'Alright, JK. Still got it in for me, then?' Rick snapped back.

'Don't you two fucking start now,' said Bobby. 'JK, he has told me all about it, and I know when it started. He just hadn't come clean till later.'

JK shook his head and viewed Rick with suspicion.

'I've changed, JK. I know you might not believe me but I've been trying really hard. It's just not easy sometimes.'

'He's trying his best, JK. That's why he's here with us now – he's not just here to support me. I meant what I said yesterday, I need to keep an eye on him, and this was the best way.'

'If you say so, Bobby. I just hope Di feels the same way,' replied JK, rolling his eyes. The subject was dropped as they continued to drink in an awkward compromise.

They had been meandering back towards their hostel in Pat Pong when they encountered JK's old friend the rat, who was subsequently introduced to Bobby and Rick. Rick in particular had been very interested and quizzed him on his local knowledge. On hearing him quote his famous welcome line, Rick became keen to know more about the local sex shows.

JK turned his back on them in disgust and walked away as Bobby chased after him.

'Hey, come on, JK. He's just curious. Weren't you?' asked Bobby.

'Not really. He's been here before, anyway. Surely it can't be much different now?'

'Well, maybe that's what he wants to find out.'

'I want another drink, that's all.'

'Look, JK. Are you OK?'

'I told you. I just want a drink.'

'Yeah, that's why I'm asking. It's not like you to drink this much normally.'

They stopped walking as JK turned to face Bobby, angrily.

'Oh, hark at my brother, acting all concerned now. It's rich coming from you, given what you got up to over the years. You're such a new man, now, are you?'

'Take it easy, JK. I'm asking because I care. Besides, doesn't it make you feel unwell with your meds?'

'I stopped taking them.'

'What? Why?'

'What's the point?'

'What... all because of... him?'

'Him? Who do you mean, Bobby? Why don't you just say it? The fucking pretence ended a long time ago. Our father, who faked his own death to leave us.'

'Yes,' said Bobby as JK remained quiet. 'I take it you found him, then?'

Eventually, JK nodded.

'And? Let me guess, he was still an asshole after all?'

Bobby saw tears begin to well up in his brother's eyes but the silence was broken as Rick returned.

'Come on, lads, the night is yet young. Let's go on somewhere. JK, your old Thai mate has told me about a very interesting establishment nearby,' said Rick, nodding over his shoulder at the rat, who remained, standing a metre behind him, grinning as ever.

'We're not going to a fucking brothel, Rick. I just got married, in case you've forgotten.'

'What do you take me for, man? Not a brothel, just a sex show. I've seen one already, years ago, but I just thought it was about time you two saw the full cultural experience while you are here. Might fucking cheer you both up.'

'Fucking hell, Rick. You have a way with words, don't you? I'm pretty sure a sex show isn't going to cheer up JK,' said Bobby, with a sigh.

'Oh, for fuck's sake, Bobby! Stop speaking on my behalf all the time,' said JK. 'You know what, Rick, fuck it. Let's go. Bobby never used to be this boring, did he?'

'OK... er, if you're sure,' said Rick. 'Bobby?'

Bobby looked at his brother in shock, pausing for a moment.

'Are you serious, JK?'

'Why the fuck shouldn't I be?' replied JK.

'Looks like I better come too, then, Rick,' said Bobby.

Shortly after, along with the rat, the three of them walked to a venue called Super Pussy Club, one of the more popular clubs of this type in Pat Pong. The rat had led them upstairs, after informing them that there was a ladyboy club downstairs, and had then spoken to an older, well-dressed woman inside. She nodded and smiled pleasantly, beckoning them through the main doors, as the rat waved goodbye and returned down to street level.

They were greeted immediately on entry by a pack of about ten to fifteen scantily clad young girls who swarmed around them, as if sensing Western money like bees to a honey pot. As they laughed and squeaked in excited expectation, JK and Bobby both felt unease, wondering if they had made a mistake by coming in.

The older lady, the maître d', pointed towards some padded leather seats against the wall. They moved their way towards them with the gang of girls still in tow. It was a very dark room, and as they sat down they had their first full view of the club. Tourists were dotted around, mostly on their own or in the odd two- or three-man group and there were no female spectators at all.

Each visitor group had two or three working girls with them. More girls were spread around three walls and at one end of the room. At the other end, a raised platform extended from the wall which was framed by tall green curtains hanging from above. The decor was very basic, some low-lit lights had green or blue lamp-shades, but it was too dark to focus on any design features. Smoke also obscured any decent view they might have had.

With so many of the girls surrounding them, they couldn't focus on any real conversation, and soon these attractive beggars became more of a nuisance. Bobby had been trying to shoe them away but as soon as Rick got some cash out of his wallet for drinks, their squawks and shrieks increased in volume again. Knowing how much it was worth to them, and how little it was to him, he began to hand around twenty-baht notes, hoping they would go away.

Of course, this turned out to be a bad choice, as several more girls then appeared on seeing Rick flaunting his money, joining the throng in the hope they would get some too. Even though Rick was laughing at all of this, JK sat looking shell-shocked and Bobby was becoming more agitated.

Just as Bobby was about to shout at them, the maître d' must have picked up on his growing impatience and barked at the girls in Thai. Most of them scurried away, some groaning disappointment as they left.

Bobby smiled at JK to try and restore calm as Rick pointed to the stage to let them know the curtains had moved. He then ordered a round of beers from one of the five girls that remained by their table, trying to ignore their provocative questioning.

'Hey, mister, I like your watch, where you get it?' said one, as Rick's eyes were drawn to the red ribbon round her neck.

'Hey, you very handsome, you smell nice – what your name?' said her friend to Bobby. This girl had striking blue eyes and an exaggerated blue eye-shadow to match.

'Do you like my hair? Is nice colour, yes? All boys say this their favourite,' said a third girl to the whole table, playfully twirling her locks of highlighted-blonde hair.

Rick would respond to some of these, while Bobby and JK others ignored them completely. They found no enjoyment in the attention when they knew exactly why they were receiving it. The insincere and repeated attempts soon became boring to them both, but then, as their drinks finally arrived, they saw Rick look longingly into the large eyes of one young girl with spectacular make-up.

'Focus on the show, Rick,' Bobby said as he nudged him. 'It's the only reason we're here, after all.'

Bobby had heard a lot about these shows, mainly from Rick, but to see it now was still a unique experience for him. They were presented with a series of freakish sights, as a succession of different objects appeared from the performing girls' genitalia.

First, they saw the release of a tiny bird. Later on heralded the retrieval of a long, thin chain that had small pins and nails attached to it. Bobby had been told of the ping pong ball trick, and was expecting more of a spectacle but the balls fell limply to the floor, as opposed to shooting across the room, as he had been led to believe.

At times, he didn't know where to look but was curious to see how his brother would react. JK just continued sitting, emotionless, staring vacantly out at the stage as he occasionally sipped his drink and smoked a cigar.

By contrast, Bobby noticed that Rick had now completely relaxed and was attempting to strike up a rapport with the girls who sat with them, trying to ask questions about their normal lives. He had been in deep conversation with one of them for several minutes.

The other girls gave an informative audience commentary on all of the events on stage, including the most dangerous trick of all, the introduction of sparklers. By this point, Bobby suddenly realised that Rick had disappeared.

'Hey, did you see where Rick went?' Bobby shouted over the background music, leaning forward over the table, as JK eventually noticed too.

'He went off with one of the girls,' replied JK.

Bobby looked around their table and noticed that the heavily made up girl had disappeared also.

'Oh god, that idiot. I fucking knew he would be tempted,' he sighed, staring all around the club to see if he could spot Rick.

'Stop worrying about him. It's his risk,' JK said, coldly, looking down at the table. With Rick gone, Bobby let his brother's reply hang in the air, and suddenly felt that JK might be ready to talk to him.

'I admire you, Bobby,' JK finally told him.

'What?' he shouted.

'I said, I admire you. I just wanted you to know that.'

'Oh, right. Er… thanks. But what the hell do you mean, JK?'

'I'm just saying that I wish I could've coped with all this – everything that's happened to us – as well as you have. You've been so much more spontaneous with your life, you've done everything you wanted to, and your life hasn't suffered at all. Now, you've got it all: a wife; a job; all the travel memories. And peace of mind, too.'

'Ah, I don't know about that, JK. You seem pretty spontaneous to me. You've left home to go travelling again. Most people are lucky to go once. This is about your third or fourth time, isn't it?'

'Only because I thought I had to. I thought I would be lucky, that I was supposed to find something. But now, I know, you're the lucky one, not me. You always were.'

'I don't know if I'm lucky. It's taken me a long time to settle down; I've wasted a lot of time and money. And just look where I am now, out here, in a seedy sex show.'

'Yeah, but only because you were worried about me.'

'I guess so. And should I be worried, JK? You don't seem right to me.'

JK stared sadly at the stage in silence.

'Come on, brother. Talk to me,' said Bobby, but JK just closed his eyes and shook his head.

'I don't know who I'm supposed to be anymore,' he said, eventually.

'Is this because of what happened when you met our father? Are you going to tell me, then?' Bobby asked, but got no further reply, suspecting JK wouldn't offer anything else now. 'Anyway, all this talking is making me thirsty. How about another drink?'

Bobby asked for another round of drinks from one of the more persistent girls hovering nearby, who then snapped an order at a barman. Just then, there was more movement on stage in readiness for their pièce de résistance: the darts show, a moment that they would never forget.

A bunch of about seven or eight balloons were being fixed to the ceiling close to their table, just a little further along the wall, but directly opposite the stage. The distance was around six metres from the edge of the platform to the balloons. As they were being attached, the girls who sat with them clapped excitedly, saying that this was their favourite part of the show.

A half-naked woman, a little older than the previous girls and with a larger physique, then appeared on stage. She was holding a short wooden bamboo tube. A chair and small table had been placed at the edge of the platform where she then sat down. On the table was a small pot, from which she pulled out a short feathered dart.

Bobby shook his head as recognition of the trick hit him. He looked for a reaction from his brother once more, but JK now held a fearful look as sweat had started to run down his face.

Taking aim, the woman on stage opened her legs, positioning her hips so that she faced towards the balloons, and then proceeded to 'load' herself with the bamboo. She then fed the dart into the tube and, after a quick shuffle on her buttocks, a dart was launched and then a loud bang was heard overhead. The exploded balloon debris fell to the floor as the audience began clapping. Bobby felt obliged to join in.

As she repeated this process, in the background, the crowd had been getting more and more excited as the stage performer reduced the size of her target. More and more balloons had popped and eventually, only three were left. She began to shoot and miss this time. One dart landed about a foot and a half away from Bobby on the sofa against the wall. One of their table girls told them to all move closer together, out of her firing range, which Bobby and JK did promptly.

Rick suddenly re-joined the table, unannounced.

'Woah there, Rick! Where the hell have you been, you pervert?' Bobby said, shoving him.

'Knock it off, Bobby, you twat,' he snapped back.

'What's up with you? Feeling guilty?'

'I just didn't wanna draw attention to myself, that's all. And I reckon we should be leaving soon, too,' Rick said, anxiously looking back in the direction he had just appeared from.

'What? Not now, surely. The final act is on,' Bobby replied.

Rick, now too preoccupied to acknowledge the show, sat with a startled expression that hadn't changed since he had returned to the table. He was a little closer to the balloons, a metre to the right of them.

A balloon popped, and another dart missed, landing on the sofa right next to Rick, who looked nervously around from one end of the club to another. Another dart flew over as the crowd were getting restless, and another balloon popped. Only one now remained – it was an impressive, relentless technique that the performer had. One more dart flew over, landing harmlessly on the floor.

In the corner, Bobby saw a bouncer talking to a girl next to one of several side doors past the bar area at the back. The girl seemed to be pointing in their direction and, as he saw her face, he noticed that it was the same girl who Rick had disappeared with earlier.

Rick pulled out a cigarette and attempted to light it with a match, but for some reason it wouldn't light. JK's eyes were suddenly transfixed by the lit match as its flame grew longer and longer the more Rick failed to get the cigarette going, swearing with each attempt.

Concerned, Bobby looked back to the stage to see the performer feed one more dart into the pipe, as concentration and sweat dominated her face. He saw the dart fly out and traced its path through the air, approaching its target. But it missed once more and, instead, ended its journey just underneath the balloons, embedding itself straight into Rick's forehead.

His delayed reaction was one of wide-eyed shock, followed by a short scream and a frantic flapping to remove the dart jutting out of his temple. But he was OK, the darts were only an inch long, and only a third of it had entered his skin anyway.

Bobby laughed out loud, and then all the table girls began to laugh with him. But their laughter was cut short as, after Rick had been struck by the errant dart, he had dropped the lit match he had been holding, lighting a fire on the alcohol-soaked table top he had been resting on. This was the catalyst for JK fainting once more: his face, despite still not managing to move a muscle whatsoever, had now started to turn an ashen grey colour and his eye-lids began to close.

Simultaneously, the girls began to scream at the fire. The final addition to the scene was two large bouncers who had stormed over to the table and roughly pushed Rick off his feet. Chaos ensued as several people rushed past and various Thai shouts and screams rang around.

Bobby quickly knelt down and shook JK. He felt his brother's face – his skin was hot to touch – and grabbed an ice cube from a nearby drink, rubbing it over his forehead and cheeks. Bobby could hear Rick arguing with the bouncers in the background as JK started to stir.

Then, the girl that Rick had been with stormed through to them, in between the bouncers, and started screaming at him. She grabbed a glass and threw it, narrowly missing him, as it crashed off the top of another table. Now the bouncers had to restrain her as she kept screaming and wriggling.

Her piercing shrieks, along with the hatred in her eyes, was more than enough to scare Rick half to death, as he cowered between the two bouncers. He looked down at Bobby like a scared rabbit as the maître d' started barking orders at the girl and the bouncers.

'What's going on?' JK mumbled as Bobby propped him up, grabbing him under his armpits. When he looked back up, it was to see Rick being lifted off his feet, a bouncer on each arm as he was carried out of the club. His earlier companion followed, still shouting at him.

By now, the small fire had been extinguished and the maître d' looked at Bobby and JK in disgust, as a few of the girls who had stayed on to watch the spectacle were gathered behind her.

'You go now!' she shouted.

Bobby tried to get JK to walk and, seeing him struggle, one of the girls approached to assist. This prompted another sharp squawk from the maître d' leading to the young girl's hasty retreat. Bobby tried to shift JK up again and, finally, he stumbled then stood on his feet. He was still slightly groggy but Bobby put his arm round him and led him towards the exit.

As he pushed the main doors open, the maître d' followed behind. Outside, the bouncers stood tall over Rick a few metres ahead, lying bruised and bloodied in a crumpled mess, but the girl was now nowhere to be seen.

Faced with a staircase to return down to street level, Bobby left JK half-standing against a railing, as he now attempted to scoop up Rick from the floor. Eventually, the three of them started to descend the stairs slowly, limping pathetically. On the final step, JK collapsed to the floor once more and began to sob uncontrollably.

'Don't worry, JK. It's all gonna be OK. We're getting out of this hell-hole as soon as possible,' Bobby said, grimly, as he looked down at his brother in pity.

Chapter Thirteen

The Lonely Shore

'How do you do it, Bobby?' asked Rick, holding a bottle of beer as he sat, shirtless, on the beach.

'Do what?' Bobby replied, also shirtless, as he sat up from his towel and lowered his sunglasses.

'Keep smiling all the time.'

Bobby took a sip from his bottle and turned his face to let the sea breeze caress his warm skin. He could still hear some kids, a group of tearaways from the local town, playing further along the beach. Only just before lunch, he had been making funny faces at them. They had laughed hysterically, uplifting him on seeing their unbridled and untainted joy, their mischievous but pure spirits shining through as they made faces back. They shouted and laughed as they chased him when he had playfully stolen their hats.

'They call it the "Land of Smiles", don't they? You should know that by now,' he replied, eventually. But even though it was easier for him nowadays, inside he knew he was still faking, just like he always did.

His smiles had always been returned here. Something about that had comforted Bobby whenever he had visited Thailand. It was almost as if he was part of one big family. Much more so than back home, where smiling was such a luxury – people there just didn't know how to receive a smile, and so they weren't that good at giving them either, in his experience, anyway, he thought.

But here it was different: everyone smiled and was inclined to be friendly. It was very disarming for those who weren't used to it, but Bobby took it all in his stride. He was good at smiling by now; for so many years he had trained himself to do it, even when he knew he wasn't smiling on the inside.

'Aye, and I know you're full of shite most of the time,' replied Rick, looking out to the sea. 'But…I'm just…I'm glad you're happy.'

'Thanks, mate,' Bobby said, surprised at Rick's unusually positive observation as he stared directly back at him. 'And you seem a lot happier yourself. I guess that's why you mentioned it.'

'Well, I'm always happy after a good lunch. Even if the setting is a bit bizarre for Christmas,' Rick replied, awkwardly changing topic. 'JK had the right idea, didn't he? I might go and have a nap now myself.'

'Yeah but an afternoon snooze on Christmas Day really isn't that bizarre, is it?'

'Aye, true.'

They had arrived at Ko Phi Phi, one of the many laid-back southern islands of Thailand, two days ago. Bobby was sure it was the right thing to do: a change of pace to the manic Bangkok, and the beach always provided a welcome change in surroundings. It was about as different a Christmas setting as he could imagine to distract his brother.

'What do you think, then, about JK? Is he going to be alright?' Rick asked.

En route from Bangkok, JK had finally told Bobby about their father's rejection. Despite his total lack of surprise, he had resisted any urge to say 'I told you so'. Now, Bobby knew he just had to be here for JK and make sure he was OK before they returned home.

'So far, so good. It all seems to be going to plan. He's slowly been cheering up since we got here. You've been enjoying yourself too, haven't you?'

'Yeah, sure.'

'Oh, come on, Rick. Don't play coy with me. I'm surprised your German friend isn't with you right now. I thought you two were joined at the hip,' said Bobby, laughing.

'Who, Esmé? Oh, she wanted to have Christmas lunch with her Swedish mate, Ilka. I'm sure we'll see them later for drinks tonight.'

'I'm sure we will,' Bobby said, as a mischievous grin spread over his face. 'And who would've thought you two would get together after your inauspicious first meeting?'

'What, you mean the snorkelling trip?'

'That poor girl, stuck on a boat in between JK, looking as miserable as ever, and you, a skin-head bean-pole with an aggressive Scottish accent, sweating profusely in a tight-fitting, knocked-off Glasgow Rangers football shirt!'

'Aye, that only cost me about fifty pence!' Rick said, laughing at the memory. 'She gave us both a pretty suspicious look.'

'Yeah, well, once she knew they were the only seats left, I saw her pleading, desperate look-back at the tour guide. It was so funny.'

'She was so pissed off when she sat down that she didn't say a word to anyone.'

'You were a lovely pale shade of green too; she must've smelled the booze on you a mile off.'

'It wasn't booze, I told you. I had really bad sea-sickness.'

'Yeah, right. Well, I was hungover so I know you must've been too. You were holding your gut with one arm and clasping the edge of the boat with the other.'

'Aye, well, if she hadn't arrived so late, she would've got a better seat!'

'I'll tell her you said that later.'

'Oh, man, and then it was so embarrassing when we finally arrived at the snorkelling spot,' Rick said, as he closed his eyes and shook his head.

'I'm glad you can laugh about it now. I certainly can, mate. As soon as the boat stopped, you lurched over the edge and threw up into the water, only for a school of fish to get really excited and circle round, then enter your puke and scavenge the remains for any tasty morsels from the contents of your stomach.' Bobby couldn't stop laughing to himself.

'Yeah, OK, Bobby, you can fuck off now.'

'Just think of all those trips, mate. We've had some good times in Thailand over the years. All those parties, those beaches. Ko Samui, Ko Pha-Ngan, Railay Beach.'

'Aye, with many more to come, I hope. I'm feeling good about myself, Bobby.'

'Because of Esmé?' Bobby replied, with a quizzical look.

'Who knows?' replied Rick, evasively.

'Well, you've never really stuck with a girl for that long, not since I've known you. Maybe that's why you're feeling so good.'

'I've only known her a couple of days, Bob.'

'I know, but you seem... different.'

'How do you mean?'

'You just do, mate. Come on, admit it, you've got feelings for her.'

'Well, I don't know about that, but I think I've found someone who is actually into the same things as me,' Rick said, giving Bobby a knowing stare and a small smile.

Bobby frowned back, as he thought for a moment, before a spark of recognition finally hit him.

'No way! You don't mean your fucking sexual perversions, do you?'

Rick slowly raised his eyebrows and tilted his head in acknowledgement.

'Oh my god!' said Bobby. 'Golden showers. You fucking sickos. After all these years, you've finally found a girl as perverted as you. Giving or receiving?'

'Both,' said Rick, smiling.

'Fucking hell. Must be true love. Or, she must be as fucked-up as you are.'

Rick looked away again, half-smiling, but Bobby knew he had touched a nerve. Not many people knew about Rick's upbringing, but he had confided in Bobby many years ago, not long after they had first met. Bobby knew that part of their friendship had always been based on a mutual respect of their own family childhood trauma. And he also knew they would always fiercely respect each other's privacy.

'Look, Rick, she seems like a nice girl. I know you won't, but don't worry about what anyone else thinks. Go with your gut feeling. You'll know when it feels right, and when it does, you should just go for it. I did with Di.'

'But how did you know?'

'It's hard to describe, but when you meet someone special, it makes you think differently about stuff. Without that someone, you can only think about your future in terms of your own memories, the ones you've already had. Just as some sort of extension to them,' said Bobby, as Rick looked on, puzzled. 'I'm probably not explaining this very well. When you meet someone new, you don't know their memories, their past. So, you don't know what your own future will hold, because it's all unknown with someone new. And that's exciting, right?'

Rick looked shell-shocked as stared out at the sea.

'Aye, I suppose. I never thought of it like that,' he replied, eventually. 'You're full of surprises, aren't you, Bobby? I can see you've thought deeply about this, about Di, haven't you?'

Bobby suddenly missed home. He felt a pang of guilt as a look of concern momentarily flashed across his face. But, just like he had done for many years, he hid his emotion, and pulled out one of his best tried-and-tested blasé smiles.

'Deep? Me? Rick, come on, how long have you known me for now? It must be all that heat getting to both of us,' he said, before abruptly standing up. 'I'm gonna go for a walk for a bit. I'm getting restless, and you know I don't do afternoon naps! Anyway, you look tired, mate. Why don't you have a sleep?'

'Aye, you're right. I might. I'll catch you later,' replied Rick, as he lay back down on his towel.

Bobby walked away, up the beach, towards town. He remembered there was a pay phone at their hostel and he wanted to call his wife on Christmas Day. The UK was seven hours behind them, so Di would just be getting up. That would be a nice treat, he thought.

En route, he approached the local kids again, who were still playing further up the beach. He waved at them and smiled, which they returned.

All apart from one of the girls. While all the others had joked and shouted back, from her there was nothing. Bobby hadn't noticed this girl earlier on, and guessed she must've been new to their group. At first he thought she was shy or upset but she just stared at Bobby, almost through him, without a glimmer of emotion.

After a few seconds, the girl walked off, along the beach and away from the other children, without looking back. And then she disappeared completely, only leaving Bobby with the memory of an unreturned smile.

At sunset, the group of five travellers sat in a humid outdoor audience of the special Christmas Day performance at Hippies bar. Fire jugglers created mesmerising circles of light as they watched, entranced and intoxicated, trapped in a world of wonder, comfortably numb without the need to bother anyone or anything.

They had enjoyed a sublime Christmas meal of Thai curry, and toasted their friends and family back home with some festive cocktails. Darkness fell, and time moved on; the show had ended and they were now deep in conversation.

'So, you're saying that nothing has ever shocked you in Thailand, Rick?' asked Ilka, a tall blonde girl from Sweden, who sat to the left of JK on their round wooden table. On her left was her travel partner, Esmé, who had Rick on her other side. Completing the circle was Bobby.

'The only thing that shocked me was how all the Thai men look so feminine,' Rick replied, as the group laughed.

'You're just so macho, aren't you, Rick?' said Ilka, rolling her eyes.

'Well, he has seen rather a lot in Thailand,' said Bobby, sending a knowing smile in Rick's direction. 'What about you two girls, then? You must've seen loads of great things in Asia over the last three weeks,' Bobby continued, quickly changing the subject.

'Oh yes, it's been the holiday of a lifetime,' replied Ilka, turning to Esmé, who smiled awkwardly.

'You must have some amazing photos?' asked Bobby.

'Er, yes, I have some,' replied Ilka, to which both Rick and Esmé shifted uncomfortably. 'Are you joking, Bobby?'

'What do you mean?' he replied.

'You mean you don't know? Rick didn't tell you?'

'Come on, Ilka. We don't need to do this now,' replied Esmé.

'Oh, I think we should. I'm sure Bobby and his brother will find it funny. They need to know what Rick has done,' Ilka replied, with a vicious smile.

'It's OK, I don't care. I've forgiven him already,' said Esmé, as she leaned over and gave Rick a lingering kiss on the lips.

'OK, now I really want to know the story,' said JK, in a rare show of excitement.

Rick looked startled as a flush rose in his cheeks.

'Me too, I don't think I've ever seen Rick blush! Come on, Ilka, what happened?' said Bobby.

'Well, Esmé did have lots of photos also. Up to a few hours ago anyway,' she replied.

'Rick went round yours first before we all went out, right?' asked JK.

'Yep. Esmé had been playing with her digital camera. It was full of photos from our trip and the memory card had run out of space. And, although you could easily get a new one in Bangkok, the shops here are pretty sparse so, in the meantime, she wanted a way of temporarily creating some space by deleting a few photos.'

Ilka took delight in telling the story, flicking her long, plaited ponytail as she turned to observe Rick, suffering and shaking his head.

'Neither of us are very technical, you see. We couldn't find a way of doing it easily, rather than just clicking one-by-one. So, Rick, the helpful gentleman from Scotland here, offered to help, seeing that he has his own digital camera. He took hers and started to play around with it. Then, sometime later, he looked up at her silently. And you know what? I remember now, he was blushing then, too. What was it he said to you again, Esmé?'

'"I'm afraid I've got some good news and some bad news." Brilliant line that, Rick!' said Esmé, laughing as she held on to Rick, squirming.

'Well, the good news was that he'd managed to create some room on the memory card like she had asked him,' Ilka said, carrying on the story. 'Unfortunately, the bad news was that he had deleted all her photos in the process.'

JK looked shocked and Bobby was laughing uncontrollably.

'Aye, I know. I'm terrible. I apologised profusely,' said Rick.

'So you should. Five hundred photos – shots of a lifetime – lost forever. Disgraceful,' said Ilka. She was smiling, but there was an undeniable tone of blame in her words.

'What did you say, Esmé?' asked JK.

'I said it was OK, and that I could always get copies of his and Ilka's photos,' she replied.

'Of course. I'm just surprised you didn't kill him there and then,' said Bobby.

'I wanted to,' said Ilka, 'But she was amazing. No tears, nothing. She just said "OK" a lot and went very quiet. Not a lot else. Are you really sure you've forgiven him, Esmé?'

'Yes, yes. Honestly, it's all fine now. It's Christmas, after all! And we made up pretty quickly afterwards,' she replied, giggling, as she kissed Rick again.

'OK, you two, get a room,' said Bobby. He turned to his brother, who was still staring ahead in silence. 'Kind of destroys your theory about karma, eh, JK?'

'It's almost unbelievable,' replied his brother.

'It wasn't funny, and I still feel bad about it. I guess I'm just very lucky that she forgave me,' said Rick.

'It's such a funny concept, luck, isn't it?' said JK, letting his reply hang in the air, as people sipped their drinks. Bobby observed his brother in trepidation as a look of confusion spread across Ilka's face.

'How so?' she said.

'Well, take these two jokers, my brother and Rick. They've both had their fair share of luck over the years. I don't know if you've heard any of their stories before. Bobby, in particular, has loads. I used to think I was the lucky one, but not anymore.'

'Really? Tell us more,' replied Esmé. 'Are you the lucky one, Bobby?'

'I don't know about that,' he replied. 'I've trotted round the world a few times. Nothing lucky about that. I chose to do it.'

'I dunno, Bob. We've both seen a hell of a lot, but you've seen your fair share of good fortune, that's for sure,' said Rick, grasping at the opportunity to deflect attention away from himself.

'People don't want to hear our boring backpacking tales. I don't want to be one of those travellers who won't shut up about how fucking great their travel experiences were. Waxing lyrical and non-stop. Smug bastards, the lot of them,' said Bobby.

'Oh, come on, Bob. Don't be so bashful, it doesn't suit you. Didn't you once get shot at by bandits, in a boat on the river Andes?' said Rick.

'Yeah, so what?' he replied, dismissively.

'And that's where a poisonous snake bit you, and the doctor told you he might have to amputate your arm? And you only just got the anti-venom in time.'

'Yes, yes,' said Bobby, sighing.

Esmé and Ilka looked at Bobby, and then back at Rick and JK, in amazement.

'Oh, trust me – there's much more,' said JK.

'Look, come on. Let's move on to someone else now. What about your fruit-picking story, Rick. That was a good one,' said Bobby.

'What, our first visit to Australia? You were there too. It was in Victoria, sweating in unbearable forty-degree heat, carrying huge plastic bags on our shoulders weighing over five kilos, smelling like death, covered in mud,' he replied, laughing.

'Exactly. Those bags were filled with resin, dust, sap and sharp thorns. Not to mention slugs, beetles and worms. All because we were *so lucky*, JK,' said Bobby, with a sarcastic smile at his brother.

'Aye, and giant spiders,' chipped in Rick. 'Rats too. Don't forget the rats. If we were really, really lucky, that is.'

'And all that for the princely sum of five dollars an hour. Yeah, we don't sound like such cool travellers anymore, do we girls?' said Bobby.

'Didn't you get into a fight with Sean Penn once?' JK asked his brother.

'What, the actor? Seriously?' asked Ilka.

'Yes, but I didn't know it was him at the time. I don't know many actors or celebs,' replied Bobby.

'But how did that happen? Where was it?' asked Esmé.

'Just some restaurant in San Francisco. He'd been arguing with several waitresses, I don't even know why now, but I just took exception to it. It never made the news.'

'Fuck,' she replied.

'And in the Pacific Islands, he gave the Fijian locals a run for their money at beach rugby. So much so they gave him the nickname "boom boom Bob" due to his electrifying pace. They even gave him their own specially made floral lei,' said Rick.

'Yes, OK. But who cares?' said Bobby, impatiently.

'I've got another one he told me about from South America. He got chased out of a village by brothers, fathers, friends, priests and elder statesman. Just because he'd been caught kissing the local horny sixteen-year-old senorita,' JK said, with glee.

'Wow. You certainly have all the stories. But I think you're just embarrassing your brother now, JK,' said Esmé.

'OK, but I just think it's amazing, that's all,' JK carried on. 'He's got all these stories after we both had a pretty hard upbringing. Yet, he's still able to carry on with life back home at the end of it all. He's got a great wife and a nice place to live. I mean, some people don't know how to cope with normal life, after experiencing all that,' he paused, looking down into his drink. 'But not you, Bobby. You'll always be remembered, that's for sure. And in a good way too.'

The girls looked at the brothers, feeling their tension.

'I don't know what you mean. I didn't set out to out-travel anyone. I was never into any sort of cock-measuring contest, like some backpackers are. I couldn't give a shit if someone else has seen all the seven natural wonders of the world, or has been to over forty countries, or whatever,' Bobby replied, defensively.

'That's a very admirable attitude, Bobby. But you have to admit that all you've seen and done is still pretty impressive,' said Esmé, staring intently at Bobby, spellbound by his amber eyes as they glistened in the evening firelight. She thought she had seen a tear begin to form in them.

'Maybe. But why does any of that matter? It doesn't to me. Never has. What difference does it make? It's just about having a good time, and having fun while it lasts. Because, at some point, it's all going to end – and we all know it,' he replied.

'Wow, that's pretty bleak, Bob. Especially for you. Are you OK?' asked Rick.

'I'm fine. Must just be the booze,' he replied, quickly, realising his mask was slipping, as he rubbed his eyes. 'Merry Christmas, everyone.'

They echoed his Christmas wishes with cheers and clinked their glasses. Bobby already knew that he'd had enough of the backpacker life for good. Not that he had needed it to, but this moment had validated the decision he had made a long time ago. Now, he just missed his wife desperately.

All he had to do was make sure his brother was OK before he could go home, back to her. It wouldn't be long now, he thought. Something inside him told him that their stay on this island would be coming to an end very soon.

They carried on drinking for a time, the girls dancing without caring, the lads playfully fighting and all were singing the cheesy, classic seasonal songs. The night temperature had dropped and a breeze followed them around as they wandered the sandy paths back to the straw huts at their beach resort.

Rick was arm in arm with Esmé. JK, who had subtly been escalating his flirting with Ilka as the night had gone on, eventually reached out to hold her hand. As they walked, they were asked by the numerous masseuses, sitting down outside their simple stall fronts, if they wanted a massage.

They laughed at the frequency and consistency of this request, among all the different old ladies: their tone, the reaction it provided each time and the ladies' willingness to laugh at themselves. Suddenly, Bobby jumped in and sat next to one of them. He joined her for five minutes, shouting out their same cry of 'you want massaaaaage?' to every other tourist that walked past them, as the rest of the group howled in laughter.

Eventually, they went their separate ways along the beach, in the moonlight. Esmé and Rick, along with Bobby, went back to the hut the boys shared, while JK and Ilka went back to the girls' hut.

JK knocked at Bobby's hut early the next morning. Bobby stumbled to open the door in confusion, his head throbbing and his eyes heavy. JK stared back at him sheepishly and in silence as he stood in the doorway.

'What?' Bobby said, grumpily. JK stared back at him, silently.

'I admire you, Bobby,' JK replied, eventually.

'Huh? Oh, fuck off, JK.'

'I know I've told you before, but I just needed you to know that.'

'Can't this wait till later?'

'No, it can't. Because I need to do something unusual, right now,' he said, waiting for a reply that didn't come, as Bobby stared vacantly back with half open eyes. 'Well, unusual for me, anyway. It's more like something you would do.'

'What are you on about? What time is it?' Bobby said, turning around to look at Esmé and Rick lying naked, asleep next to each other.

'6am. I've just come from Ilka's,' he replied, and walked past Bobby, into the hut. He quietly crept around, as he grabbed his backpack and started to pack his things into it. Eventually Rick began to stir. On seeing this, JK finished packing his bag, and walked out of the hut again, signalling to Bobby to come outside with him.

Slowly, Bobby dragged himself outside to follow his brother.

'So, what the fuck is going on?' said Bobby. 'Ilka is a stunner. Why did you leave her place so early, anyway? Is she OK?'

'She's asleep. She's fine, don't worry. After we – well, you know – I was just lying, wide awake, thinking loads, like I normally do. I couldn't sleep. So, I left her place and started walking along the beach.'

'Right. And so? Why have you packed your bag, where are you going now?'

'Well, about twenty minutes ago, I met a local fisherman. He was carrying stuff on to his boat. Then his family appeared, they were carrying loads of stuff too, so I asked him what he was doing. He told me he was leaving the island and they were packing their stuff up, ready to go. So, I thought about it, and then I asked him if I could go with them.'

'Er, what?'

'And they said yes, but only if I could go with them right now.'

Again, Bobby stared back at his brother in bewilderment.

'So, obviously, I said I needed to go and get my bag first. He said OK, but he was leaving in one hour, with or without me.'

'Where are they going?'

'No idea. Just another island.'

'You're serious, JK? You're really just going to go, right now?' said Bobby, shaking his head in disbelief.

'Yes.'

'But why?'

'Something just clicked in my head. I just suddenly thought that I've had enough of the island. Last night was amazing and I've had a great few days here with you guys. You've really helped me move on from –,' JK paused as he swallowed hard, 'Bangkok and everything that happened. And I realised I couldn't face going home right now, having to think about all the usual Christmas bullshit we go through with Mum… So, I just knew that it probably won't get any better than right now.'

'Yeah, but you can still stay here and make that feeling last. Enjoy yourself, with us,' said Bobby, scratching his stubble.

'Bobby, I'm happy, for the first time in a few weeks, or even months. I just feel that I've got to go now. It's the right time.'

'Like fuck it is. You've had an emotional roller coaster just the last few days I've been here, and maybe even longer before that. I only came out here to make sure you were OK. And now, suddenly, just like that, you say you're OK?' Bobby said in desperation.

'I know, I know. And I'm grateful for what you did for me. Really, I am. But it worked – you did your job. I'm OK now, really.'

It had started to rain and the wind had got up. Bobby, standing in only his boxer shorts, shivered and rubbed his aching head.

'I don't want to deal with this right now,' he said.

'Honestly, you don't need to worry about me, Bobby. Maybe I'll explore a few islands for a bit, like you've done in the past, and then go back to the mainland and then sort out flights for my next leg of travel. Like an African safari, I've always fancied doing that. But who knows, I could go anywhere. Why don't you come with me?'

Bobby sighed and looked along the beach and then back at his brother.

'I can't do that, JK. I need to get home, back to Di.'

'I understand,' said JK, looking disappointed. 'I guess this is role reversal, right? Finally, after all these years. Me being the spontaneous one and going; you being the one who thinks about all the stuff he needs to stay behind for.'

'Yeah, I guess so, brother… Are you really sure you're gonna be OK?'

'I'll be fine. Like I said, I admire you. That's why I'm doing this.'

They stared at each other for a moment and smiled.

'Come here, you stupid bastard,' said Bobby, embracing his brother as they said their goodbyes.

Feeling unsettled, Bobby stood and watched JK walk further along the beach. After he could no longer see his brother, he wandered back to his hut to find Rick and Esmé were still asleep. He climbed back into his bed but he was now completely unable to sleep.

Then he heard a faint sound of a motor boat and ran outside again. He saw a boat heading northwards across the waves. He could just make out his brother, along with a few other passengers, and waved frantically at them, but they couldn't see him.

One person, the father fisherman he guessed, was pointing at something in the distance on the horizon, completely the opposite direction to where they were heading, towards the west. Bobby looked over to where he was pointing, but all he could see was the ocean: no boats, no clouds, nothing unusual at all. On they went, before very quickly completely disappearing from his view.

As the rain stopped and the sun came out, he sat down on the shore, waiting to see what else would happen, looking along the beach to see if any other surprise visitors might turn up.

He began to warm up and started to snooze on the beach in the early morning sun. An occasional breeze would stir him, and eventually he went back to his hut and poured himself a glass of water.

Rick and Esmé were now half awake, still tired and hungover. But soon they were fully alert, once Bobby had told them about JK's sudden departure. They were just about to dissect the evening's events, as was customary after their nights out, when they heard a commotion outside and got up to take a look.

They could feel something strange was happening – perhaps they were all still in shock after the morning's events – but it was hard to work out exactly what it was. Various tourists and a few locals, including children, were standing around in unconnected groups between their huts, looking concerned, talking about the water. Backpacker girls put their heads in their hands. Boys ran to the edge of the shoreline to take a look.

They heard whispers: people saying to get off the beach immediately; to go and find cover. Whispers of something terrible. It spread fast.

People were running from the main stretch of shops, and Bobby, Rick and Esmé then followed, joining the masses as they ran out to the beach to see what was happening.

A sick feeling had formed in Bobby's stomach. He hadn't told Rick that the fisherman on JK's boat had been pointing at something; but somehow he knew that whatever was happening was connected to that.

Later, at around 7.45am, Bobby sat on the beach at Tonsai Bay, smiling at the alien concept of sunshine on Boxing Day. Holding a bottle of Coke in his right hand, he also smiled at the irony of what would be Ko Phi Phi's last 'thank you and goodbye' to, not only another tourist, but probably the western world as well.

He had just seen the ocean withdraw rapidly and then disappear from the shore completely, leaving him surrounded by a vast expanse of sand, a corridor of yellow between the two giant limestone ridges that made up the island of Phi Phi Don. Yesterday, this had been not even a quarter of the size it was now. Only then, JK and Bobby had walked along it in a rush to meet Rick as well as the girls at Mahoney's Bar, before moving on for the evening.

He could still hear everyone else behind him panicking. Young children wailing, loud backpackers shouting, locals snapping in Thai, a scramble of limbs scurrying across the ground, bags being hoisted on shoulders or dragged through the sand. Yet, all he was thinking was 'when will the water come back?' But he knew it wouldn't be long; it certainly would come back.

He kept smiling, trying to ignore the dread growing in his stomach. Seeing the beach, knowing that time was running out. Remembering better days, remembering Christmas holidays of his past, on what would probably turn out to be his last one.

'Happy Christmas, Bobby Jenkins,' he spoke out loud to himself, laughing at the bizarre sight in front of him.

Now, many more people rushed along the stretch of sand he sat on, but for entirely less happy reasons. And yet he found it funny that they wouldn't walk on this newly appeared stretch of beach in front of him. It's not as if the sand would hurt them; but they could only pause and stare in fearful wonder.

Merry Christmas, Mum, he thought. Merry Christmas, JK. I hope you made it back to shore in time, wherever you are.

He heard someone walking behind him but couldn't find the will power to turn around. Suddenly, a shadow hovered over his left shoulder, and he looked up to see Rick staring back at him with hurt in his eyes. Bobby had somehow known that Rick would re-join him here eventually.

'Where's Esmé?' asked Bobby.

Rick shook his head and stared back down at the sand.

'She got onto some local's fishing boat with Ilka, going the other way. It was chaos, I couldn't get on it. There were too many people and the boat was too small.'

'I'm sorry, Rick. I hope she's OK.'

'Yeah. And you, did you get through to Di?'

'No,' said Bobby, staring back over the sand. 'I tried two payphones and neither of them worked. So, I gave up and came down here to watch.'

Rick didn't reply. Eventually, he sat down next to Bobby and stared grimly out at the horizon.

'I didn't deserve her anyway,' he said, eventually.

'What?' asked Bobby.

'Esmé.'

'Don't be silly. You two are great.'

'Nah. I knew it was all too good to be true. She was the one person who finally accepted me for all my faults and didn't seem to care. She just liked me anyway. I've never met anyone like that. No one is usually willing to cope with my fucked-up life. It's no wonder I've always been alone.'

'You're not that fucked-up, Rick. I know your upbringing was difficult after your dad left. It was the same for me, remember?'

'Of course I do. That's how we became friends, isn't it? Anyway, I don't blame my father. It wasn't his fault. He only left because of my mother. It was always her fault. She was a cunt to everyone.'

'Woah, Rick, I always knew you didn't like her, but –'

'Like her? She was fucking poisonous. It should be her here now, not us. That would be fucking karma, if you ask me.'

Rick paused, expecting a reaction from Bobby. But he just stared on.

'You know what she did to me?' said Rick, as Bobby shook his head. 'Well, let me tell you. Where do you think all those perversions I've got come from in the first place?'

'Oh god, you're joking?'

'No. After Dad left, and we were stuck with her, that's when I started thinking that there was no justice in life. I couldn't get my head round it. So, I've been used to people treating me like shit all my life. And that's when I started making my own adjustments, just to balance things out. Explains a lot, right?'

'How do you mean?'

'That's why I'm the way I am. I reckon it's better to shit on someone before you get shit on yourself. May sound harsh but that's just the motto I live by. It's just self-preservation. One way or another someone, somewhere, is going to shit on you, so if you see an opportunity to get something for yourself, then you should take it.

'That's why I stole stuff. It started off small, like taking sweets from a corner shop. Then I moved on to bigger things, like magazines. And soon I got into a habit and was able to spot when people weren't looking and took their wallets.

'Good people who don't deserve to be fucking robbed get robbed and there's nothing you can do about it. So, get what you can, is what I say.

'I guess I've got a problem trusting people, as if I'm waiting for them to rip me off. I think it gets worse when I'm under pressure or if I've made a mistake. And then I get defensive and end up saying some really nasty stuff, even to my mates. I know I've done it to JK. And to you, Bob. It's not something that I'm proud of.'

'Look, it doesn't matter now, Rick. We've all made mistakes,' replied Bobby.

'Aye. Maybe that's why we're here, now.'

'What do you mean?'

'Maybe there's some bigger meaning to all this. A reason. Maybe we deserve punishment; maybe it's karma?' said Rick, with a look of frantic puzzlement. He scratched the stubble across his tanned cheek.

'I don't know how you work that one out. Punishment for what – what have we done that's so bad?'

'We've done loads over the years.'

'Not me. I stopped all that a few years ago.'

'Yeah, but before.'

'We were just normal backpackers. What rules did we break? You can't tell me it was worse than anything any other traveller has done.'

'Well, maybe not you, Bobby. But I haven't exactly been ethically sound, have I?'

'Yeah…maybe…but you've been trying to change, right?'

Rick just huffed in reply. Bobby knew he needed to be strong for Rick, seeing the tears glistening on his cheeks in the piercing low sunlight. But his words had sparked yet more memories in Bobby's mind, as he now forced back his own tears.

He presumed Rick was having similar recollections of the things he had and hadn't done, trying to piece together the chain of events that had led to them both being here now, in this moment.

Bobby's own strained upbringing was not going to beat him. He had held on to that burden for over two decades without ever letting it win, and he wasn't prepared to start now, either. He looked up at Rick to check he hadn't caught a glance of his emotional wobble and smiled at him.

'How can you smile at a time like this, Bobby?' Rick pleaded.

'Smile? That's just what Bobby Jenkins does. You should know that by now. Besides, didn't I say that's the thing they do in Thailand,' he replied confidently, like he always did. But, inside, he knew it was different this time.

'But why now?'

'Why not now? It's the only way we're gonna cope.'

'But Bob, what are we going to do…' Rick started to mumble.

'There's nothing we can do now,' he replied, grimly. He wanted to cry too, but that was just not something he did. Ever.

Despite a deepening pit of fear growing inside his gut, Bobby had to remember to show his strength. Despite everything, live by your principles, back yourself, believe in who you are and the choices you've made. That's who Bobby Jenkins is, he thought.

'Do you regret coming out here now?' said Rick. Having wiped the tears away, he now had a look of steely resolve.

Bobby pondered the question. This time, he had come for his brother, and no other reason. But that was one more reason than he was ever used to having. Besides the flights, he hadn't really planned a single thing. He never did – it was just more fun that way. He couldn't admit to anything different anyway; people just wouldn't expect that of Bobby Jenkins.

'Regret? Nah, I don't do regret. Hey, just think of the good times we've had together, even just in the last fortnight,' he said, taking a swig from his bottle of Coke. 'It's just random, what happens. We don't get to choose. Who would've had any idea about this? No one, not before it was too late, that is.'

'Random? Fuck, I can't get my head round this. It can't be fair. It wasn't meant to be. Why us? Why me?' Rick rang his hands over his shaven head.

'It is what it is. It's nothing we've done. Not you, or me, or them,' he said, pointing behind at the locals shouting and scurrying behind them. 'There is no reason.'

'So, what are you saying? We could go at any moment and should just accept it when it comes?' Bobby just shrugged in reply to Rick. 'I can't just accept that this is it. What should I have done differently?' Rick shook his head as he looked far ahead to the ocean and their approaching doom.

Bobby decided to carry on talking in the hope that it would reassure him.

'You could've done things differently, of course. We all could've. But then you wouldn't have got the memories you have now. Sometimes, you just have to take the risk, and roll with whatever life deals you. Otherwise we wouldn't have a fraction of the stories we have. Just think about all the amazing people we've met in all those countries: the jokes, the drinks we shared, the stuff we learnt. All that stuff might have been lost or, even worse, never found to start with, if we'd done anything differently. So, no, to answer your original question, I don't think I would change any of it – I'm glad we did it all.'

'Aye, all great stories and good to pass on. But we're not gonna be able to do that for much longer, are we?'

'Who cares? Point is, surely, that we lived them in the first place, and that can't be taken away from us, no matter what.'

Rick sat silently for a time, staring vacantly ahead with his hands on his head.

'No. No, no, no,' he said, shaking his head profusely. Then, he stood up and slowly wandered across the shore, towards the water's edge. Bobby could tell his mind was no longer with him in that moment.

'Rick, what are you doing, mate?' Bobby shouted out towards him. Rick just threw a hand up, with his back to Bobby, waving off his concern. He stopped and turned to his side, pensively walking across the beach and staring at the ground. He was never going to walk far; in his current state of mind, he just needed this futile attempt at solitude to compose himself.

Suddenly, Rick turned around and walked towards Bobby quickly, with a new-found purpose. He stared straight ahead to town where the hubbub of activity was.

'I can't just sit here and wait to die, Bobby,' he said glancing down, and eventually stopping a metre or so past Bobby, who could not find the right words as he stared back up at him.

But Rick didn't bother to turn around. He could only twist his neck to look at Bobby over his shoulder. He took a deep breath and his shoulders lifted then dropped.

'I've got to try something. I hope I see you later, Bobby.' Rick shut his eyes and looked ahead again. Then, after one last pause, carried on walking.

Bobby watched him for a while but then turned back to face the ocean, grateful for his own privacy. He supposed that now it was finally appropriate for him to accept this contemplative moment: his life's memories were still lingering in his head as he waited for the inevitable. It could be seconds or minutes; but either way there was nothing he could do – there wasn't enough time and he knew that the end approached.

He wanted to try and make sense of his last few days in this world. Give him a chance to get the normal Bobby Jenkins back, rather than the scared, mournful, regretful mess that he was currently in danger of becoming. Bobby Jenkins was not going to go out like that.

His strength was his mask, his persona. Everyone had pain, but he wasn't going to let that beat him. Not during his lifetime. It had taken him a long time to reconcile his father's lack of attention, his love that had always been missing. So, he had developed his own way of coping, his own style of living his life. Over the years, he had trained himself to be ready for anything that could happen.

It had always been about mental adjustment: smile on the outside; go with the flow; don't get tied down; keep moving. That was Bobby Jenkins. It might be different on the inside, but that wasn't anyone's business but his own. As long as he could cope, and he usually could. Everything that happens, you can just roll with it, so what was the point of making plans? Nothing else in your life would ever change that drastically anyway.

But he supposed that this time it had. So now, he just needed time to understand why he was left here, about to die. And still he kept smiling, on the outside at least.

Then, in the distance, Bobby saw a small figure, walking along the sand. The figure got closer and he could eventually see it was a young girl. Her features came into his view: with short black hair, it was a local girl. She looked at Bobby as she passed by.

Bobby shivered, recognising her face, seeing it was the girl from yesterday: the Thai girl who had not returned his smile. In a panicked reflex, Bobby smiled at her once more, and once again the girl refused to return it. She carried on walking along the sand and Bobby watched her until she disappeared from view for the final time, her footsteps leaving history in the sand, her history, behind.

Was I dreaming now, Bobby thought? Are these the dreams of my own history, the footsteps I was leaving behind? How did I get here?

There was a reason for this happening, he suspected. There was a reason that JK had left and yet he had stayed. But he knew that whatever it was, it wasn't good.

He watched the ocean approach. Watching the water level rising slowly in the distance, trying to remember: how did I get here?

Here he was, waiting for the inevitable. Seeing that horizon of watery death, approaching relentlessly. Trying to remember happier times.

He watched the water, waiting, alone. Rick was long gone. No one ran behind him anymore, not that he could notice, anyway. In his head, it was almost deserted on the beach. All quiet, alone with his thoughts.

It was Boxing Day on December 2004 and devastation was now on the horizon.

As quickly as the water had departed, it began to flood back in. He could see it now, growing ever taller and taller, a wall of water, distant but moving closer all the time, getting faster as it approached. He started to notice sounds and movement from behind again. People scurrying and screaming. They were all waiting for the giant wave.

But Bobby was calm. He took a sip from his bottle and grinned at fate. Somehow, he knew this was it. This was his time. This was the end. No regrets for Bobby Jenkins, the boy with the amber eyes. Not now, not ever. Because he had had fun while it lasted.

That was enough for me, he thought. That was a good a way for it to end as any, wasn't it?

Chapter Fourteen

Acacia Tree Dreams & Dysentery Nightmares

The rain tapped intermittently on the ramshackle wooden roof as JK drifted in and out of sleep. It was the mid-afternoon in Phuket and, for the last few days here at the shelter on the harbour, it had been the only time he had been able to sleep, albeit briefly. Now, every time he began to doze off, the sound of the water hitting above woke him while his dreams still lingered.

He desperately wanted to sleep, to fully embrace those dreams and escape his squalid environment, but he was surprised at the memories these interrupted dreams had brought. Now, as his memories began to clarify, he welcomed the distraction. Sleep would've been better, he thought, but then anything would be preferred to the thoughts that had been rolling round his head for so long and for every waking hour since the awful realisation of his brother's fate had set in.

He remembered one particular set of dreams, amazed that they had stayed with him all this time. They had started when he was a child and ended just before he went to university, but although at the time he hadn't had them that often, maybe once every six months, they had slowly got more and more vivid.

As a child, he had watched a nature documentary about lions hunting in the Serengeti plains of Tanzania and it had really stuck with him. The striking imagery of these huge, powerful, magnificent and beautiful beasts, in complete control of their stunning environments, had left him awestruck.

Like most children, he had been fascinated by exotic animals, the colourful scenery, or any events or behaviour that were in stark contrast to his own parental-and-school planned, carefully organised existence. This certainly applied to me, he reflected, growing up in a typically modest two-bedroom terraced house with the only company he had in the evenings being his stressed single mother and his annoying older brother.

He held back tears, and reached for the writing pad and pen that lay next to his thin mattress bed on the floor. Most of the survivors here had been given these same items, to share contact details of family or friends back home, or to perhaps write a letter to loved ones, or just to pass the time and jot down their thoughts. He had even seen some use them to record card game scores, in the hope of quickening the awful passage of time.

JK had also been given a pack of cards and had played a few games of patience without yet attempting to instigate any games with his fellow survivors. There were two other people in the small wooden booth he had been staying in and he had barely spoken to them. There was little privacy for the hundreds of survivors in the shelter: all these booths on the long wooden jetty were very similar, open on one side and with very generous spacing between the wooden slats along the walls. They all shared communal toilets and showers in one large concrete block at the start of the jetty on shore.

But now he had decided that he just wanted to write down his dreams, in an attempt to finally understand them. Today was a quiet day and so perhaps he could concentrate for a change. That had been impossible over the last few days as he had sat there, waiting for information surrounded by people screaming, crying and shouting.

Now, he could ignore that, and he began to remember the lions of his dreams again. The details of their existence captivated him, the visions of them stalking their prey with controlled, elegant movements, patiently waiting for the opportune moment. Or, following the efficient but lethal violence of an attack, supremely content after devouring their prey, they basked in the glory of the hot sun, serenity in their kingdom restored as they perused the grassy plains once more.

Cool breezes brushed past the whiskers of the male of the pride as he sat, gloriously untroubled, to complete the ultimate visualisation of being master of his own destiny, king of the jungle indeed. A tear ran freely down JK's face now. Bobby had been the alpha male, always in control. And now he was gone forever.

JK tried to think of something else, and then remembered that his dreams weren't just about lions. Nature featured heavily, the elements, how he flew and then floated above the scenery, and some obscure, singular tree that always changed colour in the light with an almost supernatural quality. He hadn't noticed this too much when he had been younger.

Now, he remembered that these dreams had started with a positive feel to them. They had hardly concerned him – they weren't exactly nightmares, and he just assumed it was some sort of fantasy, perhaps about flying, gained from watching too many movies or reading too many comic books.

But then the dreams got darker and darker in tone as he got older. When he was about twelve years old, just as he had begun secondary school and entered his teenage years, the change first began. And by the time he entered adulthood, the dreams changed again, to a more disturbing degree, on the rare occasions they surfaced. They had bothered him to the extent that he couldn't make mature, grown-up decisions.

Then, past the age of eighteen, the dreams stopped altogether. Yet, JK still didn't know why, nor why they had begun in the first place. He had ignored their existence, until now, telling no-one about them, not even his brother.

Why was he dreaming them again, now? There must be a reason, he speculated, desperately. His brother, who didn't believe in luck and had hated their father, didn't believe there was a reason for anything that happened. Maybe he had been right about our father, JK thought, but he had been wrong about luck: JK was the lucky one after all, just as their father had told him as a child. Only that could explain what had happened, why he had survived the tsunami.

JK now knew he had been wrong all along in trying to emulate his father's travels. He had wasted so much time trying to find him, and he had lost his brother in the process. Not just his brother, he realised that he had lost so much, just as the fortune teller in India had told him he would, many years ago, but he still hadn't found the fortune he was due.

Sketching on the soggy pad he clutched, he began to draw a picture of the tree from his dreams. It had always been inside his head, buried deep. That was it, he suddenly realised: that was the reason for his dreams. He just had to find that tree, to find that view, to experience that breath-taking scene of the lions in their natural habitat. It had been calling to him, all this time. It was his final destiny to achieve, he thought – that was what he needed to do. That was the fortune he was due to claim.

JK dropped his pen and cried, heartbroken that his brother had had to die for him to finally realise this. No wonder he hadn't told Bobby about these dreams; he wouldn't have understood, and now he couldn't disagree with him, anyway.

As JK rubbed his eyes, a now familiar stench surrounded him. He tried to block this by remembering another smell, of fire and smoke, when his brother had first got him to try cigars at a music festival. They had been standing round their tent, trying to keep warm, the last throes of a wild, booze-fuelled evening. Some irrelevant and nonsensical discussion about how suppressed their lives were – who would break free first. Pretentious conversations about the purity of their musical preferences and how the festival line-up compared – the usual drunken nonsense.

But it wasn't enough: the original smell remained. The terrible, pungent, inescapable and unequivocal stench of death. JK could only sit and watch, his head in his hands, as bodies were carried back and forth along the jetty.

He rushed to his feet and vomited over the side railings into the water. It provided temporary relief, but there was still no escape from his thoughts.

Where was Bobby? Was it over? How do we get home? Why did I leave him? Why didn't I just jump off that boat and swim back for him once the fisherman had first told me? Where is he? I couldn't swim for it, it was too far. I'm selfish; I was just saving my own skin. Where was he? Did he make it? I'm selfish; I could've saved him.

Over the next few days, despite his sound physical health, JK continued to think like this. Eventually, he, along with the survivors who were deemed well enough, moved away from the shelter. There were various places to get help, like the centres set up for backpackers at the hostels in the main town.

JK got to know virtually all of the hostel staff as he helped out a little, transporting the aid boxes of bedding, food, water and clothing supplied from all over the world. But he couldn't ever get used to seeing people cry: when reunited with others that they knew; on phone calls; even after reading emails they received in the internet cafes.

His mum had cried on the phone when he had first called her. He couldn't handle the conversation: she had begged for news on his brother, asking when he had seen him last, why they weren't together. But he couldn't answer, and had eventually hung up.

What was he supposed to say? He had left Bobby, on a whim, and got lucky. The luckiest he could ever be. The unluckiest Bobby would ever be.

And so, one week turned into two. The waiting was painful. Time dragged. Bodies being transported all around him, tarpaulins barely covering their faces. People collapsing with grief and shock.

He couldn't eat. He decided to play cards again. It was the perfect distraction, he thought, just like old times. He played, obsessively, to decide his next moves. Like, whether and when he should phone his mum, or his sister-in-law, Di, after receiving several desperate emails from them both.

They hate me, they must do, he thought. I would. Selfish. I could've saved him. Where is Bobby?

On the draw of the correct card, a Seven of Diamonds, he rang his mother again. Her emotional desolation was complete by then. The death counts and registers were being finalised. Bobby's name was on it, as was Rick Marshall's. But she wouldn't accept it. She said she was going to come out to Phuket and get both of her sons back.

JK knew she wouldn't. There would be Di, hopefully the voice of reason, to stop her doing that. He was surprised Di hadn't wanted to talk to him yet, but he was glad. He didn't think he would be able to cope with her rage, once she had found out about his cowardly decision to leave Bobby, the only reason he was alive now.

It was that fact that had prevented him from making the impending decision looming large over his head: to go home. He suspected he would be asked to, any day now, but he really couldn't face it.

It was the draw of the Jack of Hearts that would decide it. It represented the opportunity to fulfil his new destiny: an African safari. It was a trip of a lifetime, he had thought. What would he do at home besides mope around? Opportunities like that didn't come round very often. He had been thinking about it for a long time already, since his time on Ko Phi Phi, before the tsunami had arrived.

So, when he did eventually pull out this card, he promptly went off to a local travel agent and booked a package deal with flights that left in two weeks' time from Bangkok.

He continued to play cards as yet more emails arrived for him. His mum said that he should come home. Di had said the same. A few days later, his mum emailed to tell him that there was going to be a funeral for Bobby. But, on the same day, the draw of a Three of Spades decided that he would fly to Bangkok early and kill time for a week, which he was grateful for.

It didn't provide the escape he was looking for, as still the aura of death remained close. En route, he encountered more families at the airports, crying, looking gaunt, tired, unstable and irritable. But he kept on playing cards, ignoring all around as the emails kept arriving.

He felt guilty about his mother, about Di and about the funeral, and he toyed with the idea of cancelling his Africa flights. He knew he had to get out of Thailand: it held too many bad memories for him now. The spectacle of his father remained in his head, and he briefly considered paying him one last visit. But the cards had told him differently, and so he had to listen to them.

He also listened to his guilt, his nausea and his thoughts, over and over again: questions, questions, questions. He couldn't answer them. Why didn't I save him? He was my friend. Why am I alive? Why am I still here? Selfish. It's luck. It's fate. It was always meant to happen that way. Meant to be, nothing I could do about it, fate. Why do things happen? No need for guilt. Why do I feel guilty, then? Where is Bobby?

He drew a card, the Ace of Clubs. This was right for him: he would take control, and block Bobby out of his mind. He needed to try and get back on track. He validated his own decision, knowing, grimly, that he would not go home for the funeral, and stuck with his travel plans.

The day before his flight to Africa, four days before his brother's funeral, he drew a Queen of Spades. This was his prompt to call home and finally let them know he wouldn't be coming back.

'Hello?' a female voice answered. 'Hello? Who's there?' said the voice again. JK, staying silent in surprise, recognised it as Di, rather than his mother.

'Hello, Diana,' he said, eventually, closing his eyes in anticipation of the questions he knew were coming.

'JK! My god! Are you… are you OK? We haven't heard from you in ages! Did you get our emails? Where are you?'

'I'm fine, I'm fine. Yes, I got them. Sorry for not replying. It's been … crazy out here. I'm in Bangkok now… waiting for a flight.'

'Oh, thank god you're coming home. Your mum will be so pleased. She's not coping well, you know? That's why I'm round here, to be with her.'

'What's the matter with her?' JK said, as he felt his stomach churn.

'What do you think, JK? She's lost her son,' Di said, choking back tears, 'and then she hasn't heard from you in so long. She's been really worried.'

'Yeah, I know, I'm sorry. It's been hard for me too… Are you OK?'

'Me? I'm coping, you know. I've been through this before… I've lost people,' she replied, but JK knew her positive tone of voice was fake.

'Thank you for looking after Mum. But I need to let you know something,'

'What? Is it Bobby, have you heard from him?' Di said, desperately.

'No, no, nothing. I'm sorry.' Di stayed silent before JK continued, 'My flight from Bangkok, it's not… I'm not coming home, Di.'

'What? What do you mean?'

'I'm not going to the funeral. I can't do it.'

'It's your own brother, Jonny. What's the matter with you?'

'I'm sorry. I just can't. Please say sorry to Mum.'

'She'll be devastated, you realise that, don't you?'

'I know. Please forgive me.'

'Where are you going?'

'It doesn't matter, Di. It's just something I have to do.'

'Is it more important than your own brother's funeral? What am I supposed to tell people? Or, more to the point, your mother?'

'I don't know. I just... I just need a bit of time.'

'You're being insensitive. To your mother, to me... to all of us,' she said, sobbing. 'What happened with you and Bobby, anyway?'

JK didn't respond, trying to ignore the question he knew would come.

'Why did you leave him, JK?'

'I don't know. I just left,' he said, eventually.

'And now he's dead,' Di said. JK listened silently, paralysed by the sound of her tears.

Finally, she hung up.

JK waited in the airport, sweaty, agitated and twitching from the combined effects of no sleep, multiple caffeine tablets and Red Bull. He tried to foster a hope that he could still somehow finish his trip on a high after the agonising, heart-rending last few weeks he had suffered. And finally, as the plane rose up into the air, he could focus on what he suspected might be the last positive thing remaining in his life.

This focus didn't last as arriving at Nairobi airport, Kenya, at night was unnerving. His name was not held up by a taxi driver, as had been promised, just the name of his tour company and he had no way of knowing if he was about to be ripped off or not. Fuck knows where he's taking me, JK thought, fearing the worst. His mind raced to the worst stories he had heard about white Western tourists kidnapped by opportunist criminals.

But JK did arrive at the hotel safely and he was able to check in and unpack without any further fuss. The sanctuary and solitude in the comfort of his room provided his last release of emotion before the start of his safari. He lay on his bed as the usual thoughts began to circle round his head again.

Trying to block them, he remembered the tour brochure he had skim-read before booking this trip. Over the next four weeks, he would wear a mask of happiness and joviality in front of his companions, twenty other 'like-minded travellers', so it had said.

Where was Bobby? Why didn't I swim back for him? What do people think of me? Selfish. Could I have saved him? Dear old Lenny. Lenny Keane. Father. He doesn't want us. He doesn't want me. I'm not wanted. Selfish. People hate me. Why am I still here? I don't deserve to be here.

As a sleepless night rolled on and on, he realised that the longer he spent on his own, the more he was falling apart. No matter how enforced and restricting the safari had sounded, by morning he couldn't wait to escape the 'sanctuary' of his hotel room.

The safari began and he met the tour guides: Ewan, tall and thin, hailing from Cape Town, who was ably assisted by another guide, a young Dutch girl called Henrietta. As various hotel pick-ups around the area continued, the guides got everyone in the group to say a quick hello – the usual introductions and polite ice-breaker conversations – but he didn't really take in their names.

JK had done it a million times before and wasn't interested any more. He was going through the motions and doing a convincing job of it, as he knew he had to. It would make for an easy life over the next month and could provide some little enjoyment with the only reason he was here.

Ewan did his best to get the trip off to a positive start. An enigmatic character, he gave the impression of a man who had been through many interesting experiences, taking them all in his stride. He was a very confident man, but without being rude or confrontational, and yet incredibly laid back.

The South African guide was a fascinating contrast of personality traits. A smoker, with tattoos and a long facial scar that hinted at a free-spirited and occasionally dangerous nature, yet his demeanour was always approachable and friendly. He gave the immediate impression that he was someone you could relax around and depend on; nothing would faze him.

JK reflected that a character like this would normally be someone who he would take interest in. Under other circumstances, he could imagine investing his time getting to know him, understanding his background, sharing stories, trying to work out what made him tick. But not this time.

On the bus, they motored on, as JK half-listened to the broken group conversations, small talk about each other's 'real lives' back home. Most people had seen lions, elephants, leopards and the like on TV or in the zoo and, like JK, were genuinely excited about the prospect of seeing these animals in a natural environment. Eventually, as the six-hour drive dragged on in the heat, he began to slide into sleep again, as his thoughts wandered back to the memories of his childhood dreams.

Later, outside of Nairobi, as they got closer to the Maasai Mara National Reserve, the journey became more entertaining as the now awful, bumpy roads combined with some terrible driving and fascinating sights en route.

They drove through tiny, ramshackle towns but with sudden corporate sponsorship or brand names, such as 'Marlboro', 'Coca Cola', 'Shell' and 'Sportsman cigarettes', crudely painted on to corrugated iron shacks. With so many people and cars all around, it was chaos everywhere: market stalls, giant puddles, huge piles of mud and rubbish with goats eating from the top – all so random. Chickens, wild dogs and cows all ambled on the streets. Kids playing in the dirt, old people milling around, men and women working in barren soil plots.

They arrived at their campsite and the now wet weather meant that the prospects weren't good for an early evening safari. After a disappointing few hours getting stuck in the mud without spotting anything, they went back for a campfire meal and drinks, but JK still remained unsociable. When it came to sleep later that night, his negative and unsettled mind only served to make the impossible even more impossible.

The next day they awoke to clear skies and an expectation of a much more productive visit. And how! All in the space of 24 hours, in addition to seeing the 'big five' of lion, elephant, rhino, leopard and buffalo, they managed to spot zebras, jackals, cheetahs, giraffes, hippos, a five-metre crocodile, monkeys, a mongoose, vultures, various antelope, impala, wildebeest, hartebeest, waterbuck, gazelle, topi, eland, guinea fowl, warthog, baboons, and a tortoise.

So JK was able to stop thinking about Bobby, even if only for a day. Although he was now fully immersed in the experience, he still had some trouble socialising with his companions. But with such depth of visual material all around them, it slowly became easier and easier to find topics of conversation that directed him away from his usual, introspective view of the past few weeks.

Another long drive followed the next morning, this time to Arusha in Tanzania, via an eventful border crossing. Here, tribes people forcefully attempted to sell Western tourists their handmade souvenirs. This even occurred as they sat on their bus in a queue of traffic waiting to park, as they would come up to the window and attempt to talk to them.

These sellers were not allowed to approach the tourists as they queued to enter the customs and immigration office. But again, as soon as tourists attempted to return to their vehicles, the sellers would enthusiastically reform as a swarm and attack.

They would look at the tourists – directly into their eyes – hoping for pity, for recognition, anything, in an attempt to appeal to a generous wealthy Western nature. As JK began to climb on board his truck, one particularly aggressive and bald Maasai woman caught him unaware and snapped a bracelet onto his arm.

'A present!' she pleaded, as her eyes connected with JK. Just as he began to feel regret for a fraction of an instant, their guide, Ewan, had told him not to accept it.

'It will never be a present and they will always expect money from you,' he said.

Unexpectedly, JK's regret changed to anger in a flash as he glared back at the woman. He pulled the bracelet off his arm, discarding it on the floor, and carried on into the truck.

From Arusha, they arrived at the Serengeti National Reserve, hoping for a view of the annual migration of two million animals following the waters south from the Maasai Mara. They stopped to eat in a magnificent setting, overlooking the Ngorongoro crater conservation area.

Kite birds circled overhead as a few of the party looked up nervously from their lunch, and with good reason, as the birds began to swoop down on the group. As they attempted to eat, two girls were severely frightened as their sandwiches were snatched out of their hands by the opportunistic creatures that circled above.

They would return to enter the crater later, but now JK couldn't help feeling a sense foreboding, as if these birds of prey were stalking him.

But the feeling was wiped away soon after, at the sight of wildebeest, Thomson's gazelle, zebra, impala – animals covering the whole horizon as far as his eyes could see across a landscape completely uninhibited and unrestrained.

The group got closer and closer to the rapidly moving animal traffic, which dared to hold up their single 4x4 truck as the transient beasts leapt across the mud tracks they had left. They patiently waited for the spectacle to cross, but this patience soon gave way to necessity as they squeezed their way past, gently forcing some of the animals temporarily off track.

The spectacle stunned JK. It was one of the most untouched, natural environments on the planet, yet it was so alien to every culture he knew that it didn't feel as if it was really happening to him.

Later that evening, as the group pitched their tents in an open campsite, this detachment from reality continued. There was no fencing, meaning elephants, lions and hyenas were free to roam around their tents overnight while they were meant to sleep soundly in their sleeping bags.

The only protection they had was from a hut where a few armed guards watched – or, more likely, slept – while allegedly looking over the group through their wired windows. So surreal an experience was it that, after their evening meal finished, JK felt the need to drink his confusion away. He achieved some measure of success, finally being able to relax as he slept deeply that night.

Yet, the next morning, he recalled flashes of his dreams, fleeting images that made up the final version of the dream from his teenage years, and no thoughts of Bobby, his father or the rest of his family or friends back home. As he got up, the mist around the campsite led him to believe he was still in some hazy, dream-like setting.

The early morning mist began to clear as they drove down a windy road along steep edges entering the Ngorongoro crater. It was a vast, yet self-enclosed, ecosystem. As the walls of the crater faded quickly out of view, the group saw a variety of landscapes on display within. A large male elephant on his own, eating from the deep and vividly green vegetation. Wide flat plains, as hundreds of flamingos added a vibrant pink hue to a shimmering silver lake.

It had a magical air: the sights only magnifying as the day progressed. JK was captivated by every element of the enchanting display: rhinos, always so fleeting, were running in the distance; buffaloes, so powerful yet serene, watched them, untroubled.

A group of lions surrounded their truck as they saw two females guarding their cubs, innocently playing with the wheels and looking at the gawping faces of the watching tourists. But the parents were calm; they had seen it all before and, soon enough, they trotted away to discover some new amusements.

Later, in a large expanse of long grass, JK saw two very young lions cross in front of their vehicle. Another young male, with an underdeveloped mane, was close behind him. Ten or so metres behind this male, JK could see a female watching, sitting, with another young male standing next to her. Looking still further behind, he saw yet another lion, a second female, who was watching something far in the distance, ahead of all the young ones.

JK followed their eye line to see a small group of wildebeest that they were tracking. Ewan told the group that it was a pride of lions, and that they should look further along the line to see more. JK did this, and then saw another two females sitting closely together. He grabbed some binoculars to follow them along a diagonal to see yet another female, the ninth lion. One final, darkened shape, possibly a mound of earth, remained a few metres behind her, but he couldn't quite make out its details.

And then, after a moment, the final, tenth lion raised his head and JK could see it was the male of the pride, looking proudly across his family, across his terrain and across his prey. He was still, motionless, yet in complete control of all that was before him. JK felt deeply moved by the scene, unable to utter a single word, frozen in astonishment.

Eventually, their group moved back towards the edge of the crater and saw a rainbow over the horizon. JK's eyes fixed on this as they got closer to the edge, and a patch of greenery blended in with the background on their approach to the exit tracks. The hairs on the back of his neck tingled as he recognised the outline forming before his eyes, a familiar sight, with its distinctive branches flowing into flat canopies. It was the Acacia tree.

More Acacia trees were alongside as they filed past, seemingly in slow motion, as the rainbow remained static in the background. The clouds were darkening, and then the rainbow disappeared, yet strong light attempted to fight through these clouds. He could see one tree on its own, standing in some low rays of sunlight that caught over the edge of the truck's window frames, slicing through his vision and puncturing the image of the tree.

Light and dark shadows continued to intertwine in the background, but the black silhouette of the Acacia tree was constant. A tear began to form in JK's eye as he realised what he was seeing. Years of his dreams and ambitions spent wondering what this moment would be like had finally come to fruition. Every travel desire that he had ever had had just been satisfied with these passing few hours of beauty – and this one moment represented the pinnacle.

It should have been the happiest moment of his life. Yet he cried, realising that even though what he had found was everything he had ever hoped to find, he was still unable to enjoy it. The pain was still too recent for him to ignore, of his father's crushing rejection and of the unexpected death of his brother, for which he blamed himself.

Tears melted onto JK's face, as a cool breeze chilled his skin. He did not sob; there was no outward spectacle of emotion, and it was all he could do just to look ahead into the horizon and observe. He was waiting for the dream-like sequence of the past few hours to create some fairy-tale happy ending, a moment of magic that might ease his sorrow, but it never came.

For the rest of the day he barely said a word to his companions. After dinner, a picturesque sunset fell and then he retreated to his tent for solitary and unrestrained grief. He knew he would never be the same after that day in the crater. He would always look back at that moment as pivotal in his life, but perhaps not for the reasons he had expected after first dreaming of Africa, lions and Acacia trees as a child many years ago.

The rest of his Serengeti discovery served to pass the time for JK, who was now in a permanent state of damage limitation. He was polite but would not go out of his way to interact with people. Although he got involved with the group, it was never enough to be noticed. He wasn't sure if he wanted to be there or not, but it presented a decent enough distraction to any alternative he could think of, and so he was able to grin and bear his way through it.

Eventually they finished their safari and made their way on to Dar es Salaam, seeing more unusual sights en route: herds of cattle being beaten by young children with long wooden staffs, ushering the cows along; struggling to drive past slowly moving delivery men riding bicycles, overloaded with cargo of gigantic hay bales or plastic water canisters.

One poor man was carrying twenty-one of these large containers; even if they were empty, with a capacity of ten litres each they were still heavy. He had them stacked across three rows, with him sitting in the middle, ten balancing on one side and eleven on the other side. It looked like a giant pyramid, wobbling forward on wheels.

Their truck stopped at a service station, store and local restaurant, all in one. It was traumatic, purely for the fact that JK ended up eating the worst meal of his life. What he believed to be a local vegetable curry dish turned out, in fact, to be sheep's entrails. He had mistaken the thin pipes for runner beans, and they were mixed with miniature, and very hard, bananas. These ingredients, combined with a thick, grey sauce with rice, gave a taste sensation somewhat akin to a faeces-infused rice pudding. Two mouthfuls were enough to send JK to the extremely basic toilet facilities and vomit.

JK couldn't be sure he had food poisoning – perhaps it was purely psychological – but his stomach remained delicate for some time after that. Then he began to worry that his growing mental distress had now started to manifest itself physically. The constant disease fear among tourists in this part of Africa was malaria, but besides an annoying itch on his foot, he had no evidence to say he had been bitten by any mosquitoes, the usual carrier of this disease.

He tried to ignore further, insignificant, physical ailments he picked up, fearing paranoia was an added consequence of the continuous dream-like cycle he was now living through: sleepless nights combined with a drowsy daytime. The many interesting local characters and sights that surrounded him contributed to this feeling, as his attention dipped momentarily in and out of consciousness.

He kept seeing the colour red. He spotted red bananas, the first time he had ever seen them, as they drove past towns and tradesmen loading their ramshackle trucks with supplies. More distinctive trees, the Delonix or 'Flamboyant' tree, lined the roads with their large foliage of incredibly vibrant red flowers.

At Dar es Salaam airport, they waited two hours for a ten-minute flight to Zanzibar, the spice island off the east coast of Africa. Here, JK realised that any novelty interest in the spectacle of the locals' pursuit of their money had well and truly worn off by now.

Inevitably, they swarmed around any new arrivals of Western tourists, who they immediately assumed were wealthy and obliging; he shuddered on seeing the expectant look on children's faces, as young as three years old, who had been trained to hold up a hand for money or to grab at pockets.

On this occasion, JK could only watch and shake his head at the naïve actions of a German tourist among their group. Making the mistake of showing interest in a beaded necklace, or something similar, for sale, he then entered into a haggling battle with one of the locals before finally buying it. This, of course, opened the flood gates, prompting several other salesmen to approach and offer him more products. Yet he continued to entertain them, discussing prices and beginning another bidding process.

Eventually, he was rescued by the self-titled 'Innocent', a local tour guide with specialist knowledge of Zanzibar, supporting Ewan and Henrietta. Richard 'Innocent' Jamal had been very helpful at getting rid of these persistent local sales people and was a man determined to impress the tourists by splicing various music, comedy and film character references into his repertoire, just to show how up to date with their Western culture he was.

It was charming to begin with, and certainly JK had been impressed that he had taken the time to memorise not just British but American and Australian slang too. But, after a while, the same impressions or catchphrases, shoe-horned into every sentence, became repetitive and boring to JK.

After he had begun to get headaches, he had tried to relax on the beaches and soak in the sun, away from the hustle and bustle of the Arab stone town. In between the bouts of pain, JK's mind wandered into an even deeper, dream-like state. His memories of the next few days could only recall specific objects, smells and colours – mainly consisting of the vivid sights from a typically touristy 'Island spice tour' by good, old 'Innocent'.

Jack fruits, cardamom seeds, vanilla pods, ginger roots, chocolate and coffee beans, coconuts, custard apples, cloves, red-dye fruit, turmeric, lemon grass, cinnamon bark, peppercorns, papaya, the fresh seafood odours cooking at the fish markets, fabrics and jewellery at the stalls, the mazy streets among the old stone buildings, the stone palace ruins set among the luscious greens of the forest, old men tending to fishing boats along the shores.

He didn't even remember leaving Zanzibar, and his next coherent set of memories began again in Malawi. Somehow, they had arrived there and camped on shore of the vast Lake Malawi. On their first night, there was the most dramatic lightning storm he had ever seen. The surface of the lake spread across the whole of the horizon and was lit up by violent sparks with a deafening thunder surrounded them all for over half an hour.

It was a beguiling sight, and left JK unnerved as if a sign of impending gloom once more. Unable to sleep yet again, as the rain lashed onto his tent, he somehow knew things were only going to get worse. Whether it was paranoia or depression, JK could now only feel varying levels of dread, not excitement.

Their campsite was closed off by a tall perimeter fence, outside of which a small throng of local salesmen waited patiently every morning and lunchtime for any tourists brave enough to venture outside their comfort zone and explore. Now, JK was in no mood to do any such thing, but the reason he knew this was because their group was taken on a guided tour of the local village, meaning they had to walk past the keen young locals.

This was not just random opportunism; this was a tried-and-tested sales method. Many a tourist, every week, month or year, had been on the same walk. It was a simple consequence of supply and demand. There were so many now, there was easily enough for each tourist to have their own personal salesman for the walk, even with their group size of fifteen.

Each of the salesmen would approach and attempt to befriend JK: 'Robert De Niro', 'Superman' and 'Tom Cruise', among others; finally, 'Julius Caesar' remained with him. He made so much effort, talking and listening for the whole journey as they walked for twenty-five minutes, asking what music he liked, what football team he supported, about his family and what presents he wanted to buy them.

But JK had no intention of buying anything and he gave them limited answers. It was a lot easier for JK to lie about his circumstances, of his brother and his father, and he had been used to doing so with his fellow tourist companions anyway. He felt unease whenever he passed the salesmen around the edge of camp. Yet, still they remained, and even some days later, the spectacle of Julius Caesar disconcerted him once more. As he sunbathed on a beach, JK suddenly heard a voice call him by name. He sat up to see the salesman watching him, some fifteen metres away, behind a barricaded section of sand.

The days drew on, and JK felt his physical condition worsen. His nausea was now almost constant, occasionally interchanged with stomach cramps, intermittent headaches and mild diarrhoea. The last element was particularly unpleasant, especially when encountering the basic facilities of a campsite toilet of a small East African country.

JK queued in the sweltering heat, fighting off nausea all the time at the acrid smell of decaying human waste. The entrance to the cubicle greeted him with an even more pungent aroma. A hole in the ground was at the far end, and at the door, a big bucket filled with dark-coloured water and a smaller dipping-pot floating on top. He assumed it was for washing afterwards but there was no way he could put his hands in there. To complete his predicament, there was no toilet paper either.

One evening, JK was sitting at the campsite bar in a rare sociable moment, chatting to Ewan. Steve, the campsite manager, then joined them. He was stocky and sun-grizzled, of mixed race with a French accent and a long-term malaria sufferer. JK was worried about how relaxed Steve was about his own health condition. He had watched Steve calmly injecting himself with an antivirus, holding conversation while sweating profusely.

'Yeah, you've probably got Malaria, or at least a mild strain of it,' said Steve. 'Ewan could pick up some drugs for you at the next big stop, probably Lusaka. You'll be fine. Eventually, anyway.'

'Oh, right. Great,' JK replied, sarcastically.

'Don't worry, JK. There's a hospital in Lusaka – we can see a doctor,' said Ewan.

'Malaria isn't that bad, honestly. I get constant re-occurrences of it now, anything up to ten times a year. But I've learnt to cope with it, your body just does. Plus, a few drugs from the doc help,' Steve continued, smiling wryly.

'Well, let's hope I get lucky, then,' said JK, maintaining his previous tone.

'Or, it could be bilharzia, of course,' Steve offered.

'Oh, shut up, man. Don't scare him,' Ewan shot back.

'Why, what's that?' asked JK.

'It's when flat worms burrow into your foot. They crawl up into your bloodstream and lay eggs in your intestine. It can stay dormant for ages, or make you sick, for a long time, too. Not good, but definitely treatable. It's quite common in Africa, in the lakes and rivers, or in infected soil.'

'Well, that sounds even better. I guess it really could be my lucky day.'

'Quit worrying, man. Just get a blood test and see what the doc says… Hey! Mind your foot,' said Steve, suddenly.

'Sorry?' JK asked.

'Look down,' Ewan snapped, and pointed down at the wooden decking floor. JK looked at his bare feet and then saw a scorpion of a not-inconsiderable size approaching him. Its tail and pincers were primed in his direction. JK jumped out of the way, and the barman ran round and ushered it back to the edge of the decking, onto the sand, where it had come from.

'They tend to crawl out of the bushes after a bit of a rain,' Steve said.

'That's reassuring. I'm sure I'll sleep well again tonight,' replied JK, remembering their tents were on the sand, next to some bushes.

He didn't sleep well, as predicted, and, the next day, noticed that malaise seemed to be infectious in his current surroundings. He wondered if their campsite was an animal hospice. He saw a flea-ridden cat with only one ear and one eye, a dog with a leg missing, a skeletal cat that was constantly retching, looking like it was about to collapse and die at any second, and a dog with half of its fur falling out that hardly ever moved or made a sound, to the point where it may as well have been dead.

Later that day, just as JK began to feel worse – his head was getting heavier and he was experiencing alternating shivering mixed with hot sweats – they left the campsite and crossed into Zambia, onto its capital, Lusaka. Here, he was confident of receiving some decent medical treatment.

In town, he waited outside a small hospital building as large groups of locals walked by. Before Ewan had gone inside, he told the whole group to make sure they did not draw attention to themselves in front of the local police. Apparently, only the previous week, a group of tourists had been arrested just for taking photographs of a government building without permission and had been held in local jail cells overnight.

But there was no danger of that for JK, who couldn't focus on anything for long enough to draw any attention to himself. Eventually, Ewan re-appeared through a door and ushered him in, taking him through the building. A doctor asked him some simple questions, took his temperature and a blood sample and, then, after the briefest of warnings, injected him in the buttock with an extra strong dose of Imodium.

JK sat on a black plastic chair, surrounded by dark wooden walls with garish green curtains that filtered some of the daylight into the small empty room. He was feeling slightly light-headed again, and the hazy lighting gave the scenario the feeling of a seventies TV hospital drama. After what seemed like hours, the doctor returned to give him the results of his blood tests.

The news was good. He had a high white cell count, meaning he was fighting some infection – but it wasn't malaria. He gave JK some antibiotics, and said it was probably just a viral infection and that it would pass in a few days. This was just the boost that he had needed for some time.

But it proved to be short lived. JK had celebrated that evening by enjoying a decent-sized solid meal of pasta, minus any booze due to the antibiotics, and felt as good as he had done in about a month, before going to bed in good spirits. But, the following morning, when he should have woken refreshed, he realised it was 6am and that his stomach was now in absolute agony.

Severe cramps returned, now worse than he'd ever experienced, along with fever symptoms. Either the antibiotics had seemingly worn off, or they weren't working. But, unfortunately, he didn't have the luxury of being able to lie low in his hotel room in Lusaka. His fellow travellers remarked that JK's skin appeared to be an unhealthy grey colour but, despite this, he had to quickly pack up and board their truck to leave the city.

They were on their way through a swamp region of Zambia; their next main stop was Livingstone, via an overnight campsite on the way. JK held out as best as he could but the pain in his abdomen was changing rapidly, morphing into nausea. In truth, he didn't know what was happening to his body or what to expect next. He was frightened not to be in control of his body in this way; it was something he had never experienced before.

After a couple of hours, JK asked the driver to stop the truck. He ran out into the bushes and vomited violently, conscious that the people on board could hear him. Once again, it was commented on how ill JK looked. At this point, Ewan decided that the doctor's original prognosis was incorrect.

As he didn't want the other passengers, who were beginning to worry, to see JK in this state, Ewan took him to one side and made a suggestion. There was a small town nearby with a basic medical shelter that he could temporarily drop JK off at, while he continued with the rest of the group to the main campsite, as they were running behind schedule. However, he wasn't going to leave JK alone as his assistant, Henrietta, was happy to stay.

Ewan made a call back to Lusaka to ensure more immediate medical attention would come out to JK, and he promised that a doctor would return later in the evening to check in on them. It made sense to JK, although he was somewhat nervous being separated from the group, especially when he saw the tiny little town that would provide him with temporary shelter.

It was a bizarre assembly of a few mud and straw huts dotted around, hacked out in the middle of the forest, and there was a large red brick building visible twenty or so metres back from this main group of huts. Behind it, JK caught glimpses of other housing, some wooden, flimsy looking structures, as well as a couple of temporary corrugated iron arrangements. One old, white, pick-up truck, with empty glass bottles in the back, was parked outside.

Strange, sad-faced locals were ambling and loping around; many people, but all so slow, with strained expressions as their eyes fixed to the floor, never looking at each other. JK was immediately filled with trepidation about spending any length of time here.

Then, a man in a smart white shirt and trousers came out of the brick building to greet them, and Ewan explained the situation, pointing at JK as he stepped down from the truck. JK was about to be introduced when he suddenly felt a sharp pain hit his stomach, as if he had been stabbed. As he bent over double, Henrietta put an arm round to help him back upright. He had taken some more pain killers after vomiting earlier, and, as his head spun, JK suspected that they were not mixing well with the antibiotics.

From then, his recollection of the next few hours was patchy. Ewan had left with the group, and JK sat in a dull room with a black and white TV; a fan that provided a welcome breeze, even as flies constantly invaded his personal space and line of sight; some polite conversation with the shelter manager and Henrietta, although JK's role was mainly restricted to listening and nodding; attempting to drink water and being told to force it down, and avoiding a dinner of watery pea soup and stale bread.

The sun was setting as JK lifted himself outside, onto the decking, to visit a large concrete toilet block. Realising how weak he was, he immediately stumbled on one of the wooden slats and fell to the floor. As he sat, too weak to move, JK examined his left foot and felt it beginning to itch again. Surely, this was paranoia, he thought. But the sole of his foot was red, and he was sure he could feel a lump underneath the skin. Was it a parasitic worm? he speculated. When had this happened? Was that the cause of my sickness? JK scratched again, vigorously, until he regained some energy to stand up.

He could not face the disgusting smell coming from the toilet block, so, instead, walked to the nearer bushes to urinate, all the while questioning his health, his paranoia and many other elements about himself. When he returned to the shelter, he could see Henrietta holding a phone to her ear, and guessed from her body language that she was talking to Ewan. She confirmed this to JK shortly afterwards, to relay the bad news that the doctor from Lusaka could not come until the next morning and so he would have to stay in this hellhole overnight.

But JK was concerned about a more pressing physical matter: lasting until the morning without having to visit the toilet block again. Luckily, he was so spaced out that his body wouldn't allow him to concentrate on that issue for too long. Time and nature would conspire against him, however.

He awoke suddenly with another spike of pain in his gut, guessing it was around 5am. He quickly rose and saw the sky turning from a dark blue to brown, as the sun started to rise. He approached on the scrunched-up soles of his feet along cold wooden planks, knowing that avoidance of the foul-smelling grey concrete building ahead was no longer negotiable.

As if by way of warning, an intensely dark pool of liquid, perhaps six inches wide, lay in the thick grass next to the entrance. As the low light of sunrise reflected on its surface, JK could see its deep red colour, knowing it could only be blood. Holding his breath, he easily pushed open the flimsy, rotting wooden door to be confronted by a scene of unmitigated gross squalor.

A giant hole, perhaps the very definition of the word 'cesspit', was the centre piece of the vile enclosure. The surrounding floor was just earth, and in the middle, a concrete wall, about a foot high, formed a perimeter to the hole. Around it were three men, in varying states of dire health. One of these men was bent over the wall, retching into the hole.

A steady noise of soft moaning came from the infirm group ahead of JK. It was too dark to make out their exact features, and he didn't have time to look in any case. He saw there were three cubicles along at the back wall with more loosely fitting wooden doors. JK ran past the hole, over to the first set of cubicle doors.

Yanking them open, he immediately retched, almost losing control of his bowels in the process too, upon the sight of a giant pile of human faeces stacked at least one foot higher than the rim of the toilet seat.

He quickly turned away and, trying to ignore the smell, ran to push open the next door. He was annoyed to find it occupied and, on instinct, was about to apologise but, just before he did, took a look at the occupant's face. His eyes were shut and he had remained motionless throughout; his head was slumped against his shoulders. He realised that there was no way someone could, or would want to, sleep in this environment, and the sight of several flies crawling around the man's mouth was enough to tell JK that he was long dead. Despite the shock, JK had to grimly carry on with his simple task.

Finally, he opened the last door, now not knowing what to expect, but sweating profusely at the urgency. Again, the cubicle was occupied, but luckily, this time, the occupant was still alive. A man looked up at JK with confused eyes and shifted nervously on the seat. JK quickly judged that he was smaller than he was and so he made an on-the-spot decision.

Grabbing the man by his shoulders, JK lifted him off the seat and pushed in front of him as he twisted and slid past. He slammed the door shut on the man and heard him moaning outside and, as JK ignored both this and the state of the toilet beneath him, he pulled his trousers and boxer shorts down. Without touching the toilet seat in any way, he swiftly bent over double, just as he felt his bowels were about to collapse.

The next few moments were unforgettably unpleasant for JK, as blood, mucus and excrement exploded out of him, coating the walls behind, all the way up to the ceiling some two foot above his head. This violent diarrhoea continued, as he sweated in fear and pain. When this process was complete, JK could only shiver for a moment; there was no relief that it was over, only denial that it had happened at all. Eventually, he summoned up the strength to pull up his trousers and pushed the door open.

There was limited opportunity for light to enter the room in the absence of windows, but it did, slowly, through the ramshackle entrance. JK could make out the small man he had removed from his cubicle; he was now sitting on the edge of the wall round the central hole. Suddenly he realised what he was doing; his trousers were around his ankles and his bottom was perched over the edge.

Behind him, on an adjacent edge, the man who had been retching into the hole earlier was now vomiting, as the appalling sound echoed around the room. When he had finished, he lifted his head up, and JK squinted to make out his features. He thought he saw a skull tattoo on the man's neck, but didn't know if the lack of light or the intense and putrid smell were playing tricks on his mind. JK then saw his face, the face of Rick Marshall, and stepped forward in confusion and fear to look more closely.

JK wiped sweat from his brow and shook his head. Satisfied it was not Rick, he turned away to then see the top half of another man, on the opposite side of the hole, with his back to him, leaning up against the concrete wall.

Something compelled JK to walk around and look at this man more closely. As he approached, JK started to feel faint, and just as his legs began to buckle, the man slowly turned his head to face him.

A gaunt, skeletal face stared at JK. Yet it was a face he recognised once more, and one that filled him with terror: it was his recently departed brother, Bobby Jenkins, who now held eye contact with JK.

His jaw hung open, as a line of blood trickled from the corner of his mouth and his dead-eyed stare continued to focus on JK. He screwed his nose up and pointed, limply, laughing and grinning as JK collapsed to his knees and stared back at him.

'You look like shit,' Bobby mumbled, gurgling, as his head fell backwards. His eyes half-closed and JK's did the same. The hot and sticky air sapped JK's strength as finally he watched the face change into that of a stranger. The pungent, rancid smell forced a hoarse cough up through JK's throat and momentarily nudged him back into consciousness.

It was the same, recognisable smell, returning to haunt him once more; the inescapable and vile stench of waste, wasted human life, of death. This was now a familiar foe, an odour that he couldn't get rid of.

JK would only have to wait a few more hours for help to arrive – to heal him, cleanse him – and for him to leave this horrid place and find a place of comfort. It would last a few days, perhaps even until he arrived back home, but he knew that it wouldn't last.

No, he had a feeling that the stench would return, and that it would hang in the air for a long time to come yet.

Chapter Fifteen

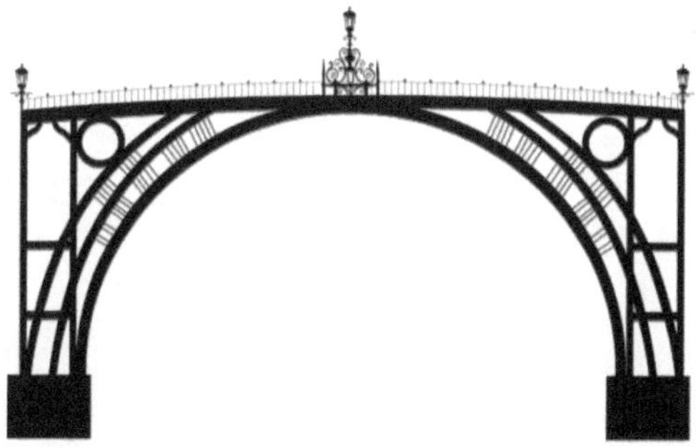

Remember Bobby Jenkins

The logs burned, crackling and spitting fire as the glowing embers mesmerised JK. When, eventually, he couldn't watch any longer, he merely had to lift his eyes up a couple of feet to see the framed photo sitting on top of the fireplace. It was the classic wedding celebration shot – the bride and groom – Diana and his brother Bobby on their happy day.

But there was so much more to the photo and only JK knew it. He had hidden his father's list of countries inside the frame, behind the picture. The worn old hand-written piece of paper which he had devoted so much of his life to, vainly trying to emulate the achievements detailed on it in tribute to his father.

After returning from Singapore a few years ago, having accidentally discovered his father, he didn't have any real reason to keep the list. Yet, he couldn't bring himself to get rid of it either. So he forgot about it, and it had stayed hidden, buried among his few remaining personal effects in the bottom of a box.

Then, just two weeks ago, on his return home from Africa, heartbroken, depressed and disillusioned with his life, he had found the list once more while going through his belongings, now out of storage, at his mother's house. Several times he had come very close to destroying it, but still he couldn't do it.

He didn't know why, but on seeing the picture of his brother on his wedding day, he had decided to hide the list within the frame. JK had run out of money and was still unwell, so he had moved back into his mother's house for now, where he was surrounded by painful memories such as this photo.

He would sit, staring – for hours at a time – like this. Wallowing in pity, thinking of his brother and whether he could've saved him, guilty at how Diana must be feeling without her husband. Remembering his father's list, and his anger at him and his mother for lying to him for so long, and the sadness of rejection. And then back to the fire, imagining the one moment that had prompted all the significant events in his life ever since; the fire that his father had started, to fake his own death, all those years ago.

It was cold outside and an extended winter in England had seen unseasonal snow and icy winds arrive. He was glad he didn't have to leave the house for work; he wasn't ready to yet, physically or mentally. His stomach still wasn't right after the health problems he had had in Africa and he had resumed his prescription for diazepam. They were a higher dosage than usual, but they still weren't working.

Without work, he was dependent on his mother who, of course, had been sympathetic to his condition. Neither did she blame him for Bobby's death, not that they had ever spoken about it. She was just grateful to have time with her one remaining son, while still being worried about him.

JK barely spoke to anyone, whether in person, phone or email, and rarely left the house, apart from doctor's appointments or quick visits to the shops. He became lethargic and sleepy, possibly as a side effect of his medication but also because his nights were filled with endless guilty thoughts about his brother.

He ate very little and would get up late, having had little sleep the night before and then, in the day, would just stare blankly at the fire, or out of the window, occasionally scratching at his foot. When Di had come over to visit a few times, he had just gone and hidden in his bedroom to avoid any awkward conversations.

JK was stuck in an endless monotony and found it hard to see any positives in his near future. He had no ambition; festering at his mother's house couldn't prompt him to doing anything constructive. He knew that he had to get out, yet couldn't quite summon the energy. Seeing his mum's face every day was an almost constant reminder of his father's deception and made him feel less like wanting to achieve anything at all, let alone work.

Everything felt like dead time to JK: filling the gaps with anything else was just extra hassle. Every decision, every moment required him to make an effort just to progress to the next ten minutes of his life.

Should I eat lunch today or could I hold on a bit longer till dinner? Should I kill some time by emailing an old friend that I hadn't heard from in years? Should I reply to friends who I just can't be bothered to speak to anymore?

Should I get up early and attempt to do something constructive at the weekend, or should I stay awake, lying in bed, trying to block out the thoughts of the past year? Should I bother to speak to my mother about that 'good old character' Lenny Keane and what he did to us all? Should I speak to someone about how I was feeling, or should I just brush over things as normal, keeping my real emotions hidden?

Then, one day, a different visitor showed up at the house. When JK's mother had announced him, from the hallway, as an old friend, someone from his brother's wedding, he had shown the briefest bit of interest.

The lounge door opened and a bronzed and skinny young man walked confidently in and grabbed a surprised JK by the hand as he stood up.

'JK, you absolute legend! How long has it been?' said Jimmy Reilly.

'Hi, Jimmy… Yeah, it's been ages. It was at my brother's wedding, right?' replied JK. 'So about five months ago?'

'Oh, yes, that's it. Look man… I … I'm so sorry for your loss. It must've been awful for you all.'

'Thanks. We're OK,' JK said, lying. They stood staring awkwardly at each other for a moment as JK's CD played in the background.

'Ah, I love the Manic Street Preachers. *La Tristesse Durera* is their best song,' said Jimmy.

'Yeah…it's my favourite,' JK said, as he hurriedly pulled down his sleeves, concealing his most recent tattoo on the inside of his left arm – the title of the song.

He didn't want to admit to Jimmy just how much it meant to him: his trip to the tattoo parlour had been a rare visit outside since he had returned home and he had been playing the song non-stop otherwise. More importantly, he didn't want Jimmy to worry about the significance of its translation: "The sadness will last forever."

'Take a seat, mate. Can I get you some tea – or something stronger?' said JK, as he finally bent over and picked up the remote control to stop the music.

'Ha, ha, it's a bit early for the sauce, even for me. I'd love a cup of tea, though.'

JK walked into the kitchen to see his mother hovering by the door.

'Do you two want some tea, dear?' she asked.

'It's OK, Mum. I can do it.'

'Don't be silly. You must have loads to catch up on. Why don't you go and sit down with him and I'll bring it in when it's ready,' she said with a smile.

'OK. Thanks, Mum,' replied JK, who then went back into the lounge and sat down opposite his surprise guest.

'Jimmy, it's good to see you,' JK said, staring at his slightly unreal, shiny and permanently youthful face. His scruffy hair was shorter and tidier than he remembered from the last time he had seen him. 'What brings you to my neck of the woods, anyway?'

'Well, I heard on the grapevine that you were around, back from your trip. I was just passing, so I thought I'd pop in on you, out of the blue,' Jimmy said, cagily.

'Uh-huh,' replied JK, suspiciously.

'Anyway, you'll never guess what, but I'm back working with those chumps at our old firm again, Mackey Finance Group.'

'Really? I thought you'd left permanently?' replied JK, surprised. Jimmy shook his head. 'How is it?'

'I guess the place is still pretty similar to when you left.'

'What, paralysed by internal politics and idiotic middle management?'

'There are still plenty of idiots around, that's for sure,' said Jimmy, laughing.

'I don't know how you still do it,' said JK, shaking his head.

'Well, I can't say I love it but I just keep my head down, do my hours and get on with it. I have my life outside of work, I take my holidays – it makes me a bit more focused. I guess I've just learnt to ignore them and – don't laugh – I like to think I've matured a little bit by now too.'

'I doubt that! Speaking of holidays, how was your trip, then? You got back from Australia before Christmas, right? I think I had an email from you while you were on Magnetic Island. About to start some jet-ski tour with your girlfriend.'

'Oh, yes, of course,' said Jimmy, laughing. 'It was amazing. We had a great time. But nothing compared to yours, mate – it was only an extended holiday after all, which I might never have done at all if you hadn't inspired me to do it. You're the seasoned travel veteran now, aren't you?'

'Don't be silly,' replied JK, as they both laughed at how ridiculous their mutual appreciation sounded.

'And Helen, do you ever hear from her?'

'My ex? No, thank god. We split up right after your brother's wedding, thanks to your little speech. She realised what was really going on soon enough.'

'Well, yes, sorry about that, mate. But it was always coming, wasn't it?'

'Yeah, I guess so. Anyway, it's good to see you too, Jonny-boy. So, how are you doing?' replied Jimmy in his broad Midlands accent.

JK smiled but didn't reply. Instead, he began scratching at the sole of his foot nonchalantly, and as he continued, the scratching became more and more vigorous. Finally, JK noticed he was being watched as he looked up to see Jimmy's shocked face.

'What on earth are you doing, JK?'

'Sorry, mate. It's some sort of gruesome, parasitic infection that I picked up in Africa,' he said, continuing to scratch.

'Gross. Didn't you sort it out when you were over there, then?'

'I should really go back to the doctor, I guess. I caught it on safari, but I thought it was all healed at the time.'

'What on earth was the infection?' Jimmy asked.

'Well the doctors weren't 100% sure, but there were loads of ideas. They thought it was dysentery, but I was never convinced. Someone else I met, a local, suggested it was something called bilharzia, I think. Nasty worms that burrow into your foot, into your blood, then lay eggs in your guts. In the end, after everything I've read since on the internet, I think he was right. Gave me the most terrible stomach pain and the worst shits you could possibly imagine. I thought I'd recovered, but I'm not sure now. I keep thinking the worms are still there, in my foot. I just keep feeling them moving around in there somewhere, so I have to scratch and scratch until it almost bleeds. I can't be satisfied until–'

'OK, enough, JK. Yeah, you do need to go back to the docs, as soon as possible.' Jimmy said, shaking his head in disgust. Then, breaking the silence, JK's mother brought in their tea.

'Thanks, Mrs Keane. Wow, cake too, amazing.'

'No problem,' she said, casting a nervous glance at her son. 'Enjoy, I'll be upstairs if you need me.'

As she disappeared out of the room, Jimmy cut a slice of cake for himself and offered one to JK, who declined. As he began eating, he smiled wryly at JK and several times he deliberately licked his lips, for effect, in between sipping his tea. They soon resumed relaxed conversation, and he feigned a cough to start a subject of a different nature.

'Well, it certainly sounds like you had an eventful trip, JK,' he said, chirpily.

JK suspected his remark was innocent enough, yet couldn't help think he wanted to know more. But how could JK possibly describe what had happened to him; he didn't know where to begin. He wasn't going to tell him about his obsession with finding his father while he was in Thailand, that was for sure.

So, instead, JK mumbled some nonsense about where he had been, what he saw, barely managing to string coherent sentences together.

'JK, what's up mate?' Jimmy said, staring at him with concern.

'I think I'm just a bit hot in here. Is it me, or is it really humid?'

'It's hot, that fire is blazing, but it's freezing outside.'

'I think I might nod off at any moment, sorry. What were you saying again?'

'You're not with it, JK. There's something not right with you, and you've lost loads of weight. What's wrong?'

'Gotta be careful about what I eat, you know. Don't know what germs might get me again. They say eggs are bad, you never know what bacteria they have. Same with milk, full of vile chemicals added in that you'll never know about. Can't eat any of it now.'

'It's psychological, JK. After you got sick in Africa, now you can't look at stuff in the same way. Am I right?'

JK felt something in his foot and began to scratch at it again. Sensing his unwillingness to open up to him, Jimmy shifted on his seat and looked outside briefly.

JK's scratching continued – intensifying as he took his sock off.

'What are you doing?' Jimmy asked, perplexed. JK had grabbed a metal pen from a side table and was now using it to violently scratch at his foot. His skin became red raw and, as blood was about to squeeze out, Jimmy's calls broke through JK's fixation.

'JK, whoa! For fuck's sake, stop it, lad! What's the matter with you?'

'What? Oh right, yeah. Sorry.' He wiped his foot and looked up embarrassedly, quickly shuffling in his chair and yanking his sock back on.

'Oh, come on, JK. Snap out of it. Look, I know, I've got an idea. You need some sort of homecoming celebration, a welcome back at least, despite, you know… everything that happened.'

'A celebration? Why?'

'Why not? Come on.'

'I don't really feel like celebrating anything, that's why.'

'Exactly. It might perk you up a little.'

'Who would come?'

'You know, our old work crew. Tom, Veronica, David. Plus my now-official girlfriend, Jenny.'

'I've kind of lost touch with that lot. In fact, I've lost touch with most of my old friends recently.'

'Yeah, well, I thought you might like it.'

Jimmy immediately recognised the gratitude in JK's eyes without having to say anything. Finally, a genuine smile formed across JK's face.

The early morning alarm sounded, heralding JK's new daily routine as he contemplated getting out of bed. Jimmy's visit a few weeks ago had given JK the impetus to look for work. After a token effort looking elsewhere, in the end, the easiest option was working back at his old firm with Jimmy.

It was a simple matter of calling up an old contact to go through a semi-formal interview, just for appearance's sake, and he was well set. The job was largely the same as what he had been doing before, only with a different group of chumps this time.

Yet, as JK lay in bed, he knew he was struggling to re-adjust to this routine. He knew that it always took time, but this still felt more of a struggle than it had ever done before. Finally, he dragged himself up, walked out of his room, and heard his mother shout good morning before he jumped in the shower.

On the surface, perhaps for his mother at least, things may have seemed like they were improving for JK. He returned to his bedroom, clean shaven, and then styled his hair and put on a smart shirt.

But he still thought about Bobby all the time, as his night-time dreams had started to take over his daytime thoughts too. Taking his medication meant that sometimes he was just too drowsy to take notice of what was happening at all.

He saw his socks and shoes by his bed, and remembered Bobby's old antics, when he used to turn up everywhere barefoot. Outside of work, JK had recently taken to do the same, just to give his bad foot some air. Everything he tried, be it socks, shoes or trainers, irritated him but other people weren't to know that: they weren't sure if he was doing it as a tribute to Bobby or as some kind of sick joke. Yet, that wasn't his intention, and he didn't laugh about it or try to draw attention to it.

He got out some polish and shined his shoes; his mind wandered aimlessly as he robotically worked the pungent-smelling cloth along the black leather surface. Eventually, this motion was interrupted as a shadow formed at his doorway. A figure stood, blocking the powerful early morning sun. JK squinted into the sun beams, as dust drifted slowly through them and he struggled to make out any features.

'Do you want tea, JK?' said the voice, a familiar voice. The figure was barefoot.

'What?' said JK, confused.

'Do you have time for breakfast? You're running late,' the voice continued, and JK could make out brown curly hair on the head of the figure.

'Bobby?' said JK, in a daze. He remembered Bobby cooking him breakfast in Sydney only a few years ago, and that his brother's hair was a lot shorter back then.

His mother, shocked at her son's reaction, walked away, downstairs, to make tea. She had seen these, now typical, moments of confusion before, even though they hadn't registered with JK. She was just glad to see him getting out of the house and speaking to people. As long as he was coping; these things were a sign of his progress.

She brought up some tea for JK and hurried him on his way to work, where he carried out his day in a sort of permanent dream-like state. It got to the point where no daily activity registered with his consciousness whatsoever.

JK had begun meeting up with Jimmy and his old work friends too. They didn't live far away, spread around the edges of the city, in Archway or Finchley. Briefly, it felt like old times to him again, as they started going back to the same old pubs where they used to watch sport and speak drunken nonsense. JK dared to feel optimistic, but he was just a passenger – the feeling never settled for long.

That evening, he walked briskly in the cold, back from Highgate tube station to his mother's house. He thought he had seen a man running several metres ahead of him. The man wore a faux-fur trapper hat, just like his brother had used to.

JK quickened his step to try and get a better view of him, but every time JK would turn a corner closer to home, he would see the man, still ahead of him, before turning off to the next road that JK was headed for. Eventually, on his road, JK saw the man again, waiting outside his mother's house, with his back to him.

JK called out to him, at which he ran up the driveway of their house and disappeared inside. JK ran and unlocked the front door. In the lounge, he found his mother, stirring sleepily in front of the fire. The TV was on and she loosely held an empty glass of sherry in her hand. In the low lighting, he could see the bottle on the side table was almost empty.

'Where is he?' shouted JK, frantically.

'Who?' she replied, jolting up in confusion.

'The man in the hat. He just came in here!' JK said, throwing his coat off and pacing up and down the hallway, looking in all the rooms.

'I don't know what you mean, JK. It's just me here, as per usual. Have you been out drinking with your work friends again?'

'Yes, so what? Looks like you've had one or two yourself.'

'Just a night-cap,' she said, flustered. 'Anyway, I made sausages for dinner. I've saved you some, you can heat them up if you want?'

'No thanks. I'm not hungry.'

'Well, suit yourself. It's late anyway. I better go to bed. Are you staying down here?'

'Yeah, for a bit. Night,' JK said, bluntly.

His mother stood up and paused at the bottom of the stairs, sheepishly. She walked back into the lounge and, with her back to JK, grabbed the bottle of sherry.

'Goodnight, JK,' she said, before walking up the stairs.

JK waited to hear her enter her room and then went to the cupboard and poured himself a brandy. He sat back in his usual chair, facing the fire, and the picture. The TV remained on in the background but he paid it little attention.

He saw movement in the corner of the room, momentarily confused, but after getting up to check, he couldn't see anything. He assumed it was the fire-light playing tricks on his eyes. He sat back down, and eventually began to nod off as the heat and the alcohol hit him.

Suddenly, he was awakened as the home phone began to ring. He got up to answer it.

'Jonny Keane, how the devil are you doing there, muchacho?' said an American voice. It sounded familiar, but JK couldn't quite place it.

'Hello, er… sorry, who is this?'

'Oh, brother, that hurts. After everything we went through in Queenstown, how can you forget me?'

And then it clicked. JK knew he was speaking to Joseph Johnson Knox – Jo-Jo – the travel buddy who he hadn't seen in five years. He had only emailed him once in the last two years.

'My god! Jo-Jo, is that you?'

'That's more like it, hombre! How are you, my man?'

'I'm in shock, that's what! Sorry for not recognising your voice. It's been so long.'

'Hey, don't sweat it. It ain't no skin off my nose, as you Brits like to say.'

'God, it's so funny. Just hearing you talk again, all the memories are flooding back.'

'Ha, correct. Queenstown, New Zealand, man. Amazing! Never to be forgotten.'

'Never. Wow. That bar crawl!'

'Exactly!' said Jo-Jo, as they both laughed, enthusiastically.

'I can't believe you're calling me. Where are you now? Do you have some news?' As soon as JK had finished asking the question, he saw movement at the back of the room again. In the shadows, a figure slowly became more visible. He saw the man from earlier, still wearing the same faux-fur trapper hat. He walked closer to JK who saw a familiar pair of eyes, even though the pupils seemed dead, the unusual amber colour reflected brilliantly against the single lightbulb that was on in the hallway.

'Oh, you know, just catching up for old time's sake,' Jo-Jo replied. 'As it's been so long I thought I'd just pick up the phone. Heck, I would've flown over to see you in person but the timing wasn't quite right. No news from me – I'm back in the States, planning my next move.'

JK momentarily ignored the figure hovering nearby to analyse the ambiguous nature of Jo-Jo's comments. They hung in the air as he considered his response.

'You're not in more trouble with the police, are you, Jo-Jo?'

'Hell-no, don't worry, JK. I've learnt my lesson.' This less-than-convincing reply gave JK something to focus on, as he managed to ignore the silent stranger lurking in his living room.

JK began to remember the awkward time after Jo-Jo had been arrested in New Zealand almost five years ago for the theft of a camera. Although he hadn't been in prison for long, it had really affected him. But, besides a few initial phone calls and emails, JK couldn't support him, having already left the country to continue his travels.

Even though he had always felt guilty about that, JK gradually lost contact with Jo-Jo. Jo-Jo had got back in touch with JK a few years later and he could still remember the email vividly, the tone of which had struck him as very different, as if Jo-Jo had changed personality completely. He had talked cynically about his plans to travel and his struggles to fund them, hinting at various illegal schemes and short cuts with no remorse.

But this had happened during a period of JK's life where he had been drifting along, aimlessly. So, he had replied to Jo-Jo, only briefly, expressing some vague ambitions of travelling to Thailand, Africa and other far-flung places himself. In reality, JK hadn't known what he was doing or saying from one day to the next at the time. And even if Jo-Jo had replied to him since, JK hadn't taken any notice.

'I hear you finally managed some more travel, JK?' said Jo-Jo, eventually breaking the silence.

'Yeah... That's right,' JK replied, hesitating once again. 'I got back in February. Who told you?'

'It was... it was your brother, actually,' Jo-Jo said, before pausing awkwardly. 'I got in touch with him after I never heard back from you. It was a couple of years ago now... I was worried about you, JK.'

As Jo-Jo's words tailed off, JK turned his head to see the stranger smiling at him from the corner of the room, standing upright, and with no shoes on. He had removed his hat now, and his smile could not hide the vacant, lifeless black centres of his eyes. JK realised that wasn't how he remembered Bobby's vibrant, vital, instinctive eyes. Confused, but intrigued, JK opened his mouth to say something to him, but no words came out.

'JK? Are you there?' Jo-Jo asked.

'Sorry... Oh, right... And since then, have you heard...' JK closed his eyes to block out the view of the stranger, but still couldn't bring himself to finish his sentence.

'Yeah, I heard... Look, JK, I'm so sorry about Bobby. It's just awful. I don't know how you must all feel.'

'But how... how did you find out?' asked JK, confused, avoiding looking at the sofa.

'His wife, Diana, she told me. Bobby must have told her about me before he... she even invited me to the funeral. But I couldn't, you know, the cost of the flights and all.'

'I see. Well, I won't lie. It's been hard but I think I'm slowly getting back to normal again now. I'm working, trying to get into a routine again.'

'Sure,' replied Jo-Jo, but JK could hear the doubt in his voice. 'What about those pills of yours? Do you still take them?'

'What, you mean my anti-depressants? Yeah, I'm still on them. My doctor just increased the dose.' JK turned his head to see the stranger was still sitting and smiling, vacantly.

'And do they help?'

'What?' said JK, still distracted.

'The pills. Do they help you feel better?'

JK paused as he thought he would try smiling back at his silent guest. On doing so, he instantly relaxed. He knew the stranger was his brother; and that he wasn't real, but now he was somehow more comfortable with him being there with him.

'A bit,' he replied, 'sometimes. Good days and bad days. But recently, I'm apathetic about everything. I don't feel or really care about anything. I'm not happy or sad or excited or nervous – about anything I do. I'm just there; I just do things.'

'Oh, man. That can't be right. What are the pills called again?'

'Diazepam.'

'Yeah, well, my uncle was on them too and I know that they're pretty addictive. You should be careful.'

'But they seem to be working.'

'Trust me, I know. There's some dangerous side effects if you were to come off them suddenly after being on them for a long time.'

'Like what?' JK watched Bobby stand and pick up the TV remote, and then sit himself down again, next to JK this time. He was about to object, when Jo-Jo spoke again.

'Panic. Paranoia. That sort of stuff. It almost killed my uncle.'

'Oh, come on, Jo-Jo. It's not like you to be such a drama queen.'

'I'm just saying, don't become dependent on them, is all. It's not healthy.'

'Well, I'm on a bit of a cocktail of drugs at the moment. I've had some other health problems after my trip to Africa.'

JK continued to describe his many ailments in detail as he watched Bobby flick through the TV channels with the remote.

'Wow, man, that is horrific. What drugs did they prescribe for your stomach infection?' asked Jo-Jo.

'Some weird tablets. Massive great green things that I had to dissolve in water. Metronidazole, I think they're called. They were just to clear up the last of the parasitic infection, if there was any left, that is. I have no idea what those things were, but they turned my piss bright fluorescent green. And they well and truly spaced me out. For a few days, I didn't know where I was.'

JK frowned at Bobby as he increased the TV volume, but he hadn't seemed to notice.

'Got any left for me, JK?' Jo-Jo said, laughing. 'And? Are they working, anyway?'

'Oh, yeah. I went back yesterday and I told the doc that I couldn't finish the whole course of tablets because they were just too strong. But he was amazed that I'd taken so many of those fuckers in the first place! Supposedly two was more than enough.'

Then, suddenly, Bobby got up and left the room in one swift movement without speaking, leaving JK feeling cold. He began to shiver.

'I think I'm gonna get on to bed now, Jo-Jo. I don't feel right.'

Jo-Jo was silent for a moment.

'OK, JK. I just wanted to make sure you were alright.'

'I'm a big boy now, Jo-Jo.'

'You said it, JK, and I know it. But, come on, shucks, man. You've gotta talk to me now!'

'Yeah… I suppose I've felt better than I do right now.'

'There is something definitely not very Jonny Keane about you at the moment, my friend! Well, not the one that I remember, anyhow.'

'Maybe… but, you know, you get older and you… you put a different value on your life experiences, things like that, don't you?'

'Hey man, we all go through it. But whatever else you're worrying about, just remember all the good stuff you've seen – and that must be a whole lot more than most folks will *ever* hope to see. That's a lot of party memories right there, and they can't ever be taken away from you, no sir. Remember, the old saying, "Better to burn out than fade away". Remember that? That's why you did it, that's why any of us did it, no? Am I wrong?'

'No, I guess not.'

'Heck, even earlier, when I first rang, remember? We were still chirpin' about New Zealand, some five years or so after the event. That ain't so bad, now, is it?'

'True, Jo-Jo. You're right,' JK said.

'*Shit,* yes, I'm right. Damn-straight.'

Eventually they said their goodbyes and JK slowly walked off to bed, thinking Bobby would re-appear again, but he never did.

A few hours later, he awoke abruptly in a cold sweat and wondered if he had imagined the whole episode. He went back downstairs for a pint of water and, passing himself in the mirror, he saw his heavy stubble, his damp, long and unkempt hair, and his face, drained of colour.

He returned to his bedroom, and drained the glass of its contents, pausing for breath halfway through. As he did so, his gaze locked upon his collection of medication on top of the bedside drawers. An assortment of pill bottles and plastic sheets of tablets, of various colours, shapes and sizes, were strewn across the surface. He continued to stare at them before eventually falling back to sleep.

Over the next few weeks, JK survived his daily routine, but nothing more. Nothing really bad or good happened to him, and he quickly realised that he felt much better whenever Bobby came to visit him. The occasional visit wasn't enough for him, though; once or twice a week wouldn't even do it – JK began to need him around all the time.

His hope was that Bobby would lift him from the constant plateau of apathy that he was living through and drag him out of the pit of despair that seemed to lurk around every corner of his life.

Recurring worries over his health were nagging at JK. Every time he was feeling good about himself, he would start to have doubts: a sick feeling would emerge in his stomach, he would get severe headaches and he would start to scratch at his foot again.

He couldn't understand why it was happening; his foot had healed after the correct treatment from the doctor. More and more he questioned the pills he was taking for depression, becoming paranoid about his state of mind.

Sleep was still largely an impossibility. So many memories played over and over in his head, real conversations and incidents, some recent but some very old ones too, merging and reforming in dream-like sequences so that he didn't know if he was awake or asleep.

I saw Bobby smiling and nodding, looking knowingly at me. 'Stop taking the medication. It's making you feel worse. You've stopped a couple of times before and survived, so how bad can it be? You just need to get used to being off them for longer. You can do it.'

'Jo-Jo said you can do it too. I have faith in you, JK; you've got the strength to do it. You're addicted to those pills. That's why you can't get rid of your problems. You need to get over your addiction first; that's how you'll get rid of them.'

Bobby's amber eyes were sparkling, but he never spoke about himself. He mentioned our father's list of countries. 'What a joke. But, still, where's your ambition gone, JK?' he asked me, but he always had more travel ambitions than me. 'Why did you try and copy him, then?' Bobby asked me, but why is that my fault? It's my father's fault he left us and since then I always wanted to know more about him and discover the world at the same time, just like you did, Bobby. 'Don't blame me,' said Bobby.

'But, what about the dog?' Bobby asked me, and I couldn't stop seeing our dog that went missing, Busby, or dogs like him. It must be cursed, the fucking thing, I must have cursed it when I was growing up, because it went missing after my dad died. Maybe I'm cursed, maybe that's why it happened in the first place; I must be cursed. Dad left us by pretending to die, then we lost our dog, then I went travelling and couldn't stop seeing a dog, then I see my father, hundreds of thousands of miles away, just after I spoke to Bobby on my birthday.

Then when I did find my dad again, he still didn't want to know me. If I hadn't met up with him, Bobby wouldn't have come out for me, and then he wouldn't have died. So, Bobby, you tell me that I'm not cursed. Every time I go away, something bad happens. Even when other good things happen, like seeing an astonishing safari and all those animals. It was a childhood ambition, a fucking trip of a lifetime, but it doesn't matter now. What's the point? I'm cursed; it's my fault. Or my dad is cursed and it's his fault.

I don't know which it is, but either way I'm fucked, am I not, Bobby? 'Don't you see, my brother?' Bobby said. 'Don't you see it? End the curse.' Bobby said.

JK sat up in bed, sweating heavily again. His head was throbbing as he vigorously scratched it. He looked at his alarm clock and saw it was 3am. He smiled grimly at the dreams that still lingered in his thoughts. They had now crystallised into a couple of decisions that he had been putting off for some time.

He got up quietly, put on his dressing gown and walked downstairs to his lounge. He walked towards the fireplace and grabbed the wedding photo of his brother and Di that was still on the shelf. How much time have I spent staring at this awful spectacle, he thought? He turned the frame over and lifted the stand at the back to pull out the glass. There, in between the photo and cardboard, was Lenny Keane's old list, still weighing JK down. He removed it and reassembled the photo frame, replacing it on the fireplace.

He held the folded piece of paper in his hand and, even now, in its frail condition, he knew what it really represented. One gigantic, long, convoluted lie that was his life. Ah, yes, that was it, he thought. A travel guide, and perhaps even a solution, for my life.

He began to remember its full influence on him: all the dreams, all his passion of youth, the memories of so many people across the world.

At the end of an evening, sitting, watching a beach sunset with a girl on his shoulder, something clicking in his head, in that one special moment, a moment that lingered as he watched candles flicker in the ocean breeze, sitting at a wooden table with sand in between their toes as they slowly finished their drinks. A smell of her perfume and the embers of a camp fire mixing together, as the light touch of her hand, or of her hair being blown across his cheek by the wind, sent a tingle down his spine. Making him believe he was special, that they were special, or that any of this time, or even all of it, meant something special, no matter how brief.

Cavorting in a freshwater pool, the cold but clean, crisp water keeping him alert and alive, energy rushing through him and all his travel companions, all on each other's side, egging each other on with funnier and funnier and more spectacular stories. Eating against a back-drop of some natural landscape of wonder, a scenic beauty making the most simple of meals taste a million times better.

Remembering the feelings from the quiet times also, alone with his thoughts as he slowly fell asleep as the world passed him by, the real travel in between destinations. Sitting on a bus, a train or a plane, reminiscing fondly, or worrying, or even just thinking, But it was his time, time that was precious and over all too quickly.

All those memories that had been so crucial to who he was had all been rendered meaningless now. He could never repeat them; and even those memories had been tainted. Because his life was now, and would forever be, a lie.

Why did I waste so much time trying to copy my father? he thought, weeping. He was underserving of the tribute that he had tried to give him. He was a deceptive, spineless and selfish criminal, JK realised. His father had stolen years of his family's life, of his own life. After everything that had happened, JK knew now he was just a petty thief.

JK angrily grabbed a box of matches from the fireplace and removed one, striking it alight. He held it to the corner of the list and watched the flame engulf the old brown paper. It quickly spread as JK had to drop it into the fireplace, watching as several pieces broke off and burned rapidly before only ashes were left. He wiped his eyes on the sleeve of his dressing gown and then briskly turned his back and walked towards the door, where he suddenly stopped. He took one last glance behind him at the fireplace, before going back upstairs to bed.

That same evening, JK had made his other decision: to come off his anti-depressant medication. To begin with, there had been no bad reaction to this at all, whether physical or emotional. JK had felt as calm as he had ever done and Bobby didn't seem to be visiting him as much anymore.

But then, slowly, he began to see small changes to his mood. His night-time thoughts became darker and deeper, re-starting the uneven sleep patterns and, when he did sleep, his dreams became more vivid.

A whole week – perhaps even two, he had lost count of the days – passed by. Suddenly, as he lay on his bed early one Saturday afternoon, a wave of emotion hit him, randomly and without warning. Out of nowhere, he felt a pit of darkness open up inside of him, as a great force of negativity flushed through him. It drained out of his head, rushed through his chest and stomach, down into this pit, filling up like some great well of insidious and incomprehensible dark liquid.

An oil of depression, a black blood, an essential body fluid; it was so vivid, almost as if it were a physical reaction. And then JK began to cry for no reason; he started sobbing, and continuously, crying again and again, for some thirty minutes.

JK couldn't move his limbs, having gone into some sort of involuntary cramp, and it was every effort just to pick himself up to try to call someone for help. He called out, over and over, and eventually his mother arrived.

When she did, JK could only see Bobby. He just stared at JK a little confused, asked what he needed and, not knowing what to say, JK just asked for water. The sobbing stopped eventually, even though he felt his body convulsing and his head throbbing, and soon he became nauseous.

Sometime later, as he dozed in and out of sleep, JK remained unnerved as his fears escalated further.

'Why did you do it, brother?' Bobby said, his amber eyes staring at me like an animal, waiting to pounce, on instinct. 'Why did you leave me?'

I miss my brother so much. I don't understand what any of it means: I'm now completely fucking clueless about everything I've ever done in my life.

Yet, I know I've done so many good things. 'Why did you do any of it, brother?' Bobby said. 'Life has been unfaithful, and it all promised so, so much.' What dreams have I got left to pursue? None, and why should I anyway? The things that really mattered to me, I had no control over.

In the end, my brother died and my father didn't want to know us, so who gives a shit how many countries I've seen, where I've been to, who I've fucked and what scenery or animals I've got photos of. My dreams are over.

'Don't you see, brother?' Bobby said, but I've got no hope left. I can't do anything about it, and that hurts more than anything else. It's like it was all one big lie; all those years of effort, planning, all that travel, all that money. But, when it came to it, fate pissed all over me, it stabbed me through the heart.

'It's the curse, brother,' Bobby said, and I knew he was right. I couldn't do anything about it, no one could. So, what's the point of carrying on? Why should I? Why can't I just find happiness some other way? Why can't I find new dreams? Everyone else finds happiness somehow, what's wrong with me?

I miss Bobby. I don't understand why these things happened to me. Why can't I start again? What's wrong with me?

'Just end the curse, brother,' Bobby said.

Later that same afternoon, JK was woken up by shouting coming from downstairs. He put on his jeans and jumper and crept slowly down the stairs to investigate. He could hear two female voices arguing from inside the kitchen, and the closed door meant he could only hear muffled details of the conversation.

He knew one of the voices was his mum's but strained to hear the other one. Eventually, after recognising her shoes and coat by the front door, he realised it belonged to his sister-in-law, Di.

He still couldn't hear what they were discussing, and resented the sudden flashbacks he was now having, sitting on his stairs as a young boy, listening to his mother arguing with his father. And he resented the fact that his family were still arguing now, probably as a result of his brother's death and his own increasingly strange behaviour.

Then Bobby appeared in his lounge once again. Despite the smiling, jovial presence of his brother, JK now felt increasingly awkward in his own house. He could feel his mood darkening further, as if he was waiting for some dark event to come and wipe everything away, once and for all. Another natural disaster to clear his head, remove all the emotional litter floating around his life; a thorough and devastating clean-up.

So, JK made one more decision, and then quickly walked down the remaining stairs to put his shoes and coat on. He opened the front door, as Bobby got up and walked out ahead of him, before JK slammed it shut on his way out. A few seconds later, the front door re-opened behind JK and both his mother and Di appeared outside to look for him.

With his head down and walking at pace, JK was focused on his destination. He didn't hear them call out and, after hurriedly putting on her coat, Di ran out to chase after him.

Just before they reached Highgate Bridge, Di caught up with JK.

'JK, wait! Hold up!' she shouted behind him.

He stopped and turned round to face her.

'Hello, Di,' he said, eventually. 'Sorry for rushing out, but I needed to get some air,' he continued, lying.

'And I'm sorry you had to hear your mum and I arguing like that. Look, JK,' she paused, 'we haven't spoken properly for ages. Why don't we… do you fancy a drink?'

JK shifted awkwardly, immediately feeling regret on seeing the desperation in her eyes. And perhaps he was curious enough to put his decision on hold for now.

'There's a pub near here, isn't there?' continued Di.

'Yeah. The Crown on Highgate Hill. It's a ten-minute walk or so.'

'Perfect. Shall we, then? I'm buying.'

'OK,' replied JK, after a while. They walked together, in stilted conversation about the weather, work and the local shops they walked past en route.

On arrival at the pub, JK asked Di for a vodka and tonic and sat down in the slightly damp, warm atmosphere inside. It was starting to get busy as the punters kept a keen eye on a TV showing football scores in the corner of the room. Two young men, probably students, played on the fruit machine in another corner. Di waited patiently as the barman wearily moved across the floor behind his unkempt and sticky bar surface to answer a phone.

JK leaned back and deliberately dug his finger nails into the green armchair sofa, resisting the urge to fall asleep. He looked for Bobby, and saw him standing near the TV, and he could only raise his arms up in a mock-helplessness gesture.

Eventually, Di joined JK at the table with their drinks. They both glanced awkwardly at each other, and then around the pub for natural distractions that could not be found from their slow and polite dialogue.

'Look, JK. No one blames you for what happened, you know?' she said, suddenly.

JK paused and thought about Bobby, picturing him as a tiny dot, sitting on the shore in Ko Phi Phi as he had watched from his fishing boat.

'Maybe,' said JK, who couldn't look at Di at all, trying to vary his gaze between the TV, the jukebox and the barman. He looked down and, on auto-pilot, took off his shoe and began to scratch his foot.

Di frowned and, trying to ignore JK's actions, carried on talking.

'No, I mean it. I don't blame you for Bobby's death. I know I wasn't very understanding to start with,' she said, looking down at the table, 'but it was a difficult time for me, for all of us.'

JK nodded at Di, and stopped scratching his foot to look at her properly. She was a lot thinner than she had been at the wedding, even though she was not overweight then. Her face was gaunt and her eyes were sunken and sorrowful, sitting above large, dark bags hanging underneath, hinting at the months of grief she had been suffering.

'I appreciate you saying that, Di,' JK said after a while. 'Really I do. But maybe I can't forgive myself.'

'You shouldn't feel that way, JK. It wasn't your fault. It wasn't anyone's. It was just bad luck.' JK could tell that Di wasn't being truthful, she was holding something back.

'But you need to talk to people. I know you're struggling at the moment, but if you talk about it you might give yourself a chance of feeling better.'

'Friends and family, yeah, I know.' JK carried on staring at his feet, waiting.

'Well, the point is, you hardly speak to your friends that much now, and that can't be healthy.' She sipped her drink and looked out the window.

'Yeah, well, I just haven't felt sociable of late. It's not been top of my priorities,' JK said, as he sat forward, pressing on his stomach and resisting the urge to scratch his foot again.

'Surely your friends are one of the most important things in life? We can all help each other. Come on, you don't need me to tell you that. Didn't Jimmy help you? Or Jo-Jo?'

Her voice faded into air as darkness filled JK completely, pushing up into his neck, arms and legs, trying to get out. His every thought was to try to contain this fluid sensation developing, but he just managed to lift his heavy head up and fix his eyes on Di once more. Suddenly, he had pieced together what had been happening.

'So, you told Jimmy Reilly and Jo-Jo to talk to me, did you? Did you feel sorry for me, Di?' he said, angrily.

'You can't blame me for being worried about you, can you, JK? They're your friends – think of all those memories, all those stories you must have. Surely talking about them must make you feel a bit better?'

JK hesitated as he looked up to the ceiling.

'A bit, maybe. But so what?'

'What do you mean?'

'I mean, all those stories have led me precisely nowhere in my life. I've come to the realisation that there was no answer to be gained from any of it. Everything is just a collection of memories now and nothing more. I can't have them again; I can't re-live them; they're in the past. So, what use are they to me now? They're not real anymore.'

And now it was JK who was holding back. What he hadn't explained was that he still couldn't stop thinking about Bobby, blaming himself for his death, or block out the fact that his father had rejected them.

'So, you tell me, Di. Does talking about it make you feel better? That it was just bad luck that was to blame for it all?' JK continued, bitterly.

Di looked at him with hurt burning in her eyes.

'I think about my luck all the time, JK. Bobby wasn't my first dose of bad luck, if you remember? I've lost people before,' she said, choking back tears. 'How exactly do you think I coped with that?'

JK merely shook his head, shocked by her aggressive response.

'Every day I cry. And I rarely eat. But I speak to my mother and my father. And sometimes I speak to your mother too. And most days, I get through OK. But no, it's not fucking easy.'

JK stared at her, silently, before taking a large gulp to finish his drink. He looked at her empty glass and then at her, raising his eyebrows, and she nodded back at him. He put his shoe back on and, as he got up to go to the bar, he noticed that she was fiddling with something in her coat pocket. While he ordered he saw her remove an envelope briefly and then she looked up to see him watching before hastily replacing it in her pocket.

'So, did you hear what your mum and I were arguing about earlier?' Di asked, after JK had returned to the table with fresh drinks.

'No. I expect she didn't know how to deal with me, right? She never has done.'

'Your mother is worried about you. We're all worried about you.' Her tone had changed to one of desperation. 'You look terrible, like a hairy, wild man. And your skin looks pale and greasy.'

'Well, thanks a lot, Di,' he replied, defiantly. 'I'm just going through a bad patch at the minute.'

'What about your work? How's that going?'

'Not great. They gave me a verbal warning last week.'

'Shit. Why? What did you do?'

'Nothing. I don't know. Just general ill health and distraction, I suppose. I guess it must've affected my performance. But I don't care.'

'What do you mean?'

'I just can't see a future there; it's not me. Nothing is, that's the problem.'

'That's a pretty pessimistic statement, JK. No future? You're still young, you're doing OK, you've got a good CV with a good firm and you should be able to spin your travels into something positive: the people you've met, your perspective on life, that sort of thing. I'd say you've got massive amounts going for you. More than most, in fact.'

JK's stomach sunk. Di's every word was pounding into his body, every utterance peppering sensitive points. He played around with his glass and avoided eye contact, stuttering to reply. He looked around the pub, wondering where Bobby had disappeared to. He needed him now.

'Di, I know what you're saying, I understand you, but I just don't feel that way. I just can't see how I'm supposed to enjoy it, how I can challenge myself. I don't even know if I want to… I can't be bothered with anything. It doesn't inspire me. The thought of thirty years of working somewhere I don't give a fuck about doesn't really make me want to make an effort. I can't see a future that's worth getting excited about.'

'Well, you could always take a break and go travelling again, JK? Save up then go. Some people do that for years.'

'Yes and I know a few idiots who still do that, but I don't want that whole yo-yo routine. They're just trying to delay the inevitable. I've achieved all my travel ambitions – and I don't want to do it anymore. It was great while it lasted but it's over now. I've done what I wanted to do and that still wasn't enough. And it probably never will be.'

Tears ran down JK's face and he could only look down at his feet again to try and ignore the pit of black emotion stirring in his stomach again.

'I'm sure it'll all work out, JK,' mumbled Di, looking uncomfortable.

'I don't know what to do next, my dreams are over and I can't do anything else. I'm just tired… tired of it all. I don't know what I'm doing anymore, Di.'

JK squirmed, feeling a hot flush. He strained to take his jacket off as a pain banged against his skull.

He was waiting and hoping still; he needed Bobby to help him through this now. Where was he? It just wasn't fair; none of this is fair, he thought.

'Like I said, all this, everything that's happened, it was just bad luck, that's all. It'll change. It always does,' said Di. 'We'll all help each other get through this.'

'Will we? So, what about Bobby, then? And what about my father? Where are they? Why can't they help me now?' JK said, his eyes stinging and his stomach churning. 'Their luck didn't change, did it? That was just their fate. And who's to say that mine will be any different?'

'I don't believe that, JK. It's not fate, of course it's not. What happened to Bobby, well, there could never be any reason for that. How could there be? No one deserved that. It's bad luck, that's all. There's nothing you could've done, about either of them.' Di crouched forward to try and get through to JK, but he couldn't fight off the swarm of emotion filling up inside of him; a battleground of bitterness, regret and sadness.

Take control, JK heard Bobby's voice tell him, suddenly. *Take control,* Bobby said again, and JK smirked. He looked straight into Di's eyes and laughed sarcastically.

JK knew the darkness had a hold of him now, and a familiar stench suddenly returned to his nostrils – the stench of death. Confusion and fear, in anticipation of the unknown, engulfed him and then he knew he had to leave, to escape from this confinement. Bobby would go with him, to show him where to go. But, even though JK had heard his voice again, he still couldn't see his saviour, Bobby.

'What does it matter? Any of it?' said JK, as he zipped up his jacket again, agitatedly looking around the pub, fidgeting on his seat.

'We all just want you to be happy. Just do whatever makes you happy,' she pleaded with JK.

And that's when JK had his final moment of clarity. Di's words finally made sense. *Take control of your happiness, JK,* said Bobby.

It was a final hint of hope, a final, warm glow of optimism. Now JK could see Bobby standing at the door, his short-sleeved shirt hanging untidily and loosely off his stocky frame. He was smiling, as ever, his hair as short as JK remembered from Thailand, wearing shorts and barefooted as per normal, ready for action; ready to save JK, to drag him from this dark malaise.

JK found the strength to stand up, abruptly turning to Di. She stared back with fear and confusion in her eyes.

'You're right, Di. I know what will make me happy now. So, thank you.'

JK walked out of the pub and faced a large church, St. Joseph's Retreat. He looked up to see the Saint's statue looking down on him, but he knew that it wouldn't provide the answers he was looking for. Instinctively, he turned right along Hornsey Lane, following Bobby, his decision remade and echoing through his head.

Bobby had always been free, JK reflected. Free to just accept the throw of the dice, to just enjoy the moment and live life for whatever it turned out to be – without trying to change anything.

As he traced Bobby's footsteps ahead, JK knew that he wasn't the person that Bobby had been. If something bad happened then so be it, but Bobby didn't spend his life worrying about it. He just got on with everything.

JK wished he had led his life like his brother, but somehow he got lost along the way, distracted trying to copy his father, trying to emulate his achievements. Trying to find meaning when there wasn't any. Now, with his hopes and dreams lost and ruined, how could he be happy living like that? That wasn't living; that was just existing – and surely that wasn't freedom?

Once the thrills in life were taken away – the glory of pursuing hope, chasing a dream – then there's no fun left, and what was the point of that, he thought? As Di had said, the most important thing was understanding how to be happy and now, finally, he thought he did.

Five minutes later, he had made his way back to Highgate Bridge. Looking south, down Archway Road, illuminated by the street lights, on the horizon he could just make out shapes from the city skyscrapers against the fading light of the evening sky.

As JK stood on the pavement, staring out at this view, an old Chinese man, with a plastic shopping bag hanging off each arm, approached him. He barely lifted his head to look as he walked past and, ever so briefly, JK thought he saw a glimpse of scorn on the man's face before looking straight ahead, down the street, to confirm JK's insignificance.

He heard Bobby's voice again. *Take control, JK. You should do it, JK. Do it, and then you can find me. We can be in peace together. Do it.*

Finally, JK could see his brother, standing across the road, waiting for him at the middle of the bridge. Here, the railings were two metres high and had a wider concrete column separating them, with tall street lamps mounted high on top.

JK stared down at the dirty pavements and heard a crushed cola can hit the grate of a drain as it was taken by the wind. He held his head in his hands as the pains grew worse, competing with the despair festering in his gut.

He was distracted by Bobby's movement as he watched him climb the wider column in the middle of the railings of the bridge. He discovered that this was the easiest place to climb up onto the ledge, but he didn't feel nervous. His pain forced him to concentrate on a plan, and Bobby seemed to lead the way the whole way through. He just had to follow his footsteps: where to tread, which leg to move, when and how far, then match his balance. If Bobby could do it barefoot, then JK knew it would work out fine. He could always trust his brother; that's why he missed him so much.

Suddenly his concentration was interrupted by an unnerving cry. Di had been attempting to catch him up and JK then turned to see her, flustered, shouting, her arms frantically waving as she ran towards him. Undeterred, JK edged along the platform, closer to Bobby, confident that he had made the right decision.

'JK, what are you doing?' she screamed.

He smiled as he reached the edge of the bridge. He looked down, and then back at Di. He watched her hesitate as she considered climbing up closer to JK. But she didn't.

'JK, please come down. What are you doing up there?'

'I think you know what I'm doing.'

'Please don't do this. Come down.'

'It was about control all along, you know? That I didn't know how to take control.'

'But you can control this, JK.'

'What about all the things you said about luck and fate?' JK said. 'Let me ask you a question. Bobby didn't care about fate, did he?'

'I don't know, JK. I suppose not.'

'Well, I did. I thought I was supposed to be lucky. And look where it got me. Nowhere. Life still fucked me over, just like it fucked Bobby over. But it's OK; I can still have the last laugh; I can still be happy – you said that was the most important thing in life, right?'

'What, by ending it? That's crazy!'

'Why? I'm doing something that'll make me happy. I want to be with Bobby again.'

JK looked across to Bobby, standing next to him, still smiling. His amber eyes had finally regained their spark now, the spark of life from old that JK remembered so fondly. On seeing this, JK let out a large sigh of relief, knowing that this was the right thing to do. His legs suddenly felt heavy as if he would drunkenly collapse, but then a cold harsh wind from the expansive view he faced brought him back to the moment.

'You won't find Bobby, JK. He's gone. This won't make you happy, JK. It won't make your friends happy, or your mum. Or me. Please, please don't do this, JK,' Di pleaded, as he stared down at her.

'I have to. It doesn't matter what I do now, does it? It doesn't make any difference. Bobby's dead, I couldn't stop it. My father left, and I couldn't bring him back. I tried so hard, Di. I've finally realised that I need to take control of my life. And that I miss Bobby. There's nothing here worth sticking around for anymore, Di.'

'Wait. Just stop and think for a moment. I miss Bobby too, so much. Every single day. More than you'll ever know. We all miss him but, sometimes, bad things just happen. To all of us. It doesn't mean you're a failure. You can control your life, JK. But not like this.'

'Well, I'll find out, wont I?'

JK edged towards the lip of the step and peered down as a cold wind slapped his face. Make sure you land central, look for a gap, avoid the cars, no need to involve anyone else, he thought. It seemed so much higher from the southern edge than the north, he suddenly thought.

He looked straight ahead as suddenly he didn't feel pain in his stomach anymore and the pain in his head lifted. He was ready and shifted slightly closer to the edge again.

'No, don't! You can't!' Di shouted from below. 'There's something you don't know yet,' she shouted out, pulling the envelope from her pocket again and holding it up at JK. But he didn't look down at her this time; he was too transfixed by the view he now faced

It was an uplifting sight, this theatre of night-time scenery in front of him. The car head lamps and street lights, the high-rise buildings that put a strange glow on the dark clouds that JK could just make out among the now night-time sky with the few dulled stars dotted around. He felt like he could almost float off the ledge, such was his confidence in his decision, along with the re-assuring presence by his side of Bobby Jenkins who he would soon be able to join.

Take control, JK. You should do it, JK. Do it, and then you can find me, once and for all. We can be in peace together. Do it.

As JK listened to Bobby, he looked into his amber eyes for the final time and watched his brother crouch and then jump off the bridge. Then, JK closed his eyes and copied the same crouching position that he had just seen his brother perform.

'Stop! It's your father. He's been in touch,' Di pleaded.

JK opened his eyes and remained still, waiting for Di to continue.

'He wrote a letter to your mum. I've got it here,' she said, waving the folded paper in the air at him.

'What?' JK replied, as he stood up straight again and stared back down.

'Your mum must've told him about Bobby's death. Then this arrived a week ago.'

'So what? I don't care what he's got to say anymore.'

'I know, that's what I was arguing with her about earlier today. Whether to tell you or not. But ... just read it. He says he regrets everything he did to you and your whole family. And he says he's sorry.'

JK shook his head and frowned in confusion, before he closed his eyes again.

'It's up to you, JK. But he says he wants to reconnect with you. At least read it.'

He stood motionless on the ledge as the strong winds rushed past him. As he felt himself sway, he considered letting nature decide his fate.

After a while, he opened his eyes and took in the view one last time. He looked down at the ledge and then took a small step away from it.

He turned his head back to look at Di. Then, he took slow, cautious steps along the bridge towards her, unsure of his future but knowing, for now at least, where he was headed.